EVERYMAN,

I WILL GO WITH THEE,

AND BE THY GUIDE,

IN THY MOST NEED

TO GO BY THY SIDE

EVERYMAN'S POCKET CLASSICS

SCOTTISH STORIES

EDITED BY GERARD CARRUTHERS

EVERYMAN'S POCKET CLASSICS

Alfred A. Knopf New York London Toronto

This selection by Gerard Carruthers first published in
Everyman's Library, 2023
Copyright © 2023 by Everyman's Library

A list of acknowledgments to copyright owners appears at
the back of this volume.

everymanslibrary.com
www.everymanslibrary.co.uk

ISBN 978-0-593-53628-5 (US)
978-1-84159-635-1 (UK)

A CIP catalogue reference for this book is available from the
British Library

Typography by Peter B. Willberg
Typeset in the UK by Input Data Services Ltd, Isle Abbotts, Somerset
Printed and bound in Germany by GGP Media GmbH, Pössneck

Contents

PREFACE

Short stories are perhaps the Cinderella of literary genres compared to poetry, the novel and drama. However, shorter fiction is as rich thematically and formally as any of these others, and this is as true for Scotland as for many other nations.

One of the places where the short story came into being, in fact, was Scotland. In part, this had to do with the periodical press, including *Blackwood's Magazine* (founded in 1817) in Edinburgh with which writers like Walter Scott and James Hogg were associated. *Blackwood's*, indeed, was part of an international centre of periodical magazine production in the Scottish capital including its rival, the *Edinburgh Review* and *Tait's*, also, from 1832, a powerful producer of the short story. Often at the cutting edge of new literary development throughout the nineteenth century, *Blackwood's* was an important shop-window for new writing talent including Charles Dickens, George Eliot, Edgar Allan Poe and Joseph Conrad among many others. Stretching a point, we might almost have claimed for this anthology some of these writers in their Scottish/*Blackwood's* context. Like other post-Enlightenment publications servicing a burgeoning urban population, *Blackwood's* channelled the exotic and the supernatural-gothic, and in both its fiction and non-fiction articles gave readers a glimpse of alternative, marginalized, 'primitive' lives and experiences in general. Broadly, this context helps explain Walter Scott in 'The Two

Drovers' comparing and contrasting different cultural ways of living within Britain (English and Scottish, which equally have their historical hinterland: Robin Hood as much as Rob Roy). Might it be, Scott asks in his text, that as we rush headlong into modern progress (a worry then as now), we do not properly consider older ways of living, diverse codes of human behaviour? His is a story that asks us to empathize all round amid this clash of cultures: we need law and order, we need civilization but we need to understand the different formative circumstances of peoples within a multifarious nation state: the United Kingdom.

Similarly, James Hogg in 'The Cameronian Preacher's Tale' asks us to take seriously the possibility of something we might usually dismiss, the supernatural. Do we believe in this or not, we – like the original readerly audience – are asked to consider. How 'modern' are we? Are we post-Enlightenment people who have done away with more 'primitive' or 'savage' beliefs? The supernatural features here in stories by Robert Louis Stevenson, Margaret Oliphant, Eric Linklater, Muriel Spark, Dorothy K. Haynes and George Mackay Brown. In each of them, however, the other-worldly is insinuated within human action that is very real-worldly, and all abound with reflections upon morality, religion, human avarice and how we narrate stories. Since the Romantic period, the rise of anthropological and psychological insight in our culture and in our literature has taught us that in many ways we remain not particularly rational, progressive creatures, but rather – as so many of the stories in this collection demonstrate – tied to beliefs and prejudices that will not go away or even might be more sympathetically viewed as part of our human nature, warts and all.

Literature following the Romantic period of the late eighteenth and early nineteenth centuries makes much of the quotidian, the seemingly unremarkable incidents and people of everyday life. We see this in John Galt's 'The Gudewife' where ordinary domestic circumstances are the occasion both for comedy and for thoughtful consideration of married life and gender (arguably, the text has feminist elements in it as it nicely reverses the scenario of Shakespeare's *The Taming of the Shrew*). We might also think here of Lewis Grassic Gibbon's 'Smeddum', a century after Galt, where a strong female presence – arguably a riff on mythic Mother Nature – again features in a story which is likewise powerfully comical but also profound in its depiction of a 'common' person. The short story genre is part of that shift in literary history where the seemingly insignificant episode or 'common' occurrence becomes of interest to us, especially if well-written and with some level of absorbing colour, tone or tension, which all of the texts chosen here exemplify.

The form of the short story has also lent itself very well to vignettes (or close-up, small-scale portraiture), both serious and comic, sometimes both simultaneously. Stories here by Iain Crichton Smith, Alasdair Gray and Irvine Welsh are side-splittingly funny, poking fun at their own cultures, suggesting that we wryly observe the idiosyncrasies of the human character and the humour of life as much as its gravity. James Robertson's 'Old Mortality' reprises the title of a Walter Scott novel and has resonances with the nineteenth-century supernatural mode. However, it also reflects on connectedness, in this case ancestry, on how we relate to place and family both in the present and in the past. Connectedness is a concern of many of the stories here, including the offering by William McIlvanney, a brilliant stylist long associated with Scottish 'urban realism'. The arched irony in the writing suggests as much as any supernatural literary text that 'realism' or 'reality' is seldom to be consumed in straightforward fashion.

Female experiences and writing are a prominent part of the Scottish short-story tradition. That experience is reflected in male writers such as Galt, Gibbon and Mackay Brown as well as in the work of Oliphant, Muriel Spark, Janice Galloway, A. L. Kennedy, Jackie Kay and Ali Smith. Diverse intersections between race and sexuality complicate identity here, Spark being of Jewish origin, Kay and Smith gay, Kay also black. Scottish identity as revealed through its writers and literature is no more straightforward or uniform than anywhere else. Into the mix of a Scotland that remains one of Europe's less ethnically diverse countries comes work by Bernard MacLaverty, from Northern Ireland but resident for most of his life in Glasgow, and Leila Aboulela, Sudanese-Egyptian in her origins but based for much of her writing career in Aberdeen. Both are superb prose stylists and are adroit in the little ironies and tender poignances of human life that transcend place and nationality. Scottish writers often happily write about or inhabit geographies other than Scotland's. In this collection, Scott's story is largely set in England, with Conan Doyle we go to sea and to Africa, Spark's story occurs beside the River Zambesi, and Ali Smith bestrides two different continents culturally as she riffs on the composers Beethoven and Gershwin. Andrew O'Hagan, like Arthur Conan Doyle and (sometimes) Robert Louis Stevenson before him, is a Scottish writer writing from London and for international magazines. O'Hagan and Conan Doyle share a background of Irish-Catholic emigration to Scotland. Many of the other writers here are cradled in Scotland's dominant Presbyterian Christianity. O'Hagan's story takes the working-class life of Glasgow and presents it in the *New York Times Magazine*, exemplifying our common human curiosity about other lives and places. In a way it takes us back to the origins of the short story in *Blackwood's Magazine*.

Scottish regions with their own distinctive historic culture, the traditionally Gaelic-speaking highlands (Iain Crichton Smith) or the Orkney Islands (George Mackay Brown) or the south west (John Buchan) feature alongside 'central' Scotland. The Scots language (for instance, Galt and Welsh) is on show in this anthology alongside English. History, geography, religion and politics are all contemplated in one way or another. There is no one 'Scottishness' that binds the writers altogether easily or at all, but every one of them has a Scottish footprint or accent. Perhaps more importantly, they are masters of their form, managing the short story to entertain and engage readers, regardless of background, anywhere in the world.

Gerard Carruthers

WALTER SCOTT

THE TWO DROVERS

CHAPTER I

IT WAS THE day after the Doune Fair when my story commences. It had been a brisk market, several dealers had attended from the northern and midland counties in England, and the English money had flown so merrily about as to gladden the hearts of the Highland farmers. Many large droves were about to set off for England, under the protection of their owners, or of the topsmen whom they employed in the tedious, laborious, and responsible office of driving the cattle for many hundred miles, from the market where they had been purchased to the fields or farmyards where they were to be fattened for the shambles.

The Highlanders in particular are masters of this difficult trade of driving, which seems to suit them as well as the trade of war. It affords exercise for all their habits of patient endurance and active exertion. They are required to know perfectly the drove-roads, which lie over the wildest tracts of the country, and to avoid as much as possible the highways, which distress the feet of the bullocks, and the turnpikes, which annoy the spirit of the drover; whereas on the broad green or grey track, which leads across the pathless moor, the herd not only move at ease and without taxation, but, if they mind their business, may pick up a mouthful of food by the way. At night, the drovers usually sleep along with their cattle, let the weather be what it will; and many of these hardy men do not once rest under a roof during a journey on foot from Lochaber to Lincolnshire. They are paid very highly, for the trust reposed is of the last importance, as it depends on their prudence, vigilance, and honesty, whether the cattle reach the final market in good order, and afford a profit to the grazier. But as they maintain themselves at their own expense, they are especially economical in that particular. At the period we speak of, a Highland drover was victualled for his long and toilsome journey with a few handfulls of oatmeal and two or three onions, renewed from time to time, and a ram's horn filled with whisky, which he used regularly, but sparingly, every night and morning. His dirk, or *skene-dhu*, (*i.e.* black knife,) so worn as to be concealed beneath the arm, or by the folds of the plaid, was his only weapon, excepting the cudgel with which he directed the movements of the cattle. A Highlander was never so happy as on these occasions. There was a variety in the whole journey, which exercised the Celt's natural curiosity and love of motion; there were the constant change of place and scene, the petty adventures incidental to the traffic, and the intercourse with the various farmers, graziers, and traders, intermingled with occasional merrymakings, not the less acceptable to Donald that they were void of expense; – and there was the consciousness of superior skill; for the Highlander, a child amongst flocks, is a prince amongst herds, and his natural habits induce him to disdain the shepherd's slothful life, so that he feels himself nowhere more at home than when following a gallant drove of his country cattle in the character of their guardian.

Of the number who left Doune in the morning, and with the purpose we have described, not a *Glunamie* of them all cocked his bonnet more briskly, or gartered his tartan hose under knee over a pair of more promising *spiogs*, (legs,) than did Robin Oig McCombich, called familiarly Robin Oig, that is Young, or the Lesser, Robin. Though small of stature, as the epithet Oig implies, and not very strongly limbed, he was as light and alert as one of the deer of his mountains. He had an elasticity of step, which, in the course of a long march, made many a stout fellow envy him; and the manner in which he busked his plaid and adjusted his bonnet, argued a consciousness that so smart a John Highlandman as himself would not pass unnoticed among the Lowland lasses. The ruddy cheek, red lips, and white teeth, set off a countenance which had gained by exposure to the weather a healthful and hardy rather than a rugged hue. If Robin Oig did not laugh, or even smile frequently, as indeed is not the practice among his countrymen, his bright eyes usually gleamed from under his bonnet with an expression of cheerfulness ready to be turned into mirth.

The departure of Robin Oig was an incident in the little town, in and near which he had many friends male and female. He was a topping person in his way, transacted considerable business on his own behalf, and was intrusted by the best farmers in the Highlands, in preference to any other drover in that district. He might have increased his business to any extent had he condescended to manage it by deputy; but except a lad or two, sister's sons of his own, Robin rejected the idea of assistance, conscious, perhaps, how much his reputation depended upon his attending in person to the practical discharge of his duty in every instance. He remained, therefore, contented with the highest premium given to persons of his description, and comforted himself with the hopes that a few journeys to England might enable him to conduct business on his own account, in a manner becoming his birth. For Robin Oig's father, Lachlan McCombich, (or, *son of my friend*, his actual clan-surname being MacGregor,) had been so called by the celebrated Rob Roy, because of the particular friendship which had subsisted between the grandsire of Robin and that renowned cateran. Some people even say, that Robin Oig derived his Christian name from a man, as renowned in the wilds of Lochlomond, as ever was his namesake Robin Hood, in the precincts of merry Sherwood. 'Of such ancestry,' as James Boswell says, 'who would not be proud?' Robin Oig was proud accordingly; but his frequent visits to England and to the Lowlands had given him tact enough to know that pretensions, which still gave him a little right to distinction in his own lonely glen, might be both obnoxious and ridiculous if preferred elsewhere. The pride of birth, therefore, was like the miser's treasure, the secret subject of his contemplation, but never exhibited to strangers as a subject of boasting.

Many were the words of gratulation and good-luck which were bestowed on Robin Oig. The judges commended his drove, especially the best of them, which were Robin's own property. Some thrust out their snuff-mulls for the parting pinch – others tendered the *dock-an-dorrach*, or parting cup. All cried – 'Good-luck travel out with you and come home with you. – Give you luck in the Saxon market – brave notes in the *leabhar-dhu*, (black pocket-book,) and plenty of English gold in the *sporran* (pouch of goatskin).'

The bonny lasses made their adieus more modestly, and more than one, it was said, would have given her best brooch to be certain that it was upon her that his eye last rested as he turned towards his road.

Robin Oig had just given the preliminary '*Hoo-hoo!*' to urge forward the loiterers of the drove, when there was a cry behind him.

'Stay, Robin – bide a blink. Here is Janet of Tomahourich – auld Janet, your father's sister.'

'Plague on her, for an auld Highland witch and spaewife,'

said a farmer from the Carse of Stirling; 'she'll cast some of her cantrips on the cattle.'

'She canna do that,' said another sapient of the same profession – 'Robin Oig is no the lad to leave any of them, without tying Saint Mungo's knot on their tails, and that will put to her speed the best witch that ever flew over Dimayet upon a broomstick.'

It may not be indifferent to the reader to know, that the Highland cattle are peculiarly liable to be *taken*, or infected, by spells and witchcraft, which judicious people guard against by knitting knots of peculiar complexity on the tuft of hair which terminates the animal's tail.

But the old woman who was the object of the farmer's suspicion seemed only busied about the drover, without paying any attention to the drove. Robin, on the contrary, appeared rather impatient of her presence.

'What auld-world fancy,' he said, 'has brought you so early from the ingle-side this morning, Muhme? I am sure I bid you good even, and had your God-speed, last night.'

'And left me more siller than the useless old woman will use till you come back again, bird of my bosom,' said the sibyl. 'But it is little I would care for the food that nourishes me, or the fire that warms me, or for God's blessed sun itself, if aught but weal should happen to the grandson of my father. So let me walk the *deasil* round you, that you may go safe out into the far foreign land, and come safe home.'

Robin Oig stopped, half embarrassed, half laughing, and signing to those around that he only complied with the old woman to soothe her humour. In the meantime, she traced around him, with wavering steps, the propitiation, which some have thought has been derived from the Druidical mythology. It consists, as is well known, in the person who makes the *deasil*, walking three times round the person who is the object of the ceremony, taking care to move according to the course of the sun. At once, however, she stopped short, and exclaimed, in a voice of alarm and horror, 'Grandson of my father, there is blood on your hand.'

'Hush, for God's sake, aunt,' said Robin Oig; 'you will bring more trouble on yourself with this Taishataragh (second sight) than you will be able to get out of for many a day.'

The old woman only repeated, with a ghastly look, 'There is blood on your hand, and it is English blood. The blood of the Gael is richer and redder. Let us see – let us—'

Ere Robin Oig could prevent her, which, indeed, could only have been by positive violence, so hasty and peremptory were her proceedings, she had drawn from his side the dirk which lodged in the folds of his plaid, and held it up, exclaiming, although the weapon gleamed clear and bright in the sun, 'Blood, blood – Saxon blood again. Robin Oig McCombich, go not this day to England!'

'Prutt, trutt,' answered Robin Oig, 'that will never do neither – it would be next thing to running the country. For shame, Muhme – give me the dirk. You cannot tell by the colour the difference betwixt the blood of a black bullock and a white one, and you speak of knowing Saxon from Gaelic blood. All men have their blood from Adam, Muhme. Give me my skene-dhu, and let me go on my road. I should have been half way to Stirling brig by this time – Give me my dirk, and let me go.'

'Never will I give it to you,' said the old woman – 'Never will I quit my hold on your plaid, unless you promise me not to wear that unhappy weapon.'

The women around him urged him also, saying few of his aunt's words fell to the ground; and as the Lowland farmers continued to look moodily on the scene, Robin Oig determined to close it at any sacrifice.

'Well, then,' said the young drover, giving the scabbard of the weapon to Hugh Morrison, 'you Lowlanders care nothing for these freats. Keep my dirk for me. I cannot give it you, because it was my father's; but your drove follows ours, and I am content it should be in your keeping, not in mine. – Will this do, Muhme?'

'It must,' said the old woman – 'that is, if the Lowlander is mad enough to carry the knife.'

The strong westlandman laughed aloud.

'Goodwife,' said he, 'I am Hugh Morrison from Glenae, come of the Manly Morrisons of auld langsyne, that never took short weapon against a man in their lives. And neither needed they: They had their broadswords, and I have this bit supple (showing a formidable cudgel) – for dirking ower the board, I leave that to John Highlandman. – Ye needna snort, none of you Highlanders, and you in especial, Robin. I'll keep the bit knife, if you are feared for the auld spaewife's tale, and give it back to you whenever you want it.'

Robin was not particularly pleased with some part of Hugh Morrison's speech; but he had learned in his travels more patience than belonged to his Highland constitution originally, and he accepted the service of the descendant of the Manly Morrisons, without finding fault with the rather depreciating manner in which it was offered.

'If he had not had his morning in his head, and been but a Dumfries-shire hog into the boot, he would have spoken more like a gentleman. But you cannot have more of a sow than a grumph. It's shame my father's knife should ever slash a haggis for the like of him.'

Thus saying, (but saying it in Gaelic,) Robin drove on his cattle, and waved farewell to all behind him. He was in the greater haste, because he expected to join at Falkirk a comrade and brother in profession, with whom he proposed to travel in company.

Robin Oig's chosen friend was a young Englishman, Harry Wakefield by name, well known at every northern market, and in his way as much famed and honoured as our Highland driver of bullocks. He was nearly six feet high, gallantly formed to keep the rounds at Smithfield, or maintain the ring at a wrestling match; and although he might have been overmatched, perhaps, among the regular professors of the Fancy, yet, as a chance customer, he was able to give a bellyful to any amateur of the pugilistic art. Doncaster races saw him in his glory, betting his guinea, and generally successfully; nor was there a main fought in Yorkshire, the feeders being persons of celebrity, at which he was not to be seen, if business permitted. But though a *sprack* lad, and fond of pleasure and its haunts, Harry Wakefield was steady, and not the cautious Robin Oig McCombich himself was more attentive to the main chance. His holidays were holidays indeed; but his days of work were dedicated to steady and persevering labour. In countenance and temper, Wakefield was the model of Old England's merry yeomen, whose clothyard shafts, in so many hundred battles, asserted her superiority over the nations, and whose good sabres, in our own time, are her cheapest and most assured defence. His mirth was readily excited; for, strong in limb and constitution, and fortunate in circumstances, he was disposed to be pleased with everything about him; and such difficulties as he might occasionally encounter, were, to a man of his energy, rather matter of amusement than serious annoyance. With all the merits of a sanguine temper, our young English drover was not without its defects. He was irascible, and sometimes to the verge of being quarrelsome; and perhaps not the less inclined to bring his disputes to a pugilistic decision, because he found few antagonists able to stand up to him in the boxing ring.

It is difficult to say how Henry Wakefield and Robin Oig first became intimates; but it is certain a close acquaintance had taken place betwixt them, although they had apparently few common topics of conversation or of interest, so soon as their talk ceased to be of bullocks. Robin Oig, indeed, spoke the English language rather imperfectly upon any other topics but stots and kyloes, and Harry Wakefield could never bring his broad Yorkshire tongue to utter a single word of Gaelic. It was in vain Robin spent a whole morning, during a walk over Minch-Moor, in attempting to teach his companion to utter, with true precision, the shibboleth *Llhu*, which is the Gaelic for a calf. From Traquair to Murder-cairn, the hill rung with the discordant attempts of the Saxon upon the unmanageable monosyllable, and the heartfelt laugh which followed every failure. They had, however, better modes of awakening the echoes; for Wakefield could sing many a ditty to the praise of Moll, Susan, and Cicely, and Robin Oig had a particular gift at whistling interminable pibrochs through all their involutions, and what was more agreeable to his companion's southern ear, knew many of the northern airs, both lively and pathetic, to which Wakefield learned to pipe a bass. Thus, though Robin could hardly have comprehended his companion's stories about horse-racing, cock-fighting, or fox-hunting, and although his own legends of clan-fights and *creaghs*, varied with talk of Highland goblins and fairy folk, would have been caviare to his companion, they contrived nevertheless to find a degree of pleasure in each other's company, which had for three years back induced them to join company and travel together, when the direction of their journey permitted. Each, indeed, found his advantage in this companionship; for where could the Englishman have found a guide through the Western Highlands like Robin Oig McCombich? and when they were on what Harry called the *right* side of the Border, his patronage, which was extensive, and his purse, which was heavy, were at all times at the service of his Highland friend, and on many occasions his liberality did him genuine yeoman's service.

CHAPTER II

Were ever two such loving friends: –
    How could they disagree?
O thus it was, he loved him dear,
    And thought how to requite him,
And having no friend left but he,
    He did resolve to fight him.
                                    Duke upon Duke

The pair of friends had traversed with their usual cordiality the grassy wilds of Liddesdale, and crossed the opposite part of Cumberland, emphatically called The Waste. In these solitary regions, the cattle under the charge of our drovers subsisted themselves cheaply, by picking their food as they went along the drove-road, or sometimes by the tempting opportunity of a *start and owerloup*, or invasion of the neighbouring pasture, where an occasion presented itself. But now the scene changed before them; they were descending towards a fertile and enclosed country, where no such liberties could be taken with impunity, or without a previous arrangement and bargain with the possessors of the ground. This was more especially the case, as a great northern fair was upon the eve of taking place, where both the Scotch and English drover expected to dispose of a part of their cattle, which it was desirable to produce in the market, rested and in good order. Fields were therefore difficult to be obtained, and only upon high terms. This necessity occasioned a temporary separation betwixt the two friends, who went to bargain, each as he could, for the separate accommodation of his herd. Unhappily it chanced that both of them, unknown to each other, thought of bargaining for the ground they wanted on the property of a country gentleman of some fortune, whose estate lay in the neighbourhood. The English drover applied to the bailiff on the property, who was known to him. It chanced that the Cumbrian Squire, who had entertained some suspicions of his manager's honesty, was taking occasional measures to ascertain how far they were well founded, and had desired that any inquiries about his enclosures, with a view to occupy them for a temporary purpose, should be referred to himself. As, however, Mr Ireby had gone the day before upon a journey of some miles' distance to the northward, the bailiff chose to consider the check upon his full powers as for the time removed, and concluded that he should best consult his master's interest, and perhaps his own, in making an agreement with Harry Wakefield. Meanwhile, ignorant of what his comrade was doing, Robin Oig, on his side, chanced to be overtaken by a well-looked smart little man upon a pony, most knowingly hogged and cropped, as was then the fashion, the rider wearing tight leather breeches, and long-necked bright spurs. This cavalier asked one or two pertinent questions about markets and the price of stock. So Robin, seeing him a well-judging civil gentleman, took the freedom to ask him whether he could let him know if there was any grass-land to be let in that neighbourhood, for the temporary accommodation of his drove. He could not have put the question to more willing ears. The gentleman of the buckskins was the proprietor, with whose bailiff Harry Wakefield had dealt, or was in the act of dealing.

'Thou art in good luck, my canny Scot,' said Mr Ireby, 'to have spoken to me, for I see thy cattle have done their day's work, and I have at my disposal the only field within three miles that is to be let in these parts.'

'The drove can pe gang two, three, four miles very pratty weel indeed –' said the cautious Highlander; 'put what would his honour pe axing for the peasts pe the head, if she was to tak the park for twa or three days?'

'We won't differ, Sawney, if you let me have six stots for winterers, in the way of reason.'

'And which peasts wad your honour pe for having?'

'Why – let me see – the two black – the dun one – yon doddy – him with the twisted horn – the brockit – How much by the head?'

'Ah,' said Robin, 'your honour is a shudge – a real shudge – I couldna have set off the pest six peasts petter mysell, me that ken them as if they were my pairns, puir things.'

'Well, how much per head, Sawney,' continued Mr Ireby.

'It was high markets at Doune and Falkirk,' answered Robin.

And thus the conversation proceeded, until they had agreed on the *prix juste* for the bullocks, the Squire throwing in the temporary accommodation of the enclosure for the cattle into the boot, and Robin making, as he thought, a very good bargain, providing the grass was but tolerable. The Squire walked his pony alongside of the drove, partly to show him the way, and see him put into possession of the field, and partly to learn the latest news of the northern markets.

They arrived at the field, and the pasture seemed excellent.

But what was their surprise when they saw the bailiff quietly inducting the cattle of Harry Wakefield into the grassy Goshen which had just been assigned to those of Robin Oig McCombich by the proprietor himself. Squire Ireby set spurs to his horse, dashed up to his servant, and learning what had passed between the parties, briefly informed the English drover that his bailiff had let the ground without his authority, and that he might seek grass for his cattle wherever he would, since he was to get none there. At the same time he rebuked his servant severely for having transgressed his commands, and ordered him instantly to assist in ejecting the hungry and weary cattle of Harry Wakefield, which were just beginning to enjoy a meal of unusual plenty, and to introduce those of his comrade, whom the English drover now began to consider as a rival.

The feelings which arose in Wakefield's mind would have induced him to resist Mr Ireby's decision; but every Englishman has a tolerably accurate sense of law and justice, and John Fleecebumpkin, the bailiff, having acknowledged that he had exceeded his commission, Wakefield saw nothing else for it than to collect his hungry and disappointed charge, and drive them on to seek quarters elsewhere. Robin Oig saw what had happened with regret, and hastened to offer to his English friend to share with him the disputed possession. But Wakefield's pride was severely hurt, and he answered disdainfully, 'Take it all, man – take it all – never make two bites of a cherry – thou canst talk over the gentry, and blear a plain man's eye – Out upon you, man – I would not kiss any man's dirty latchets for leave to bake in his oven.'

Robin Oig, sorry but not surprised at his comrade's displeasure, hastened to entreat his friend to wait but an hour till he had gone to the Squire's house to receive payment for the cattle he had sold, and he would come back and help him to drive the cattle into some convenient place of rest, and explain to him the whole mistake they had both of them fallen into. But the Englishman continued indignant: 'Thou hast been selling, hast thou? Ay, ay – thou is a cunning lad for kenning the hours of bargaining. Go to the devil with thyself, for I will ne'er see thy fause loon's visage again – thou should be ashamed to look me in the face.'

'I am ashamed to look no man in the face,' said Robin Oig, something moved; 'and, moreover, I will look you in the face this blessed day, if you will bide at the Clachan down yonder.'

'Mayhap you had as well keep away,' said his comrade; and turning his back on his former friend, he collected his unwilling associates, assisted by the bailiff, who took some real and some affected interest in seeing Wakefield accommodated.

After spending some time in negotiating with more than one of the neighbouring farmers, who could not, or would not, afford the accommodation desired, Henry Wakefield at last, and in his necessity, accomplished his point by means of the landlord of the alehouse at which Robin Oig and he had agreed to pass the night, when they first separated from each other. Mine host was content to let him turn his cattle on a piece of barren moor, at a price little less than the bailiff had asked for the disputed inclosure; and the wretchedness of the pasture, as well as the price paid for it, were set down as exaggerations of the breach of faith and friendship of his Scottish crony. This turn of Wakefield's passions was encouraged by the bailiff, (who had his own reasons for being offended against poor Robin, as having been the unwitting cause of his falling into disgrace with his master,) as well as by the innkeeper, and two or three chance guests, who stimulated the drover in his resentment against his quondam associate, – some from the ancient grudge against the Scots, which, when it exists anywhere, is to be found lurking in the Border counties, and some from the general love of mischief, which characterizes mankind in all ranks of life, to the honour of Adam's children be it spoken. Good John Barleycorn also, who always heightens and exaggerates the prevailing passions, be they angry or kindly, was not wanting in his offices on this occasion; and confusion to false friends and hard masters, was pledged in more than one tankard.

In the meanwhile Mr Ireby found some amusement in detaining the northern drover at his ancient hall. He caused a cold round of beef to be placed before the Scot in the butler's pantry, together with a foaming tankard of home-brewed, and took pleasure in seeing the hearty appetite with which these unwonted edibles were discussed by Robin Oig McCombich. The Squire himself lighting his pipe, compounded between his patrician dignity and his love of agricultural gossip, by walking up and down while he conversed with his guest.

'I passed another drove,' said the Squire, 'with one of your countrymen behind them – they were something less beasts than your drove, doddies most of them – a big man was with them – none of your kilts though, but a decent pair of breeches – D'ye know who he may be?'

'Hout ay – that might, could, and would pe Hughie Morrison – I didna think he could hae peen sae weel up. He has made a day on us; put his Argyleshires will have wearied shanks. How far was he pehind?'

'I think about six or seven miles,' answered the Squire, 'for I passed them at the Christenbury Cragg, and I overtook you at the Hollan Bush. If his beasts be leg-weary, he will be maybe selling bargains.'

'Na, na, Hughie Morrison is no the man for pargains – ye

maun come to some Highland body like Robin Oig hersell for the like of these – put I maun pe wishing you goot night, and twenty of them let alane ane, and I maun down to the Clachan to see if the lad Henry Waakfelt is out of his humdudgeons yet.'

The party at the alehouse were still in full talk, and the treachery of Robin Oig still the theme of conversation, when the supposed culprit entered the apartment. His arrival, as usually happens in such a case, put an instant stop to the discussion of which he had furnished the subject, and he was received by the company assembled with that chilling silence, which, more than a thousand exclamations, tells an intruder that he is unwelcome. Surprised and offended, but not appalled by the reception which he experienced, Robin entered with an undaunted and even a haughty air, attempted no greeting as he saw he was received with none, and placed himself by the side of the fire, a little apart from a table, at which Harry Wakefield, the bailiff, and two or three other persons, were seated. The ample Cumbrian kitchen would have afforded plenty of room even for a larger separation.

Robin, thus seated, proceeded to light his pipe, and call for a pint of twopenny.

'We have no twopence ale,' answered Ralph Heskett the landlord; 'but as thou find'st thy own tobacco, it's like thou may'st find thy own liquor too – it's the wont of thy country, I wot.'

'Shame, goodman,' said the landlady, a blithe bustling housewife, hastening herself to supply the guest with liquor – 'Thou knowest well enow what the strange man wants, and it's thy trade to be civil, man. Thou shouldst know, that if the Scot likes a small pot, he pays a sure penny.'

Without taking any notice of this nuptial dialogue, the

Highlander took the flagon in his hand, and addressing the company generally, drank the interesting toast of 'Good markets,' to the party assembled.

'The better that the wind blew fewer dealers from the north,' said one of the farmers, 'and fewer Highland runts to eat up the English meadows.'

'Saul of my pody, put you are wrang there, my friend,' answered Robin, with composure; 'it is your fat Englishmen that eat up our Scots cattle, puir things.'

'I wish there was a summat to eat up their drovers,' said another; 'a plain Englishman canna make bread within a kenning of them.'

'Or an honest servant keep his master's favour, but they will come sliding in between him and the sunshine,' said the bailiff.

'If these pe jokes,' said Robin Oig, with the same composure, 'there is ower mony jokes upon one man.'

'It is no joke, but downright earnest,' said the bailiff. 'Harkye, Mr Robin Ogg, or whatever is your name, it's right we should tell you that we are all of one opinion, and that is, that you, Mr Robin Ogg, have behaved to our friend Mr Harry Wakefield here, like a raff and a blackguard.'

'Nae doubt, nae doubt,' answered Robin, with great composure; 'and you are a set of very feeling judges, for whose prains or pehaviour I wad not gie a pinch of sneeshing. If Mr Harry Waakfelt kens where he is wranged, he kens where he may be righted.'

'He speaks truth,' said Wakefield, who had listened to what passed, divided between the offence which he had taken at Robin's late behaviour, and the revival of his habitual habits of friendship.

He now rose, and went towards Robin, who got up from his seat as he approached, and held out his hand.

'That's right, Harry – go it – serve him out,' resounded on all sides – 'tip him the nailer – show him the mill.'

'Hold your peace all of you, and be—,' said Wakefield; and then addressing his comrade, he took him by the extended hand, with something alike of respect and defiance. 'Robin,' he said, 'thou hast used me ill enough this day; but if you mean, like a frank fellow, to shake hands, and take a tussle for love on the sod, why I'll forgie thee, man, and we shall be better friends than ever.'

'And would it not pe petter to be cood friends without more of the matter?' said Robin; 'we will be much petter friendships with our panes hale than proken.'

Harry Wakefield dropped the hand of his friend, or rather threw it from him.

'I did not think I had been keeping company for three years with a coward.'

'Coward pelongs to none of my name,' said Robin, whose eyes began to kindle, but keeping the command of his temper. 'It was no coward's legs or hands, Harry Waakfelt, that drew you out of the fords of Frew, when you was drifting ower the plack rock, and every eel in the river expected his share of you.'

'And that is true enough, too,' said the Englishman, struck by the appeal.

'Adzooks!' exclaimed the bailiff – 'sure Harry Wakefield, the nattiest lad at Whitson Tryste, Wooler Fair, Carlisle Sands, or Stagshaw Bank, is not going to show white feather? Ah, this comes of living so long with kilts and bonnets – men forget the use of their daddles.'

'I may teach you, Master Fleecebumpkin, that I have not lost the use of mine,' said Wakefield, and then went on. 'This will never do, Robin. We must have a turn-up, or we shall be the talk of the country side. I'll be d—d if I hurt thee – I'll put on the gloves gin thou like. Come, stand forward like a man.'

'To pe peaten like a dog,' said Robin; 'is there any reason in that? If you think I have done you wrong, I'll go before your shudge, though I neither know his law nor his language.'

A general cry of 'No, no – no law, no lawyer! a bellyful and be friends,' was echoed by the bystanders.

'But,' continued Robin, 'if I am to fight, I have no skill to fight like a jackanapes, with hands and nails.'

'How would you fight then?' said his antagonist; 'though I am thinking it would be hard to bring you to the scratch anyhow.'

'I would fight with proadswords, and sink point on the first plood drawn – like a gentlemans.'

A loud shout of laughter followed the proposal, which indeed had rather escaped from poor Robin's swelling heart, than been the dictates of his sober judgment.

'Gentleman, quotha!' was echoed on all sides, with a shout of unextinguishable laughter; 'a very pretty gentleman, God wot – Canst get two swords for the gentleman to fight with, Ralph Heskett?'

'No, but I can send to the armoury at Carlisle, and lend them two forks, to be making shift with in the meantime.'

'Tush, man,' said another, 'the bonny Scots come into the world with the blue bonnet on their heads, and dirk and pistol at their belt.'

'Best send post,' said Mr Fleecebumpkin, 'to the Squire of Corby Castle, to come and stand second to the *gentleman*.'

In the midst of this torrent of general ridicule, the Highlander instinctively griped beneath the folds of his plaid.

'But it's better not,' he said in his own language. 'A hundred curses on the swine-eaters, who know neither decency nor civility!'

'Make room, the pack of you,' he said, advancing to the door.

But his former friend interposed his sturdy bulk, and opposed his leaving the house; and when Robin Oig attempted to make his way by force, he hit him down on the floor, with as much ease as a boy bowls down a nine-pin.

'A ring, a ring!' was now shouted, until the dark rafters, and the hams that hung on them, trembled again, and the very platters on the *bink* clattered against each other. 'Well done, Harry' – 'Give it him home, Harry' – 'Take care of him now – he sees his own blood!'

Such were the exclamations, while the Highlander, starting from the ground, all his coldness and caution lost in frantic rage, sprung at his antagonist with the fury, the activity, and the vindictive purpose, of an incensed tiger-cat. But when could rage encounter science and temper? Robin Oig again went down in the unequal contest; and as the blow was necessarily a severe one, he lay motionless on the floor of the kitchen. The landlady ran to offer some aid, but Mr Fleecebumpkin would not permit her to approach.

'Let him alone,' he said, 'he will come to within time, and come up to the scratch again. He has not got half his broth yet.'

'He has got all I mean to give him, though,' said his antagonist, whose heart began to relent towards his old associate; 'and I would rather by half give the rest to yourself, Mr Fleecebumpkin, for you pretend to know a thing or two, and Robin had not art enough even to peel before setting to, but fought with his plaid dangling about him. – Stand up, Robin, my man! all friends now; and let me hear the man that will speak a word against you, or your country, for your sake.'

Robin Oig was still under the dominion of his passion,

and eager to renew the onset; but being withheld on the one side by the peace-making Dame Heskett, and on the other, aware that Wakefield no longer meant to renew the combat, his fury sunk into gloomy sullenness.

'Come, come, never grudge so much at it, man,' said the brave-spirited Englishman, with the placability of his country, 'shake hands, and we will be better friends than ever.'

'Friends!' exclaimed Robin Oig with strong emphasis – 'friends! – Never. Look to yourself, Harry Waakfelt.'

'Then the curse of Cromwell on your proud Scots stomach, as the man says in the play, and you may do your worst, and be d—; for one man can say nothing more to another after a tussle, than that he is sorry for it.'

On these terms the friends parted; Robin Oig drew out, in silence, a piece of money, threw it on the table, and then left the alehouse. But turning at the door, he shook his hand at Wakefield, pointing with his fore-finger upwards, in a manner which might imply either a threat or a caution. He then disappeared in the moonlight.

Some words passed after his departure, between the bailiff, who piqued himself on being a little of a bully, and Harry Wakefield, who, with generous inconsistency, was now not indisposed to begin a new combat in defence of Robin Oig's reputation, 'although he could not use his daddles like an Englishman, as it did not come natural to him.' But Dame Heskett prevented this second quarrel from coming to a head by her peremptory interference. 'There should be no more fighting in her house,' she said; 'there had been too much already. – And you, Mr Wakefield, may live to learn,' she added, 'what it is to make a deadly enemy out of a good friend.'

'Pshaw, dame! Robin Oig is an honest fellow, and will never keep malice.'

'Do not trust to that – you do not know the dour temper of the Scotch, though you have dealt with them so often. I have a right to know them, my mother being a Scot.'

'And so is well seen on her daughter,' said Ralph Heskett.

This nuptial sarcasm gave the discourse another turn; fresh customers entered the tap-room or kitchen, and others left it. The conversation turned on the expected markets, and the report of prices from different parts both of Scotland and England – treaties were commenced, and Harry Wakefield was lucky enough to find a chap for a part of his drove, and at a very considerable profit; an event of consequence more than sufficient to blot out all remembrances of the unpleasant scuffle in the earlier part of the day. But there remained one party from whose mind that recollection could not have been wiped away by possession of every head of cattle betwixt Esk and Eden.

This was Robin Oig McCombich. – 'That I should have had no weapon,' he said, 'and for the first time in my life! – Blighted be the tongue that bids the Highlander part with the dirk – the dirk – ha! the English blood! – My muhme's word – when did her word fall to the ground?'

The recollection of the fatal prophecy confirmed the deadly intention which instantly sprang up in his mind.

'Ha! Morrison cannot be many miles behind; and if it were an hundred, what then!'

His impetuous spirit had now a fixed purpose and motive of action, and he turned the light foot of his country towards the wilds, through which he knew, by Mr Ireby's report, that Morrison was advancing. His mind was wholly engrossed by the sense of injury – injury sustained from a friend; and by the desire of vengeance on one whom he now accounted his most bitter enemy. The treasured ideas of self-importance and self-opinion – of ideal birth and quality, had become more precious to him, (like the hoard to the miser,) because he could only enjoy them in secret. But that hoard was pillaged, the idols which he had secretly worshipped had been desecrated and profaned. Insulted, abused, and beaten, he was no longer worthy, in his own opinion, of the name he bore, or the lineage which he belonged to – nothing was left to him – nothing but revenge; and, as the reflection added a galling spur to every step, he determined it should be as sudden and signal as the offence.

When Robin Oig left the door of the alehouse, seven or eight English miles at least lay betwixt Morrison and him. The advance of the former was slow, limited by the sluggish pace of his cattle; the last left behind him stubble-field and hedge-row, crag and dark heath, all glittering with frost-rhime in the broad November moonlight, at the rate of six miles an hour. And now the distant lowing of Morrison's cattle is heard; and now they are seen creeping like moles in size and slowness of motion on the broad face of the moor; and now he meets them – passes them, and stops their conductor.

'May good betide us,' said the Southlander – 'Is this you, Robin McCombich, or your wraith?'

'It is Robin Oig McCombich,' answered the Highlander, 'and it is not. – But never mind that, put pe giving me the skene-dhu.'

'What! you are for back to the Highlands – The devil! – Have you selt all off before the fair? This beats all for quick markets.'

'I have not sold – I am not going north – May pe I will never go north again. – Give me pack my dirk, Hugh Morrison, or there will pe words petween us.'

'Indeed, Robin, I'll be better advised or I gie it back to you – it is a wanchancy weapon in a Highlandman's hand,

and I am thinking you will be about some barns-breaking.'

'Pratt, trutt! let me have my weapon,' said Robin Oig impatiently.

'Hooly and fairly,' said his well-meaning friend. 'I'll tell you what will do better than these dirking doings – Ye ken Highlander and Lowlander, and Border-men, are a' ae man's bairns when you are over the Scots dyke. See, the Eskdale callants, and fighting Charlie of Liddesdale, and the Lockerby lads, and the four Dandies of Lustruther, and a wheen mair grey plaids, are coming up behind; and if you are wranged, there is the hand of a Manly Morrison, we'll see you righted, if Carlisle and Stanwix baith took up the feud.'

'To tell you the truth,' said Robin Oig, desirous of eluding the suspicions of his friend, 'I have enlisted with a party of the Black Watch, and must march off to-morrow morning.'

'Enlisted! Were you mad or drunk? – You must buy yourself off – I can lend you twenty notes, and twenty to that, if the drove sell.'

'I thank you – thank ye, Hughie; but I go with good will the gate that I am going, – so the dirk – the dirk!'

'There it is for you then, since less wunna serve. But think on what I was saying. – Wae's me, it will be sair news in the braes of Balquidder, that Robin Oig McCombich should have run an ill gate, and ta'en on.'

'Ill news in Balquidder, indeed!' echoed poor Robin; 'put Cot speed you, Hughie, and send you good marcats. Ye winna meet with Robin Oig again either at tryste or fair.'

So saying, he shook hastily the hand of his acquaintance, and set out in the direction from which he had advanced, with the spirit of his former pace.

'There is something wrang with the lad,' muttered the Morrison to himself; 'but we will maybe see better into it the morn's morning.'

But long ere the morning dawned, the catastrophe of our tale had taken place. It was two hours after the affray had happened, and it was totally forgotten by almost every one, when Robin Oig returned to Heskett's inn. The place was filled at once by various sorts of men, and with noises corresponding to their character. There were the grave, low sounds of men engaged in busy traffic, with the laugh, the song, and the riotous jest of those who had nothing to do but to enjoy themselves. Among the last was Harry Wakefield, who, amidst a grinning group of smock-frocks, hobnailed shoes, and jolly English physiognomies, was trolling forth the old ditty,

> What though my name be Roger,
> Who drives the plough and cart –

when he was interrupted by a well known voice, saying in a high and stern voice, marked by the sharp Highland accent, 'Harry Waakfelt – if you be a man, stand up!'

'What is the matter? – what is it?' the guests demanded of each other.

'It is only a d—d Scotsman,' said Fleecebumpkin, who was by this time very drunk, 'whom Harry Wakefield helped to his broth to-day, who is now come to have *his cauld kail* het again.'

'Harry Waakfelt,' repeated the same ominous summons, 'stand up, if you be a man!'

There is something in the tone of deep and concentrated passion, which attracts attention and imposes awe, even by the very sound. The guests shrunk back on every side, and gazed at the Highlander, as he stood in the middle of them, his brows bent, and his features rigid with resolution.

'I will stand up with all my heart, Robin, my boy, but it shall be to shake hands with you, and drink down all unkindness. It is not the fault of your heart, man, that you don't know how to clench your hands.'

By this time he stood opposite to his antagonist; his open and unsuspecting look strangely contrasted with the stern purpose, which gleamed wild, dark, and vindictive in the eyes of the Highlander.

''Tis not thy fault, man, that, not having the luck to be an Englishman, thou canst not fight more than a school-girl.'

'I *can* fight,' answered Robin Oig sternly, but calmly, 'and you shall know it. You, Harry Waakfelt, showed me to-day how the Saxon churls fight – I show you now how the Highland Dunniewassal fights.'

He seconded the word with the action, and plunged the dagger, which he suddenly displayed, into the broad breast of the English yeoman, with such fatal certainty and force, that the hilt made a hollow sound against the breast-bone, and the double-edged point split the very heart of his victim. Harry Wakefield fell, and expired with a single groan. His assassin next seized the bailiff by the collar, and offered the bloody poniard to his throat, whilst dread and surprise rendered the man incapable of defence.

'It were very just to lay you beside him,' he said, 'but the blood of a base pick-thank shall never mix on my father's dirk, with that of a brave man.'

As he spoke, he cast the man from him with so much force that he fell on the floor, while Robin, with his other hand, threw the fatal weapon into the blazing turf-fire.

'There,' he said, 'take me who likes – and let fire cleanse blood if it can.'

The pause of astonishment still continuing, Robin Oig asked for a peace-officer, and a constable having stepped out, he surrendered himself to his custody.

'A bloody night's work you have made of it,' said the constable.

'Your own fault,' said the Highlander. 'Had you kept his hands off me twa hours since, he would have been now as well and merry as he was twa minutes since.'

'It must be sorely answered,' said the peace-officer.

'Never you mind that – death pays all debts; it will pay that too.'

The horror of the bystanders began now to give way to indignation; and the sight of a favourite companion murdered in the midst of them, the provocation being, in their opinion, so utterly inadequate to the excess of vengeance, might have induced them to kill the perpetrator of the deed even upon the very spot. The constable, however, did his duty on this occasion, and with the assistance of some of the more reasonable persons present, procured horses to guard the prisoner to Carlisle, to abide his doom at the next assizes. While the escort was preparing, the prisoner neither expressed the least interest, nor attempted the slightest reply. Only, before he was carried from the fatal apartment, he desired to look at the dead body, which, raised from the floor, had been deposited upon the large table, (at the head of which Harry Wakefield had presided but a few minutes before, full of life, vigour, and animation,) until the surgeons should examine the mortal wound. The face of the corpse was decently covered with a napkin. To the surprise and horror of the bystanders, which displayed itself in a general *Ah!* drawn through clenched teeth and half-shut lips, Robin Oig removed the cloth, and gazed with a mournful but steady eye on the lifeless visage, which had been so lately animated, that the smile of good humoured confidence in his own strength, of conciliation at once, and contempt towards his enemy, still curled his lip. While those present expected that the wound, which had so lately flooded the apartment with gore, would send forth fresh streams at the touch of the homicide, Robin Oig replaced the covering, with the brief exclamation – 'He was a pretty man!'

My story is nearly ended. The unfortunate Highlander stood his trial at Carlisle. I was myself present, and as a young Scottish lawyer, or barrister at least, and reputed a man of some quality, the politeness of the Sheriff of Cumberland offered me a place on the bench. The facts of the case were proved in the manner I have related them; and whatever might be at first the prejudice of the audience against a crime so un-English as that of assassination from revenge, yet when the rooted national prejudices of the prisoner had been explained, which made him consider himself as stained with indelible dishonour, when subjected to personal violence; when his previous patience, moderation, and endurance, were considered, the generosity of the English audience was inclined to regard his crime as the wayward aberration of a false idea of honour rather than as flowing from a heart naturally savage, or perverted by habitual vice. I shall never forget the charge of the venerable Judge to the jury, although not at that time liable to be much affected either by that which was eloquent or pathetic.

'We have had,' he said, 'in the previous part of our duty, (alluding to some former trials,) to discuss crimes which infer disgust and abhorrence, while they call down the well-merited vengeance of the law. It is now our still more melancholy duty to apply its salutary though severe enactments to a case of a very singular character, in which the crime (for a crime it is, and a deep one) arose less out of the malevolence of the heart, than the error of the understanding – less from any idea of committing wrong, than from an unhappily perverted notion of that which is right. Here we have two men, highly esteemed, it has been stated, in their rank of life, and attached, it seems, to each other as friends, one of whose lives has been already sacrificed to a punctilio, and the other is about to prove the vengeance of the offended laws; and yet both may claim our commiseration at least, as men acting in ignorance of each other's national prejudices, and unhappily misguided rather than voluntarily erring from the path of right conduct.

'In the original cause of the misunderstanding, we must in justice give the right to the prisoner at the bar. He had acquired possession of the inclosure, which was the object of competition, by a legal contract with the proprietor Mr Ireby; and yet, when accosted with reproaches undeserved in themselves, and galling doubtless to a temper at least sufficiently susceptible of passion, he offered notwithstanding to yield up half his acquisition, for the sake of peace and good neighbourhood, and his amicable proposal was rejected with scorn. Then follows the scene at Mr Heskett the publican's, and you will observe how the stranger was treated by the deceased, and I am sorry to observe, by those around, who seem to have urged him in a manner which was aggravating in the highest degree. While he asked for peace and for composition, and offered submission to a magistrate, or to a mutual arbiter, the prisoner was insulted by a whole company, who seem on this occasion to have forgotten the national maxim of "fair play;" and while attempting to escape from the place in peace, he was intercepted, struck down, and beaten to the effusion of his blood.

'Gentlemen of the Jury, it was with some impatience that I heard my learned brother, who opened the case for the crown, give an unfavourable turn to the prisoner's conduct on this occasion. He said the prisoner was afraid to encounter his antagonist in fair fight, or to submit to the laws of the ring; and that therefore, like a cowardly Italian, he had recourse to his fatal stiletto, to murder the man whom he dared not meet in manly encounter. I observed the prisoner shrink from this part of the accusation with the abhorrence natural to a brave man; and as I would wish to make my words impressive, when I point his real crime, I must secure his opinion of my impartiality, by rebutting everything that seems to me a false accusation. There can be no doubt that the prisoner is a man of resolution – too much resolution – I wish to Heaven that he had less, or rather that he had had a better education to regulate it.

'Gentlemen, as to the laws my brother talks of, they may be known in the Bull-ring, or the Bear-garden, or the Cockpit, but they are not known here. Or, if they should be so far admitted as furnishing a species of proof, that no malice was intended in this sort of combat, from which fatal accidents do sometimes arise, it can only be so admitted when both parties are *in pari casu*, equally acquainted with, and equally willing to refer themselves to, that species of arbitrement. But will it be contended that a man of superior rank and education is to be subjected, or is obliged to subject himself, to this coarse and brutal strife, perhaps in opposition to a younger, stronger, or more skilful opponent? Certainly even the pugilistic code, if founded upon the fair play of Merry Old England, as my brother alleges it to be, can contain nothing so preposterous. And, gentlemen of the jury, if the laws would support an English gentleman, wearing, we will suppose, his sword, in defending himself by force against a violent personal aggression of the nature offered to this prisoner, they will not less protect a foreigner and a stranger, involved in the same unpleasing circumstances. If, therefore, gentlemen of the jury, when thus pressed by a *vis major*, the object of obloquy to a whole company, and of direct violence

46

from one at least, and as he might reasonably apprehend, from more, the panel had produced the weapon which his countrymen, as we are informed, generally carry about their persons, and the same unhappy circumstance had ensued which you have heard detailed in evidence, I could not in my conscience have asked from you a verdict of murder. The prisoner's personal defence might indeed, even in that case, have gone more or less beyond the boundary of the *Moderamen inculpatæ tutelæ*, spoken of by lawyers, but the punishment incurred would have been that of manslaughter, not of murder. I beg leave to add, that I should have thought this milder species of charge was demanded in the case supposed, notwithstanding the statute of James I. cap. 8, which takes the case of slaughter by stabbing with a short weapon, even without malice prepense, out of the benefit of clergy. For this statute of stabbing, as it is termed, arose out of a temporary cause; and as the real guilt is the same, whether the slaughter be committed by the dagger, or by sword or pistol, the benignity of the modern law places them all on the same, or nearly the same footing.

'But, gentlemen of the jury, the pinch of the case lies in the interval of two hours interposed betwixt the reception of the injury and the fatal retaliation. In the heat of affray and *chaude mêlée,* law, compassionating the infirmities of humanity, makes allowance for the passions which rule such a stormy moment – for the sense of present pain, for the apprehension of further injury, for the difficulty of ascertaining with due accuracy the precise degree of violence which is necessary to protect the person of the individual, without annoying or injuring the assailant more than is absolutely necessary. But the time necessary to walk twelve miles, however speedily performed, was an interval sufficient for the prisoner to have recollected himself; and the violence with which he carried his purpose into effect, with so many circumstances of deliberate determination, could neither be induced by the passion of anger, nor that of fear. It was the purpose and the act of predetermined revenge, for which law neither can, will, nor ought to have sympathy or allowance.

'It is true, we may repeat to ourselves, in alleviation of this poor man's unhappy action, that his case is a very peculiar one. The country which he inhabits was, in the days of many now alive, inaccessible to the laws, not only of England, which have not even yet penetrated thither, but to those to which our neighbours of Scotland are subjected, and which must be supposed to be, and no doubt actually are, founded upon the general principles of justice and equity which pervade every civilized country. Amongst their mountains, as among the North American Indians, the various tribes were wont to make war upon each other, so that each man was obliged to go armed for his own protection, and for the offence of his neighbour. These men, from the ideas which they entertained of their own descent and of their own consequence, regarded themselves as so many cavaliers or men-at-arms, rather than as the peasantry of a peaceful country. Those laws of the ring, as my brother terms them, were unknown to the race of warlike mountaineers; that decision of quarrels by no other weapons than those which nature has given every man, must to them have seemed as vulgar and as preposterous as to the Noblesse of France. Revenge, on the other hand, must have been as familiar to their habits of society as to those of the Cherokees or Mohawks. It is, indeed, as described by Bacon, at bottom a kind of wild untutored justice; for the fear of retaliation must withhold the hands of the oppressor where there is no regular law to check daring violence. But though all this may be granted, and though we may allow that, such having been the case of the Highlands in the days of the prisoner's fathers, many of the opinions and sentiments must still continue to influence the present generation, it cannot, and ought not, even in this most painful case, to alter the administration of the law, either in your hands, gentlemen of the jury, or in mine. The first object of civilization is to place the general protection of the law, equally administered, in the room of that wild justice, which every man cut and carved for himself, according to the length of his sword and the strength of his arm. The law says to the subjects, with a voice only inferior to that of the Deity, "Vengeance is mine." The instant that there is time for passion to cool, and reason to interpose, an injured party must become aware, that the law assumes the exclusive cognizance of the right and wrong betwixt the parties, and opposes her inviolable buckler to every attempt of the private party to right himself. I repeat, that this unhappy man ought personally to be the object rather of our pity than our abhorrence, for he failed in his ignorance, and from mistaken notions of honour. But his crime is not the less that of murder, gentlemen, and, in your high and important office, it is your duty so to find. Englishmen have their angry passions as well as Scots; and should this man's action remain unpunished, you may unsheath, under various pretences, a thousand daggers betwixt the Land's-end and the Orkneys.'

The venerable Judge thus ended what, to judge by his apparent emotion, and by the tears which filled his eyes, was really a painful task. The jury, according to his instructions, brought in a verdict of Guilty; and Robin Oig McCombich, *alias* MacGregor, was sentenced to death, and left for execution, which took place accordingly. He met his fate with great firmness, and acknowledged the justice of his sentence.

But he repelled indignantly the observations of those who accused him of attacking an unarmed man. 'I give a life for the life I took,' he said, 'and what can I do more?'

JOHN GALT

THE GUDEWIFE

INTRODUCTION

I AM INDITING the good matter of this book for the instruction of our only daughter when she comes to years of discretion, as she soon will, for her guidance when she has a house of her own, and has to deal with the kittle temper of a gudeman in so couthy a manner as to mollify his sour humour when any thing out of doors troubles him. Thanks be and praise I am not ill qualified! indeed, it is a clear ordinance that I was to be of such a benefit to the world; for it would have been a strange thing if the pains taken with my education had been purposeless in the decrees of Providence.

Mr Desker, the schoolmaster, was my father; and, as he was reckoned in his day a great teacher, and had a pleasure in opening my genie for learning, it is but reasonable to suppose that I in a certain manner profited by his lessons, and made a progress in parts of learning that do not fall often into the lot of womankind. This much it behoves me to say, for there are critical persons in the world that might think it was very upsetting of one of my degree to write a book, especially a book which has for its end the bettering of the conjugal condition. If I did not tell them, as I take it upon me to do, how well I have been brought up for the work, they might look down upon my endeavours with a doubtful eye; but when they read this, they will have a new tout to their old horn, and reflect with more reverence of others who may be in some things their inferiors, superiors, or equals.

It would not become me to say to which of these classes I belong, though I am not without an inward admonition on that head.

It fell out, when I was in my twenties, that Mr Thrifter came, in the words of the song of Auld Robin Gray, 'a-courting to me'; and, to speak a plain matter of fact, in some points he was like that bald-headed carle. For he was a man, considering my juvenility, well stricken in years; besides being a bachelor, with a natural inclination (as all old bachelors have) to be dozened, and fond of his own ayes and nays. For my part, when he first came about the house, I was as dawty as Jeanie – as I thought myself entitled to a young man, and did not relish the apparition of him coming in at the gloaming, when the day's darg was done, and before candles were lighted. However, our lot in life is not of our own choosing. I will say – for he is still to the fore – that it could not have been thought he would have proved himself such a satisfactory gudeman as he has been. To be sure, I put my shoulder to the wheel, and likewise prayed to Jupiter; for there never was a rightful head of a family without the concurrence of his wife. These are words of wisdom that my father taught, and I put in practice.

Mr Thrifter, when he first came about me, was a bein man. He had parts in two vessels, besides his own shop, and was sponsible for a nest-egg of lying money: so that he was not, though rather old, a match to be, as my father thought, discomfited with a flea in the lug instanter. I therefore, according to the best advice, so comported myself, that it came to pass in the course of time that we were married; and of my wedded life and experience I intend to treat in this book.

CHAPTER I

Among the last words that my sagacious father said when I took upon me to be the wedded wife of Mr Thrifter were, that a man never throve unless his wife would let, which is a text that I have not forgotten; for though in a way, and in obedience to the customs of the world, women acknowledge men as their head, yet we all know in our hearts that this is but diplomatical. Do not we see that men work for us, which shews that they are our servants? do not we see that men protect us, are they not therefore our soldiers? do not we see that they go hither and yon at our bidding, which shews that they have that within their nature that teaches them to obey? and do not we feel that we have the command of them in all things, just as they had the upper hand in the world till woman was created? No clearer proof do I want that, although in a sense for policy we call ourselves the weaker vessels – and in that very policy there is power – we know well in our hearts that, as the last made creatures, we necessarily are more perfect, and have all that was made before us, by hook or crook, under our thumb. Well does Robin Burns sing of this truth in the song where he has –

> Her 'prentice hand she tried on man,
> And syne she made the lassies oh!

Accordingly having a proper conviction of the superiority of my sex, I was not long of making Mr Thrifter, my gudeman, to know into what hands he had fallen, by correcting many of the bad habits of body to which he had become addicted in his bachelor loneliness. Among these was a custom that I did think ought not to be continued after he had surrendered himself into the custody of a wife, and that was an usage with him in the morning before breakfast to toast his shoes against the fender and forenent the fire. This he did not tell me till I saw it with my own eyes the morning after we were married, which when I beheld gave me a sore heart, because, had I known it before we were everlastingly made one, I will not say but there might have been a dubiety as to the paction; for I have ever had a natural dislike to men who toasted their shoes, thinking it was a hussie fellow's custom. However, being endowed with an instinct of prudence, I winked at it for some days; but it could not be borne any longer, and I said in a sweet manner, as it were by the by,

'Dear Mr Thrifter, that servant lass that we have gotten has not a right notion of what is a genteel way of living. Do you see how the misleart creature sets up your shoes in the inside of the fender, keeping the warmth from our feet? really I'll thole this no longer; it's not a custom in a proper house. If a stranger were accidentally coming in and seeing your shoes in that situation, he would not think of me as it is well known he ought to think.'

Mr Thrifter did not say much, nor could he; for I judiciously laid all the wyte and blame of the thing to the servant; but he said, in a diffident manner, that it was not necessary to be so particular.

'No necessary! Mr Thrifter, what do you call a particularity, when you would say that toasting shoes is not one? It might do for you when you were a bachelor, but ye should remember that you're so no more, and it's a custom I will not allow.'

'But,' replied he with a smile, 'I am the head of the house; and, to make few words about it, I say, Mrs Thrifter, I will have my shoes warmed any how, whether or no.'

'Very right, my dear,' quo' I; 'I'll ne'er dispute that you are the head of the house; but I think that you need not make a poor wife's life bitter by insisting on toasting your shoes.'

And I gave a deep sigh. Mr Thrifter looked very solemn on hearing this, and as he was a man not void of understanding, he said to me.

'My dawty,' said he, 'we must not stand on trifles; if you do not like to see my shoes within the parlour fender, they can be toasted in the kitchen.'

I was glad to hear him say this; and, ringing the bell, I told the servant-maid at once to take them away and place them before the kitchen-fire, well pleased to have carried my point with such debonair suavity; for if you get the substance of a thing, it is not wise to make a piece of work for the shadow likewise. Thus it happened I was conqueror in the controversy; but Mr Thrifter's shoes have to this day been toasted every morning in the kitchen; and I daresay the poor man is vogie with the thoughts of having gained a victory; for the generality of men have, like parrots, a good conceit of themselves, and cry 'Pretty Poll!' when every body sees they have a crooked neb.

CHAPTER II

But what I have said was nothing to may other calamities that darkened our honeymoon. Mr Thrifter having been a long-keepit bachelor, required a consideration in many things besides his shoes; for men of that stamp are so long accustomed to their own ways, that it is not easy to hammer them into docility, far less to make them obedient husbands. So that although he is the best of men, yet I cannot say on my conscience that he was altogether free of an ingrained temper, requiring my canniest hand to manage properly. It could not be said that I suffered much from great faults; but he was fiky, and made more work about trifles that didna just please him than I was willing to conform to. Some excuse, however, might be pleaded for him, because he felt that infirmities were growing upon him, which was the cause that made him think of taking a wife; and I was not in my younger days quite so thoughtful, may be, as was necessary: for I will take blame to myself, when it would be a great breach of truth in me to deny a fault that could be clearly proven.

Mr Thrifter was a man of great regularity; he went to the shop, and did his business there in a most methodical manner; he returned to the house and ate his meals like clockwork; and he went to bed every night at half-past nine o'clock, and slept there like a door-nail. In short, all he did and said was as orderly as commodities on chandler-pins; but for all that, he was at times of a crunkly spirit, fractiously making faults about nothing at all: by which he was neither so smooth as oil nor so sweet as honey to me, whose duty it was to govern him.

At the first outbreaking of the original sin that was in him, I was vexed and grieved, watering my plants in the solitude of my room, when he was discoursing on the news of the day with customers in the shop. At last I said to myself, 'This will never do; one of two must obey: and it is not in the course of nature that a gudeman should rule a house, which is the province of a wife, and becomes her nature to do.'

So I set a stout heart to the steybrae, and being near my time with our daughter, I thought it would be well to try how he would put up with a little sample of womanhood. So that day when he came in to his dinner, I was, maybe, more incommoded with my temper than might be, saying to him, in a way as if I could have fought with the wind, that it was very unsettled weather.

'My dawty,' said he, 'I wonder what would content you! we have had as delightful a week as ever made the sight of the sun heartsome.'

'Well, but,' said I, 'good weather that is to you may not be so to me; and I say again, that this is most ridiculous weather.'

'What would you have, my dawty? Is it not known by a better what is best for us?'

'Oh,' cried I, 'we can never speak of temporal things but you haul in the grace of the Maker by the lug and the horn. Mr Thrifter, ye should set a watch on the door of your lips; especially as ye have now such a prospect before you of being the father of a family.'

'Mrs Thrifter,' said he, 'what has that to do with the state of the weather?'

'Every thing,' said I. 'Isn't the condition that I am in a visibility that I cannot look after the house as I should do? which is the cause of your having such a poor dinner to-day; for the weather wiled out the servant lass, and she has in consequence not been in the kitchen to see to her duty. Doesn't that shew you that, to a woman in the state that I am, fine sunshiny weather is no comfort?'

'Well,' said he, 'though a shower is at times seasonable, I will say that I prefer days like this.'

'What you, Mr Thrifter, prefer, can make no difference to me; but I will uphold, in spite of every thing you can allege to the contrary, that this is not judicious weather.'

'Really now, gudewife,' said Mr Thrifter, 'what need we quarrel about the weather? neither of us can make it better or worse.'

'That's a truth,' said I; 'but what need you maintain that dry weather is pleasant weather, when I have made it plain to you that it is a great affliction? And how can you say the contrary? does not both wet and dry come from Providence? Which of them is the evil? – for they should be in their visitations both alike.'

'Mrs Thrifter,' said he, 'what would you be at, summering and wintering on nothing?'

Upon which I said, 'Oh, Mr Thrifter, if ye were like me, ye would say any thing; for I am not in a condition to be spoken to. I'll not say that ye're far wrong, but till my time is a bygone ye should not contradict me so; for I am no in a state to be contradicted: it may go hard with me if I am. So I beg you to think, for the sake of the baby unborn, to let me have my own way in all things for a season.'

'I have no objection,' said he, 'if there is a necessity for complying; but really, gudewife, ye're at times a wee fashous just now; and this house has not been a corner in the king-dom of heaven for some time.'

Thus, from less to more, our argolbargoling was put an end to; and from that time I was the ruling power in our domicile, which has made it the habitation of quiet ever since; for from that moment I never laid down the rod of authority, which I achieved with such a womanly sleight of hand.

CHAPTER III

Though from the time of the conversation recorded in the preceding chapter I was, in a certain sense, the ruling power in our house, as a wedded wife should be, we did not slide down a glassy brae till long after. For though the gudeman in a compassionate manner allowed me to have my own way till my fulness of time was come, I could discern by the tail of my eye that he meditated to usurp the authority again, when he saw a fit time to effect the machination. Thus it came to pass, when I was delivered of our daughter, I had, as I lay on my bed, my own thoughts anent the evil that I saw barming within him; and I was therefore determined to keep the upper hand, of which I had made a conquest with such dexterity, and the breaking down of difficulties.

So when I was some days in a recumbent posture, but in a well-doing way, I said nothing; it made me, however, often grind my teeth in a secrecy, when I saw from the bed many a thing that I treasured in remembrance should never be again. But I was very thankful for my deliverance, and assumed a blitheness in my countenance that was far from my heart. In short, I could see that the gudeman, in whose mouth you would have thought sugar would not have melted, had from day to day a stratagem in his head subversive of the regency that I had won in my tender state; and as I saw it would never do to let him have his own will, I had recourse to the usual diplomaticals of womankind.

It was a matter before the birth that we settled, him and me, that the child should be baptised on the eighth day after, in order that I might be up, and a partaker of the ploy; which, surely, as the mother, I was well entitled to. But from what I saw going on from the bed and jaloused, it occurred to me that the occasion should be postponed, and according as Mr Thrifter should give his consent, or withhold it, I should comport myself; determined, however, I was to have the matter postponed, just to ascertain the strength and durability of what belonged to me.

On the fifth day I therefore said to him, as I was sitting in the easy chair by the fire, with a cod at my shoulders and my mother's fur-cloak about me – the baby was in the cradle close by, but not rocking, for the keeper said it was yet too young – and sitting as I have said, Mr Thrifter forenent me,

'My dear,' said I, 'it will never do to have the christening on the day we said.'

'What for no?' was the reply; 'isn't it a very good day?'

So I, seeing that he was going to be upon his peremptors, replied, with my usual meekness,

'No human being, my dear, can tell what sort of day it will be; but be it good or be it bad, the christening is not to be on that day.'

'You surprise me!' said he. 'I considered it a settled point, and have asked Mr Sweetie, the grocer, to come to his tea.'

'Dear me!' quo' I; 'ye should not have done that without my consent; for although we set the day before my time was come, it was not then in the power of man to say how I was to get through; and therefore it was just a talk we had on the subject, and by no manner of means a thing that could be fixed.'

'In some sort,' said Mr Thrifter, 'I cannot but allow that you are speaking truth; but I thought that the only impediment to the day was your illness. Now you have had a most blithe time o't, and there is nothing in the way of an obstacle.'

'Ah, Mr Thrifter!' said I, 'it's easy for you, who have such a barren knowledge of the nature of women, so to speak, but I know that I am no in a condition to have such a handling as a christening; and besides, I have a scruple of conscience well worth your attention concerning the same – and it's my opinion, formed in the watches of the night, when I was in my bed, that the baby should be christened in the kirk on the Lord's-day.'

'Oh,' said he, 'that's but a fashion, and you'll be quite well by the eighth; the howdie told me that ye had a most pleasant time o't, and cannot be ill on the eighth day.'

I was just provoked into contumacy to hear this; for to

tell a new mother that childbirth is a pleasant thing, set me almost in a passion; and I said to him, that he might entertain Mr Sweetie himself, for that I was resolved the christening should not be as had been set.

In short, from less to more I gained my point; as, indeed, I always settled it in my own mind before broaching the subject; first, by letting him know that I had latent pains, which made me very ill, though I seemed otherwise; and, secondly, that it was very hard, and next to a martyrdom, to be controverted in religion, as I would be if the bairn was baptised any where but in the church.

CHAPTER IV

In due time the christening took place in the kirk, as I had made a point of having; and for some time after we passed a very happy married life. Mr Thrifter saw that it was of no use to contradict me, and in consequence we lived in great felicity, he never saying nay to me; and I, as became a wife in the rightful possession of her prerogatives, was most condescending. But still he shewed, when he durst, the bull-horn; and would have meddled with our householdry, to the manifest detriment of our conjugal happiness, had I not continued my interdict in the strictest manner. In truth, I was all the time grievously troubled with nursing Nance, our daughter, and could not take the same pains about things that I otherwise would have done; and it is well known that husbands are like mice, that know when the cat is out of the house, or her back turned, they take their own way: and I assure the courteous reader, to say no ill of my gudeman, that he was one of the mice genus.

But at last I had a trial, that was not to be endured with

such a composity as if I had been a black snail. It came to pass that our daughter was to be weaned, and on the day settled – a Sabbath-day – we had, of course, much to do, for it behoved in this ceremony that I should keep out of sight; and keeping out of sight, it seemed but reasonable, considering his parentage to the wean, that Mr Thrifter should take my place. So I said to him in the morning, that he must do so, and keep Nance for that day; and, to do the poor man justice, he consented at once, for he well knew that it would come to nothing to be contrary.

So I went to the kirk, leaving him rocking the cradle and singing hush, ba! as he saw need. But oh, dule! scarcely had I left the house when the child screamed up in a panic, and would not be pacified. He thereupon lifted it out of the cradle, and with it in his arms went about the house; but it was such a roaring buckie, that for a long time he was like to go distracted. Over what ensued I draw the curtain, and must only say, that when I came from the church, there he was, a spectacle, and as sour as a crab-apple, blaming me for leaving him with such a devil.

I was really woful to see him, and sympathised in the most pitiful manner with him, on account of what had happened; but the more I condoled with him the more he would not be comforted, and for all my endeavours to keep matters in a propriety, I saw my jurisdiction over the house was in jeopardy; and every now and then the infant cried out, just as if it had been laid upon a heckle. Oh! such a day as that was for Mr Thrifter, when he heard the tyrant bairn shrieking like mad, and every now and then drumming with its wee feetie like desperation, he cried,

'For the love of God, give it a drop of the breast! or it will tempt me to wring off its ancles or its head.'

But I replied composedly that it could not be done, for

the wean must be speant, and what he advised was even-down nonsense.

'What has come to pass, both my mother and other sagacious carlines told me I had to look for; and so we must bow the head of resignation to our lot. You'll just,' said I, 'keep the bairn this afternoon; it will not be a long fashery.'

He said nothing, but gave a deep sigh.

At this moment, the bells of the kirk were ringing for the afternoon's discourse, and I lifted my bonnet to put it on and go; but ere I knew where I was, Mr Thrifter was out of the door and away, leaving me alone with the torment in the cradle, which the bells at that moment wakened: and it gave a yell that greatly discomposed me.

Once awa and aye awa, Mr Thrifter went into the fields, and would not come back when I lifted the window and called to him, but walked faster and faster, and was a most demented man; so that I was obligated to stay at home, and would have had my own work with the termagant baby, if my mother had not come in and advised me to give it sweetened rum and water for a pacificator.

CHAPTER V

Mr Thrifter began in time to be a very complying husband, and we had, after the trial of the weaning, no particular con-fabulation; indeed he was a very reasonable man, and had a rightful instinct of the reverence that is due to the opinion of a wife of discernment. I do not think, to the best of my recollection, that between the time Nance was weaned till she got her walking shoes and was learning to walk, that we had a single controversy; nor can it be said that we had a great ravelment on that occasion. Indeed, saving our daily higling about trifles not worth remembering, we passed a pleasant life. But when Nance came to get her first walking shoes that was a catastrophe well worthy of being rehearsed for her behoof now.

It happened that for some months before, she had, in place of shoes, red worsted socks; but as she began, from the character of her capering, to kithe that she was coming to her feet, I got a pair of yellow slippers for her; and no mother could take more pains that I did to learn her how to handle her feet. First I tried to teach her to walk by putting a thimble or an apple beyond her reach, at least a chair's breadth off; and then I endeavoured to make the cutty run from me to her father, across the hearth, and he held out his hands to catch her.

This, it will be allowed, was to us pleasant pastime. But it fell out one day, when we were diverting ourselves by making Nance run to and fro between us across the hearth, that the glaiket baudrons chanced to see the seal of her father's watch glittering, and, in coming from him to me, she drew it after her, as if it had been a turnip. He cried, 'Oh, Christal and –' I lifted my hands in wonderment; but the tottling creature, with no more sense than a sucking turkey, whirled the watch, the Almighty knows how! into the fire, and giggled as if she had done an exploit.

'Take it out with the tongs,' said I.

'She's an ill-brought-up wean,' cried he.

The short and the long of it was, before the watch could be got out, the heat broke the glass and made the face of it dreadful; besides, he wore a riband chain – that was in a bleeze before we could make a redemption.

When the straemash was over, I said to him that he could expect no better by wearing his watch in such a manner.

'It is not,' said he, 'the watch that is to blame, but your bardy bairn, that ye have spoiled in the bringing up.'

'Mr Thrifter,' quo' I, 'this is not a time for upbraiding; for if ye mean to insinuate any thing to my disparagement, it is what I will not submit to.'

'E'en as you like, my dawty,' said he; 'but what I say is true – that your daughter will just turn out a randy like her mother.'

'What's that ye say?' quo' I, and I began to wipe my eyes with the corner of my shawl – saying in a pathetic manner, 'If I am a randy, I ken who has made me one.'

'Ken,' said he, 'ken! every body kens that ye are like a clubby foot, made by the hand of God, and passed the remede of doctors.'

Was not this most diabolical to hear? Really my corruption rose at such blasphemy; and starting from my seat, I put my hands on my haunches, and gave a stamp with my foot that made the whole house dirl: 'What does the man mean?' said I.

But he replied with a composity as if he had been in liquor, saying, with an ill-faured smile, 'Sit down, my dawty; you'll do yourself a prejudice if ye allow your passion to get the better of you.'

Could mortal woman thole the like of this; it stunned me speechless, and for a time I thought my authority knocked on the head. But presently the spirit that was in my nature mustered courage, and put a new energy within me, which caused me to say nothing, but to stretch out my feet, and stiffen back, with my hands at my sides, as if I was a dead corpse. Whereupon the good man ran for a tumbler of water to jaup on my face; but when he came near me in this posture, I dauded the glass of water in his face, and drummed with my feet and hands in a delirious manner, which convinced him that I was going by myself. Oh, but he was in an awful terrification! At last, seeing his fear and contrition, I began to moderate, as it seemed; which made him as softly and kindly as if I had been a true frantic woman; which I was not, but a practiser of the feminine art, to keep the ruling power.

Thinking by my state that I was not only gone daft, but not without the need of a soothing, he began to ask my pardon in a proper humility, and with a most pitiful penitence. Whereupon I said to him, that surely he had not a right knowledge of my nature: and then he began to confess a fault, and was such a dejected man, that I took the napkin from my eyes and gave a great guffaw, telling him that surely he was silly daft and gi'en to pikerry, if he thought he could daunton me. 'No, no, Mr Thrifter,' quo' I, 'while I live, and the iron tongs are by the chumly lug, never expect to get the upper hand of me.'

From that time he was as bidable a man as any reasonable woman could desire; but he gave a deep sigh, which was a testificate to me that the leaven of unrighteousness was still within him, and might break out into treason and rebellion if I was not on my guard.

JAMES HOGG

THE CAMERONIAN
PREACHER'S TALE

SIT NEAR ME, my children, and come nigh, all ye who are not of my kindred, though of my flock; for my days and hours are numbered; death is with me dealing, and I have a sad and a wonderful story to relate. I have preached and ye have profited; but what I am about to say is far better than man's preaching, it is one of those terrible sermons which God preaches to mankind, of blood unrighteously shed, and most wondrously avenged. The like has not happened in these our latter days. His presence is visible in it; and I reveal it that its burthen may be removed from my soul, so that I may die in peace; and I disclose it, that you may lay it up in your hearts and tell it soberly to your children, that the warning memory of a dispensation so marvellous may live and not perish. Of the deed itself, some of you have heard a whispering; and some of you know the men of whom I am about to speak; but the mystery which covers them up as with a cloud I shall remove; listen, therefore, my children, to a tale of truth, and may you profit by it!

On Dryfe Water, in Annandale, lived Walter Johnstone, a man open hearted and kindly, but proud withal and warm tempered; and on the same water lived John Macmillan, a man of a nature grasping and sordid, and as proud and hot tempered as the other. They were strong men, and vain of their strength; lovers of pleasant company, well to live in the world, extensive dealers in corn and cattle; married too, and both of the same age – five and forty years. They often met, yet they were not friends; nor yet were they companions, for bargain making and money seeking narroweth the heart and shuts up generosity of soul. They were jealous, too, of one another's success in trade, and of the fame they had each acquired for feats of personal strength and agility, and skill with the sword – a weapon which all men carried, in my youth, who were above the condition of a peasant. Their mutual and growing dislike was inflamed by the whisperings of evil friends, and confirmed by the skilful manner in which they negotiated bargains over each other's heads. When they met, a short and surly greeting was exchanged, and those who knew their natures looked for a meeting between them, when the sword or some other dangerous weapon would settle for ever their claims for precedence in cunning and in strength.

They met at the fair of Longtown, and spoke, and no more – with them both it was a busy day, and mutual hatred subsided for a time, in the love of turning the penny and amassing gain. The market rose and fell, and fell and rose; and it was whispered that Macmillan, through the superior skill or good fortune of his rival, had missed some bargains which were very valuable, while some positive losses touched a nature extremely sensible of the importance of wealth. One was elated and the other depressed – but not more depressed than moody and incensed, and in this temper they were seen in the evening in the back room of a public inn, seated apart and silent, calculating losses and gains, drinking deeply, and exchanging dark looks of hatred and distrust. They had been observed, during the whole day, to watch each other's movements, and now when they were met face to face, the labours of the day over, and their natures inflamed by liquor as well as by hatred, their companions looked for personal strife between them, and wondered not a little when they saw Johnstone rise, mount his horse, and ride homewards, leaving his rival in Longtown. Soon afterwards Macmillan started up from a moody fit, drank off a large draught of brandy, threw down a half-guinea, nor waited for change – a thing uncommon with him; and men said, as his horse's feet struck fire from the pavement, that if he overtook Johnstone, there would be a living soul less in the land before sunrise.

Before sunrise next morning the horse of Walter Johnstone came with an empty saddle to his stable door. The bridle was trampled to pieces amongst its feet, and its saddle and sides were splashed over with blood as if a bleeding body had been carried across its back. The cry arose in the country, an instant search was made, and on the side of the public road was found a place where a deadly contest seemed to have happened. It was in a small green field, bordered by a wood, in the farm of Andrew Pattison. The sod was dinted deep with men's feet, and trodden down and trampled and sprinkled over with blood as thickly as it had ever been with dew. Blood drops, too, were traced to some distance, but nothing more was discovered; the body could not be found, though every field was examined and every pool dragged. His money and bills, to the amount of several thousand pounds, were gone, so was his sword – indeed nothing of him could be found on earth save his blood, and for its spilling a strict account was yet to be sought.

Suspicion instantly and naturally fell on John Macmillan, who denied all knowledge of the deed. He had arrived at his own house in due course of time, no marks of weapon or warfare were on him, he performed family worship as was his custom, and he sang the psalm as loudly and prayed as fervently as he was in the habit of doing. He was apprehended and tried, and saved by the contradictory testimony of the witnesses against him, into whose hearts the spirit of falsehood seemed to have entered in order to perplex and confound the judgment of men – or rather that man might have no hand in the punishment, but that God should bring it about in his own good time and way. 'Revenge is mine, saith the Lord,' which meaneth not because it is too sweet a morsel for man, as the scoffer said, but because it is too dangerous. A glance over this conflicting testimony will show how little was then known of this foul offence, and how that little was rendered doubtful and dark by the imperfections of human nature.

Two men of Longtown were examined. One said that he saw Macmillan insulting and menacing Johnstone, laying his hand on the hilt of his sword with a look dark and ominous; while the other swore that he was present at the time, but that it was Johnstone who insulted and menaced Macmillan, and laid his hand on the hilt of his sword and pointed to the road homewards. A very expert and searching examination could make no more of them; they were both respectable men with characters above suspicion. The next witnesses were of another stamp, and their testimony was circuitous and contradictory. One of them was a shepherd – a reluctant witness. His words were these: 'I was frae hame on the night of the murder, in the thick of the wood, no just at the place which was bloody and trampled, but gaye and near hand it. I canna say I can just mind what I was doing; I had somebody to see I jalouse, but wha it was is naebody's business but my ain. There was maybe ane forbye myself in the wood, and maybe twa; there was ane at ony rate, and I am no sure but it was an auld acquaintance. I see nae use there can be in questioning me. I saw nought, and therefore can say nought. I canna but say that I heard something – the trampling of horses, and a rough voice saying, "Draw and defend yourself." Then followed the clashing of swords and half smothered sort of work, and then the sound of horses' feet was heard again, and that's a' I ken about it; only I thought the voice was Walter Johnstone's, and so thought Kate Pennie, who was with me and kens as meikle as me.' The examination of Katherine Pennie, one of the Pennies of Pennieland, followed, and she declared that she had heard the evidence of Dick Purdie with surprise and anger. On that night she was not over the step of her father's door for more than five minutes, and that was to look at the sheep in the fauld; and she neither heard the clashing of swords nor the word of man or woman. And with respect to Dick Purdie, she scarcely knew him even by sight; and if all tales were true that were told of him, she would not venture into a lonely wood with him, under the cloud of night, for a gown of silk with pearls on each sleeve. The shepherd, when recalled, admitted that Kate Pennie might be right, 'For after a',' said he, 'it happened in the dark, when a man like me, no that gleg of the uptauk, might confound persons. Somebody was with me, I am gaye and sure, frae what took place – if it was nae Kate, I kenna wha it was, and it couldna weel be Kate either, for Kate's a douce quean, and besides is married.' The judge dismissed the witnesses with some indignant words, and, turning to the prisoner, said, 'John Macmillan, the prevarications of these witnesses have saved you; mark my words – saved you from man, but not from God. On the murderer, the Most High will lay his hot right hand, visibly and before men, that we may know that blood unjustly shed will be avenged. You are at liberty to depart.' He left the bar and resumed his station and his pursuits as usual; nor did he appear sensible to the feeling of the country, which was strong against him.

A year passed over his head, other events happened, and the murder of Walter Johnstone began to be dismissed from men's minds. Macmillan went to the fair of Longtown, and when evening came he was seated in the little back room which I mentioned before, and in company with two men of the names of Hunter and Hope. He sat late, drank deeply, but in the midst of the carousal a knock was heard at the door, and a voice called sharply, 'John Macmillan.' He started up, seemed alarmed, and exclaimed, 'What in Heaven's name can *he* want with me?' and opening the door hastily, went into the garden, for he seemed to dread another summons lest his companions should know the voice. As soon as he was gone, one said to the other, 'If that was not the voice of Walter Johnstone, I never heard it in my life; he is either come back in the flesh or in the spirit, and in either way John Macmillan has good cause to dread him.' They listened – they heard Macmillan speaking in great agitation; he was answered only by a low sound, yet he appeared to understand what was said, for his concluding words were, 'Never! never! I shall rather submit to His judgment who cannot err.' When he returned he was pale and shaking, and he sat down and seemed buried in thought. He spread his palms on his knees, shook his head often, then, starting up, said, 'The judge was a fool and no prophet – to mortal man is not given the wisdom of God – so neighbours let us ride.' They mounted their horses and rode homewards into Scotland at a brisk pace.

The night was pleasant, neither light nor dark; there were few travellers out, and the way winded with the hills and with the streams, passing through a pastoral and beautiful country. Macmillan rode close by the side of his companions, closer than was desirable or common; yet he did not speak, nor make answer when he was spoken to; but looked keenly and earnestly before and behind him, as if he expected the coming of some one, and every tree and bush seemed to alarm and startle him. Day at last dawned, and with the growing light his alarm subsided, and he began to converse with his companions, and talk with a levity which surprised them more than his silence had done before. The sun was all but risen when they approached the farm of Andrew Pattison, and here and there the top of a high tree and the summit of a hill had caught light upon them. Hope looked to Hunter silently, when they came nigh the bloody spot where it was believed the murder had been committed. Macmillan sat looking resolutely before him, as if determined not to look upon it; but his horse stopt at once, trembled violently, and then sprung aside, hurling its rider headlong to the ground. All this passed in a moment; his companions sat astonished; the horse rushed forward, leaving him on the ground, from whence he never rose in life, for his neck was broken by the fall, and with a convulsive shiver or two he expired. Then did the prediction of the judge, the warning voice and summons of the preceding night, and the spot and the time, rush upon their recollection; and they firmly believed that a murderer and robber lay dead beside them. 'His horse saw something,' said Hope to Hunter; 'I never saw such flashing eyes in a horse's head;' – 'and *he* saw something too,' replied Hunter, 'for the glance that he gave to the bloody spot, when his horse started, was one of terror. I never saw such a look, and I wish never to see such another again.'

When John Macmillan perished, matters stood thus with his memory. It was not only loaded with the sin of blood and the sin of robbery, with the sin of making a faithful woman a widow and her children fatherless, but with the grievous sin also of having driven a worthy family to ruin and beggary. The sum which was lost was large, the creditors were merciless; they fell upon the remaining substance of Johnstone, sweeping it wholly away; and his widow sought shelter in a miserable cottage among the Dryfesdale hills, where she supported her children by gathering and spinning wool. In a far different state and condition remained the family of John Macmillan. He died rich and unincumbered, leaving an evil name and an only child, a daughter, wedded to one whom many knew and esteemed, Joseph Howatson by name, a man sober and sedate; a member, too, of our own broken remnant of Cameronians.

Now, my dear children, the person who addresses you was then, as he is yet, God's preacher for the scattered kirk of Scotland, and his tent was pitched among the green hills of Annandale. The death of the transgressor appeared unto me the manifest judgment of God, and when my people gathered around me I rejoiced to see so great a multitude, and, standing in the midst of them, I preached in such a wise that they were deeply moved. I took for my text these words, 'Hath there been evil in the land and the Lord hath not known it?' I discoursed on the wisdom of Providence in guiding the affairs of men. How he permitted our evil passions to acquire the mastery over us, and urge us to deeds of darkness; allowing us to flourish for a season, that he might strike us in the midst of our splendour in a way so visible and awful that the wildest would cry out, 'Behold the finger of God.' I argued the matter home to the heart; I named no names, but I saw Joseph Howatson hide his face in his hands, for he felt and saw from the eyes which were turned towards him that I alluded to the judgment of God upon his relative.

Joseph Howatson went home heavy and sad of heart, and somewhat touched with anger at God's servant for having so pointedly and publicly alluded to his family misfortune; for he believed his father-in-law was a wise and a worthy man. His way home lay along the banks of a winding and beautiful stream, and just where it entered his own lands there was a rustic gate, over which he leaned for a little space, ruminating upon earlier days, on his wedded wife, on his children, and finally his thoughts settled on his father-in-law. He thought of his kindness to himself and to many others, on his fulfilment of all domestic duties, on his constant performance of family worship, and on his general reputation for honesty and fair dealing. He then dwelt on the circumstances of Johnstone's disappearance, on the singular summons his father-in-law received in Longtown, and the catastrophe which followed on the spot and on the very day of the year that the murder was supposed to be committed. He was in sore perplexity, and said aloud, 'Would to God that I knew the truth; but the doors of eternity, alas! are shut on the secret for ever.' He looked up and John Macmillan stood before him – stood with all the calmness and serenity and meditative air which a grave man wears when he walks out on a sabbath eve.

'Joseph Howatson,' said the apparition, 'on no secret are the doors of eternity shut – of whom were you speaking?' 'I was speaking,' answered he, 'of one who is cold and dead, and to whom you bear a strong resemblance.' 'I am he,' said the shape; 'I am John Macmillan.' 'God of heaven!' replied Joseph Howatson, 'how can that be; did I not lay his head in the grave; see it closed over him; how, therefore, can it be? Heaven permits no such visitations.' 'I entreat you, my son,' said the shape, 'to believe what I say; the end of man is not when his body goes to dust; he exists in another state, and from that state am I permitted to come to you; waste not time, which is brief, with vain doubts, I am John Macmillan.' 'Father, father,' said the young man, deeply agitated, 'answer me, did you kill and rob Walter Johnstone?' 'I did,' said the Spirit, 'and for that have I returned to earth; listen to me.'

The young man was so much overpowered by a revelation thus fearfully made, that he fell insensible on the ground; and when he recovered, the moon was shining, the dews of night were upon him, and he was alone.

Joseph Howatson imagined that he had dreamed a fearful dream; and conceiving that Divine Providence had presented the truth to his fancy, he began to consider how he could secretly make reparation to the wife and children of Johnstone for the double crime of his relative. But on more mature reflection he was impressed with the belief that a spirit had appeared to him, the spirit of his father-in-law, and that his own alarm had hindered him from learning fully the secret of his visit to earth; he therefore resolved to go to the same place next sabbath night, seek rather than avoid an interview, acquaint himself with the state of bliss or woe in which the spirit was placed, and learn if by acts of affection and restitution he could soften his sufferings or augment his happiness. He went accordingly to the little rustic gate by the side of the lonely stream; he walked up and down; hour passed after hour, but he heard nothing and saw nothing save the murmuring of the brook and the hares running among the wild clover. He had resolved to return home, when something seemed to rise from the ground, as shapeless as a cloud at first, but moving with life. It assumed a form, and the appearance of John Macmillan was once more before him. The young man was nothing daunted, but looking on the spirit, said, 'I thought you just and upright and devout, and incapable of murder and robbery.' The spirit seemed to dilate as it made answer. 'The death of Walter Johnstone sits lightly upon me. We had crossed each other's purposes, we had lessened each other's gains, we had vowed revenge, we met on fair terms, tied our horses to a gate, and fought fairly and long; and when I slew him, I but did what he sought to do to me. I threw him over his horse, carried him far into the country, sought out a deep quagmire on the north side of the Snipe Knowe, in Crake's Moss, and having secured his bills and other perishable property, with the purpose of returning all to his family, I buried him in the moss, leaving his gold in his purse, and laying his cloak and his sword above him.

'Now listen, Joseph Howatson. In my private desk you will find a little key tied with red twine, take it and go to the house of Janet Mathieson in Dumfries, and underneath the hearthstone in my sleeping room you will get my strong-box, open it, it contains all the bills and bonds belonging to Walter Johnstone. Restore them to his widow. I would have restored them but for my untimely death. Inform her privily and covertly where she will find the body of her husband, so that she may bury him in the churchyard with his ancestors. Do these things, that I may have some assuagement of misery; neglect them, and you will become a world's wonder.' The spirit vanished with these words, and was seen no more.

Joseph Howatson was sorely troubled. He had communed with a spirit, he was impressed with the belief that early death awaited him; he felt a sinking of soul and a misery of body, and he sent for me to help him with counsel, and comfort him in his unexampled sorrow. I loved him and hastened to him; I found him weak and woe-begone, and the hand of God seemed to be sore upon him. He took me out to the banks of the little stream where the shape appeared to him, and having desired me to listen without interrupting him, told me how he had seen his father-in-law's spirit, and related the revelations which it had made and the commands it had laid upon him. 'And now,' he said, 'look upon me. I am young, and ten days ago I had a body strong and a mind buoyant, and gray hairs and the honours of old age seemed to await me. But ere three days pass I shall be as the clod of the valley, for he who converses with a spirit, a spirit shall he soon become. I have written down the strange tale I have told you and I put it into your hands, perform for me and for my wretched parent, the instructions which the grave yielded up its tenant to give; and may your days be long in the land, and may you grow gray-headed among your people.' I listened to his words with wonder and with awe, and I promised to obey him in all his wishes with my best and most anxious judgment. We went home together: we spent the evening in prayer. Then he set his house in order, spoke to all his children cheerfully and with a mild voice, and falling on the neck of his wife, said, 'Sarah Macmillan, you were the choice of my young heart, and you have been a wife to me kind, tender, and gentle.' He looked at his children and he looked at his wife, for his heart was too full for more words, and retired to his chamber. He was found next morning kneeling by his bedside, his hands held out as if repelling some approaching object, horror stamped on every feature, and cold and dead.

Then I felt full assurance of the truth of his communications; and as soon as the amazement which his untimely death occasioned had subsided, and his wife and little ones were somewhat comforted, I proceeded to fulfil his dying request. I found the small key tied with red twine, and I went to the house of Janet Mathieson in Dumfries, and I held up the key and said, 'Woman, knowest thou that?' and when she saw it she said, 'Full well I know it, it belonged to a jolly man and a douce, and mony a merry hour has he whiled away wi' my servant maidens and me.' And when she saw me lift the hearthstone, open the box, and spread out the treasure which it contained, she held up her hands,

'Eh! what o' gowd! what o' gowd! but half's mine, be ye saint or sinner; John Macmillan, douce man, aye said he had something there which he considered as not belonging to him but to a quiet friend; weel I wot he meant me, for I have been a quiet friend to him and his.' I told her I was commissioned by his daughter to remove the property, that I was the minister of that persecuted remnant of the true kirk called Cameronians, and she might therefore deliver it up without fear. 'I ken weel enough wha ye are,' said this worthless woman, 'd'ye think I dinna ken a minister of the kirk; I have seen meikle o' their siller in my day, frae eighteen to fifty and aught have I caroused with divines, Cameronians, I trow, as well as those of a freer kirk. But touching this treasure, give me twenty gowden pieces, else I'se gar three stamps of my foot bring in them that will see me righted, and send you awa to the mountains bleating like a sheep shorn in winter.' I gave the imperious woman twenty pieces of gold, and carried away the fatal box.

Now, when I got free of the ports of Dumfries, I mounted my little horse and rode away into the heart of the country, among the pastoral hills of Dryfesdale. I carried the box on the saddle before me, and its contents awakened a train of melancholy thoughts within me. There were the papers of Walter Johnstone, corresponding to the description which the spirit gave, and marked with his initials in red ink by the hand of the man who slew him. There were two gold watches and two purses of gold, all tied with red twine, and many bills and much money to which no marks were attached. As I rode along pondering on these things, and casting about in my own mind how and by what means I should make restitution, I was aware of a morass, broad and wide, which with all its quagmires glittered in the moonlight before me. I knew I had penetrated into the centre of Dryfesdale, but

I was not well acquainted with the country; I therefore drew my bridle, and looked around to see if any house was nigh, where I could find shelter for the night. I saw a small house built of turf and thatched with heather, from the window of which a faint light glimmered. I rode up, alighted, and there I found a woman in widow's weeds, with three sweet children, spinning yarn from the wool which the shepherds shear in spring from the udders of the ewes. She welcomed me, spread bread and placed milk before me. I asked a blessing, and ate and drank, and was refreshed.

Now it happened that, as I sat with the solitary woman and her children, there came a man to the door, and with a loud yell of dismay burst it open and staggered forward crying, 'There's a corse candle in Crake's Moss, and I'll be a dead man before the morning.' 'Preserve me! piper,' said the widow, 'ye're in a piteous taking; here is a holy man who will speak comfort to you, and tell you how all these are but delusions of the eye or exhalations of nature.' 'Delusions and exhalations, Dame Johnstone,' said the piper, 'd'ye think I dinna ken a corse light from an elf candle, an elf candle from a will-o'-wisp, and a will-o'-wisp from all other lights of this wide world.' The name of the morass and the woman's name now flashed upon me, and I was struck with amazement and awe. I looked on the widow, and I looked on the wandering piper, and I said, 'Let me look on those corse lights, for God creates nothing in vain; there is a wise purpose in all things, and a wise aim.' And the piper said, 'Na, na; I have nae wish to see ony mair on't, a dead light bodes the living nae gude; and I am sure if I gang near Crake's Moss it will lair me amang the hags and quags.' And I said, 'Foolish old man, you are equally safe every where; the hand of the Lord reaches round the earth, and strikes and protects according as it was foreordained, for nothing is hid from his eyes – come with me.' And the piper looked strangely upon me and stirred not a foot; and I said, 'I shall go by myself;' and the woman said, 'Let me go with you, for I am sad of heart, and can look on such things without fear; for, alas! since I lost my own Walter Johnstone, pleasure is no longer pleasant: and I love to wander in lonesome places and by old churchyards.' 'Then,' said the piper, 'I darena bide my lane with the bairns; I'll go also; but O! let me strengthen my heart with ae spring on my pipes before I venture.' 'Play,' I said, 'Clavers and his Highlandmen, it is the tune to cheer ye and keep your heart up.' 'Your honour's no cannie,' said the old man; 'that's my favourite tune.' So he played it and said, 'Now I am fit to look on lights of good or evil.' And we walked into the open air.

All Crake's Moss seemed on fire; not illumined with one steady and uninterrupted light, but kindled up by fits like the northern sky with its wandering streamers. On a little bank which rose in the centre of the morass, the supernatural splendour seemed chiefly to settle; and having continued to shine for several minutes, the whole faded and left but one faint gleam behind. I fell on my knees, held up my hands to heaven, and said, 'This is of God; behold in that fearful light the finger of the Most High. Blood has been spilt, and can be no longer concealed; the point of the mariner's needle points less surely to the north than yon living flame points to the place where man's body has found a bloody grave. Follow me,' and I walked down to the edge of the moss and gazed earnestly on the spot. I knew now that I looked on the long hidden resting place of Walter Johnstone, and considered that the hand of God was manifest in the way that I had been thus led blindfold into his widow's house. I reflected for a moment on these things; I wished to right the fatherless, yet spare the feelings of the innocent; the supernatural light partly showed me the way, and the words which I now heard whispered by my companions aided in directing the rest.

'I tell ye, Dame Johnstone,' said the piper, 'the man's no cannie; or what's waur, he may belong to the spiritual world himself, and do us a mischief. Saw ye ever mortal man riding with ae spur and carrying a silver-headed cane for a whip, wi' sic a fleece of hair about his haffets and sic a wild ee in his head; and then he kens a' things in the heavens aboon and the earth beneath. He kenned my favourite tune Clavers; I'se uphaud he's no in the body, but ane of the souls made perfect of the auld Covenanters whom Grahame or Grierson slew; we're daft to follow him.' 'Fool body,' I heard the widow say, 'I'll follow him; there's something about that man, be he in the spirit or in the flesh, which is pleasant and promising. O! could he but, by prayer or other means of lawful knowledge, tell me about my dear Walter Johnstone; thrice has he appeared to me in dream or vision with a sorrowful look, and weel ken I what that means.' We had now reached the edge of the morass, and a dim and uncertain light continued to twinkle about the green knoll which rose in its middle. I turned suddenly round and said, 'For a wise purpose am I come; to reveal murder; to speak consolation to the widow and the fatherless, and to soothe the perturbed spirits of those whose fierce passions ended in untimely death. Come with me; the hour is come, and I must not do my commission negligently.' 'I kenned it, I kenned it,' said the piper, 'he's just one of the auld persecuted worthies risen from his red grave to right the injured, and he'll do't discreetly; follow him, Dame, follow him.' 'I shall follow,' said the widow, 'I have that strength given me this night which will bear me through all trials which mortal flesh can endure.'

When we reached the little green hillock in the centre of the morass, I looked to the north and soon distinguished the place described by my friend Joseph Howatson, where the body of Walter Johnstone was deposited. The moon shone clear, the stars aided us with their light, and some turfcutters having left their spades standing near, I ordered the piper to take a spade and dig where I placed my staff. 'O dig carefully,' said the widow, 'do not be rude with mortal dust.' We dug and came to a sword; the point was broken and the blade hacked. 'It is the sword of my Walter Johnstone,' said his widow, 'I could swear to it among a thousand.' 'It is my father's sword,' said a fine dark haired boy who had followed us unperceived, 'it is my father's sword, and were he living who wrought this, he should na be lang in rueing it.' 'He is dead, my child,' I said, 'and beyond your reach, and vengeance is the Lord's.' 'O, Sir,' cried his widow, in a flood of tears, 'ye ken all things; tell me, is this my husband or no?' 'It is the body of Walter Johnstone,' I answered, 'slain by one who is passed to his account, and buried here by the hand that slew him, with his gold in his purse and his watch in his pocket.' So saying we uncovered the body, lifted it up, laid it on the grass; the embalming nature of the morass had preserved it from decay, and mother and child, with tears and with cries, named his name and lamented over him. His gold watch and his money, his cloak and his dress, were untouched and entire, and we bore him to the cottage of his widow, where with clasped hands she sat at his feet and his children at his head till the day drew nigh the dawn; I then rose and said, 'Woman, thy trials have been severe and manifold; a good wife, a good mother, and a good widow hast thou been, and thy reward will be where the blessed alone are admitted. It was revealed to me by a mysterious revelation that thy husband's body was where we found it; and I was commissioned by a voice, assuredly not of this world, to deliver thee this treasure, which is thy own, that thy children may be educated, and that bread and raiment may be thine.' And I delivered her husband's wealth into her hands, refused gold which she offered, and mounting my horse, rode over the hills and saw her no more. But I soon heard of her, for there rose a strange sound in the land, that a Good Spirit had appeared to the widow of Walter Johnstone, had disclosed where her husband's murdered body lay, had enriched her with all his lost wealth, had prayed by her side till the blessed dawn of day, and then vanished with the morning light. I closed my lips on the secret till now; and I reveal it to you, my children, that you may know there is a God who ruleth this world by wise and invisible means, and punisheth the wicked, and cheereth the humble of heart and the lowly minded.

Such was the last sermon of the good John Farley, a man whom I knew and loved. I think I see him now, with his long white hair and his look mild, eloquent, and sagacious. He was a giver of good counsel, a sayer of wise sayings, with wit at will, learning in abundance, and a gift in sarcasm which the wildest dreaded.

ROBERT LOUIS STEVENSON

THRAWN JANET

THE REVEREND MURDOCH SOULIS was long minister of the moorland parish of Balweary, in the vale of Dule. A severe, bleak-faced old man, dreadful to his hearers, he dwelt in the last years of his life, without relative or servant or any human company, in the small and lonely manse under the Hanging Shaw. In spite of the iron composure of his features, his eye was wild, scared, and uncertain; and when he dwelt, in private admonition, on the future of the impenitent, it seemed as if his eye pierced through the storms of time to the terrors of eternity. Many young persons, coming to prepare themselves against the season of the Holy Communion, were dreadfully affected by his talk. He had a sermon on 1st Peter v. and 8th, 'The devil as a roaring lion,' on the Sunday after every seventeenth of August, and he was accustomed to surpass himself upon that text both by the appalling nature of the matter and the terror of his bearing in the pulpit. The children were frightened into fits, and the old looked more than usually oracular, and were, all that day, full of those hints that Hamlet deprecated. The manse itself, where it stood by the water of Dule among some thick trees, with the Shaw overhanging it on the one side, and on the other many cold, moorish hill-tops rising toward the sky, had begun, at a very early period of Mr Soulis's ministry, to be avoided in the dusk hours by all who valued themselves upon their prudence; and guidmen sitting at the clachan alehouse shook their heads together at the thought of passing late by that uncanny neighbourhood. There was one spot, to be more particular, which was regarded with especial awe. The manse stood between the highroad and the water of Dule, with a gable to each; its back was towards the kirktown of Balweary, nearly half a mile away; in front of it, a bare garden, hedged with thorn, occupied the land between the river and the road. The house was two stories high, with two large rooms on each. It opened not directly on the garden, but on a causewayed path, or passage, giving on the road on the one hand, and closed on the other by the tall willows and elders that bordered on the stream. And it was this strip of causeway that enjoyed among the young parishioners of Balweary so infamous a reputation. The minister walked there often after dark, sometimes groaning aloud in the instancy of his unspoken prayers; and when he was from home, and the manse door was locked, the more daring schoolboys ventured, with beating hearts, to 'follow my leader' across that legendary spot.

This atmosphere of terror, surrounding, as it did, a man of God of spotless character and orthodoxy, was a common cause of wonder and subject of inquiry among the few strangers who were led by chance or business into that unknown, outlying country. But many even of the people of the parish were ignorant of the strange events which had marked the first year of Mr Soulis's ministrations; and among those who were better informed, some were naturally reticent, and others shy of that particular topic. Now and again, only, one of the older folk would warm into courage over his third tumbler, and recount the cause of the minister's strange looks and solitary life.

Fifty years syne, when Mr Soulis cam' first into Ba'weary, he was still a young man – a callant, the folk said – fu' o' book-learnin' an' grand at the exposition, but, as was natural in sae young a man, wi' nae leevin' experience in religion. The younger sort were greatly taken wi' his gifts and his gab; but auld, concerned, serious men and women were moved even to prayer for the young man, whom they took to be a self-deceiver, and the parish that was like to be sae ill-supplied. It was before the days o' the moderates – weary fa' them; but ill things are like guid – they baith come bit by bit, a pickle at a time; and there were folk even then that said the Lord had left the college professors to their ain devices, an' the lads that went to study wi' them wad hae done mair an' better sittin' in a peat-bog, like their forbears of the persecution, wi' a Bible under their oxter an' a speerit o' prayer in their heart. There was nae doubt onyway, but that Mr Soulis had been ower lang at the college. He was careful and troubled for mony things besides the ae thing needful. He had a feck o' books wi' him – mair than had ever been seen before in a' that presbytery; and a sair wark the carrier had wi' them, for they were a' like to have smoored in the De'il's Hag between this and Kilmackerlie. They were books o' divinity, to be sure, or so they ca'd them; but the serious were o' opinion there was little service for sae mony, when the hail o' God's Word would gang in the neuk o' a plaid. Then he wad sit half the day and half the nicht forbye, which was scant decent – writin', nae less; an' first they were feared he wad read his sermons; an' syne it proved he was writin' a book himsel', which was surely no' fittin' for ane o' his years an' sma' experience.

Onyway it behoved him to get an auld, decent wife to keep the manse for him an' see to his bit denners; an' he was recommended to an auld limmer – Janet M'Clour, they ca'd her – an' sae far left to himsel' as to be ower persuaded. There was mony advised him to the contrar, for Janet was mair than suspeckit by the best folk in Ba'weary. Lang or that, she had had a wean to a dragoon; she hadna come forrit* for maybe thretty year; and bairns had seen her mumblin' to hersel' up on Key's Loan in the gloamin', whilk was an unco time an' place for a God-fearin' woman. Howsoever, it was the laird himsel' that had first tauld the minister o' Janet; an' in thae days he wad hae gane a far gate to pleesure the laird. When folk tauld him that Janet was sib to the de'il, it was a' superstition by his way o' it; an' when they cast up the Bible to him an' the witch of Endor, he wad threep it doun their thrapples that thir days were a' gane by, an' the de'il was mercifully restrained.

Weel, when it got about the clachan that Janet M'Clour was to be servant at the manse, the folk were fair mad wi' her an' him thegither; an' some o' the guidwives had nae better to dae than get round her door-cheeks and chairge her wi' a' that was ken't again' her, frae the sodger's bairn to John Tamson's twa kye. She was nae great speaker; folk usually let her gang her ain gate, an' she let them gang theirs, wi' neither Fair-guid-een nor Fair-guid-day; but when she buckled to, she had a tongue to deave the miller. Up she got, an' there wasna an auld story in Ba'weary but she gart somebody lowp for it that day; they couldna say ae thing but she could say twa to it; till, at the hinder end, the guidwives up an' claught haud of her, an' clawed the coats aff her back, and pu'd her doun the clachan to the water o' Dule, to see if she were a witch or no, soom or droun. The carline skirled till ye could hear at the Hangin' Shaw, an' she focht like ten; there was mony a guidwife bure the mark o' her neist day an' mony a lang day after; an' just in the hettest o' the collieshangie, wha suld come up (for his sins) but the new minister!

* 'To come forrit' – to offer oneself as a communicant.

'Women,' said he (an' he had a grand voice), 'I charge you in the Lord's name to let her go.'

Janet ran to him – she was fair wud wi' terror – an' clang to him, an' prayed him, for Christ's sake, save her frae the cummers; an' they, for their pairt, tauld him a' that was ken't, an' maybe mair.

'Woman,' says he to Janet, 'is this true?'

'As the Lord sees me,' says she, 'as the Lord made me, no' a word o't. Forbye the bairn,' says she, 'I've been a decent woman a' my days.'

'Will you,' says Mr Soulis, 'in the name of God, and before me, His unworthy minister, renounce the devil and his works?'

Weel, it wad appear that when he askit that, she gave a girn that fairly frichit them that saw her, an' they could hear her teeth play dirl thegither in her chafts; but there was naething for it but the ae way or the ither; an' Janet lifted up her hand an' renounced the de'il before them a'.

'And now,' says Mr Soulis to the guidwives, 'home with ye, one and all, and pray to God for His forgiveness.'

An' he gied Janet his arm, though she had little on her but a sark, and took her up the clachan to her ain door like a leddy o' the land; an' her screighin' an' laughin' as was a scandal to be heard.

There were mony grave folk lang ower their prayers that nicht; but when the morn cam' there was sic a fear fell upon a' Ba'weary that the bairns hid theirsels, an' even the menfolk stood an' keekit frae their doors. For there was Janet comin' doun the clachan – her or her likeness, nane could tell – wi' her neck thrawn, an' her heid on ae side, like a body that has been hangit, an' a girn on her face like an unstreakit corp. By an' by they got used wi' it, an' even sneered at her to ken what was wrang; but frae that day forth

95

she couldna speak like a Christian woman, but slavered an' played click wi' her teeth like a pair o' shears; an' frae that day forth the name o' God cam' never on her lips. Whiles she wad try to say it, but it michtna be. Them that kenned best said least; but they never gied that Thing the name o' Janet M'Clour; for the auld Janet, by their way o't, was in muckle hell that day. But the minister was neither to haud nor to bind; he preached about naething but the folk's cruelty that had gi'en her a stroke of the palsy; he skelpit the bairns that meddled her; an' he had her up to the manse that same nicht, an' dwalled there a' his lane wi' her under the Hangin' Shaw.

Weel, time gaed by: and the idler sort commenced to think mair lichtly o' that black business. The minister was weel thocht o'; he was aye late at the writing, folk wad see his can'le doon by the Dule water after twal' at e'en; and he seemed pleased wi' himsel' an' upsitten as at first, though a' body could see that he was dwining. As for Janet she cam' an' she gaed; if she didna speak muckle afore, it was reason she should speak less then; she meddled naebody; but she was an eldritch thing to see, an' nane wad hae mistrysted wi' her for Ba'weary glebe.

About the end o' July there cam' a spell o' weather, the like o't never was in that country-side; it was lown an' het an' heartless; the herds couldna win up the Black Hill, the bairns were ower weariet to play; an' yet it was gousty too, wi' claps o' het wund that rumm'led in the glens, and bits o' shouers that slockened naething. We aye thocht it büt to thun'er on the morn; but the morn cam', an' the morn's morning, an' it was aye the same uncanny weather, sair on folks and bestial. O' a' that were the waur, nane suffered like Mr Soulis; he could neither sleep nor eat, he tauld his elders; an' when he wasna writin' at his weary book, he wad be stravaguin' ower a' the country-side like a man possessed, when a' body else was blithe to keep caller ben the house.

Abune Hangin' Shaw, in the bield o' the Black Hill, there's a bit enclosed grund wi' an iron yett: an' it seems, in the auld days, that was the kirkyaird o' Ba'weary, an' consecrated by the Papists before the blessed licht shone upon the kingdom. It was a great howff, o' Mr Soulis's onyway; there he wad sit an' consider his sermons; an' indeed it's a bieldy bit. Weel, as he cam' ower the wast end o' the Black Hill, ae day, he saw first twa, an' syne fower, an' syne seeven corbie craws fleein' round an' round abune the auld kirkyaird. They flew laigh an' heavy, an' squawked to ither as they gaed; an' it was clear to Mr Soulis that something had put them frae their ordinar. He wasna easy fleyed, an' gaed straucht up to the wa's; an' what suld he find there but a man, or the appearance o' a man, sittin' in the inside upon a grave. He was of a great stature, an' black as hell, and his e'en were singular to see.* Mr Soulis had heard tell o' black men, mony's the time; but there was something unco about this black man that daunted him. Het as he was, he took a kind o' cauld grue in the marrow o' his banes; but up he spak for a' that; an' says he: 'My friend, are you a stranger in this place?' The black man answered never a word; he got upon his feet, an' begoud on to hirsle to the wa' on the far side; but he aye lookit at the minister; an' the minister stood an' lookit back; till a' in a meenit the black man was ower the wa' an' rinnin' for the bield o' the trees. Mr Soulis, he hardly kenned why, ran after him; but he was fair forjeskit wi' his walk an' the het, unhalesome weather; an' rin as he likit, he got nae mair than

* It was a common belief in Scotland that the devil appeared as a black man. This appears in several witch trials and I think in Law's *Memorials*, that delightful storehouse of the quaint and grisly.

a glisk o' the black man amang the birks, till he won doun to the foot o' the hillside, an' there he saw him ance mair, gaun, hap-step-an'-lowp, ower Dule water to the manse.

Mr Soulis wasna weel pleased that this fearsome gangrel suld mak' sae free wi' Ba'weary manse; an' he ran the harder, an', wet shoon, ower the burn, an' up the walk; but the de'il a black man was there to see. He stepped out upon the road, but there was naebody there; he gaed a' ower the garden, but na, nae black man. At the hinder end, an' a bit feared as was but natural, he lifted the hasp an' into the manse; and there was Janet M'Clour before his e'en, wi' her thrawn craig, an' nane sae pleased to see him. An' he aye minded sinsyne, when first he set his e'en upon her, he had the same cauld and deidly grue.

'Janet,' says he, 'have you seen a black man?'

'A black man!' quo' she. 'Save us a'! Ye're no wise, minister. There's nae black man in a' Ba'weary.'

But she didna speak plain, ye maun understand; but yam-yammered, like a powney wi' the bit in its moo.

'Weel,' says he, 'Janet, if there was nae black man, I have spoken with the Accuser of the Brethren.'

An' he sat doun like ane wi' a fever, an' his teeth chittered in his heid.

'Hoots,' says she, 'think shame to yoursel', minister'; an' gied him a drap brandy that she keept aye by her.

Syne Mr Soulis gaed into his study amang a' his books. It's a lang, laigh, mirk chalmer, perishin' cauld in winter, an' no' very dry even in the top o' the simmer, for the manse stands near the burn. Sae doun he sat, and thocht of a' that had come an' gane since he was in Ba'weary, an' his hame, an' the days when he was a bairn an' ran daffin' on the braes; an' that black man aye ran in his heid like the owercome of a sang. Aye the mair he thocht, the mair he thocht o' the black man. He tried the prayer, an' the words wouldna come to him; an' he tried, they say, to write at his book, but he couldna mak' nar mair o' that. There was whiles he thocht the black man was at his oxter, an' the swat stood upon him cauld as well-water; and there was ither whiles, when he cam' to himsel' like a christened bairn an' minded naething.

The upshot was that he gaed to the window an' stood glowrin' at Dule water. The trees are unco thick, an' the water lies deep an' black under the manse; an' there was Janet washin' the cla'es wi' her coats kilted. She had her back to the minister, an' he, for his pairt, hardly kenned what he was lookin' at. Syne she turned round, an' shawed her face; Mr Soulis had the same cauld grue as twice that day afore, an' it was borne in upon him what folk said, that Janet was deid lang syne, an' this was a bogle in her clay-cauld flesh. He drew back a pickle and he scanned her narrowly. She was tramp-trampin' in the cla'es croonin' to hersel'; and eh! Gude guide us, but it was a fearsome face. Whiles she sang louder, but there was nae man born o' woman that could tell the words o' her sang; an' whiles she lookit side-lang doun, but there was naething there for her to look at. There gaed a scunner through the flesh upon his banes; an' that was Heeven's advertisement. But Mr Soulis just blamed himsel', he said, to think sae ill o' a puir, auld afflicted wife that hadna a freend forbye himsel'; an' he put up a bit prayer for him an' heir, an' drank a little caller water – for his heart rose again' the meat – an' gaed up to his naked bed in the gloamin'.

That was a nicht that has never been forgotten in Ba'weary, the nicht o' the seeventeenth o' August, seeventeen hun'er' an' twal'. It had been het afore, as I hae said, but that nicht it was hetter than ever. The sun gaed doun amang unco-lookin' clouds; it fell as mirk as the pit; no' a star, no' a breath o' wund; ye couldna see your han' afore your face, an' even the

99

auld folk cuist the covers frae their beds an' lay pechin' for their breath. Wi' a' that he had upon his mind, it was gey an' unlikely Mr Soulis wad get muckle sleep. He lay an' he tummled; the gude, caller bed that he got into brunt his very banes; whiles he slept, an' whiles he waukened; whiles he heard the time o' nicht, an' whiles a tyke yowlin' up the muir, as if somebody was deid; whiles he thocht he heard bogles claverin' in his lug, an' whiles he saw spunkies in the room. He behoved, he judged, to be sick; an' sick he was – little he jaloosed the sickness.

At the hinder end, he got a clearness in his mind, sat up in his sark on the bed-side, an' fell thinkin' ance mair o' the black man an' Janet. He couldna weel tell how – maybe it was the cauld to his feet – but it cam' in upon him wi' a spate that there was some connection between thir twa, an' that either or baith o' them were bogles. An' just at that moment, in Janet's room, which was neist to his, there cam' a stramp o' feet as if men were wars'lin', an' then a loud bang; an' then a wund gaed reishling round the fower quarters o' the house; an' then a' was ance mair as seelent as the grave.

Mr Soulis was feared for neither man nor de'il. He got his tinder-box, an' lit a can'le, an' made three steps o't ower to Janet's door. It was on the hasp, an' he pushed it open, an' keeked bauldly in. It was a big room, as big as the minister's ain, an' plenished wi grand, auld solid gear, for he had naething else. There was a fower-posted bed wi' auld tapestry; an' a braw cabinet o' aik, that was fu' o' the minister's divinity books, an' put there to be out o' the gate; an' a wheen duds o' Janet's lying here an' there about the floor. But nae Janet could Mr Soulis see; nor ony sign o' a contention. In he gaed (an' there's few that wad hae followed him) an' lookit a' round, an' listened. But there was naething to be heard, neither inside the manse nor in a' Ba'weary parish, an' naething to be seen but the muckle shadows turnin' round the can'le. An' then, a' at aince, the minister's heart played dunt an' stood stock-still; an' a cauld wund blew amang the hairs o' his heid. Whaten a weary sicht was that for the puir man's e'en! For there was Janet hangin' frae a nail beside the auld aik cabinet: her heid aye lay on her shouther, her e'en were steekit, the tongue projected frae her mouth, an' her heels were twa feet clear abune the floor.

'God forgive us all!' thocht Mr Soulis, 'poor Janet's dead.'

He cam' a step nearer to the corp; an' then his heart fair whammled in his inside. For by what cantrip it wad ill beseem a man to judge, she was hangin' frae a single nail an' by a single wursted thread for darnin' hose.

It 's a awfu' thing to be your lane at nicht wi' siccan prodigies o' darkness; but Mr Soulis was strong in the Lord. He turned an' gaed his ways oot o' that room, an' lockit the door ahint him; an' step by step, doun the stairs, as heavy as leed; and set doun the can'le on the table at the stairfoot. He couldna pray, he couldna think, he was dreepin' wi' caul' swat, an' naething could he hear but the dunt-dunt-duntin' o' his ain heart. He micht maybe hae stood there an hour, or maybe twa, he minded sae little; when a' o' a sudden, he heard a laigh, uncanny steer up-stairs; a foot gaed to an' fro in the chalmer whaur the corp was hangin'; syne the door was opened, though he minded weel that he had lockit it; an' syne there was a step upon the landin', an' it seemed to him as if the corp was lookin' ower the rail and doun upon him whaur he stood.

He took up the can'le again (for he couldna want the licht), an' as saftly as ever he could, gaed straucht oot o' the manse an' to the far end o' the causeway. It was aye pit-mirk; the flame o' the can'le, when he set it on the grund, brunt steedy and clear as in a room; naething moved, but the Dule water seepin' and sabbin' doun the glen, an' yon unhaly footstep that cam' ploddin' doun the stairs inside the manse. He kenned the foot ower weel, for it was Janet's; an' at ilka step that cam' a wee thing nearer, the cauld got deeper in his vitals. He commended his soul to Him that made an' keepit him; 'and, O Lord,' said he, 'give me strength this night to war against the powers of evil.'

By this time the foot was comin' through the passage for the door; he could hear a hand skirt alang the wa', as if the fearsome thing was feelin' for its way. The saughs tossed an' maned thegither, a long sigh cam' ower the hills, the flame o' the can'le was blawn aboot; an' there stood the corp of Thrawn Janet, wi' her grogram goun an' her black mutch, wi' the heid aye upon the shouther, an' the girn still upon the face o't – leevin', ye wad hae said – deid, as Mr Soulis weel kenned – upon the threshold o' the manse.

It's a strange thing that the soul of a man should be that thirled into his perishable body; but the minister saw that, an' his heart didna break.

She didna stand there lang; she began to move again an' cam' slowly towards Mr Soulis whaur he stood under the saughs. A' the life o' his body, a' the strength o' his speerit, were glowerin' frae his e'en. It seemed she was gaun to speak, but wanted words, an' made a sign wi' the left hand. There cam' a clap o' wund, like a cat's fuff; oot gaed the can'le, the saughs skreighed like folk; an' Mr Soulis kenned that, live or die, this was the end o't.

'Witch, beldame, devil!' he cried, 'I charge you, by the power of God, begone – if you be dead, to the grave – if you be damned, to hell.'

An' at that moment the Lord's ain hand out o' the Heevens struck the Horror whaur it stood; the auld, deid, desecrated corp o' the witch-wife, sae lang keepit frae the grave and hirsled round by de'ils, lowed up like a brunstane spunk an' fell in ashes to the grund; the thunder followed, peal on dirlin' peal, the rairin' rain upon the back o' that; and Mr Soulis lowped through the garden hedge, an' ran, wi' skelloch upon skelloch, for the clachan.

That same mornin', John Christie saw the Black Man pass the Muckle Cairn as it was chappin' six; before eicht, he gaed by the change-house at Knockdow; an' no' lang after, Sandy M'Lellan saw him gaun linkin' doun the braes frae Kilmackerlie. There's little doubt but it was him that dwalled sae lang in Janet's body; but he was awa' at last; an' sinsyne the de'il has never fashed us in Ba'weary.

But it was a sair dispensation for the minister; lang, lang he lay ravin' in his bed; an' frae that hour to this, he was the man ye ken the day.

MARGARET OLIPHANT

THE OPEN DOOR

I TOOK THE house of Brentwood on my return from India in 18–, for the temporary accommodation of my family, until I could find a permanent home for them. It had many advantages which made it peculiarly appropriate. It was within reach of Edinburgh, and my boy Roland, whose education had been considerably neglected, could go in and out to school, which was thought to be better for him than either leaving home altogether or staying there always with a tutor. The first of these expedients would have seemed preferable to me, the second commended itself to his mother. The doctor, like a judicious man, took the midway between. 'Put him on his pony and let him ride into the Academy every morning; it will do him all the good in the world,' Dr Simson said; 'and when it is bad weather there is the train.' His mother accepted this solution of the difficulty more easily than I could have hoped; and our pale-faced boy, who had never known anything more invigorating than Simla, began to encounter the brisk breezes of the North in the subdued severity of the month of May. Before the time of the vacation in July we had the satisfaction of seeing him begin to acquire something of the brown and ruddy complexion of his schoolfellows. The English system did not commend itself to Scotland in these days. There was no little Eton at Fettes; nor do I think, if there had been, that a genteel exotic of that class would have tempted either my wife or me. The lad was doubly precious to us, being the only one left us of many; and he was fragile in body, we believed, and deeply sensitive in mind. To keep him at home, and yet to send him to school – to combine the advantages of the two systems – seemed to be everything that could be desired. The two girls also found at Brentwood everything they wanted. They were near enough to Edinburgh to have masters and lessons as many as they required for completing that never-ending education which the young people seem to require nowadays. Their mother married me when she was younger than Agatha, and I should like to see them improve upon their mother! I myself was then no more than twenty-five – an age at which I see the young fellows now groping about them, with no notion what they are going to do with their lives. However, I suppose every generation has a conceit of itself which elevates it, in its own opinion, above that which comes after it. Brentwood stands on that fine and wealthy slope of country, one of the richest in Scotland, which lies between the Pentland Hills and the Firth. In clear weather you could see the blue gleam – like a bent bow, embracing the wealthy fields and scattered houses – of the great estuary on one side of you; and on the other the blue heights, not gigantic like those we had been used to, but just high enough for all the glories of the atmosphere, the play of clouds, and sweet reflections, which give to a hilly country an interest and a charm which nothing else can emulate. Edinburgh, with its two lesser heights – the Castle and the Calton Hill – its spires and towers piercing through the smoke, and Arthur's Seat, lying crouched behind, like a guardian no longer very needful, taking his repose beside the well-beloved charge, which is now, so to speak, able to take care of itself without him – lay at our right hand. From the lawn and drawing-room windows we could see all these varieties of landscape. The colour was sometimes a little chilly, but sometimes, also, as animated and full of vicissitude as a drama. I was never tired of it. Its colour and freshness revived the eyes which had grown weary of arid plains and blazing skies. It was always cheery, and fresh, and full of repose.

The village of Brentwood lay almost under the house, on the other side of the deep little ravine, down which a stream – which ought to have been a lovely, wild, and frolicsome little river – flowed between its rocks and trees. The river, like so many in that district, had, however, in its earlier life been sacrificed to trade, and was grimy with paper-making. But this did not affect our pleasure in it so much as I have known it to affect other streams. Perhaps our water was more rapid – perhaps less clogged with dirt and refuse. Our side of the dell was charmingly *accidenté*, and clothed with fine trees, through which various paths wound down to the river-side and to the village bridge which crossed the stream. The village lay in the hollow, and climbed, with very prosaic houses, the other side. Village architecture does not flourish in Scotland. The blue slates and the grey stone are sworn foes to the picturesque; and though I do not, for my own part, dislike the interior of an old-fashioned pewed and galleried church, with its little family settlements on all sides, the square box outside, with its bit of a spire like a handle to lift it by, is not an improvement to the landscape. Still a cluster of houses on differing elevations, with scraps of garden coming in between, a hedgerow with clothes laid out to dry, the opening of a street with its rural sociability, the women at their doors, the slow waggon lumbering along – gives a centre to the landscape. It was cheerful to look at, and convenient in a hundred ways. Within ourselves we had walks in plenty, the glen being always beautiful in all its phases, whether the woods were green in the spring or ruddy in the autumn. In the park which surrounded the house were the ruins of the former mansion of Brentwood, a much smaller and less important house than the solid Georgian edifice which we inhabited. The ruins were picturesque, however, and gave importance to the place. Even we, who were but temporary tenants, felt a vague pride in them, as if they somehow reflected a certain consequence upon ourselves. The old building had the remains of a tower, an indistinguishable mass of mason-work, overgrown with ivy, and the shells of walls attached to this were half filled up with soil. I had never examined it closely, I am ashamed to say. There was a large room, or what had been a large room, with the lower part of the windows still existing, on the principal floor, and underneath other windows, which were perfect, though half filled up with fallen soil, and waving with a wild growth of brambles and chance growths of all kinds. This was the oldest part of all. At a little distance were some very commonplace and disjointed fragments of building, one of them suggesting a certain pathos by its very commonness and the complete wreck which it showed. This was the end of a low gable, a bit of grey wall, all encrusted with lichens, in which was a common doorway. Probably it had been a servants' entrance, a back-door, or opening into what are called 'the offices' in Scotland. No offices remained to be entered – pantry and kitchen had all been swept out of being; but there stood the doorway open and vacant, free to all the winds, to the rabbits, and every wild creature. It struck my eye, the first time I went to Brentwood, like a melancholy comment upon a life that was over. A door that led to nothing – closed once, perhaps, with anxious care, bolted and guarded, now void of any meaning. It impressed me, I remember, from the first; so perhaps it may be said that my mind was prepared to attach to it an importance which nothing justified.

The summer was a very happy period of repose for us all. The warmth of Indian suns was still in our veins, and we did not feel the cold. It seemed to us that we could never have enough of the greenness, the dewiness, the freshness of the northern landscape. Even its mists were pleasant to us, taking all the fever out of us, and pouring in vigour and refreshment. In autumn we followed the fashion of the time, and went away for change, which we did not in the least require. It was when the family had settled down for the winter, when the days were short and dark, and the rigorous reign of frost upon us, that the incidents occurred which alone could justify me in intruding upon the world my private affairs. These incidents were, however, of so curious a character, that I hope my inevitable references to my own family and pressing personal interests will meet with a general pardon.

I was absent in London when these events began. In London an old Indian plunges back into the interests with which all his previous life has been associated, and meets old friends at every step. I had been circulating among some half-dozen of these – enjoying the return of my former life in shadow, though I had been so thankful in substance to throw it aside – and had missed some of my home letters, what with going down from Friday to Monday to old Benbow's place in the country, and stopping on the way back to dine and sleep at Sellar's, and to take a look into Cross's stables, which occupied another day. It is never safe to miss one's letters. In this transitory life, as the Prayer-book says, how can one ever be certain what is going to happen? All was perfectly well at home. I knew very well (I thought) what they would have to say to me: 'The weather has been so fine, that Roland has not once gone by train, and he enjoys the ride beyond anything.' 'Dear papa, be sure that you don't forget anything, but bring us so-and-so, and so-and-so' – a list as long as my arm. Dear girls and dearer mother! I would not for the world have forgotten their commissions, or given the sight of their little letters, for all the Benbows and Crosses in the world.

But I was confident in my home-comfort and peacefulness. When I got back to my club, however, three or four letters were lying for me, upon some of which I noticed the 'immediate', 'urgent', which old-fashioned people and anxious people still believe will influence the post-office and quicken the speed of the mails. I was about to open one of these, when the club porter brought me two telegrams, one of which, he said, had arrived the night before. I opened, as was to be expected, the last first, and this was what I read: 'Why don't you come or answer? For God's sake, come. He is much worse.' This was a thunderbolt to fall upon a man's head who had one only son, and he the light of his eyes! The other telegram, which I opened with hands trembling so much that I lost time by my haste, was to much the same purport: 'No better; doctor afraid of brain-fever. Calls for you day and night. Let nothing detain you.' The first thing I did was to look up the time-tables to see if there was any way of getting off sooner than by the night-train, though I knew well enough there was not; and then I read the letters, which furnished, alas! too clearly, all the details. They told me that the boy had been pale for some time, with a scared look. His mother had noticed it before I left home, but would not say anything to alarm me. This look had increased day by day; and soon it was observed that Roland came home at a wild gallop through the park, his pony panting and in foam, himself 'as white as a sheet', but with the perspiration streaming from his forehead. For a long time he had resisted all questioning, but at length had developed such strange changes of mood, showing a reluctance to go to school, a desire to be fetched in the carriage at night – which was a ridiculous piece of luxury – an unwillingness to go out in the grounds, and nervous start at every sound, that his mother had insisted upon an explanation. When the boy – our boy Roland, who had never known what fear was – began to talk to her of voices he had heard in the park, and shadows that had appeared to him among the ruins, my wife promptly put him to bed and sent for Dr Simson – which, of course, was the only thing to do.

I hurried off that evening, as may be supposed, with an anxious heart. How I got through the hours before the starting of the train, I cannot tell. We must all be thankful for the quickness of the railway when in anxiety; but to have thrown myself into a post-chaise as soon as horses could be put to, would have been a relief. I got to Edinburgh very early in the blackness of the winter morning, and scarcely dared look the man in the face, at whom I gasped 'What news?' My wife had sent the brougham for me, which I concluded, before the man spoke, was a bad sign. His answer was that stereotyped answer which leaves the imagination so wildly free – 'Just the same.' Just the same! What might that mean? The horses seemed to me to creep along the long dark country-road. As we dashed through the park, I thought I heard some one moaning among the trees, and clenched my fist at them (whoever they might be) with fury. Why had the fool of a woman at the gate allowed any one to come in to disturb the quiet of the place? If I had not been in such hot haste to get home, I think I should have stopped the carriage and got out to see what tramp it was that had made an entrance, and chosen my grounds, of all places in the world, – when my boy was ill! – to grumble and groan in. But I had no reason to complain of our slow pace here. The horses flew like lightning along the intervening path, and drew up at the door all panting, as if they had run a race. My wife stood at the open door with a pale face, and a candle in her hand, which made her look paler still as the wind blew the flame about. 'He is sleeping,' she said in a whisper, as if her voice might wake him. And I replied, when I could find my voice, also in a whisper, as though the jingling of the horses' furniture and the sound of their hoofs must not have been more dangerous. I stood on the steps with her a moment, almost afraid to go in, now that I was here; and it seemed to me that I saw without observing, if I may say so, that the horses were unwilling to turn round, though their stables lay that way, or that the men were unwilling. These things occurred to me afterwards, though at the moment I was not capable of anything but to ask questions and to hear of the condition of the boy.

I looked at him from the door of his room, for we were afraid to go near, lest we should disturb that blessed sleep. It looked like actual sleep – not the lethargy into which my wife told me he would sometimes fall. She told me everything in the next room, which communicated with his, rising now and then and going to the door of communication; and in this there was much that was very startling and confusing to the mind. It appeared that ever since the winter began, since it was early dark, and night had fallen before his return from school, he had been hearing voices among the ruins – at first only a groaning, he said, at which his pony was as much alarmed as he was, but by degrees a voice. The tears ran down my wife's cheeks as she described to me how he would start up in the night and cry out, 'Oh, mother, let me in! oh, mother, let me in!' with a pathos which rent her heart. And she sitting there all the time, only longing to do everything his heart could desire! But though she would try to soothe him, crying, 'You are at home, my darling. I am here. Don't you know me? Your mother is here!' he would only stare at her, and after a while spring up again with the same cry. At other times he would be quite reasonable, she said, asking eagerly when I was coming, but declaring that he must go with me as soon as I did so, 'to let them in.' 'The doctor thinks his nervous system must have received a shock,' my wife said. 'Oh, Henry, can it be that we have pushed him on too much with his work – a delicate boy like Roland? – and what is his work in comparison with his health? Even you would think little of honours or prizes if it hurt the boy's health.' Even I! as if I were an inhuman father sacrificing my child to my ambition. But I would not increase her trouble by taking any notice. After a while they persuaded me to lie down, to rest, and to eat – none of which things had been possible since one received their letters. The mere fact of being on the spot of course, in itself was a great thing; and when I knew that I could be called in a moment, as soon as he was awake and wanted me, I felt capable, even in the dark, chill morning twilight, to snatch an hour or two's sleep. As it happened, I was so worn out with the strain of anxiety, and he so quieted and consoled by knowing I had come, that I was not disturbed till the afternoon, when the twilight had again settled down. There was just daylight enough to see his face when I went to him; and what a change in a fortnight! He was paler and more worn, I thought, than even in those dreadful days in the plains before we left India. His hair seemed to me to have grown long and lank; his eyes were like blazing lights projecting out of his white face. He got hold of my hand in a cold and tremulous clutch, and waved to everybody to go away. 'Go away – even mother,' he said, – 'go away.' This went to her heart, for she did not like that even I should have more of the boy's confidence than herself;

but my wife has never been a woman to think of herself, and she left us alone. 'Are they all gone?' he said, eagerly. 'They would not let me speak. The doctor treated me as if I was a fool. You know I am not a fool, papa.'

'Yes, yes, my boy, I know; but you are ill, and quiet is so necessary. You are not only not a fool, Roland, but you are reasonable and understand. When you are ill you must deny yourself; you must not do everything that you might do being well.'

He waved his thin hand with a sort of indignation. 'Then, father, I am not ill,' he cried. 'Oh, I thought when you came you would not stop me, – you would see the sense of it! What do you think is the matter with me, all of you? Simson is well enough, but he is only a doctor. What do you think is the matter with me? I am no more ill than you are. A doctor, of course, he thinks you are ill the moment he looks at you – that's what he's there for – and claps you into bed.'

'Which is the best place for you at present, my dear boy.'

'I made up my mind,' cried the little fellow, 'that I would stand it till you came home. I said to myself, I won't frighten mother and the girls. But now, father,' he cried, half jumping out of the bed, 'it's not illness, – it's a secret.'

His eyes shone so wildly, his face was so swept with strong feeling, that my heart sank within me. It could be nothing but fever that did it, and fever had been so fatal. I got him into my arms to put him back into bed. 'Roland,' I said, humouring the poor child, which I knew was the only way, 'if you are going to tell me this secret to do any good, you know you must be quite quiet, and not excite yourself. If you excite yourself, I must not let you speak.'

'Yes, father,' said the boy. He was quiet directly, like a man, as if he quite understood. When I had laid him back on his pillow, he looked up at me with that grateful sweet look with which children, when they are ill, break one's heart, the water coming into his eyes in his weakness. 'I was sure as soon as you were here you would know what to do,' he said.

'To be sure, my boy. Now keep quiet, and tell it all out like a man.' To think I was telling lies to my own child! for I did it only to humour him, thinking, poor little fellow, his brain was wrong.

'Yes, father. Father, there is some one in the park, – some one that has been badly used.'

'Hush, my dear; you remember, there is to be no excitement. Well, who is this somebody, and who has been ill-using him? We will soon put a stop to that.'

'Ah,' cried Roland, 'but it is not so easy as you think. I don't know who it is. It is just a cry. Oh, if you could hear it! It gets into my head in my sleep. I heard it as clear – as clear; – and they think that I am dreaming – or raving perhaps,' the boy said, with a sort of disdainful smile.

This look of his perplexed me; it was less like fever than I thought. 'Are you quite sure you have not dreamt it, Roland!' I said.

'Dreamt? – that!' He was springing up again when he suddenly bethought himself, and lay down flat with the same sort of smile on his face. 'The pony heard it too,' he said. 'She jumped as if she had been shot. If I had not grasped at the reins, – for I was frightened, father—'

'No shame to you, my boy,' said I, though I scarcely knew why.

'If I hadn't held to her like a leech, she'd have pitched me over her head, and never drew breath till we were at the door. Did the pony dream it?' he said, with a soft disdain, yet indulgence for my foolishness. Then he added slowly: 'It was only a cry the first time, and all the time before you went

117

away. I wouldn't tell you, for it was so wretched to be frightened. I thought it might be a hare or a rabbit snared, and I went in the morning and looked, but there was nothing. It was after you went I heard it really first, and this is what it says.' He raised himself on his elbow close to me, and looked me in the face. ' "Oh, mother, let me in! oh, mother, let me in!" ' As he said the words a mist came over his face, the mouth quivered, the soft features all melted and changed, and when he had ended these pitiful words, dissolved in a shower of heavy tears.

Was it a hallucination? Was it the fever of the brain? Was it the disordered fancy caused by great bodily weakness? How could I tell? I thought it wisest to accept it as if it were all true.

'This is very touching, Roland,' I said.

'Oh, if you had just heard it, father! I said to myself, if father heard it he would do something; but mamma, you know, she's given over to Simson, and that fellow's a doctor, and never thinks of anything but clapping you into bed.'

'We must not blame Simson for being a doctor, Roland.'

'No, no,' said my boy, with delightful toleration and indulgence; 'oh no; that's the good of him – that's what he's for; I know that. But you – you are different; you are just father, and you'll do something, – directly, papa, directly, – this very night.'

'Surely,' I said. 'No doubt it is some little lost child.'

He gave me a sudden, swift look, investigating my face as if to see if, after all, this was everything my eminence as 'father' came to, – no more than that? Then he got hold of my shoulder, clutching it with his thin hand: 'Look here,' he said, with a quiver in his voice; 'suppose it wasn't living at all!'

'My dear boy, how then could you have heard it?' I said.

He turned away from me with a pettish exclamation – 'As if you didn't know better than that!'

'Do you want to tell me it is a ghost?' I said.

Roland withdrew his hand; his countenance assumed an aspect of great dignity and gravity; a slight quiver remained about his lips. 'Whatever it was – you always said we were not to call names. It was something – in trouble. Oh, father, in terrible trouble!'

'But, my boy,' I said – I was at my wits' end – 'if it was a child that was lost, or any poor human creature – but, Roland, what do you want me to do?'

'I should know if I was you,' said the child, eagerly. 'That is what I always said to myself – Father will know. Oh, papa, papa, to have to face it night after night, in such terrible, terrible trouble! and never to be able to do it any good. I don't want to cry; it's like a baby, I know; but I can't help it; – out there all by itself in the ruin, and nobody to help it. I can't bear it, I can't bear it!' cried my generous boy. And in his weakness he burst out, after many attempts to restrain it, into a great childish fit of sobbing and tears.

I do not know that I ever was in a greater perplexity in my life; and afterwards, when I thought of it, there was something comic in it too. It is bad enough to find your child's mind possessed with the conviction that he has seen – or heard – a ghost. But that he should require you to go instantly and help that ghost, was the most bewildering experience that had ever come my way. I am a sober man myself, and not superstitious – at least any more than everybody is superstitious. Of course I do not believe in ghosts; but I don't deny any more than other people, that there are stories, which I cannot pretend to understand. My blood got a sort of chill in my veins at the idea that Roland should be a ghost-seer; for that generally means a hysterical temperament and weak health, and all that men most hate and fear for their children. But that I should take up his ghost and right its wrongs, and save it from its trouble, was such a mission as was enough to confuse any man. I did my best to console my boy without giving any promise of this astonishing kind; but he was too sharp for me. He would have none of my caresses. With sobs breaking in at intervals upon his voice, and the rain-drops hanging on his eyelids, he yet returned to the charge.

'It will be there now – it will be there all the night. Oh, think, papa, think, if it was me! I can't rest for thinking of it. Don't!' he cried, putting away my hand – 'don't! You go and help it, and mother can take care of me.'

'But, Roland, what can I do?'

My boy opened his eyes, which were large with weakness and fever, and gave me a smile such, I think, as sick children only know the secret of. 'I was sure you would know as soon as you came. I always said – Father will know: and mother,' he cried, with a softening of repose upon his face, his limbs relaxing, his form sinking with a luxurious repose in his bed – 'mother can come and take care of me.'

I called her, and saw him turn to her with the complete dependence of a child, and then I went away and left them, as perplexed a man as any in Scotland. I must say, however, I had this consolation, that my mind was greatly eased about Roland. He might be under a hallucination, but his head was clear enough, and I did not think him so ill as everybody else did. The girls were astonished even at the ease with which I took his illness. 'How do you think he is?' they said in a breath, coming round me, laying hold of me. 'Not half so ill as I expected,' I said; 'not very bad at all.' 'Oh, papa, you are a darling!' cried Agatha, kissing me, and crying upon my shoulder; while little Jeanie, who was as pale as Roland, clasped both her arms round mine, and could not speak at all. I knew nothing about it, not half so much as Simson, but they believed in me; they had a feeling that all would go right now. God is very good to you when your children look to you like that. It makes one humble, not proud. I was not worthy of it; and then I recollected that I had to act the part of a father to Roland's ghost, which made me almost laugh, though I might just as well have cried. It was the strangest mission that ever was intrusted to mortal man.

It was then I remembered suddenly the looks of the men when they turned to take the brougham to the stables in the dark that morning: they had not liked it, and the horses had not liked it. I remembered that even in my anxiety about Roland I had heard them tearing along the avenue back to the stables, and had made a memorandum mentally that I must speak of it. It seemed to me that the best thing I could do was to go to the stables now and make a few inquiries. It is impossible to fathom the minds of rustics; there might be some deviltry of practical joking, for anything I knew; or they might have some reason in getting up a bad reputation for the Brentwood avenue. It was getting dark by the time I went out, and nobody who knows the country will need to be told how black is the darkness of a November night under high laurel-bushes and yew-trees. I walked into the heart of the shrubberies two or three times, not seeing a step before me, till I came out upon the broader carriage-road, where the trees opened a little, and there was a faint grey glimmer of sky visible, under which the great limes and elms stood darkling like ghosts; but it grew black again as I approached the corner where the ruins lay. Both eyes and ears were on the alert, as may be supposed; but I could see nothing in the absolute gloom, and, so far as I can recollect, I heard nothing. Nevertheless there came a strong impression upon me that somebody was there. It is a sensation which most people have felt. I have seen when it has been strong enough to awake you out of sleep, the sense of some one looking at you. I suppose my imagination had been affected by Roland's story; and the mystery of the darkness is always full of suggestions. I stamped my feet violently on the gravel to rouse myself, and called out sharply, 'Who's there?' Nobody answered, nor did I expect any one to answer, but the impression had been made. I was so foolish that I did not like to look back, but went sideways, keeping an eye on the gloom behind. It was with great relief that I spied the light in the stables, making a sort of oasis in the darkness. I walked very quickly into the midst of that lighted and cheerful place, and thought the clank of the groom's pail one of the pleasantest sounds I had ever heard. The coachman was the head of this little colony, and it was to his house I went to pursue my investigations. He was a native of the district, and had taken care of the place in the absence of the family for years; it was impossible but that he must know everything that was going on, and all the traditions of the place. The men, I could see, eyed me anxiously when I thus appeared at such an hour among them, and followed me with their eyes to Jarvis's house, where he lived alone with his old wife, their children being all married and out in the world. Mrs Jarvis met me with anxious questions. How was the poor young gentleman? but the others knew, I could see by their faces, that not even this was the foremost thing in my mind.

'Noises? – ou ay, there'll be noises – the wind in the trees, and the water soughing down the glen. As for tramps, Cornel, no, there's little o' that kind o' cattle about here; and Merran at the gate's a careful body.' Jarvis moved about with some embarrassment from one leg to another as he spoke. He kept in the shade, and did not look at me more than he could help. Evidently his mind was perturbed, and he had reasons for keeping his own counsel. His wife sat by, giving him a quick look now and then, but saying nothing. The kitchen was very snug, and warm, and bright – as different as could be from the chill and mystery of the night outside.

'I think you are trifling with me, Jarvis,' I said.

'Triflin', Cornel? no me. What would I trifle for? If the deevil himsel was in the auld hoose, I have no interest in't one way or another—'

'Sandy, hold your peace!' cried his wife, imperatively.

'And what am I to hold my peace for, wi' the Cornel standing there asking a' thae questions? I'm saying, if the deevil himsel—'

'And I'm telling ye hold your peace!' cried the woman, in great excitement. 'Dark November weather and lang nichts, and us that ken a' we ken. How daur ye name – a name that shouldna be spoken?' She threw down her stocking and got up, also in great agitation. 'I tellt ye you never could keep it. It's no a thing that will hide; and the haill toun kens as weel as you or me. Tell the Cornel straight out, or see, I'll do it. I dinna hold wi' your secrets: and a secret that the haill toun kens!' She snapped her fingers with an air of large disdain. As for Jarvis, ruddy and big as he was, he shrank to nothing before this decided woman. He repeated to her two or three times her own adjuration, 'Hold your peace!' then, suddenly changing his tone, cried out, 'Tell him then, confound ye! I'll wash my hands o't. If a' the ghosts in Scotland were in the auld hoose, is that ony concern o' mine?'

After this I elicited without much difficulty the whole story. In the opinion of the Jarvises, and of everybody about, the certainty that the place was haunted was beyond all doubt. As Sandy and his wife warmed to the tale, one tripping up another in their eagerness to tell everything, it gradually developed as distinct a superstition as I ever heard, and not without poetry and pathos. How long it was since the voice had been heard first, nobody could tell with certainty. Jarvis's opinion was that his father, who had been coachman at Brentwood before him, had never heard anything about it, and that the whole thing had arisen within the last ten years, since the complete dismantling of the old house: which was a wonderfully modern date for a tale so well authenticated. According to these witnesses, and to several whom I questioned afterwards, and who were all in perfect agreement, it was only in the months of November and December that 'the visitation' occurred. During these months, the darkest of the year, scarcely a night passed without the recurrence of these inexplicable cries. Nothing, it was said, had ever been seen – at least nothing that could be identified. Some people, bolder or more imaginative than the others, had seen the darkness moving, Mrs Jarvis said, with unconscious poetry. It began when night fell, and continued, at intervals, till day broke. Very often it was only an inarticulate cry and moaning, but sometimes the words which had taken possession of my poor boy's fancy had been distinctly audible – 'Oh, mother, let me in!' The Jarvises were not aware that there had ever been any investigation into it. The estate of Brentwood had lapsed into the hands of a distant branch of the family, who had lived but little there; and of the many people who had taken it, as I had done, few had remained through two Decembers. And nobody had taken the trouble to make a very close examination into the facts. 'No, no,' Jarvis said, shaking his head, 'no, no, Cornel. Wha wad set themsels up for a laughin'-stock to a' the country-side, making a wark about a ghost? Naebody believes in ghosts. It bid to be the wind in the trees, the last gentleman said, or some effec' o' the water wrastlin' among the rocks. He said it was a' quite easy explained: but he gave up the hoose. And when you cam, Cornel, we were awfu' anxious you should never hear. What for should I have spoiled the bargain and hairmed the property for no-thing?'

'Do you call my child's life nothing?' I said in the trouble of the moment, unable to restrain myself. 'And instead of telling this all to me, you have told it to him – to a delicate boy, a child unable to sift evidence, or judge for himself, a tender-hearted young creature—'

I was walking about the room with an anger all the hotter that I felt it to be most likely quite unjust. My heart was full of bitterness against the stolid retainers of a family who were content to risk other people's children and comfort rather than let a house lie empty. If I had been warned I might have taken precautions, or left the place, or sent Roland away, a hundred things which now I could not do; and here I was with my boy in brain-fever, and his life, the most precious life on earth, hanging in the balance, dependent on whether or not I could get to the reason of a *banal*, commonplace ghost-story! I paced about in high wrath, not seeing what I was to do; for, to take Roland away, even if he were able to travel, would not settle his agitated mind; and I feared even that a scientific explanation of refracted sound, or reverberation, or any other of the easy certainties with which we elder men are silenced, would have very little effect upon the boy.

'Cornel,' said Jarvis, solemnly, 'and she'll bear me witness – the young gentleman never heard a word from me – no, nor from either groom or gardener; I'll gie ye my word for that. In the first place, he's no a lad that invites ye to talk. There are some that are, and some that arena. Some will draw ye on, till ye've tellt them a' the clatter of the toun, and a' ye ken, and whiles mair. But Maister Roland, his mind's fu' of his books. He's aye civil and kind, and a fine lad; but no that sort. And ye see it's for a' our interest, Cornel, that you should stay at Brentwood. I took it upon me mysel to pass the word – "No a syllable to Maister Roland, nor to the young leddies – no a syllable." The women-servants, that have little reason to be out at night, ken little or nothing about it. And some think it grand to have a ghost so long as they're no in the way of coming across it. If you had been tellt the story to begin with, maybe ye would have thought so yoursel?'

This was true enough, though it did not throw any light upon my perplexity. If we had heard of it to start with, it is possible that all the family would have considered the possession of a ghost a distinct advantage. It is the fashion of the times. We never think what a risk it is to play with young imaginations, but cry out, in the fashionable jargon, 'A ghost! – nothing else was wanted to make it perfect.' I should not have been above this myself. I should have smiled, of course, at the idea of the ghost at all, but then to feel that it was mine would have pleased my vanity. Oh yes, I claim no exemption. The girls would have been delighted. I could fancy their eagerness, their interest, and excitement. No; if we had been told, it would have done no good – we should have made the bargain all the more eagerly, the fools that we are. 'And there has been no attempt to investigate it,' I said, 'to see what it really is?'

'Eh, Cornel,' said the coachman's wife, 'wha would investigate, as ye call it, a thing that nobody believes in? Ye would be the laughin'-stock of a' the country-side, as my man says.'

'But you believe in it,' I said, turning upon her hastily. The woman was taken by surprise. She made a step backward out of my way.

'Lord, Cornel, how ye frichten a body! Me! – there's awfu'

strange things in this world. An unlearned person doesna ken what to think. But the minister and the gentry they just laugh in your face. Inquire into the thing that is not! Na, na, we just let it be—'

'Come with me, Jarvis,' I said, hastily, 'and we'll make an attempt at least. Say nothing to the men or to anybody. I'll come back after dinner, and we'll make a serious attempt to see what it is, if it is anything. If I hear it – which I doubt – you may be sure I shall never rest till I make it out. Be ready for me about ten o'clock.'

'Me, Cornel!' Jarvis said, in a faint voice. I had not been looking at him in my own preoccupation, but when I did so, I found that the greatest change had come over the fat and ruddy coachman. 'Me, Cornel!' he repeated, wiping the perspiration from his brow. His ruddy face hung in flabby folds, his knees knocked together, his voice seemed half extinguished in his throat. Then he began to rub his hands and smile upon me in a deprecating, imbecile way. 'There's no-thing I wouldna do to pleasure ye, Cornel,' taking a step further back. 'I'm sure, *she* kens I've aye said I never had to do with a mair fair, weel-spoken gentleman—' Here Jarvis came to a pause, again looking at me, rubbing his hands.

'Well?' I said.

'But eh, sir!' he went on, with the same imbecile yet insinuating smile, 'if ye'll reflect that I am no used to my feet. With a horse atween my legs, or the reins in my hand, I'm maybe nae worse than other men; but on fit, Cornel— It's no the – bogles; – but I've been cavalry, ye see,' with a little hoarse laugh, 'a' my life. To face a thing ye didna understan' – on your feet, Cornel.'

'Well, sir, if *I* do it,' said I, tartly, 'why shouldn't you?'

'Eh, Cornel, there's an awfu' difference. In the first place, ye tramp about the haill country-side, and think naething of it, but a walk tires me mair than a hunard miles' drive: and then ye're a gentleman, and do your ain pleasure; and you're no so auld as me; and it's for your ain bairn, ye see, Cornel; and then—'

'He believes in it, Cornel, and you dinna believe in it,' the woman said.

'Will you come with me?' I said, turning to her.

She jumped back, upsetting her chair in her bewilderment. 'Me!' with a scream, and then fell into a sort of hysterical laugh. 'I wouldna say but what I would go; but what would the folk say to hear of Cornel Mortimer with an auld silly woman at his heels?'

The suggestion made me laugh too, though I had little inclination for it. 'I'm sorry you have so little spirit, Jarvis,' I said. 'I must find some one else, I suppose.'

Jarvis, touched by this, began to remonstrate, but I cut him short. My butler was a soldier who had been with me in India, and was not supposed to fear anything – man or devil, – certainly not the former; and I felt that I was losing time. The Jarvises were too thankful to get rid of me. They attended me to the door with the most anxious courtesies. Outside, the two grooms stood close by, a little confused by my sudden exit. I don't know if perhaps they had been listening – at least standing as near as possible, to catch any scrap of the conversation. I waved my hand to them as I went past, in answer to their salutations, and it was very apparent to me that they also were glad to see me go.

And it will be thought very strange, but it would be weak not to add, that I myself, though bent on the investigation I have spoken of, pledged to Roland to carry it out, and feeling that my boy's health, perhaps his life, depended on the result of my inquiry, – I felt the most unaccountable reluctance to pass these ruins on my way home. My curiosity was intense;

and yet it was all my mind could do to pull my body along. I daresay the scientific people would describe it the other way, and attribute my cowardice to the state of my stomach. I went on; but if I had followed my impulse I should not have gone on, I should have turned and bolted. Everything in me seemed to cry out against it; my heart thumped, my pulses all began, like sledge-hammers, beating against my ears and every sensitive part. It was very dark, as I have said; the old house, with its shapeless tower, loomed a heavy mass through the darkness, which was only not entirely so solid as itself. On the other hand, the great dark cedars of which we were so proud seemed to fill up the night. My foot strayed out of the path in my confusion and the gloom together, and I brought myself up with a cry as I felt myself knock against something solid. What was it? The contact with hard stone and lime, and prickly bramble-bushes, restored me a little to myself. 'Oh, it's only the old gable,' I said aloud, with a little laugh to reassure myself. The rough feeling of the stones reconciled me. As I groped about thus, I shook off my visionary folly. What so easily explained as that I should have strayed from the path in the darkness? This brought me back to common existence, as if I had been shaken by a wise hand out of all the silliness of superstition. How silly it was, after all! What did it matter which path I took? I laughed again, this time with better heart – when suddenly, in a moment, the blood was chilled in my veins, a shiver stole along my spine, my faculties seemed to forsake me. Close by me at my side, at my feet, there was a sigh. No, not a groan, not a moaning, not anything so tangible – a perfectly soft, faint, inarticulate sigh. I sprung back, and my heart stopped beating. Mistaken! no, mistake was impossible. I heard it as clearly as I hear myself speak; a long, soft, weary sigh, as if drawn to the utmost, and emptying out a load of sadness that filled the breast. To hear this in the solitude, in the dark, in the night (though it was still early), had an effect which I cannot describe. I feel it now – something cold creeping over me, up into my hair, and down to my feet, which refused to move. I cried out, with a trembling voice, 'Who is there?' as I had done before – but there was no reply.

I got home I don't quite know how; but in my mind there was no longer any indifference as to the thing, whatever it was, that haunted these ruins. My scepticism disappeared like a mist. I was as firmly determined that there was something as Roland was. I did not for a moment pretend to myself that it was possible I could be deceived; there were movements and noises which I understood all about, cracklings of small branches in the frost, and little rolls of gravel on the path, such as have a very eerie sound sometimes, and perplex you with wonder as to who has done it, *when there is no real mystery*; but I assure you all these little movements of nature don't affect you one bit *when there is something*. I understood *them*. I did not understand the sigh. That was not simple nature; there was meaning in it – feeling, the soul of a creature invisible. This is the thing that human nature trembles at – a creature invisible, yet with sensations, feelings, a power somehow of expressing itself. I had not the same sense of unwillingness to turn my back upon the scene of the mystery which I had experienced in going to the stables; but I almost ran home, impelled by eagerness to get everything done that had to be done, in order to apply myself to finding it out. Bagley was in the hall as usual when I went in. He was always there in the afternoon, always with the appearance of perfect occupation, yet, so far as I know, never doing anything. The door was open, so that I hurried in without any pause, breathless; but the sight of his calm regard, as he came to help me off with my overcoat, subdued me in a moment. Anything out of the way, anything incomprehensible, faded to nothing in the presence of Bagley. You saw and wondered how *he* was made: the parting of his hair, the tie of his white neckcloth, the fit of his trousers, all perfect as works of art; but you could see how they were done, which makes all the difference. I flung myself upon him, so to speak, without waiting to note the extreme unlikeness of the man to anything of the kind I meant. 'Bagley,' I said, 'I want you to come out with me tonight to watch for—'

'Poachers, Colonel,' he said, a gleam of pleasure running all over him.

'No, Bagley; a great deal worse,' I cried.

'Yes, Colonel; at what hour, sir?' the man said; but then I had not told him what it was.

It was ten o'clock when we set out. All was perfectly quiet indoors. My wife was with Roland, who had been quite calm, she said, and who (though the fever of course must run its course) had been better ever since I came. I told Bagley to put on a thick greatcoat over his evening coat, and did the same myself – with strong boots; for the soil was like a sponge, or worse. Talking to him, I almost forgot what we were going to do. It was darker even than it had been before, and Bagley kept very close to me as we went along. I had a small lantern in my hand, which gave us partial guidance. We had come to the corner where the path turns. On one side was the bowling-green, which the girls had taken possession of for their croquet-lawn – a wonderful enclosure surrounded by high hedges of holly, three hundred years old and more; on the other, the ruins. Both were black as night; but before we got so far, there was a little opening in which we could just discern the trees and the lighter line of the road. I thought it best to pause there and take breath. 'Bagley,' I said, 'there is something about these ruins I don't understand. It is there

I am going. Keep your eyes open and your wits about you. Be ready to pounce upon any stranger you see – anything, man or woman. Don't hurt, but seize – anything you see.' 'Colonel,' said Bagley, with a little tremor in his breath, 'they do say there's things there – as is neither man nor woman.' There was no time for words. 'Are you game to follow me, my man? that's the question,' I said. Bagley fell in without a word, and saluted. I knew then I had nothing to fear.

We went, so far as I could guess, exactly as I had come, when I heard that sigh. The darkness, however, was so complete that all marks, as of trees or paths, disappeared. One moment we felt our feet on the gravel, another sinking noiselessly into the slippery grass, that was all. I had shut up my lantern, not wishing to scare any one, whoever it might be. Bagley followed, it seemed to me, exactly in my footsteps as I made my way, as I supposed, towards the mass of the ruined house. We seemed to take a long time groping along seeking this; the squash of the wet soil under our feet was the only thing that marked our progress. After a while I stood still to see, or rather feel, where we were. The darkness was very still, but no stiller than is usual in a winter's night. The sounds I have mentioned – the crackling of twigs, the roll of a pebble, the sound of some rustle in the dead leaves, or creeping creature on the grass – were audible when you listened, all mysterious enough when your mind is disengaged, but to me cheering now as signs of the livingness of nature, even in the death of the frost. As we stood still there came up from the trees in the glen the prolonged hoot of an owl. Bagley started with alarm, being in a state of general nervousness, and not knowing what he was afraid of. But to me the sound was encouraging and pleasant, being so comprehensible. 'An owl,' I said, under my breath. 'Y–es, Colonel,' said Bagley, his teeth chattering. We stood still about five minutes, while it broke into the still brooding of the air, the sound widening out in circles, dying upon the darkness. This sound, which is not a cheerful one, made me almost gay. It was natural, and relieved the tension of the mind. I moved on with new courage, my nervous excitement calming down.

When all at once, quite suddenly, close to us, at our feet, there broke out a cry. I made a spring backwards in the first moment of surprise and horror, and in doing so came sharply against the same rough masonry and brambles that had struck me before. This new sound came upwards from the ground – a low, moaning, wailing voice, full of suffering and pain. The contrast between it and the hoot of the owl was indescribable; the one with a wholesome wildness and naturalness that hurt nobody – the other, a sound that made one's blood curdle, full of human misery. With a great deal of fumbling – for in spite of everything I could do to keep up my courage my hands shook, I managed to remove the slide of my lantern. The light leaped out like something living, and made the place visible in a moment. We were what would have been inside the ruined building had anything remained but the gable-wall which I have described. It was close to us, the vacant doorway in it going out straight into the blackness outside. The light showed the bit of wall, the ivy glistening upon it in clouds of dark green, the bramble branches waving, and below, the open door – a door that led to nothing. It was from this the voice came which died out just as the light flashed upon this strange scene. There was a moment's silence, and then it broke forth again. The sound was so near, so penetrating, so pitiful, that, in the nervous start I gave, the light fell out of my hand. As I groped for it in the dark my hand was clutched by Bagley, who I think must have dropped upon his knees; but I was too much perturbed myself to think much of this. He clutched at me in the confusion of his terror, forgetting all his usual decorum. 'For God's sake, what is it, sir?' he gasped. If I yielded, there was evidently an end of both of us. 'I can't tell,' I said, 'any more than you; that's what we've got to find out: up, man, up!' I pulled him to his feet. 'Will you go round and examine the other side, or will you stay here with the lantern?' Bagley gasped at me with a face of horror. 'Can't we stay together, Colonel?' he said – his knees were trembling under him. I pushed him against the corner of the wall, and put the light into his hands. 'Stand fast till I come back; shake yourself together, man; let nothing pass you,' I said. The voice was within two or three feet of us, of that there could be no doubt.

I went myself to the other side of the wall, keeping close to it. The light shook in Bagley's hand, but, tremulous though it was, shone out through the vacant door, one oblong block of light marking all the crumbling corners and hanging masses of foliage. Was that something dark huddled in a heap by the side of it? I pushed forward across the light in the doorway, and fell upon it with my hands; but it was only a juniper-bush growing close against the wall. Meanwhile, the sight of my figure crossing the doorway had brought Bagley's nervous excitement to a height: he flew at me, gripping my shoulder. 'I've got him, Colonel! I've got him!' he cried, with a voice of sudden exultation. He thought it was a man, and was at once relieved. But at that moment the voice burst forth again between us, at our feet – more close to us than any separate being could be. He dropped off from me, and fell against the wall, his jaw dropping as if he were dying. I suppose, at the same moment, he saw that it was I whom he had clutched. I, for my part, had scarcely more command of myself. I snatched the light out of his hand, and flashed it all about me wildly. Nothing, – the juniper-bush, which I thought I had never seen before, the heavy growth of the glistening ivy, the brambles waving. It was close to my ears now, crying, crying, pleading as if for life. Either I heard the same words Roland had heard, or else, in my excitement, his imagination got possession of mine. The voice went on, growing into distinct articulation, but waving about, now from one point, now from another, as if the owner of it were moving slowly back and forward. 'Mother! mother!' and then an outburst of wailing. As my mind steadied, getting accustomed (as one's mind gets accustomed to anything), it seemed to me as if some uneasy, miserable creature was pacing up and down before a closed door. Sometimes – but that must have been excitement – I thought I heard a sound like knocking, and then another burst, 'Oh, mother! mother!' All this close, close to the space where I was standing with my lantern – now before me, now behind me: a creature restless, unhappy, moaning, crying, before the vacant doorway, which no one could either shut or open more.

'Do you hear it, Bagley? do you hear what it is saying?' I cried, stepping in through the doorway. He was lying against the wall – his eyes glazed, half dead with terror. He made a motion of his lips as if to answer me, but no sounds came; then lifted his hand with a curious imperative movement as if ordering me to be silent and listen. And how long I did so I cannot tell. It began to have an interest, an exciting hold upon me, which I could not describe. It seemed to call up visibly a scene any one could understand – a something shut out, restlessly wandering to and fro; sometimes the voice dropped, as if throwing itself down – sometimes wandered off a few paces, growing sharp and clear. 'Oh, mother, let me in! oh, mother, mother, let me in! oh, let me in!' every word was clear to me. No wonder the boy had gone wild with pity. I tried to steady my mind upon Roland, upon his conviction that I could do something, but my head swam with the excitement, even when I partially overcame the terror. At last the words died away, and there was a sound of sobs and moaning. I cried out, 'In the name of God who are you?' with a kind of feeling in my mind that to use the name of God was profane, seeing that I did not believe in ghosts or anything supernatural; but I did it all the same, and waited, my heart giving a leap of terror lest there should be a reply. Why this should have been I cannot tell, but I had a feeling that if there was an answer it would be more than I could bear. But there was no answer; the moaning went on, and then, as if it had been real, the voice rose a little higher again, the words recommenced, 'Oh, mother, let me in! oh, mother, let me in!' with an expression that was heart-breaking to hear.

As if it had been real! What do I mean by that? I suppose I got less alarmed as the thing went on. I began to recover the use of my senses – I seemed to explain it all to myself by saying that this had once happened, that it was a recollection of a real scene. Why there should have seemed something quite satisfactory and composing in this explanation I cannot tell, but so it was. I began to listen almost as if it had been a play, forgetting Bagley, who, I almost think, had fainted, leaning against the wall. I was startled out of this strange spectatorship that had fallen upon me by the sudden rush of something which made my heart jump once more, a large black figure in the doorway waving its arms. 'Come in! come in! come in!' it shouted out hoarsely at the top of a deep bass voice, and then poor Bagley fell down senseless across the threshold. He was less sophisticated than I, – he had not been able to bear it any longer. I took him for something supernatural, as he took me, and it was some time before

I awoke to the necessities of the moment. I remembered only after, that from the time I began to give my attention to the man, I heard the other voice no more. It was some time before I brought him to. It must have been a strange scene; the lantern making a luminous spot in the darkness, the man's white face lying on the black earth, I over him, doing what I could for him. Probably I should have been thought to be murdering him had any one seen us. When at last I succeeded in pouring a little brandy down his throat, he sat up and looked about him wildly. 'What's up?' he said; then recognising me, tried to struggle to his feet with a faint 'Beg your pardon, Colonel.' I got him home as best I could, making him lean upon my arm. The great fellow was as weak as a child. Fortunately he did not for some time remember what had happened. From the time Bagley fell the voice had stopped, and all was still.

'You've got an epidemic in your house, Colonel,' Simson said to me next morning. 'What's the meaning of it all? Here's your butler raving about a voice. This will never do, you know; and so far as I can make out, you are in it too.'

'Yes, I am in it, doctor. I thought I had better speak to you. Of course you are treating Roland all right – but the boy is not raving, he is as sane as you or I. It's all true.'

'As sane as – I – or you. I never thought the boy insane. He's got cerebral excitement, fever. I don't know what you've got. There's something very queer about the look of your eyes.'

'Come,' said I, 'you can't put us all to bed, you know. You had better listen and hear the symptoms in full.'

The doctor shrugged his shoulders, but he listened to me patiently. He did not believe a word of the story, that was clear; but he heard it all from beginning to end. 'My dear fellow,' he said, 'the boy told me just the same. It's an epi-demic. When one person falls a victim to this sort of thing, it's as safe as can be – there's always two or three.'

'Then how do you account for it?' I said.

'Oh, account for it! – that's a different matter; there's no accounting for the freaks our brains are subject to. If it's delusion; if it's some trick of the echoes or the winds – some phonetic disturbance or other—'

'Come with me to-night, and judge for yourself,' I said.

Upon this he laughed aloud, then said, 'That's not such a bad idea; but it would ruin me for ever if it were known that John Simson was ghost-hunting.'

'There it is,' said I; 'you dart down on us who are unlearned with your phonetic disturbances, but you daren't examine what the thing really is for fear of being laughed at. That's science!'

'It's not science – it's common-sense,' said the doctor. 'The thing has delusion on the front of it. It is encouraging an unwholesome tendency even to examine. What good could come of it? Even if I am convinced, I shouldn't believe.'

'I should have said so yesterday; and I don't want you to be convinced or to believe,' said I. 'If you prove it to be a delusion, I shall be very much obliged too, for one. Come; somebody must go with me.'

'You are cool,' said the doctor. 'You've disabled this poor fellow of yours, and made him – on that point – a lunatic for life; and now you want to disable me. But for once, I'll do it. To save appearance, if you'll give me a bed, I'll come over after my last rounds.'

It was agreed that I should meet him at the gate, and that we should visit the scene of last night's ocurrences before we came to the house, so that nobody might be the wiser. It was scarcely possible to hope that the cause of Bagley's sudden illness should not somehow steal into the knowledge of the servants at least, and it was better that all should be done as quietly as possible. The day seemed to me a very long one. I had to spend a certain part of it with Roland, which was a terrible ordeal for me – for what could I say to the boy? The improvement continued, but he was still in a very precarious state, and the trembling vehemence with which he turned to me when his mother left the room, filled me with alarm. 'Father?' he said, quietly. 'Yes, my boy; I am giving my best attention to it – all is being done that I can do. I have not come to any conclusion – yet. I am neglecting nothing you said,' I cried. What I could not do was to give his active mind any encouragement to dwell upon the mystery. It was a hard predicament, for some satisfaction had to be given him. He looked at me very wistfully, with the great blue eyes which gazed so large and brilliant out of his white and worn face. 'You must trust me,' I said. 'Yes, father. Father knows – father knows,' he said to himself, as if to soothe some inward doubt. I left him as soon as I could. He was about the most precious thing I had on earth, and his health my first thought; but yet somehow, in the excitement of this other subject, I put it aside, and preferred not to dwell upon Roland, which was the most curious part of it all.

That night at eleven I met Simson at the gate. He had come by train, and I let him in gently myself. I had been so much absorbed in the coming experiment that I passed the ruins in going to meet him, almost without thought, if you can understand that. I had my lantern; and he showed me a coil of taper which he had ready for use. 'There is nothing like light,' he said, in his scoffing tone. It was a very still night, scarcely a sound, but not so dark. We could keep the path without difficulty as we went along. As we approached the spot we could hear a low moaning, broken occasionally by a bitter cry. 'Perhaps that is your voice,' said the doctor; 'I thought it must be something of the kind. That's a poor brute caught in some of these infernal traps of yours; you'll find it among the bushes somewhere.' I said nothing. I felt no particular fear, but a triumphant satisfaction in what was to follow. I led him to the spot where Bagley and I had stood on the previous night. All was silent as a winter night could be – so silent that we heard far off the sound of the horses in the stables, the shutting of a window at the house. Simson lighted his taper and went peering about, poking into all the corners. We looked like two conspirators lying in wait for some unfortunate traveller; but not a sound broke the quiet. The moaning had stopped before we came up; a star or two shone over us in the sky, looking down as if surprised at our strange proceedings. Dr Simson did nothing but utter subdued laughs under his breath. 'I thought as much,' he said. 'It is just the same with tables and all other kinds of ghostly apparatus; a sceptic's presence stops everything. When I am present nothing ever comes off. How long do you think it will be necessary to stay here? Oh, I don't complain; only, when *you* are satisfied, *I* am – quite.'

I will not deny that I was disappointed beyond measure by this result. It made me look like a credulous fool. It gave the doctor such a pull over me as nothing else could. I should point all his morals for years to come, and his materialism, his scepticism would be increased beyond endurance. 'It seems, indeed,' I said, 'that there is to be no—' 'Manifestation', he said, laughing; 'that is what all the mediums say. No manifestations, in consequence of the presence of an unbeliever.' His laugh sounded very uncomfortable to me in the silence; and it was now near midnight. But that laugh seemed the signal; before it died away the moaning we had heard before was resumed. It started from some distance off, and came towards us, nearer and nearer, like some one walking along and moaning to himself. There could be no idea now that it was a hare caught in a trap. The approach was slow, like that of a weak person with little halts and pauses. We heard it coming along the grass straight towards the vacant doorway. Simson had been a little startled by the first sound. He said hastily, 'That child has no business to be out so late.' But he felt, as well as I, that this was no child's voice. As it came nearer, he grew silent, and, going to the doorway with his taper, stood looking out towards the sound. The taper being unprotected blew about in the night air, though there was scarcely any wind. I threw the light of my lantern steady and white across the same space. It was in a blaze of light in the midst of the blackness. A little icy thrill had gone over me at the first sound, but as it came close, I confess that my only feeling was satisfaction. The scoffer could scoff no more. The light touched his own face, and showed a very perplexed countenance. If he was afraid, he concealed it with great success, but he was perplexed. And then all that had happened on the previous night was enacted once more. It fell strangely upon me with a sense of repetition. Every cry, every sob seemed the same as before. I listened almost without any emotion at all in my own person, thinking of its effect upon Simson. He maintained a very bold front on the whole. All that coming and going of the voice was, if our ears could be trusted, exactly in front of the vacant, blank doorway, blazing full of light, which caught and shone in the glistening leaves of the great hollies at a little distance. Not a rabbit could have crossed the turf without being seen; – but there was nothing. After a time, Simson, with a certain caution and bodily reluctance, as it seemed to me, went out with his roll of taper into this space. His figure showed against the holly in full outline. Just at this moment the voice sank, as was its custom, and seemed to fling itself down at the door. Simson recoiled violently, as if some one had come up against him, then turned, and held his taper low as if examining something. 'Do you see anybody?' I cried in a whisper, feeling the chill of nervous panic steal over me at this action. 'It's nothing but a— confounded juniper-bush,' he said. This I knew very well to be nonsense, for the juniper-bush was on the other side. He went about after this round and round, poking his taper everywhere, then returned to me on the inner side of the wall. He scoffed no longer; his face was contracted and pale. 'How long does this go on?' he whispered to me, like a man who does not wish to interrupt some one who is speaking. I had become too much perturbed myself to remark whether the successions and changes of the voice were the same as last night. It suddenly went out in the air almost as he was speaking, with a soft reiterated sob dying away. If there had been anything to be seen, I should have said that the person was at that moment crouching on the ground close to the door.

We walked home very silent afterwards. It was only when we were in sight of the house that I said, 'What do you think of it?' 'I can't tell what to think of it,' he said quickly. He took – though he was a very temperate man – not the claret I was going to offer him, but some brandy from the tray, and swallowed it almost undiluted. 'Mind you, I don't believe a word of it,' he said, when he had lighted his candle; 'but I can't tell what to think of it,' he turned round to add, when he was half-way upstairs.

All of this, however, did me no good with the solution of my problem. I was to help this weeping, sobbing thing, which was already to me as distinct a personality as anything I knew – or what should I say to Roland? It was on my heart that my boy would die if I could not find some way of help-ing this creature. You may be surprised that I should speak of it in this way. I did not know if it was man or woman; but I no more doubted that it was a soul in pain than I doubted my own being; and it was my business to soothe this pain – to deliver it, if that was possible. Was ever such a task given to an anxious father trembling for his only boy? I felt in my heart, fantastic as it may appear, that I must fulfil this somehow, or part with my child; and you may conceive that rather than do that I was ready to die. But even my dying would not have advanced me – unless by bringing me into the same world with that seeker at the door.

Next morning Simson was out before breakfast, and came in with evident signs of the damp grass on his boots, and a look of worry and weariness, which did not say much for the night he had passed. He improved a little after breakfast, and visited his two patients, for Bagley was still an invalid. I went out with him on his way to the train, to hear what he had to say about the boy. 'He is going on very well,' he said; 'there are no complications as yet. But mind you, that's not a boy to be trifled with, Mortimer. Not a word to him about last night.' I had to tell him then of my last interview with Roland, and of the impossible demand he had made upon me – by which, though he tried to laugh, he was much discomposed, as I could see. 'We must just perjure ourselves all round,' he said, 'and swear you exorcised it;' but the man was too kind-hearted to be satisfied with that. 'It's frightfully serious for you, Mortimer. I can't laugh as I should like to. I wish I saw a way out of it, for your sake. By the way,' he added shortly, 'didn't you notice that juniper-bush on the left-hand side?' 'There was one on the right hand of the door. I noticed you made that mistake last night.' 'Mistake!' he cried, with a curious low laugh, pulling up the collar of his coat as though he felt the cold, – 'there's no juniper there this morning, left or right. Just go and see.' As he stepped into the train a few minutes after, he looked back upon me and beckoned me for a parting word. 'I'm coming back to-night,' he said.

I don't think I had any feeling about this as I turned away from that common bustle of the railway which made my private preoccupations feel so strangely out of date. There had been a distinct satisfaction in my mind before that his scepticism had been so entirely defeated. But the more serious part of the matter pressed upon me now. I went straight from the railway to the manse, which stood on a little plateau on the side of the river opposite to the woods of Brentwood. The minister was one of a class which is not so common in Scotland as it used to be. He was a man of good family, well educated in the Scotch way, strong in philosophy, not so strong in Greek, strongest of all in experience, – a man who had 'come across', in the course of his life, most people of note that had ever been in Scotland – and who was said to be very sound in doctrine, without infringing the toleration to which old men, who are good men, so often come. He was old-fashioned; perhaps he did not think so much about the troublous problems of theology as many of the young men, nor ask himself any hard questions upon the Confession of Faith – but he understood human nature, which is perhaps better. He received me with a cordial welcome. 'Come away, Colonel Mortimer,' he said; 'I'm all the more glad to see you, that I feel it's a good sign for the boy. He's doing well? – God be praised – and the Lord bless him and keep him. He has many a poor body's prayers – and that can do nobody harm.'

'He will need them all, Dr Moncrieff,' I said, 'and your counsel too.' And I told him the story – more than I had told Simson. The old clergyman listened to me with many suppressed exclamations, and at the end the water stood in his eyes.

'That's just beautiful,' he said. 'I do not mind to have heard anything like it; it's as fine as Burns when he wished deliverance to one – that is prayed for in no kirk. Ay, ay! so he would have you console the poor lost spirit? God bless the boy! There's something more than common in that, Colonel Mortimer. And also the faith of him in his father! – I would like to put that into a sermon.' Then the old gentleman gave me an alarmed look, and said, 'No, no; I was not meaning a sermon; but I must write it down for the "Children's Record." ' I saw the thought that passed through his mind. Either he thought, or he feared I would think, of a funeral sermon. You may believe this did not make me more cheerful.

I can scarcely say that Dr Moncrieff gave me any advice. How could any one advise on such a subject? But he said, 'I think I'll come too. I'm an old man; I'm less liable to be frighted than those that are further off the world unseen. It behoves me to think of my own journey there. I've no cut-and-dry beliefs on the subject. I'll come too: and maybe at the moment the Lord will put it into our heads what to do.'

This gave me a little comfort – more than Simson had given me. To be clear about the cause of it was not my grand desire. It was another thing that was in my mind – my boy. As for the poor soul at the open door, I had no more doubt, as I have said, of its existence than I had of my own. It was no ghost to me. I knew the creature, and it was in trouble. That was my feeling about it, as it was Roland's. To hear it first was a great shock to my nerves, but not now; a man will get accustomed to anything. But to do something for it was the great problem; how was I to be serviceable to a being that was invisible, that was mortal no longer? 'Maybe at the moment the Lord will put it into our heads.' This is very old-fashioned phraseology, and a week before, most likely, I should have smiled (though always with kindness) at Dr Moncrieff's credulity; but there was a great comfort, whether rational or otherwise I cannot say, in the mere sound of the words.

The road to the station and the village lay through the glen – not by the ruins; but though the sunshine and the fresh air, and the beauty of the trees, and the sound of the water were all very soothing to the spirits, my mind was so full of my own subject that I could not refrain from turning to the right hand as I got to the top of the glen, and going straight to the place which I may call the scene of all my thoughts. It was lying full in the sunshine, like all the rest of the world. The ruined gable looked due east, and in the present aspect of the sun the light streamed down through the doorway as our lantern had done, throwing a flash of light upon the damp grass beyond. There was a strange suggestion in the open door – so futile, a kind of emblem of vanity – all free around, so that you could go where you pleased, and yet that semblance of an enclosure – that way of entrance, unnecessary, leading to nothing. And why any creature should pray and weep to get in – to nothing: or be kept out – by nothing! You could not dwell upon it, or it made your brain go round. I remembered, however, what Simson said about the juniper, with a little smile on my own mind as to the inaccuracy of recollection, which even a scientific man will be guilty of. I could see now the light of my lantern gleaming upon the wet glistening surface of the spiky leaves at the right hand – and he ready to go to the stake for it that it was the left! I went round to make sure. And then I saw what he had said. Right or left there was no juniper at all. I was confounded by

146

this, though it was entirely a matter of detail: nothing at all: a bush of brambles waving, the grass growing up to the very walls. But after all, though it gave me a shock for a moment, what did that matter? There were marks as if a number of footsteps had been up and down in front of the door; but these might have been our steps; and all was bright, and peaceful, and still. I poked about the other ruin – the larger ruins of the old house – for some time, as I had done before. There were marks upon the grass here and there, I could not call them footsteps, all about; but that told for nothing one way or another. I had examined the ruined rooms closely the first day. They were half filled up with soil and *débris*, without brackens and bramble – no refuge for any one there. It vexed me that Jarvis should see me coming from that spot when he came up to me for his orders. I don't know whether my nocturnal expeditions had got wind among the servants. But there was a significant look in his face. Something in it I felt was like my own sensations when Simson in the midst of his scepticism was struck dumb. Jarvis felt satisfied that his veracity had been put beyond question. I never spoke to a servant of mine in such a peremptory tone before. I sent him away 'with a flea in his lug', as the man described it afterwards. Interference of every kind was intolerable to me at such a moment.

But what was strangest of all was, that I could not face Roland. I did not go up to his room as I would have naturally done at once. This the girls could not understand. They saw there was some mystery in it. 'Mother has gone to lie down,' Agatha said; 'he has had such a good night.' 'But he wants you so, papa!' cried little Jeanie, always with her two arms embracing mine in a pretty way she had. I was obliged to go at last – but what could I say? I could only kiss him, and tell him to keep still – that I was doing all I could. There is something mystical about the patience of a child. 'It will come all right, won't it, father?' he said. 'God grant it may! I hope so, Roland.' 'Oh yes, it will come all right.' Perhaps he understood that in the midst of my anxiety I could not stay with him as I should have done otherwise. But the girls were more surprised than it is possible to describe. They looked at me with wondering eyes. 'If I were ill, papa, and you only stayed with me a moment, I should break my heart,' said Agatha. But the boy had a sympathetic feeling. He knew that of my own will I would not have done it. I shut myself up in the library, where I could not rest, but kept pacing up and down like a caged beast. What could I do? and if I could do nothing, what would become of my boy? These were the questions that, without ceasing, pursued each other through my mind.

Simson came out to dinner, and when the house was all still, and most of the servants in bed, we went out and met Dr Moncrieff, as we had appointed, at the head of the glen. Simson, for his part, was disposed to scoff at the Doctor. 'If there are to be any spells, you know, I'll cut the whole concern,' he said. I did not make him any reply. I had not invited him; he could go or come as he pleased. He was very talkative, far more so than suited my humour, as we went on. 'One thing is certain, you know, there must be some human agency,' he said. 'It is all bosh about apparitions. I never have investigated the laws of sound to any great extent, and there's a great deal in ventriloquism that we don't know much about.' 'If it's the same to you,' I said, 'I wish you'd keep all that to yourself, Simson, it doesn't suit my state of mind.' 'Oh, I hope I know how to respect idiosyncrasy,' he said. The very tone of his voice irritated me beyond measure. These scientific fellows, I wonder people put up with them as they do, when you have no mind for their cold-blooded confidence. Dr Moncrieff met us about eleven o'clock, the same time as on the previous night. He was a large man, with a venerable countenance and white hair – old, but in full vigour, and thinking less of a cold night walk than many a younger man. He had his lantern as I had. We were fully provided with means of lighting the place, and we were all of us resolute men. We had a rapid consultation as we went up, and the result was that we divided to different posts. Dr Moncrieff remained inside the wall – if you can call that inside where there was no wall but one. Simson placed himself on the side next the ruins, so as to intercept any communication with the old house, which was what his mind was fixed upon. I was posted on the other side. To say that nothing could come near without being seen was self-evident. It had been so also on the previous night. Now, with our three lights in the midst of the darkness, the whole place seemed illuminated. Dr Moncrieff's lantern, which was a large one, without any means of shutting up – an old-fashioned lantern with a pierced and ornamental top – shone steadily, the rays shooting out of it upward into the gloom. He placed it on the grass, where the middle of the room, if this had been a room, would have been. The usual effect of the light streaming out of the doorway was prevented by the illumination which Simson and I on either side supplied. With these differences, everything seemed as on the previous night.

And what occurred was exactly the same, with the same air of repetition, point for point, as I had formerly remarked. I declare that it seemed to me as if I were pushed against, put aside, by the owner of the voice as he paced up and down in his trouble, – though these are perfectly futile words, seeing that the stream of light from my lantern, and that from Simson's taper, lay broad and clear, without a shadow, without the smallest break, across the entire breadth of the grass. I had ceased even to be alarmed, for my part. My heart was rent with pity and trouble – pity for the poor suffering human creature that moaned and pleaded so, and trouble for myself and my boy. God! if I could not find any help – and what help could I find? – Roland would die.

We were all perfectly still till the first outburst was exhausted, as I knew (by experience) it would be. Dr Moncrieff, to whom it was new, was quite still on the other side of the wall, as we were in our places. My heart had remained almost at its usual beating during the voice. I was used to it; it did not rouse all my pulses as it did at first. But just as it threw itself sobbing at the door (I cannot use other words), there suddenly came something which sent the blood coursing in my veins and my heart into my mouth. It was a voice inside the wall – the minister's well-known voice. I would have been prepared for it in any kind of adjuration, but I was not prepared for what I heard. It came out with a sort of stammering, as if too much moved for utterance. 'Willie, Willie! Oh, God preserve us! is it you?'

These simple words had an effect upon me that the voice of the invisible creature had ceased to have. I thought the old man, whom I had brought into this danger, had gone mad with terror. I made a dash round to the other side of the wall, half crazed myself with the thought. He was standing where I had left him, his shadow thrown vague and large upon the grass by the lantern which stood at his feet. I lifted my own light to see his face as I rushed forward. He was very pale, his eyes wet and glistening, his mouth quivering with parted lips. He neither saw nor heard me. We that had gone through this experience before, had crouched towards each other to get a little strength to bear it. But he was not even aware that I was there. His whole being seemed absorbed in anxiety and tenderness. He held out his hands, which trembled, but it seemed to me with eagerness, not fear. He went on speaking all the time. 'Willie, if it is you – and it's you, if it is not a delusion of Satan, – Willie, lad! why come ye here frighting them that know you not? Why came ye not to me?'

He seemed to wait for an answer. When his voice ceased, his countenance, every line moving, continued to speak. Simson gave me another terrible shock, stealing into the open doorway with his light, as much awestricken, as wildly curious, as I. But the minister resumed, without seeing Simson, speaking to some one else. His voice took a tone of expostulation –

'Is this right to come here? Your mother's gone with your name on her lips. Do you think she would ever close her door on her own lad? Do ye think the Lord will close the door, ye faint-hearted creature? No! – I forbid ye! I forbid ye!' cried the old man. The sobbing voice had begun to resume its cries. He made a step forward, calling out the last words in a voice of command. 'I forbid ye! Cry out no more to man. Go home, ye wandering spirit! go home! Do you hear me? – me that christened ye, that have struggled with ye, that have wrestled for ye with the Lord!' Here the loud tones of his voice sank into tenderness. 'And her too, poor woman! poor woman! her you are calling upon. She's no here. You'll find her with the Lord. Go there and seek her, not here. Do you hear me, lad? go after her there. He'll let you in, though it's late. Man, take heart! if you will lie and sob and greet, let it be at heaven's gate, and no your poor mother's ruined door.'

He stopped to get his breath: and the voice had stopped, not as it had done before, when its time was exhausted and all its repetitions said, but with a sobbing catch in the breath as if overruled. Then the minister spoke again. 'Are you hearing me, Will? Oh, laddie, you've liked the beggarly elements all your days. Be done with them now. Go home to the Father – the Father! Are you hearing me?' Here the old man sank down upon his knees, his face raised upwards, his hands held up with a tremble in them, all white in the light in the midst of the darkness. I resisted as long as I could, though I cannot tell why, – then I, too, dropped upon my knees. Simson all the time stood in the doorway, with an expression in his face such as words could not tell, his underlip dropped, his eyes wild, staring. It seemed to be to him, that image of blank ignorance and wonder, that we were praying. All the time the voice, with a low arrested sobbing, lay just where he was standing, as I thought.

'Lord,' the minister said – 'Lord, take him into Thy everlasting habitations. The mother he cries to is with Thee. Who can open to him but Thee? Lord, when is it too late for Thee, or what is too hard for Thee? Lord, let that woman there draw him inower! Let her draw him inower!'

I sprang forward to catch something in my arms that flung itself wildly within the door. The illusion was so strong, that I never paused till I felt my forehead graze against the wall and my hands clutch the ground – for there was nobody there to save from falling, as in my foolishness I thought. Simson held out his hand to me to help me up. He was trembling and cold, his lower lip hanging, his speech almost inarticulate. 'It's gone,' he said, stammering, – 'it's gone!' We leant upon each other for a moment, trembling so much both of us that the whole scene trembled as if it were going to dissolve and disappear; and yet as long as I live I will never forget it – the shining of the strange lights, the blackness all round, the kneeling figure with all the whiteness of the light concentrated on its white venerable head and uplifted hands. A strange solemn stillness seemed to close all round us. By intervals a single syllable, 'Lord! Lord!' came from the old minister's lips. He saw none of us, nor thought of us. I never knew how long we stood, like sentinels guarding him at his prayers, holding our lights in a confused dazed way, not knowing what we did. But at last he rose from his knees, and standing up at his full height, raised his arms, as the Scotch manner is at the end of a religious service, and solemnly gave the apostolical benediction – to what? to the silent earth, the dark woods, the wide breathing atmosphere – for we were but spectators gasping an Amen!

It seemed to me that it must be the middle of the night, as we all walked back. It was in reality very late. Dr Moncrieff put his arm into mine. He walked slowly, with an air of exhaustion. It was as if we were coming from a death-bed. Something hushed and solemnised the very air. There was that sense of relief in it which there always is at the end of a death-struggle. And nature, persistent, never daunted, came back in all of us, as we returned into the ways of life. We said nothing to each other, indeed, for a time; but when we got clear of the trees and reached the opening near the house, where we could see the sky, Dr Moncrieff himself was the first to speak. 'I must be going,' he said; 'it's very late, I'm afraid. I will go down the glen, as I came.'

'But not alone. I am going with you, Doctor.'

'Well, I will not oppose it. I am an old man, and agitation wearies more than work. Yes; I'll be thankful of your arm. Tonight, Colonel, you've done me more good turns than one.'

I pressed his hand on my arm, not feeling able to speak. But Simson, who turned with us, and who had gone along all this time with his taper flaring, in entire unconsciousness, came to himself, apparently at the sound of our voices, and put out that wild little torch with a quick movement, as if of shame. 'Let me carry your lantern,' he said; 'it is heavy.' He recovered with a spring, and in a moment, from the awe-stricken spectator he had been, became himself, sceptical and cynical. 'I should like to ask you a question,' he said. 'Do you believe in Purgatory, Doctor? It's not in the tenets of the Church; so far as I know.'

'Sir,' said Dr Moncrieff, 'an old man like me is sometimes not very sure what he believes. There is just one thing I am certain of – and that is the loving-kindness of God.'

'But I thought that was in this life. I am no theologian—'

'Sir,' said the old man again, with a tremor in him which I could feel going over all his frame, 'if I saw a friend of mine within the gates of hell, I would not despair but his Father would find him still – if he cried like *yon*.'

'I allow it is very strange – very strange. I cannot see through it. That there must be human agency, I feel sure. Doctor, what made you decide upon the person and the name?'

The minister put out his hand with the impatience which a man might show if he were asked how he recognised his brother. 'Tuts!' he said, in familiar speech – then more solemnly, 'how should I not recognise a person that I know better – far better – than I know you?'

'Then you saw the man?'

Dr Moncrieff made no reply. He moved his hand again with a little impatient movement, and walked on, leaning heavily on my arm. And we went on for a long time without another word, threading the dark paths, which were steep and slippery with the damp of the winter. The air was very still – not more than enough to make a faint sighing in the branches, that mingled with the sound of the water to which we were descending. When we spoke again, it was about different matters – about the height of the river, and the recent rains. We parted with the minister at his own door, where his old housekeeper appeared in great perturbation, waiting for him. 'Eh me, minister! the young gentleman will be worse?' she cried.

'Far from that – better. God bless him!' Dr Moncrieff said.

I think if Simson had begun again to me with his questions, I should have pitched him over the rocks as we returned up the glen; but he was silent, by a good inspiration. And the sky was clearer than it had been for many nights, shining high over the trees, with here and there a star faintly gleaming through the wilderness of dark and bare branches. The air, as I have said, was very soft in them, with a subdued and peaceful cadence. It was real, like every natural sound, but came to us like a hush of peace and relief. I thought there was a sound in it as of the breath of a sleeper, and it seemed clear to me that Roland must be sleeping, satisfied and calm. We went up to his room when we went in. There we found the complete hush of rest. My wife looked up out of a doze, and gave me a smile; 'I think he is a great deal better: but you are very late,' she said in a whisper, shading the light with her hand that the doctor might see his patient. The boy had got back something like his own colour. He woke as we stood all round his bed. His eyes had the happy half-awakened look of childhood, glad to shut again, yet pleased with the interruption and glimmer of the light. I stooped over him and kissed his forehead, which was moist and cool. 'It is all well, Roland,' I said. He looked up at me with a glance of pleasure, and took my hand and laid his cheek upon it, and so went to sleep.

For some nights after, I watched among the ruins, spending all the dark hours up to midnight patrolling about the bit of wall which was associated with so many emotions; but I heard nothing, and saw nothing beyond the quiet course of nature: nor, so far as I am aware, has anything been heard again. Dr Moncrieff gave me the history of the youth, whom he never hesitated to name. I did not ask, as Simson did, how he recognised him. He had been a prodigal – weak, foolish, easily imposed upon, and 'led away', as people say. All that we had heard had passed actually in life, the doctor said. The young man had come home thus a day or two after his mother died – who was no more than the housekeeper in the old house – and distracted with the news, had thrown himself down at the door and called upon her to let him in. The old man could scarcely speak of it for tears. To me it seemed as if – Heaven help us, how little do we know about anything! – a scene like that might impress itself somehow upon the hidden heart of nature. I do not pretend to know how, but the repetition had struck me at the time as, in its terrible strangeness and incomprehensibility, almost mechanical – as if the unseen actor could not exceed or vary, but was bound to re-enact the whole. One thing that struck me, however, greatly, was the likeness between the old minister and my boy in the manner of regarding these strange phenomena. Dr Moncrieff was not terrified, as I had been myself, and all the rest of us. It was no 'ghost', as I fear we all vulgarly considered it, to him – but a poor creature whom he knew under these conditions, just as he had known him in the flesh, having no doubt of his identity. And to Roland it was the same. This spirit in pain – if it was a spirit – this voice out of the unseen – was a poor fellow-creature in misery, to be succoured and helped out of his trouble, to my boy. He spoke to me quite frankly about it when he got better. 'I knew father would find out some way,' he said. And this was when he was strong and well, and all idea that he would turn hysterical or become a seer of visions had happily passed away.

I must add one curious fact which does not seem to me to have any relation to the above, but which Simson made great use of, as the human agency which he was determined to find somehow. We had examined the ruins very closely at the time of these occurrences; but afterwards, when all was over, as we went casually about them one Sunday afternoon in the idleness of that unemployed day, Simson with his stick penetrated an old window which had been entirely blocked up with fallen soil. He jumped down into it in great excitement, and called me to follow. There we found a little hole – for it was more a hole than a room – entirely hidden under the ivy and ruins, in which there was a quantity of straw laid in a corner, as if some one had made a bed there, and some remains of crusts about the floor. Some one had lodged there, and not very long before, he made out; and that this unknown being was the author of all the mysterious sounds we heard he is convinced. 'I told you it was human agency,' he said triumphantly. He forgets, I suppose, how he and I stood with our lights seeing nothing while the space between us was audibly traversed by something that could speak, and sob, and suffer. There is no argument with men of this kind. He is ready to get up a laugh against me on this slender ground. 'I was puzzled myself – I could not make it out – but I always felt convinced human agency was at the bottom of it. And here it is – and a clever fellow he must have been,' the doctor says.

Bagley left my service as soon as he got well. He assured me it was no want of respect; but he could not stand 'them kind of things'. And the man was so shaken and ghastly that I was glad to give him a present and let him go. For my own part, I made a point of staying out the time, two years, for which I had taken Brentwood; but I did not renew my tenancy. By that time we had settled, and found for ourselves a pleasant home of our own.

I must add that when the doctor defies me, I can always bring back gravity to his countenance, and a pause in his railing, when I remind him of the juniper-bush. To me that was a matter of little importance. I could believe I was mistaken. I did not care about it one way or other; but on his mind the effect was different. The miserable voice, the spirit in pain, he could think of as the result of ventriloquism, or reverberation, or – anything you please: an elaborate prolonged hoax executed somehow by the tramp that had found a lodging in the old tower. But the juniper-bush staggered him. Things have effects so different on the minds of different men.

JOHN BUCHAN

THE BLACK FISHERS

ONCE UPON A TIME, as the story goes, there lived a man in Gledsmuir, called Simon Hay, who had born to him two sons. They were all very proper men, tall, black-avised, formed after the right model of stalwart folk, and by the account of the place in fear of neither God nor devil. He himself had tried many trades before he found the one which suited his talent; but in the various professions of herd, gamekeeper, drover, butcher, and carrier he had not met with the success he deserved. Some makeshift for a conscience is demanded sooner or later in all, and this Simon could not supply. So he flitted from one to the other with decent haste, till his sons came to manhood and settled the matter for themselves. Henceforth all three lived by their wits in defiance of the law, snaring game, poaching salmon, and working evil over the green earth. Hard drinkers and quick fighters, all men knew them and loved them not. But with it all they kept up a tincture of reputability, foreseeing their best interest. Ostensibly their trade was the modest one of the small crofter, and their occasional attendance at the kirk kept within bounds the verdict of an uncensorious parish.

It chanced that in spring, when the streams come down steely-blue and lipping over their brims, there came the most halcyon weather that ever man heard of. The air was mild as June, the nights soft and clear, and winter fled hotfoot in dismay. Then these three girded themselves and went to the salmon-poaching in the long shining pools of the Callowa in the haughlands below the Dun Craigs. The place was far enough and yet not too far from the town, so that an active walker could go there, have four hours' fishing, and return, all well within the confines of the dark.

On this night their sport was good, and soon the sacks were filled with glittering backs. Then, being drowsy from many nights out o' bed, they bethought them of returning. It would be well to get some hours of sleep before the morning, for they must be up betimes to dispose of their fish. The hardship of such pursuits lies not in the toil but the fate which hardens expediency into necessity.

At the strath which leads from the Callowa vale to Gled they halted. By crossing the ridge of hill they would save three good miles and find a less frequented path. The argument was irresistible; without delay they left the highway and struck over the bent and heather. The road was rough, but they were near its end, and a serene glow of conscious labour began to steal over their minds.

Near the summit is a drystone dyke which girdles the breast of the hill. It was a hard task to cross with a great load of fish, even for the young men. The father, a man of corpulent humours and maturing years, was nigh choked with his burden. He mounted slowly and painfully on the loose stones, and prepared to jump. But his foothold was insecure, and a stone slipped from its place. Then something terrible followed. The sack swung round from his neck, and brought him headlong to the ground. When the sons ran forward he was dead as a herring, with a broken neck.

The two men stood staring at one another in hopeless bewilderment. Here was something new in their experience, a disturbing element in their plans. They had just the atom of affection for the fellow-worker to make them feel the practical loss acutely. If they went for help to the nearest town, time would be lost and the salmon wasted; and indeed, it was not unlikely that some grave suspicion would attach to their honourable selves.

They held a hurried debate. At first they took refuge in mutual recriminations and well-worn regrets. They felt that some such sentiments were due to the modicum of respectability in their reputations. But their minds were too practical to linger long in such barren ground. It was demanded by common feeling of decency that they should have their father's body taken home. But were there any grounds for such feeling? None. It could not matter much to their father, who was the only one really concerned, whether he was removed early or late. On the other hand, they had trysted to meet a man seven miles down the water at five in the morning. Should he be disappointed? Money was money; it was a hard world, where one had to work for beer and skittles; death was a misfortune, but not exactly a deterrent. So picking up the old man's sack, they set out on their errand.

It chanced that the shepherd of the Lowe Moss returned late that night from a neighbour's house, and in crossing the march dyke came on the body. He was much shocked, for he recognized it well as the mortal remains of one who had once been a friend. The shepherd was a dull man and had been drinking; so as the subject was beyond his special domain he dismissed its consideration till some more convenient season. He did not trouble to inquire into causes – there were better heads than his for the work – but set out with all speed for the town.

The Procurator-fiscal had been sitting up late reading in the works of M. de Maupassant, when he was aroused by a constable, who told him that a shepherd had come from the Callowa with news that a man lay dead at the back of a dyke. The Procurator-fiscal rose with much grumbling, and wrapped himself up for the night errand. Really, he reflected with Hedda Gabler, people should not do these things nowadays. But, once without, his feelings changed. The clear high space of the sky and the whistling airs of night were strange and beautiful to a town-bred man. The round hills and grey whispering river touched his poetic soul. He began to feel some pride in his vocation.

When he came to the spot he was just in the mood for high sentiment. The sight gave him a shudder. The full-blown face ashen with the grip of death jarred on his finer sensibilities. He remembered to have read of just such a thing in the works of M. Guy. He felt a spice of anger at fate and her cruel ways.

'How sad!' he said; 'this old man, still hale and fit to enjoy life, goes out into the hills to visit a friend. On returning he falls in with those accursed dykes of yours; there is a slip in the darkness, a cry, and then – he can taste of life no more. Ah, Fate, to men how bitter a taskmistress,' he quoted with a far-off classical reminiscence.

The constable said nothing. He knew Simon Hay well, and guessed shrewdly how he had come by his death, but he kept his own counsel. He did not like to disturb fine sentiment, being a philosopher in a small way.

The two fishers met their man and did their business all in the most pleasant fashion. On their way they had discussed their father's demise. It would interfere little with their profits, for of late he had grown less strong and more exacting. Also, since death must come to all, it was better that it should have taken their father unawares. Otherwise he might have seen fit to make trouble about the cottage which was his, and which he had talked of leaving elsewhere. On the whole, the night's events were good; it only remained to account for them.

It was with some considerable trepidation that they returned to the town in the soft spring dawning. As they entered, one or two people looked out and pointed to them, and nodded significantly to one another. The two men grew hotly uncomfortable. Could it be possible? No. All must have happened as they expected. Even now they would be bringing their father home. His finding would prove the manner of his death. Their only task was to give some reason for its possibility.

At the bridge-end a man came out and stood before them.

'Stop,' he cried. 'Tam and Andra Hay, prepare to hear bad news. Your auld faither was fund this morning on the back o' Callowa hill wi' a broken neck. It's a sair affliction. Try and thole it like men.'

The two grew pale and faltering. 'My auld faither,' said the chorus. 'Oh ye dinna mean it. Say it's no true. I canna believe it, and him aye sae guid to us. What'll we dae wi'oot him?'

'Bear up, my poor fellows,' and the minister laid a hand on the shoulder of one. 'The Lord gave and the Lord has taken away.' He had a talent for inappropriate quotation.

But for the two there was no comfort. With dazed eyes and drawn faces, they asked every detail, fervently, feverishly. Then with faltering voices they told of how their father had gone the night before to the Harehope shepherd's, who was his cousin, and proposed returning in the morn. They bemoaned their remissness, they bewailed his kindness; and then, attended by condoling friends, these stricken men went down the street, accepting sympathy in every public.

ARTHUR CONAN DOYLE

J. HABAKUK JEPHSON'S STATEMENT

IN THE MONTH of December in the year 1873, the British ship *Dei Gratia* steered into Gibraltar, having in tow the derelict brigantine *Marie Celeste*, which had been picked up in latitude 38° 40', longitude 17° 15' W. There were several circumstances in connection with the condition and appearance of this abandoned vessel which excited considerable comment at the time, and aroused a curiosity which has never been satisfied. What these circumstances were was summed up in an able article which appeared in the *Gibraltar Gazette*. The curious can find it in the issue for January 4, 1874, unless my memory deceives me. For the benefit of those, however, who may be unable to refer to the paper in question, I shall subjoin a few extracts which touch upon the leading features of the case.

'We have ourselves,' says the anonymous writer in the *Gazette*, 'been over the derelict *Marie Celeste*, and have closely questioned the officers of the *Dei Gratia* on every point which might throw light on the affair. They are of opinion that she had been abandoned several days, or perhaps weeks, before being picked up. The official log, which was found in the cabin, states that the vessel sailed from Boston to Lisbon, starting upon October 16. It is, however, most imperfectly kept, and affords little information. There is no reference to rough weather, and, indeed, the state of the vessel's paint and rigging excludes the idea that she was abandoned for any such reason. She is perfectly watertight. No signs of a struggle or of violence are to be detected, and there is absolutely nothing to account for the disappearance of the crew. There are several indications that a lady was present on board, a sewing-machine being found in the cabin and some articles of female attire. These probably belonged to the captain's wife, who is mentioned in the log as having accompanied her husband. As an instance of the mildness of the weather, it may be remarked that a bobbin of silk was found standing upon the sewing-machine, though the least roll of the vessel would have precipitated it to the floor. The boats were intact and slung upon the davits; and the cargo, consisting of tallow and American clocks, was untouched. An old-fashioned sword of curious workmanship was discovered among some lumber in the forecastle, and this weapon is said to exhibit a longitudinal striation on the steel, as if it had been recently wiped. It has been placed in the hands of the police, and submitted to Dr Monaghan, the analyst, for inspection. The result of his examination has not yet been published. We may remark, in conclusion, that Captain Dalton, of the *Dei Gratia*, an able and intelligent seaman, is of opinion that the *Marie Celeste* may have been abandoned a considerable distance from the spot at which she was picked up, since a powerful current runs up in that latitude from the African coast. He confesses his inability, however, to advance any hypothesis which can reconcile all the facts of the case. In the utter absence of a clue or grain of evidence, it is to be feared that the fate of the crew of the *Marie Celeste* will be added to those numerous mysteries of the deep which will never be solved until the great day when the sea shall give up its dead. If crime has been committed, as is much to be suspected, there is little hope of bringing the perpetrators to justice.'

I shall supplement this extract from the *Gibraltar Gazette* by quoting a telegram from Boston, which went the round of the English papers, and represented the total amount of information which had been collected about the *Marie Celeste*. 'She was,' it said, 'a brigantine of 170 tons burden, and belonged to White, Russell & White, wine importers, of this city. Captain J. W. Tibbs was an old servant of the firm, and was a man of known ability and tried probity. He was accompanied by his wife, aged thirty-one, and their youngest child, five years old. The crew consisted of seven hands, including two coloured seamen, and a boy. There were three passengers, one of whom was the well-known Brooklyn specialist on consumption, Dr Habakuk Jephson, who was a distinguished advocate for Abolition in the early days of the movement, and whose pamphlet, entitled "Where is thy Brother?" exercised a strong influence on public opinion before the war. The other passengers were Mr J. Harton, a writer in the employ of the firm, and Mr Septimius Goring, a half-caste gentleman, from New Orleans. All investigations have failed to throw any light upon the fate of these fourteen human beings. The loss of Dr Jephson will be felt both in political and scientific circles.'

I have here epitomised, for the benefit of the public, all that has been hitherto known concerning the *Marie Celeste* and her crew, for the past ten years have not in any way helped to elucidate the mystery. I have now taken up my pen with the intention of telling all that I know of the ill-fated voyage. I consider that it is a duty which I owe to society, for symptoms which I am familiar with in others lead me to believe that before many months my tongue and hand may be alike incapable of conveying information. Let me remark, as a preface to my narrative, that I am Joseph Habakuk Jephson, Doctor of Medicine of the University of Harvard, and ex-Consulting Physician of the Samaritan Hospital of Brooklyn.

Many will doubtless wonder why I have not proclaimed myself before, and why I have suffered so many conjectures and surmises to pass unchallenged. Could the ends of justice have been served in any way by my revealing the facts in my possession I should unhesitatingly have done so. It seemed to me, however, that there was no possibility of such a result; and when I attempted, after the occurrence, to state my case to an English official, I was met with such offensive incredulity that I determined never again to expose myself to the chance of such an indignity. I can excuse the discourtesy of the Liverpool magistrate, however, when I reflect upon the treatment which I received at the hands of my own relatives, who, though they knew my unimpeachable character, listened to my statement with an indulgent smile as if humouring the delusion of a monomaniac. This slur upon my veracity led to a quarrel between myself and John Vanburger, the brother of my wife, and confirmed me in my resolution to let the matter sink into oblivion – a determination which I have only altered through my son's solicitations. In order to make my narrative intelligible, I must run lightly over one or two incidents in my former life which throw light upon subsequent events.

My father, William K. Jephson, was a preacher of the sect called Plymouth Brethren, and was one of the most respected citizens of Lowell. Like most of the other Puritans of New England, he was a determined opponent of slavery, and it was from his lips that I received those lessons which tinged every action of my life. While I was studying medicine at Harvard University, I had already made a mark as an advanced Abolitionist; and when, after taking my degree, I bought a third share of the practice of Dr Willis, of Brooklyn, I managed,

172

in spite of my professional duties, to devote a considerable time to the cause which I had at heart, my pamphlet, 'Where is thy Brother?'(Swarburgh, Lister & Co., 1849) attracting considerable attention.

When the war broke out I left Brooklyn and accompanied the 113th New York Regiment through the campaign. I was present at the second battle of Bull's Run and at the battle of Gettysburg. Finally, I was severely wounded at Antietam, and would probably have perished on the field had it not been for the kindness of a gentleman named Murray, who had me carried to his house and provided me with every comfort. Thanks to his charity, and to the nursing which I received from his black domestics, I was soon able to get about the plantation with the help of a stick. It was during this period of convalescence that an incident occurred which is closely connected with my story.

Among the most assiduous of the negresses who had watched my couch during my illness there was one old crone who appeared to exert considerable authority over the others. She was exceedingly attentive to me, and I gathered from the few words that passed between us that she had heard of me, and that she was grateful to me for championing her oppressed race.

One day as I was sitting alone in the verandah, basking in the sun, and debating whether I should rejoin Grant's army, I was surprised to see this old creature hobbling towards me. After looking cautiously around to see that we were alone, she fumbled in the front of her dress and produced a small chamois leather bag which was hung round her neck by a white cord.

'Massa,' she said, bending down and croaking the words into my ear, 'me die soon. Me very old woman. Not stay long on Massa Murray's plantation.'

'You may live a long time yet, Martha,' I answered. 'You know I am a doctor. If you feel ill let me know about it, and I will try to cure you.'

'No wish to live – wish to die. I'm gwine to join the heavenly host.' Here she relapsed into one of those half-heathenish rhapsodies in which negroes indulge. 'But, massa, me have one thing must leave behind me when I go. No able to take it with me across the Jordan. That one thing very precious, more precious and more holy than all thing else in the world. Me, a poor old black woman, have this because my people, very great people, 'spose they was back in the old country. But you cannot understand this same as black folk could. My fader give it me, and his fader give it him, but now who shall I give it to? Poor Martha hab no child, no relation, nobody. All round I see black man very bad man. Black woman very stupid woman. Nobody worthy of the stone. And so I say, Here is Massa Jephson who write books and fight for coloured folk – he must be good man, and he shall have it though he is white man, and nebber can know what it mean or where it came from.' Here the old woman fumbled in the chamois leather bag and pulled out a flattish black stone with a hole through the middle of it. 'Here, take it,' she said, pressing it into my hand; 'take it. No harm nebber come from anything good. Keep it safe – nebber lose it!' and with a warning gesture the old crone hobbled away in the same cautious way as she had come, looking from side to side to see if we had been observed.

I was more amused than impressed by the old woman's earnestness, and was only prevented from laughing during her oration by the fear of hurting her feelings. When she was gone I took a good look at the stone which she had given me. It was intensely black, of extreme hardness, and oval in shape – just such a flat stone as one would pick up on the seashore if one wished to throw a long way. It was about three inches long, and an inch and a half broad at the middle, but rounded off at the extremities. The most curious part about it was several well-marked ridges which ran in semicircles over its surface, and gave it exactly the appearance of a human ear. Altogether I was rather interested in my new possession, and determined to submit it, as a geological specimen, to my friend Professor Shroeder of the New York Institute, upon the earliest opportunity. In the meantime I thrust it into my pocket, and rising from my chair started off for a short stroll in the shrubbery, dismissing the incident from my mind.

As my wound had nearly healed by this time, I took my leave of Mr Murray shortly afterwards. The Union armies were everywhere victorious and converging on Richmond, so that my assistance seemed unnecessary, and I returned to Brooklyn. There I resumed my practice, and married the second daughter of Josiah Vanburger, the well-known wood engraver. In the course of a few years I built up a good connection and acquired considerable reputation in the treatment of pulmonary complaints. I still kept the old black stone in my pocket, and frequently told the story of the dramatic way in which I had become possessed of it. I also kept my resolution of showing it to Professor Shroeder, who was much interested both by the anecdote and the specimen. He pronounced it to be a piece of meteoric stone, and drew my attention to the fact that its resemblance to an ear was not accidental, but that it was most carefully worked into that shape. A dozen little anatomical points showed that the worker had been as accurate as he was skilful. 'I should not wonder,' said the Professor, 'if it were broken off from some larger statue, though how such hard material could be so perfectly worked is more than I can understand. If there is a statue to correspond I should like to see it!' So I thought at the time, but I have changed my opinion since.

The next seven or eight years of my life were quiet and uneventful. Summer followed spring, and spring followed winter, without any variation in my duties. As the practice increased I admitted J. S. Jackson as partner, he to have one-fourth of the profits. The continued strain had told upon my constitution, however, and I became at last so unwell that my wife insisted upon my consulting Dr Kavanagh Smith, who was my colleague at the Samaritan Hospital. That gentleman examined me, and pronounced the apex of my left lung to be in a state of consolidation, recommending me at the same time to go through a course of medical treatment and to take a long sea-voyage.

My own disposition, which is naturally restless, predisposed me strongly in favour of the latter piece of advice, and the matter was clinched by my meeting young Russell, of the firm of White, Russell & White, who offered me a passage in one of his father's ships, the *Marie Celeste*, which was just starting from Boston. 'She is a snug little ship,' he said, 'and Tibbs, the captain, is an excellent fellow. There is nothing like a sailing ship for an invalid.' I was very much of the same opinion myself, so I closed with the offer on the spot.

My original plan was that my wife should accompany me on my travels. She has always been a very poor sailor, however, and there were strong family reasons against her exposing herself to any risk at the time, so we determined that she should remain at home. I am not a religious or an effusive man; but oh, thank God for that! As to leaving my practice, I was easily reconciled to it, as Jackson, my partner, was a reliable and hard-working man.

I arrived in Boston on October 12, 1873, and proceeded immediately to the office of the firm in order to thank them for their courtesy. As I was sitting in the counting-house waiting until they should be at liberty to see me, the words *Marie Celeste* suddenly attracted my attention. I looked round and saw a very tall, gaunt man, who was leaning across the polished mahogany counter asking some questions of the clerk at the other side. His face was turned half towards me, and I could see that he had a strong dash of negro blood in him, being probably a quadroon or even nearer akin to the black. His curved aquiline nose and straight lank hair showed the white strain; but the dark restless eye, sensuous mouth, and gleaming teeth all told of his African origin. His complexion was of a sickly unhealthy yellow, and as his face was deeply pitted with small-pox, the general impression was so unfavourable as to be almost revolting. When he spoke, however, it was in a soft, melodious voice, and in well-chosen words, and he was evidently a man of some education.

'I wished to ask a few questions about the *Marie Celeste*,' he repeated, leaning across to the clerk. 'She sails the day after to-morrow, does she not?'

'Yes, sir,' said the young clerk, awed into unusual politeness by the glimmer of a large diamond in the stranger's shirt front.

'Where is she bound for?'

'Lisbon.'

'How many of a crew?'

'Seven, sir.'

'Passengers?'

'Yes, two. One of our young gentlemen, and a doctor from New York.'

'No gentleman from the South?' asked the stranger eagerly.

'No, none, sir.'

'Is there room for another passenger?'

'Accommodation for three more,' answered the clerk.

'I'll go,' said the quadroon decisively; 'I'll go, I'll engage my passage at once. Put it down, will you – Mr Septimius Goring, of New Orleans.'

The clerk filled up a form and handed it over to the stranger, pointing to a blank space at the bottom. As Mr Goring stooped over to sign it I was horrified to observe that the fingers of his right hand had been lopped off, and that he was holding the pen between his thumb and the palm. I have seen thousands slain in battle, and assisted at every conceivable surgical operation, but I cannot recall any sight which gave me such a thrill of disgust as that great brown sponge-like hand with the single member protruding from it. He used it skilfully enough, however, for dashing off his signature, he nodded to the clerk and strolled out of the office just as Mr White sent out word that he was ready to receive me.

I went down to the *Marie Celeste* that evening, and looked over my berth, which was extremely comfortable considering the small size of the vessel. Mr Goring, whom I had seen in the morning, was to have the one next mine. Opposite was the captain's cabin and a small berth for Mr John Harton, a gentleman who was going out in the interests of the firm. These little rooms were arranged on each side of the passage which led from the main-deck to the saloon. The latter was a comfortable room, the panelling tastefully done in oak and mahogany, with a rich Brussels carpet and luxurious settees. I was very much pleased with the accommodation, and also with Tibbs the captain, a bluff, sailor-like fellow, with a loud voice and hearty manner, who welcomed me to the ship with effusion, and insisted upon our splitting a bottle of wine in his cabin. He told me that he intended to take his wife and youngest child with him on the voyage, and that he hoped with good luck to make Lisbon in three weeks. We had a pleasant chat and parted the best of friends, he warning me to make the last of my preparations next morning, as he intended to make a start by the midday tide, having now shipped all his cargo. I went back to my hotel, where I found a letter from my wife awaiting me, and, after a refreshing night's sleep, returned to the boat in the morning. From this point I am able to quote from the journal which I kept in order to vary the monotony of the long sea-voyage. If it is somewhat bald in places I can at least rely upon its accuracy in details, as it was written conscientiously from day to day.

October 16th. – Cast off our warps at half-past two and were towed out into the bay, where the tug left us, and with all sail set we bowled along at about nine knots an hour. I stood upon the poop watching the low land of America sinking gradually upon the horizon until the evening haze hid it from my sight. A single red light, however, continued to blaze balefully behind us, throwing a long track like a trail of blood upon the water, and it is still visible as I write, though reduced to a mere speck. The Captain is in a bad humour, for two of his hands disappointed him at the last moment, and he was compelled to ship a couple of negroes who happened to be on the quay. The missing men were steady, reliable fellows, who had been with him several voyages, and their non-appearance puzzled as well as irritated him. Where a crew of seven men have to work a fair-sized ship the loss of two experienced seamen is a serious one, for though the negroes may take a spell at the wheel or swab the decks, they are of little or no use in rough weather. Our cook is also a black man, and Mr Septimius Goring has a little darkie servant, so that we are rather a piebald community. The accountant, John Harton, promises to be an acquisition, for he is a cheery, amusing young fellow. Strange how little wealth has to do with happiness! He has all the world before him and is seeking his fortune in a far land, yet he is as transparently happy as a man can be. Goring is rich, if I am not mistaken, and so am I; but I know that I have a lung, and Goring has some deeper trouble still, to judge by his features. How poorly do we both contrast with the careless, penniless clerk!

October 17th. – Mrs Tibbs appeared upon deck for the first time this morning – a cheerful, energetic woman, with a dear little child just able to walk and prattle. Young Harton pounced on it at once, and carried it away to his cabin, where no doubt he will lay the seeds of future dyspepsia in the child's stomach. Thus medicine doth make cynics of us all! The weather is still all that could be desired, with a fine fresh breeze from the west-sou'-west. The vessel goes so steadily that you would hardly know that she was moving were it not for the creaking of the cordage, the bellying of the sails, and the long white furrow in our wake. Walked the quarter-deck all morning with the Captain, and I think the keen fresh air has already done my breathing good, for the exercise did not fatigue me in any way. Tibbs is a remarkably intelligent man, and we had an interesting argument about Maury's observations on ocean currents, which we terminated by going down into his cabin to consult the original work. There we found Goring, rather to the Captain's surprise, as it is not usual for passengers to enter that sanctum unless specially invited. He apologised for his intrusion, however, pleading his ignorance of the usages of ship life; and the good-natured sailor simply laughed at the incident, begging him to remain and favour us with his company. Goring pointed to the chronometers, the case of which he had opened, and remarked that he had been admiring them. He has evidently some practical knowledge of mathematical instruments, as he told at a glance which was the most trustworthy of the three, and also named their price within a few dollars. He had a discussion with the Captain too upon the variation of the compass, and when we came back to the ocean currents he showed a thorough grasp of the subject. Altogether he rather improves upon acquaintance, and is a man of decided culture and refinement. His voice harmonises with his conversation, and both are the very antithesis of his face and figure.

The noonday observation shows that we have run two hundred and twenty miles. Towards evening the breeze freshened up, and the first mate ordered reefs to be taken in the topsails and top-gallant sails in expectation of a windy night. I observe that the barometer has fallen to twenty-nine. I trust our voyage will not be a rough one, as I am a poor sailor, and my health would probably derive more harm than good from a stormy trip, though I have the greatest confidence in the Captain's seamanship and in the soundness of the vessel. Played cribbage with Mrs Tibbs after supper, and Harton gave us a couple of tunes on the violin.

October 18th. – The gloomy prognostications of last night were not fulfilled, as the wind died away again, and we are lying now in a long greasy swell, ruffled here and there by a fleeting catspaw which is insufficient to fill the sails. The air is colder than it was yesterday, and I have put on one of the thick woollen jerseys which my wife knitted for me. Harton came into my cabin in the morning, and we had a cigar together. He says that he remembers having seen Goring in Cleveland, Ohio, in '69. He was, it appears, a mystery then as now, wandering about without any visible employment, and extremely reticent on his own affairs. The man interests me as a psychological study. At breakfast this morning I suddenly had that vague feeling of uneasiness which comes over some people when closely stared at, and, looking quickly up, I met his eyes bent upon me with an intensity which amounted to ferocity, though their expression instantly softened as he made some conventional remark upon the weather. Curiously enough, Harton says that he had a very similar experience yesterday upon deck. I observe that Goring frequently talks to the coloured seamen as he strolls about – a trait which I rather admire, as it is common to find half-breeds ignore their dark strain and treat their black kinsfolk with greater intolerance than a white man would do. His little page is devoted to him, apparently, which speaks well for his treatment of him. Altogether, the man is a curious mixture of incongruous qualities, and unless I am deceived in him will give me food for observation during the voyage.

The Captain is grumbling about his chronometers, which do not register exactly the same time. He says it is the first time that they have ever disagreed. We were unable to get a noonday observation on account of the haze. By dead reckoning, we have done about a hundred and seventy miles in the twenty-four hours. The dark seamen have proved, as the skipper prophesied, to be very inferior hands, but as they can both manage the wheel well they are kept steering, and so leave the more experienced men to work the ship. These details are trivial enough, but a small thing serves as food for gossip aboard ship. The appearance of a whale in the evening caused quite a flutter among us. From its sharp back and forked tail, I should pronounce it to have been a rorqual, or 'finner,' as they are called by the fishermen.

October 19th. – Wind was cold, so I prudently remained in my cabin all day, only creeping out for dinner. Lying in my bunk I can, without moving, reach my books, pipes, or anything else I may want, which is one advantage of a small apartment. My old wound began to ache a little to-day, probably from the cold. Read *Montaigne's Essays* and nursed myself. Harton came in in the afternoon with Doddy, the Captain's child, and the skipper himself followed, so that I held quite a reception.

October 20th and 21st. – Still cold, with a continual drizzle of rain, and I have not been able to leave the cabin. This confinement makes me feel weak and depressed. Goring came in to see me, but his company did not tend to cheer me up much, as he hardly uttered a word, but contented himself with staring at me in a peculiar and rather irritating manner. He then got up and stole out of the cabin without saying anything. I am beginning to suspect that the man is a lunatic. I think I mentioned that his cabin is next to mine. The two are simply divided by a thin wooden partition which is cracked in many places, some of the cracks being so large that I can hardly avoid, as I lie in my bunk, observing his motions in the adjoining room. Without any wish to play the spy, I see him continually stooping over what appears to be a chart and working with a pencil and compasses. I have remarked the interest he displays in matters connected with navigation, but I am surprised that he should take the trouble to work out the course of the ship. However, it is a harmless amusement enough, and no doubt he verifies his results by those of the Captain.

I wish the man did not run in my thoughts so much. I had a nightmare on the night of the 20th, in which I thought my bunk was a coffin, that I was laid out in it, and that Goring was endeavouring to nail up the lid, which I was frantically pushing away. Even when I woke up, I could hardly persuade myself that I was not in a coffin. As a medical man, I know that a nightmare is simply a vascular derangement of the cerebral hemispheres, and yet in my weak state I cannot shake off the morbid impression which it produces.

October 22nd. – A fine day, with hardly a cloud in the sky, and a fresh breeze from the sou'-west which wafts us gaily on our way. There has evidently been some heavy weather near us, as there is a tremendous swell on, and the ship lurches until the end of the fore-yard nearly touches the water. Had a refreshing walk up and down the quarter-deck, though I have hardly found my sea-legs yet. Several small birds – chaffinches, I think – perched in the rigging.

4.40 P.M. – While I was on deck this morning I heard a sudden explosion from the direction of my cabin, and, hurrying down, found that I had very nearly met with a serious accident. Goring was cleaning a revolver, it seems, in his cabin, when one of the barrels which he thought was unloaded went off. The ball passed through the side partition and imbedded itself in the bulwarks in the exact place where my head usually rests. I have been under fire too often to magnify trifles, but there is no doubt that if I had been in the bunk it must have killed me. Goring, poor fellow, did not know that I had gone on deck that day, and must therefore have felt terribly frightened. I never saw such emotion in a man's face as when, on rushing out of his cabin with the smoking pistol in his hand, he met me face to face as I came down from deck. Of course, he was profuse in his apologies, though I simply laughed at the incident.

11 P.M. – A misfortune has occurred so unexpected and so horrible that my little escape of the morning dwindles into insignificance. Mrs Tibbs and her child have disappeared – utterly and entirely disappeared. I can hardly compose myself to write the sad details. About half-past eight Tibbs rushed into my cabin with a very white face and asked me if I had seen his wife. I answered that I had not. He then ran wildly into the saloon and began groping about for any trace of her, while I followed him, endeavouring vainly to

persuade him that his fears were ridiculous. We hunted over the ship for an hour and a half without coming on any sign of the missing woman or child. Poor Tibbs lost his voice completely from calling her name. Even the sailors, who are generally stolid enough, were deeply affected by the sight of him as he roamed bareheaded and dishevelled about the deck, searching with feverish anxiety the most impossible places, and returning to them again and again with a piteous pertinacity. The last time she was seen was about seven o'clock, when she took Doddy on to the poop to give him a breath of fresh air before putting him to bed. There was no one there at the time except the black seaman at the wheel, who denies having seen her at all. The whole affair is wrapped in mystery. My own theory is that while Mrs Tibbs was holding the child and standing near the bulwarks it gave a spring and fell overboard, and that in her convulsive attempt to catch or save it, she followed it. I cannot account for the double disappearance in any other way. It is quite feasible that such a tragedy should be enacted without the knowledge of the man at the wheel, since it was dark at the time, and the peaked skylights of the saloon screen the greater part of the quarter-deck. Whatever the truth may be it is a terrible catastrophe, and has cast the darkest gloom upon our voyage. The mate has put the ship about, but of course there is not the slightest hope of picking them up. The Captain is lying in a state of stupor in his cabin. I gave him a powerful dose of opium in his coffee that for a few hours at least his anguish may be deadened.

October 23rd. – Woke with a vague feeling of heaviness and misfortune, but it was not until a few moments' reflection that I was able to recall our loss of the night before. When I came on deck I saw the poor skipper standing gazing back at the waste of waters behind us which contains everything dear to him upon earth. I attempted to speak to him, but he turned brusquely away, and began pacing the deck with his head sunk upon his breast. Even now, when the truth is so clear, he cannot pass a boat or an unbent sail without peering under it. He looks ten years older than he did yesterday morning. Harton is terribly cut up, for he was fond of little Doddy, and Goring seems sorry too. At least he has shut himself up in his cabin all day, and when I got a casual glance at him his head was resting on his two hands as if in a melancholy reverie. I fear we are about as dismal a crew as ever sailed. How shocked my wife will be to hear of our disaster! The swell has gone down now, and we are doing about eight knots with all sail set and a nice little breeze. Hyson is practically in command of the ship, as Tibbs, though he does his best to bear up and keep a brave front, is incapable of applying himself to serious work.

October 24th. – Is the ship accursed? Was there ever a voyage which began so fairly and which changed so disastrously? Tibbs shot himself through the head during the night. I was awakened about three o'clock in the morning by an explosion, and immediately sprang out of bed and rushed into the Captain's cabin to find out the cause, though with a terrible presentiment in my heart. Quickly as I went, Goring went more quickly still, for he was already in the cabin stooping over the dead body of the Captain. It was a hideous sight, for the whole front of his face was blown in, and the little room was swimming in blood. The pistol was lying beside him on the floor, just as it had dropped from his hand. He had evidently put it to his mouth before pulling the trigger. Goring and I picked him reverently up and laid him on his bed. The crew had all clustered into his cabin, and the six white men were deeply grieved, for they were old hands who had sailed with him many years. There were dark looks and murmurs among them too, and one of them openly declared that the ship was haunted. Harton helped to lay the poor skipper out, and we did him up in canvas between us. At twelve o'clock the foreyard was hauled aback, and we committed his body to the deep, Goring reading the Church of England burial service. The breeze has freshened up, and we have done ten knots all day and sometimes twelve. The sooner we reach Lisbon and get away from this accursed ship the better pleased shall I be. I feel as though we were in a floating coffin. Little wonder that the poor sailors are superstitious when I, an educated man, feel it so strongly.

October 25th. – Made a good run all day. Feel listless and depressed.

October 26th. – Goring, Harton, and I had a chat together on deck in the morning. Harton tried to draw Goring out as to his profession, and his object in going to Europe, but the quadroon parried all his questions and gave us no information. Indeed, he seemed to be slightly offended by Harton's pertinacity, and went down into his cabin. I wonder why we should both take such an interest in this man! I suppose it is his striking appearance, coupled with his apparent wealth, which piques our curiosity. Harton has a theory that he is really a detective, that he is after some criminal who has got away to Portugal, and that he chooses this peculiar way of travelling that he may arrive unnoticed and pounce upon his quarry unawares. I think the supposition is rather a far-fetched one, but Harton bases it upon a book which Goring left on deck, and which he picked up and glanced over. It was a sort of scrap-book it seems, and contained a large number of newspaper cuttings. All these cuttings related to murders which had been committed at various times in the States during the last twenty years or so. The curious thing which Harton observed about them, however, was that they were invariably murders the authors of which had never been brought to justice. They varied in every detail, he says, as to the manner of execution and the social status of the victim, but they uniformly wound up with the same formula that the murderer was still at large, though, of course, the police had every reason to expect his speedy capture. Certainly the incident seems to support Harton's theory, though it may be a mere whim of Goring's, or, as I suggested to Harton, he may be collecting materials for a book which shall outvie De Quincey. In any case it is no business of ours.

October 27th, 28th. – Wind still fair, and we are making good progress. Strange how easily a human unit may drop out of its place and be forgotten! Tibbs is hardly ever mentioned now; Hyson has taken possession of his cabin, and all goes on as before. Were it not for Mrs Tibbs's sewing-machine upon a side-table we might forget that the unfortunate family had ever existed. Another accident occurred on board to-day, though fortunately not a very serious one. One of our white hands had gone down the afterhold to fetch up a spare coil of rope, when one of the hatches which he had removed came crashing down on the top of him. He saved his life by springing out of the way, but one of his feet was terribly crushed, and he will be of little use for the remainder of the voyage. He attributes the accident to the carelessness of his negro companion, who had helped him to shift the hatches. The latter, however, puts it down to the roll of the ship. Whatever be the cause, it reduces our short-handed crew still further. This run of ill-luck seems to be depressing Harton, for he has lost his usual good spirits and joviality. Goring is the only one who preserves his cheerfulness. I see him still working at his chart in his own cabin. His nautical knowledge would be useful should anything happen to Hyson – which God forbid!

October 29th, 30th. – Still bowling along with a fresh breeze. All quiet and nothing of note to chronicle.

October 31st. – My weak lungs, combined with the exciting episodes of the voyage, have shaken my nervous system so much that the most trivial incident affects me. I can hardly believe that I am the same man who tied the external iliac artery, an operation requiring the nicest precision, under a heavy rifle fire at Antietam. I am as nervous as a child. I was lying half dozing last night about four bells in the middle watch trying in vain to drop into a refreshing sleep. There was no light inside my cabin, but a single ray of moonlight streamed in through the port-hole, throwing a silvery flickering circle upon the door. As I lay I kept my drowsy eyes upon this circle, and was conscious that it was gradually becoming less well-defined as my senses left me, when I was suddenly recalled to full wakefulness by the appearance of a small dark object in the very centre of the luminous disc. I lay quietly and breathlessly watching it. Gradually it grew larger and plainer, and then I perceived that it was a human hand which had been cautiously inserted through the chink of the half-closed door – a hand which, as I observed with a thrill of horror, was not provided with fingers. The door swung cautiously backwards, and Goring's head followed his hand. It appeared in the centre of the moonlight, and was framed as it were in a ghastly uncertain halo, against which his features showed out plainly. It seemed to me that I had never seen such an utterly fiendish and merciless expression upon a human face. His eyes were dilated and glaring, his lips drawn back so as to show his white fangs, and his straight black hair appeared to bristle over his low forehead like the hood of a cobra. The sudden and noiseless apparition had such an effect upon me that I sprang up in bed trembling in every limb, and held out my hand towards my revolver. I was heartily ashamed of my hastiness when he explained the object of his intrusion, as he immediately did in the most courteous language. He had been suffering from toothache, poor fellow! and had come in to beg some laudanum, knowing that I possessed a medicine chest. As to a sinister expression he is never a beauty, and what with my state of nervous tension and the effect of the shifting moonlight it was easy to conjure up something horrible. I gave him twenty drops, and he went off again with many expressions of gratitude. I can hardly say how much this trivial incident affected me. I have felt unstrung all day.

A week's record of our voyage is here omitted, as nothing eventful occurred during the time, and my log consists merely of a few pages of unimportant gossip.

November 7th. – Harton and I sat on the poop all the morning, for the weather is becoming very warm as we come into southern latitudes. We reckon that we have done two-thirds of our voyage. How glad we shall be to see the green banks of the Tagus, and leave this unlucky ship for ever! I was endeavouring to amuse Harton to-day and to while away the time by telling him some of the experiences of my past life. Among others I related to him how I came into the possession of my black stone, and as a finale I rummaged in the side pocket of my old shooting coat and produced the identical object in question. He and I were bending over it together, I pointing out to him the curious ridges upon its surface, when we were conscious of a shadow falling between us and the sun, and looking round saw Goring standing behind us glaring over our shoulders at the stone. For some reason or other he appeared to be powerfully excited, though he was evidently trying to control himself and to conceal his emotion. He pointed once or twice at my relic with his stubby thumb before he could recover himself sufficiently to ask what it was and how I obtained it – a question put in such a brusque manner that I should have been offended had I not known the man to be an eccentric. I told him the story very much as I had told it to Harton. He listened with the deepest interest, and then asked me if I had any idea what the stone was. I said I had not, beyond that it was meteoric. He asked me if I had ever tried its effect upon a negro. I said I had not. 'Come,' said he, 'we'll see what our black friend at the wheel thinks of it.' He took the stone in his hand and went across to the sailor, and the two examined it carefully. I could see the man gesticulating and nodding his head excitedly as if making some assertion, while his face betrayed the utmost astonishment, mixed, I think, with some reverence. Goring came across the deck to us presently, still holding the stone in his hand. 'He says it is a worthless, useless thing,' he said, 'and fit only to be chucked overboard,' with which he raised his hand and would most certainly have made an end of my relic, had the black sailor behind him not rushed forward and seized him by the wrist. Finding himself secured Goring dropped the stone and turned away with a very bad grace to avoid my angry remonstrances at his breach of faith. The black picked up the stone and handed it to me with a low bow and every sign of profound respect. The whole affair is inexplicable. I am rapidly coming to the conclusion that Goring is a maniac or something very near one. When I compare the effect produced by the stone upon the sailor, however, with the respect shown to Martha on the plantation, and the surprise of Goring on its first produc-tion, I cannot but come to the conclusion that I have really got hold of some powerful talisman which appeals to the whole dark race. I must not trust it in Goring's hands again.

November 8th, 9th. – What splendid weather we are having! Beyond one little blow, we have had nothing but fresh breezes the whole voyage. These two days we have made better runs than any hitherto. It is a pretty thing to watch the spray fly up from our prow as it cuts through the waves. The sun shines through it and breaks it up into a number of miniature rainbows – 'sun-dogs,' the sailors call them. I stood on the fo'c'sle-head for several hours to-day watching the effect, and surrounded by a halo of prismatic colours. The steersman has evidently told the other blacks about my wonderful stone, for I am treated by them all with the greatest respect. Talking about optical phenomena, we had a curious one yesterday evening which was pointed out to me by Hyson. This was the appearance of a triangular well-defined object high up in the heavens to the north of us. He explained that it was exactly like the Peak of Teneriffe as seen from a great distance – the peak was, however, at that moment at least five hundred miles to the south. It may have been a cloud, or it may have been one of those strange reflections of which one reads. The weather is very warm. The mate says that he never knew it so warm in these latitudes. Played chess with Harton in the evening.

November 10th. – It is getting warmer and warmer. Some land birds came and perched in the rigging today, though we are still a considerable way from our destination. The heat is so great that we are too lazy to do anything but lounge about the decks and smoke. Goring came over to me to-day and asked me some more questions about my stone; but I answered him rather shortly, for I have not quite forgiven him yet for the cool way in which he attempted to deprive me of it.

November 11th, 12th. – Still making good progress. I had

no idea Portugal was ever as hot as this, but no doubt it is cooler on land. Hyson himself seemed surprised at it, and so do the men.

November 13th. – A most extraordinary event has happened, so extraordinary as to be almost inexplicable. Either Hyson has blundered wonderfully, or some magnetic influence has disturbed our instruments. Just about daybreak the watch on the fo'c'sle-head shouted out that he heard the sound of surf ahead, and Hyson thought he saw the loom of land. The ship was put about, and, though no lights were seen, none of us doubted that we had struck the Portuguese coast a little sooner than we had expected. What was our surprise to see the scene which was revealed to us at break of day! As far as we could look on either side was one long line of surf, great, green billows rolling in and breaking into a cloud of foam. But behind the surf what was there! Not the green banks nor the high cliffs of the shores of Portugal, but a great sandy waste which stretched away and away until it blended with the skyline. To right and left, look where you would, there was nothing but yellow sand, heaped in some places into fantastic mounds, some of them several hundred feet high, while in other parts were long stretches as level apparently as a billiard board. Harton and I, who had come on deck together, looked at each other in astonishment, and Harton burst out laughing. Hyson is exceedingly mortified at the occurrence, and protests that the instruments have been tampered with. There is no doubt that this is the mainland of Africa, and that it was really the Peak of Teneriffe which we saw some days ago upon the northern horizon. At the time when we saw the land birds we must have been passing some of the Canary Islands. If we continued on the same course, we are now to the north of Cape Blanco, near the unexplored country which skirts the great Sahara. All we can do is to rectify our instruments as far as possible and start afresh for our destination.

8.30 P.M. – Have been lying in a calm all day. The coast is now about a mile and a half from us. Hyson has examined the instruments, but cannot find any reason for their extraordinary deviation.

This is the end of my private journal, and I must make the remainder of my statement from memory. There is little chance of my being mistaken about facts which have seared themselves into my recollection. That very night the storm which had been brewing so long burst over us, and I came to learn whither all those little incidents were tending which I had recorded so aimlessly. Blind fool that I was not to have seen it sooner! I shall tell what occurred as precisely as I can.

I had gone into my cabin about half-past eleven, and was preparing to go to bed, when a tap came at my door. On opening it I saw Goring's little black page, who told me that his master would like to have a word with me on deck. I was rather surprised that he should want me at such a late hour, but I went up without hesitation. I had hardly put my foot on the quarter-deck before I was seized from behind, dragged down upon my back, and a handkerchief slipped round my mouth. I struggled as hard as I could, but a coil of rope was rapidly and firmly wound round me, and I found myself lashed to the davit of one of the boats, utterly powerless to do or say anything, while the point of a knife pressed to my throat warned me to cease my struggles. The night was so dark that I had been unable hitherto to recognise my assailants, but as my eyes became accustomed to the gloom, and the moon broke out through the clouds that obscured it, I made out that I was surrounded by the two negro sailors, the black cook, and my fellow-passenger Goring. Another man was crouching on the deck at my feet, but he was in the shadow and I could not recognise him.

All this occurred so rapidly that a minute could hardly have elapsed from the time I mounted the companion until I found myself gagged and powerless. It was so sudden that I could scarce bring myself to realise it, or to comprehend what it all meant. I heard the gang round me speaking in short, fierce whispers to each other, and some instinct told me that my life was the question at issue. Goring spoke authoritatively and angrily – the others doggedly and all together, as if disputing his commands. Then they moved away in a body to the opposite side of the deck, where I could still hear them whispering, though they were concealed from my view by the saloon skylights.

All this time the voices of the watch on deck chatting and laughing at the other end of the ship were distinctly audible, and I could see them gathered in a group, little dreaming of the dark doings which were going on within thirty yards of them. Oh! That I could have given them one word of warning, even though I had lost my life in doing it! but it was impossible. The moon was shining fitfully through the scattered clouds, and I could see the silvery gleam of the surge, and beyond it the vast weird desert with its fantastic sand hills. Glancing down, I saw that the man who had been crouching on the deck was still lying there, and as I gazed at him, a flickering ray of moonlight fell full upon his upturned face. Great heaven! even now, when more than twelve years have elapsed, my hand trembles as I write that, in spite of distorted features and projecting eyes, I recognised the face of Harton, the cheery young clerk who had been my companion during the voyage. It needed no medical eye to see that he was quite dead, while the twisted handkerchief round the neck, and the gag in his mouth, showed the silent way in which the hell-hounds had done their work. The clue which explained every event of our voyage came upon me like a flash of light as I gazed on poor Harton's corpse. Much was dark and unexplained, but I felt a great dim perception of the truth.

I heard the striking of a match at the other side of the skylights, and then I saw the tall, gaunt figure of Goring standing up on the bulwarks and holding in his hands what appeared to be a dark lantern. He lowered this for a moment over the side of the ship, and, to my inexpressible astonishment, I saw it answered instantaneously by a flash among the sand-hills on shore, which came and went so rapidly, that unless I had been following the direction of Goring's gaze, I should never have detected it. Again he lowered the lantern, and again it was answered from the shore. He then stepped down from the bulwarks, and in doing so slipped, making such a noise, that for a moment my heart bounded with the thought that the attention of the watch would be directed to his proceedings. It was a vain hope. The night was calm and the ship motionless, so that no idea of duty kept them vigilant. Hyson, who after the death of Tibbs was in command of both watches, had gone below to snatch a few hours' sleep, and the boatswain who was left in charge was standing with the other two men at the foot of the foremast. Powerless, speechless, with the cords cutting into my flesh and the murdered man at my feet, I awaited the next act in the tragedy.

The four ruffians were standing up now at the other side of the deck. The cook was armed with some sort of a cleaver, the others had knives, and Goring had a revolver. They were all leaning against the rail and looking out over the water as if watching for something. I saw one of them grasp another's arm and point as if at some object, and following the direction I made out the loom of a large moving mass making towards the ship. As it emerged from the gloom I saw that it was a great canoe crammed with men and propelled by at least a score of paddles. As it shot under our stern the watch caught sight of it also, and raising a cry hurried aft. They were too late, however. A swarm of gigantic negroes clambered over the quarter, and led by Goring swept down the deck in an irresistible torrent. All opposition was overpowered in a moment, the unarmed watch were knocked over and bound, and the sleepers dragged out of their bunks and secured in the same manner. Hyson made an attempt to defend the narrow passage leading to his cabin, and I heard a scuffle, and his voice shouting for assistance. There was none to assist, however, and he was brought on to the poop with the blood streaming from a deep cut in his forehead. He was gagged like the others, and a council was held upon our fate by the negroes. I saw our black seamen pointing towards me and making some statement, which was received with murmurs of astonishment and incredulity by the savages. One of them then came over to me, and plunging his hand into my pocket took out my black stone and held it up. He then handed it to a man who appeared to be a chief, who examined it as minutely as the light would permit, and muttering a few words passed it on to the warrior beside him, who also scrutinised it and passed it on until it had gone from hand to hand round the whole circle. The chief then said a few words to Goring in the native tongue, on which the quadroon addressed me in English. At this moment I seem to see the scene. The tall masts of the ship with the moonlight streaming down, silvering the yards and bringing the network of cordage into hard relief; the group of dusky warriors leaning on their spears; the dead man at my feet; the line of white-faced prisoners, and in front of me the loathsome half-breed, looking in his white linen and elegant clothes a strange contrast to his associates.

'You will bear me witness,' he said in his softest accents, 'that I am no party to sparing your life. If it rested with me you would die as these other men are about to do. I have no personal grudge against either you or them, but I have devoted my life to the destruction of the white race, and you are the first that has ever been in my power and has escaped me. You may thank that stone of yours for your life. These poor fellows reverence it, and indeed if it really be what they think it is they have cause. Should it prove when we get ashore that they are mistaken, and that its shape and material is a mere chance, nothing can save your life. In the meantime we wish to treat you well, so if there are any of your possessions which you would like to take with you, you are at liberty to get them.' As he finished he gave a sign, and a couple of the negroes unbound me, though without removing the gag. I was led down into the cabin, where I put a few valuables into my pockets, together with a pocket-compass and my journal of the voyage. They then pushed me over the side into a small canoe, which was lying beside the large one, and my guards followed me, and shoving off began paddling for the shore. We had got about a hundred yards or so from the ship when our steersman held up his hand, and the paddlers paused for a moment and listened. Then on the silence of the night I heard a sort of dull, moaning sound, followed by a succession of splashes in the water. That is all I know of the fate of my poor shipmates. Almost immediately afterwards the large canoe followed us, and the deserted ship was left drifting about – a dreary, spectre-like hulk. Nothing was taken from her by the savages. The whole fiendish transaction was carried through as decorously and temperately as though it were a religious rite.

The first grey of daylight was visible in the east as we passed through the surge and reached the shore. Leaving half-a-dozen men with the canoes, the rest of the negroes set off through the sand-hills, leading me with them, but treating me very gently and respectfully. It was difficult walking, as we sank over our ankles into the loose, shifting sand at every step, and I was nearly dead beat by the time we reached the native village, or town rather, for it was a place of considerable dimensions. The houses were conical structures not unlike bee-hives, and were made of compressed seaweed cemented over with a rude form of mortar, there being neither stick nor stone upon the coast nor anywhere within many hundreds of miles. As we entered the town an enormous crowd of both sexes came swarming out to meet us, beating tom-toms and howling and screaming. On seeing me they redoubled their yells and assumed a threatening attitude, which was instantly quelled by a few words shouted by my escort. A buzz of wonder succeeded the war-cries and yells of the moment before, and the whole dense mass proceeded down the broad central street of the town, having my escort and myself in the centre.

My statement hitherto may seem so strange as to excite doubt in the minds of those who do not know me, but it was the fact which I am now about to relate which caused my own brother-in-law to insult me by disbelief. I can but relate the occurrence in the simplest words, and trust to chance and time to prove their truth. In the centre of this main street there was a large building, formed in the same primitive way as the others, but towering high above them; a stockade of beautifully polished ebony rails was planted all round it, the framework of the door was formed by two magnificent elephant's tusks sunk in the ground on each side and meeting at the top, and the aperture was closed by a screen of native cloth richly embroidered with gold. We made our way to this imposing-looking structure, but on reaching the opening in the stockade, the multitude stopped and squatted down upon their hams, while I was led through into the enclosure by a few of the chiefs and elders of the tribe, Goring accompanying us, and in fact directing the proceedings. On reaching the screen which closed the temple – for such it evidently was – my hat and my shoes were removed, and I was then led in, a venerable old negro leading the way carrying in his hand my stone, which had been taken from my pocket. The building was only lit up by a few long slits in the roof, through which the tropical sun poured, throwing broad golden bars upon the clay floor, alternating with intervals of darkness.

The interior was even larger than one would have imagined from the outside appearance. The walls were hung with native mats, shells, and other ornaments, but the remainder of the great space was quite empty, with the exception of a single object in the centre. This was the figure of a colossal negro, which I at first thought to be some real king or high priest of titanic size, but as I approached it I saw by the way in which the light was reflected from it that it was a statue admirably cut in jet-black stone. I was led up to this idol, for such it seemed to be, and looking at it closer I saw that though it was perfect in every other respect, one of its ears had been broken short off. The grey-haired negro who held my relic mounted upon a small stool, and stretching up his arm fitted Martha's black stone on to the jagged surface on the side of the statue's head. There could not be a doubt that the one had been broken off from the other. The parts dovetailed together so accurately that when the old man removed his hand the ear stuck in its place for a few seconds before dropping into his open palm. The group round me prostrated themselves upon the ground at the sight with a cry of reverence, while the crowd outside, to whom the result was communicated, set up a wild whooping and cheering.

In a moment I found myself converted from a prisoner into a demi-god. I was escorted back through the town in triumph, the people pressing forward to touch my clothing and to gather up the dust on which my foot had trod. One of the largest huts was put at my disposal, and a banquet of every native delicacy was served me. I still felt, however, that I was not a free man, as several spearmen were placed as a guard at the entrance of my hut. All day my mind was occupied with plans of escape, but none seemed in any way feasible. On the one side was the great arid desert stretching away to Timbuctoo, on the other was a sea untraversed by vessels. The more I pondered over the problem the more hopeless did it seem. I little dreamed how near I was to its solution.

Night had fallen, and the clamour of the negroes had died gradually away. I was stretched on the couch of skins which had been provided for me, and was still meditating over my future, when Goring walked stealthily into the hut. My first idea was that he had come to complete his murderous holocaust by making away with me, the last survivor, and I sprang up upon my feet, determined to defend myself to the last. He smiled when he saw the action, and motioned me down again while he seated himself upon the other end of the couch.

'What do you think of me?' was the astonishing question with which he commenced our conversation.

'Think of you!' I almost yelled. 'I think you the vilest, most unnatural renegade that ever polluted the earth. If we were away from these black devils of yours I would strangle you with my hands!'

'Don't speak so loud,' he said, without the slightest appearance of irritation. 'I don't want our chat to be cut short. So you would strangle me, would you!' he went on, with an amused smile. 'I suppose I am returning good for evil, for I have come to help you to escape.'

'You!' I gasped incredulously.

'Yes, I,' he continued. 'Oh, there is no credit to me in the matter. I am quite consistent. There is no reason why I should not be perfectly candid with you. I wish to be king over these fellows – not a very high ambition, certainly, but you know what Cæsar said about being first in a village in Gaul. Well, this unlucky stone of yours has not only saved your life, but has turned all their heads, so that they think you are come down from heaven, and my influence will be gone until you are out of the way. That is why I am going to help you to escape, since I cannot kill you' – this in the most natural and dulcet voice, as if the desire to do so were a matter of course.

'You would give the world to ask me a few questions,' he went on, after a pause; 'but you are too proud to do it. Never mind, I'll tell you one or two things, because I want your fellow white men to know them when you go back – if you are lucky enough to get back. About that cursed stone of yours, for instance. These negroes, or at least so the legend goes, were Mahometans originally. While Mahomet himself was still alive, there was a schism among his followers, and the smaller party moved away from Arabia, and eventually crossed Africa. They took away with them, in their exile, a valuable relic of their old faith in the shape of a large piece of the black stone of Mecca. The stone was a meteoric one, as you may have heard, and in its fall upon the earth it broke into two pieces. One of these pieces is still at Mecca. The larger piece was carried away to Barbary, where a skilful worker modelled it into the fashion which you saw to-day. These men are the descendants of the original seceders from Mahomet, and they have brought their relic safely through all their wanderings until they settled in this strange place, where the desert protects them from their enemies.'

'And the ear?' I asked, almost involuntarily.

'Oh, that was the same story over again. Some of the tribe wandered away to the south a few hundred years ago, and one of them, wishing to have good luck for the enterprise, got into the temple at night and carried off one of the ears. There has been a tradition among the negroes ever since that the ear would come back some day. The fellow who carried it was caught by some slaver, no doubt, and that was how it got into America, and so into your hands – and you have had the honour of fulfilling the prophecy.'

He paused for a few minutes, resting his head upon his hands, waiting apparently for me to speak. When he looked up again, the whole expression of his face had changed. His features were firm and set, and he changed the air of half levity with which he had spoken before for one of sternness and almost ferocity.

'I wish you to carry a message back,' he said, 'to the white race, the great dominating race whom I hate and defy. Tell them that I have battened on their blood for twenty years, that I have slain them until even I became tired of what had once been a joy, that I did this unnoticed and unsuspected in the face of every precaution which their civilisation could suggest. There is no satisfaction in revenge when your enemy does not know who has struck him. I am not sorry, therefore, to have you as a messenger. There is no need why I should tell you how this great hate became born in me. See this,' and he held up his mutilated hand; 'that was done by a white man's knife. My father was white, my mother was a slave. When he died she was sold again, and I, a child then, saw her lashed to death to break her of some of the little airs and graces which her late master had encouraged in her. My young wife, too, oh, my young wife!' a shudder ran through his whole frame. 'No matter! I swore my oath, and I kept it. From Maine to Florida, and from Boston to San Francisco, you could track my steps by sudden deaths which baffled the police. I warred against the whole white race as they for centuries had warred against the black one. At last, as I tell you, I sickened of blood. Still, the sight of a white face was abhorrent to me, and I determined to find some bold free black people and to throw in my lot with them, to cultivate their latent powers, and to form a nucleus for a great coloured nation. This idea possessed me, and I travelled over the world for two years seeking for what I desired. At last I almost despaired of finding it. There was no hope of regeneration in the slave-dealing Soudanese, the debased Fantee, or the Americanised negroes of Liberia. I was returning from my quest when chance brought me in contact with this magnificent tribe of dwellers in the desert, and I threw in my lot with them. Before doing so, however, my old instinct of revenge prompted me to make one last visit to the United States, and I returned from it in the *Marie Celeste*.

'As to the voyage itself, your intelligence will have told you by this time that, thanks to my manipulation, both compasses and chronometers were entirely untrustworthy. I alone worked out the course with correct instruments of my own, while the steering was done by my black friends under my guidance. I pushed Tibbs's wife overboard. What! You look surprised and shrink away. Surely you had guessed that by this time. I would have shot you that day through the partition, but unfortunately you were not there. I tried again afterwards, but you were awake. I shot Tibbs. I think the idea of suicide was carried out rather neatly. Of course when once we got on the coast the rest was simple. I had bargained that all on board should die; but that stone of yours upset my plans. I also bargained that there should be no plunder. No one can say we are pirates. We have acted from principle, not from any sordid motive.'

I listened in amazement to the summary of his crimes which this strange man gave me, all in the quietest and most composed of voices, as though detailing incidents of everyday occurrence. I still seem to see him sitting like a hideous nightmare at the end of my couch, with the single rude lamp flickering over his cadaverous features.

'And now,' he continued, 'there is no difficulty about your escape. These stupid adopted children of mine will say that you have gone back to heaven from whence you came. The wind blows off the land. I have a boat all ready for you, well stored with provisions and water. I am anxious to be rid of you, so you may rely that nothing is neglected. Rise up and follow me.'

I did what he commanded, and he led me through the door of the hut. The guards had either been withdrawn, or Goring had arranged matters with them. We passed unchallenged through the town and across the sandy plain. Once more I heard the roar of the sea, and saw the long white line of the surge. Two figures were standing upon the shore arranging the gear of a small boat. They were the two sailors who had been with us on the voyage.

'See him safely through the surf,' said Goring. The two men sprang in and pushed off, pulling me in after them. With mainsail and jib we ran out from the land and passed safely over the bar. Then my two companions without a word of farewell sprang overboard, and I saw their heads like black dots on the white foam as they made their way back to the shore, while I scudded away into the blackness of the night. Looking back I caught my last glimpse of Goring. He was standing upon the summit of a sand-hill, and the rising moon behind him threw his gaunt angular figure into hard relief. He was waving his arms frantically to and fro; it may have been to encourage me on my way, but the gestures seemed to me at the time to be threatening ones, and I have often thought that it was more likely that his old savage instinct had returned when he realised that I was out of his power. Be that as it may, it was the last that I ever saw or ever shall see of Septimius Goring.

There is no need for me to dwell upon my solitary voyage. I steered as well as I could for the Canaries, but was picked up upon the fifth day by the British and African Steam Navigation Company's boat *Monrovia*. Let me take this opportunity of tendering my sincerest thanks to Captain Stornoway and his officers for the great kindness which they showed me from that time till they landed me in Liverpool, where I was enabled to take one of the Guion boats to New York.

From the day on which I found myself once more in the bosom of my family I have said little of what I have undergone. The subject is still an intensely painful one to me, and the little which I have dropped has been discredited. I now put the facts before the public as they occurred, careless how far they may be believed, and simply writing them down because my lung is growing weaker, and I feel the responsibility of holding my peace longer. I make no vague statement. Turn to your map of Africa. There above Cape Blanco, where the land trends away north and south from the westernmost point of the continent, there it is that

Septimius Goring still reigns over his dark subjects, unless retribution has overtaken him; and there, where the long green ridges run swiftly in to roar and hiss upon the hot yellow sand, it is there that Harton lies with Hyson and the other poor fellows who were done to death in the *Marie Celeste*.

LEWIS GRASSIC GIBBON

SMEDDUM

SHE'D HAD NINE of a family in her time, Mistress Menzies, and brought the nine of them up, forbye – some near by the scruff of the neck, you would say. They were sniftering and weakly, two–three of the bairns, sniftering in their cradles to get into their coffins; but she'd shake them to life, and dose them with salts and feed them up till they couldn't but live. And she'd plonk one down – finishing the wiping of the creature's neb or the unco dosing of an ill bit stomach or the binding of a broken head – with a look on her face as much as to say *Die on me now and see what you'll get!*

Big-boned she was by her fortieth year, like a big roan mare, and *If ever she was bonny 'twas in Noah's time*, Jock Menzies, her eldest son would say. She'd reddish hair and a high, skeugh nose, and a hand that skelped her way through life; and if ever a soul had seen her at rest when the dark was done and the day was come he'd died of the shock and never let on.

For from morn till night she was at it, work, work, on that ill bit croft that sloped to the sea. When there wasn't a mist on the cold, stone parks there was more than likely the wheep of the rain, wheeling and dripping in from the sea that soughed and plashed by the land's stiff edge. Kinneff lay north, and at night in the south, if the sky was clear on the gloaming's edge, you'd see in that sky the Bervie lights come suddenly lit, far and away, with the quiet about you as you stood and looked, nothing to hear but a sea-bird's cry.

But feint the much time to look or to listen had Margaret Menzies of Tocherty toun. Day blinked and Meg did the same, and was out, up out of her bed, and about the house, making the porridge and rousting the bairns, and out to the byre to milk the three kye, the morning growing out in the east and a wind like a hail of knives from the hills. Syne back to the kitchen again she would be, and catch Jock, her eldest, a clour in the lug that he hadn't roused up his sisters and brothers; and rouse them herself, and feed them and scold, pull up their breeks and straighten their frocks, and polish their shoes and set their caps straight. *Off you get and see you're not late*, she would cry, *and see you behave yourselves at the school. And tell the Dominie I'll be down the night to ask him what the mischief he meant by leathering Jeannie and her not well.*

They'd cry *Ay, Mother*, and go trotting away, a fair flock of the creatures, their faces red-scoured. Her own as red, like a meikle roan mare's, Meg'd turn at the door and go prancing in; and then at last, by the closet-bed, lean over and shake her man half-awake. *Come on, then, Willie, it's time you were up.*

And he'd groan and say *Is't?* and crawl out at last, a little bit thing like a weasel, Will Menzies, though some said that weasels were decent beside him. He was drinking himself into the grave, folk said, as coarse a little brute as you'd meet, bone-lazy forbye, and as sly as sin. Rampageous and ill with her tongue though she was, you couldn't but pity a woman like Meg tied up for life to a thing like *that*. But she'd more than a soft side still to the creature, she'd half-skelp the backside from any of the bairns she found in the telling of a small bit lie; but when Menzies would come paiching in of a noon and groan that he fair was tashed with his work, he'd mended all the ley fence that day and he doubted he'd need to be off to his bed – when he'd told her that and had ta'en to the blankets, and maybe in less than the space of an hour she'd hold out for the kye and see that he'd lied, the fence neither mended nor letten a-be, she'd just purse up her meikle wide mouth and say nothing, her eyes with a glint as though she half-laughed. And when he came drunken home from a mart she'd shoo the children out of the room, and take off his clothes and put him to bed, with an extra nip to keep off a chill.

She did half his work in the Tocherty parks, she'd yoke up the horse and the sholtie together, and kilt up her skirts till you'd see her great legs, and cry *Wissh!* like a man and turn a fair drill, the sea-gulls cawing in a cloud behind, the wind in her hair and the sea beyond. And Menzies with his sly-like eyes would be off on some drunken ploy to Kineff or Stonehive. Man, you couldn't but think as you saw that steer it was well that there was a thing like marriage, folk held together and couldn't get apart; else a black look-out it well would be for the fusionless creature of Tocherty toun.

Well, he drank himself to his grave at last, less smell on the earth if maybe more in it. But she broke down and wept, it was awful to see, Meg Menzies weeping like a stricken horse, her eyes on the dead, quiet face of her man. And she ran from the house, she was gone all that night, though the bairns cried and cried her name up and down the parks in the sound of the sea. But next morning they found her back in their midst, brisk as ever, like a great-boned mare, ordering here and directing there, and a fine feed set the next day for the folk that came to the funeral of her orra man.

She'd four of the bairns at home when he died, the rest were in kitchen-service or fee'd, she'd seen to the settling of the queans herself; and twice when two of them had come home, complaining-like of their mistresses' ways, she'd thrashen the queans and taken them back – near scared the life from the doctor's wife, her that was mistress to young Jean Menzies. *I've skelped the lassie and brought you her back. But don't you ill-use her, or I'll skelp you as well.*

There was a fair speak about that at the time, Meg Menzies and the vulgar words she had used, folk told that she'd even said what was the place where she'd skelp the bit doctor's wife. And faith! that fair must have been a sore shock to the doctor's wife that was that genteel she'd never believed she'd a place like that.

Be that as it might, her man new dead, Meg wouldn't hear of leaving the toun. It was harvest then and she drove the reaper up and down the long, clanging clay rigs by the sea, she'd jump down smart at the head of a bout and go gathering and binding swift as the wind, syne wheel in the horse to the cutting again. She led the stooks with her bairns to help, you'd see them at night a drowsing cluster under the moon on the harvesting cart.

And through that year and into the next and so till the speak died down in the Howe Meg Menzies worked the Tocherty toun; and faith, her crops came none so ill. She rode to the mart at Stonehive when she must, on the old box-cart, the old horse in the shafts, the cart behind with a sheep for sale or a birn of old hens that had finished with laying. And a butcher once tried to make a bit joke. *That's a sheep like yourself, fell long in the tooth.* And Meg answered up, neighing like a horse, and all heard: *Faith, then, if you've got a spite against teeth I've a clucking hen in the cart outbye. It's as toothless and senseless as you are, near.*

Then word got about of her eldest son, Jock Menzies that was fee'd up Allardyce way. The creature of a loon had had fair a conceit since he'd won a prize at a ploughing match – not for his ploughing, but for good looks; and the queans about were as daft as himself, he'd only to nod and they came to his heel; and the stories told they came further than that. Well, Meg'd heard the stories and paid no heed, till the last one came, she was fell quick then.

Soon's she heard it she hove out the old bit bike that her daughter Kathie had bought for herself, and got on the thing and went cycling away down through the Bervie braes in that Spring, the sun was out and the land lay green with a blink of mist that was blue on the hills, as she came to the toun where Jock was fee'd she saw him out in a park by the road, ploughing, the black loam smooth like a ribbon turning and wheeling at the tail of the plough. Another billy came ploughing behind, Meg Menzies watched till they reached the rig-end, her great chest heaving like a meikle roan's, her eyes on the shape of the furrows they made. And they drew to the end and drew the horse out, and Jock cried *Ay*, and she answered back *Ay*, and looked at the drill, and gave a bit snort, *If your looks win prizes, your ploughing never will.*

Jock laughed, *Fegs, then, I'll not greet for that,* and chirked to his horses and turned them about. But she cried him. *Just bide a minute, my lad. What's this I hear about you and Ag Grant?*

He drew up short then, and turned right red, the other childe as well, and they both gave a laugh, as plough-childes do when you mention a quean they've known overwell in more ways than one. And Meg snapped *It's an answer I want, not a cockerel's cackle: I can hear that at home on my own dunghill. What are you to do about Ag and her pleiter?*

And Jock said *Nothing,* impudent as you like, and next minute Meg was in over the dyke and had hold of his lug and shook him and it till the other childe ran and caught at her nieve. *Faith, mistress, you'll have his lug off!* he cried. But

Meg Menzies turned like a mare on new grass, *Keep off or I'll have yours off as well!*

So he kept off and watched, fair a story he'd to tell when he rode out that night to go courting his quean. For Meg held to the lug till it near came off and Jock swore that he'd put things right with Ag Grant. She let go the lug then and looked at him grim: *See that you do and get married right quick, you're the like that needs loaded with a birn of bairns – to keep you out of the jail, I jaloose. It needs smeddum to be either right coarse or right kind.*

They were wed before the month was well out, Meg found them a cottar house to settle and gave them a bed and a press she had, and two–three more sticks from Tocherty toun. And she herself led the wedding dance, the minister in her arms, a small bit childe; and 'twas then as she whirled him about the room, he looked like a rat in the teeth of a tyke, that he thanked her for seeing Ag out of her soss, *There's nothing like a marriage for redding things up.* And Meg Menzies said *EH?* and then she said *Ay*, but queer-like, he supposed she'd no thought of the thing. Syne she slipped off to sprinkle thorns in the bed and to hang below it the great hand-bell that the bothy-billies took them to every bit marriage.

Well, that was Jock married and at last off her hands. But she'd plenty left still, Dod, Kathleen and Jim that were still at school, Kathie a limner that alone tongued her mother, Jeannie that next led trouble to her door. She'd been found at her place, the doctor's it was, stealing some money and they sent her home. Syne news of the thing got into Stonehive, the police came out and tormented her sore, she swore she never had stolen a meck, and Meg swore with her, she was black with rage. And folk laughed right hearty, fegs! that was a clour for meikle Meg Menzies, her daughter a thief!

But it didn't last long, it was only three days when folk

saw the doctor drive up in his car. And out he jumped and went striding through the close and met face to face with Meg at the door. And he cried *Well, mistress, I've come over for Jeannie.* And she glared at him over her high, skeugh nose, *Ay, have you so then? And why, may I speir?*

So he told her why, the money they'd missed had been found at last in a press by the door; somebody or other had left it there, when paying a grocer or such at the door. And Jeannie – he'd come over to take Jean back.

But Meg glared *Ay, well, you've made another mistake. Out of this, you and your thieving suspicions together!* The doctor turned red, *You're making a miserable error* – and Meg said *I'll make you mince-meat in a minute.*

So he didn't wait that, she didn't watch him go, but went ben to the kitchen where Jeannie was sitting, her face chalk-white as she'd heard them speak. And what happened then a story went round, Jim carried it to school, and it soon spread out, Meg sank in a chair, they thought she was greeting; syne she raised up her head and they saw she was laughing, near as fearsome the one as the other, they thought. *Have you any cigarettes?* she snapped sudden at Jean, and Jean quavered *No*, and Meg glowered at her cold. *Don't sit there and lie. Gang bring them to me.* And Jean brought them, her mother took the pack in her hand. *Give's hold of a match till I light up the thing. Maybe smoke'll do good for the crow that I got in the throat last night by the doctor's house.*

Well, in less than a month she'd got rid of Jean – packed off to Brechin the quean was, and soon got married to a creature there – some clerk that would have left her sore in the lurch but that Meg went down to the place on her bike, and there, so the story went, kicked the childe so that he couldn't sit down for a fortnight, near. No doubt that was just a bit lie that they told, but faith! Meg Menzies had herself to blame, the reputation she'd gotten in the Howe, folk said, *She'll meet with a sore heart yet.* But devil a sore was there to be seen, Jeannie was married and was fair genteel.

Kathleen was next to leave home at the term. She was tall, like Meg, and with red hair as well, but a thin fine face, long eyes blue-grey like the hills on a hot day, and a mouth with lips you thought over thick. And she cried *Ah well, I'm off then, mother.* And Meg cried *See you behave yourself.* And Kathleen cried *Maybe; I'm not at school now.*

Meg stood and stared after the slip of a quean, you'd have thought her half-angry, half near to laughing, as she watched that figure, so slender and trig, with its shoulders square-set, slide down the hill on the wheeling bike, swallows were dipping and flying by Kinneff, she looked light and free as a swallow herself, the quean, as she biked away from her home, she turned at the bend and waved and whistled, she whistled like a loon and as loud, did Kath.

Jim was the next to leave from the school, he bided at home and he took no fee, a quiet-like loon, and he worked the toun, and, wonder of wonders, Meg took a rest. Folk said that age was telling a bit on even Meg Menzies at last. The grocer made hints at that one night, and Meg answered up smart as ever of old: *Damn the age! But I've finished the trauchle of the bairns at last, the most of them married or still over young. I'm as swack as ever I was, my lad. But I've just got the notion to be a bit sweir.*

Well, she'd hardly begun on that notion when faith! ill the news that came up to the place from Segget. Kathleen her quean that was fee'd down there, she'd ta'en up with some coarse old childe in a bank, he'd left his wife, they were off together, and she but a bare sixteen years old.

And that proved the truth of what folk were saying, Meg Menzies she hardly paid heed to the news, just gave a bit laugh like a neighing horse and went on with the work of park and byre, cool as you please – ay, getting fell old.

No more was heard of the quean or the man till a two years or more had passed and then word came up to the Tocherty someone had seen her – and where do you think? Out on a boat that was coming from Australia. She was working as stewardess on that bit boat, and the childe that saw her was young John Robb, an emigrant back from his uncle's farm, near starved to death he had been down there. She hadn't met in with him near till the end, the boat close to Southampton the evening they met. And she'd known him at once, though he not her, she'd cried *John Robb?* and he'd answered back *Ay?* and looked at her canny in case it might be the creature was looking for a tip from him. Syne she'd laughed *Don't you know me, then, you gowk? I'm Kathie Menzies you knew long syne – it was me ran off with the banker from Segget!*

He was clean dumbfounded, young Robb, and he gaped, and then they shook hands and she spoke some more, though she hadn't much time, they were serving up dinner for the first-class folk, aye dirt that are ready to eat and to drink. *If ever you get near to Tocherty toun tell Meg I'll get home and see her sometime. Ta-ta!* And then she was off with a smile, young Robb he stood and he stared where she'd been, he thought her the bonniest thing that he'd seen all the weary weeks that he'd been from home.

And this was the tale that he brought to Tocherty, Meg sat and listened and smoked like a tink, forbye herself there was young Jim there, and Jock and his wife and their three bit bairns, he'd fair changed with marriage, had young Jock Menzies. For no sooner had he taken Ag Grant to his bed than he'd started to save, grown mean as dirt, in a three–four years he'd finished with feeing, now he rented a fell big farm himself, well stocked it was, and he fee'd two men. Jock himself had grown thin in a way, like his father but worse his bothy childes said, old Menzies at least could take a bit dram and get lost to the world but the son was that mean he might drink rat-poison and take no harm, 'twould feel at home in a stomach like his.

Well, that was Jock, and he sat and heard the story of Kath and her stay on the boat. *Ay, still a coarse bitch, I have not a doubt. Well if she never comes back to the Mearns, in Segget you cannot but redden with shame when a body will ask 'Was Kath Menzies your sister?'*

And Ag, she'd grown a great sumph of a woman, she nodded to that, it was only too true, a sore thing it was on decent bit folks that they should have any relations like Kath.

But Meg just sat there and smoked and said never a word, as though she thought nothing worth a yea or a nay. Young Robb had fair ta'en a fancy to Kath and he near boiled up when he heard Jock speak, him and the wife that he'd married from her shame. So he left them short and went raging home, and wished for one that Kath would come back, a Summer noon as he cycled home, snipe were calling in the Auchindreich moor where the cattle stood with their tails a-switch, the Grampians rising far and behind, Kinraddie spread like a map for show, its ledges veiled in a mist from the sun. You felt on that day a wild, daft unease, man, beast and bird: as though something were missing and lost from the world, and Kath was the thing that John Robb missed, she'd something in her that minded a man of a house that was builded upon a hill.

Folk thought that maybe the last they would hear of young Kath Menzies and her ill-getted ways. So fair stammy-gastered they were with the news she'd come back to the Mearns, she was down in Stonehive, in a grocer's shop, as calm as could be, selling out tea and cheese and such-like with no blush of shame on her face at all, to decent women that were properly wed and had never looked on men but their own, and only on them with their braces buttoned.

It just showed you the way that the world was going to allow an ill quean like that in a shop, some folk protested to the creature that owned it, but he just shook his head, *Ah well, she works fine; and what else she does is no business of mine.* So you well might guess there was more than business between the man and Kath Menzies, like.

And Meg heard the news and went into Stonehive, driving her sholtie, and stopped at the shop. And some in the shop knew who she was and minded the things she had done long syne to other bit bairns of hers that went wrong; and they waited with their breaths held up with delight. But all that Meg did was to nod to Kath, *Ay, well, then, it's you – Ay, mother, just that – Two pounds of syrup and see that it's good.*

And not another word passed between them, Meg Menzies that once would have ta'en such a quean and skelped her to rights before you could wink. Going home from Stonehive she stopped by the farm where young Robb was fee'd, he was out in the hayfield coling the hay, and she nodded to him grim, with her high horse face. *What's this that I hear about you and Kath Menzies?*

He turned right red, but he wasn't ashamed. *I've no idea – though I hope it's the worse—. It fell near is—. Then I wish it was true, she might marry me, then, as I've prigged her to do.*

Oh, have you so, then? said Meg, and drove home, as though the whole matter was a nothing to her.

But next Tuesday the postman brought a bit note, from Kathie it was to her mother at Tocherty. *Dear mother, John Robb's going out to Canada and wants me to marry him and go with him. I've told him instead I'll go with him and see what he's like as a man – and then marry him at leisure, if I feel in the mood. But he's hardly any money, and we want to borrow some, so he and I are coming over on Sunday. I hope that you'll have dumpling for tea. Your own daughter, Kath.*

Well, Meg passed that letter over to Jim, he glowered at it dour, *I know – near all the Howe's heard. What are you going to do, now, mother?*

But Meg just lighted a cigarette and said nothing, she'd smoked like a tink since that steer with Jean. There was promise of strange on-goings at Tocherty by the time that the Sabbath day was come. For Jock came there on a visit as well, him and his wife, and besides him was Jeannie, her that had married the clerk down in Brechin, and she brought the bit creature, he fair was a toff; and he stepped like a cat through the sharn in the close; and when he had heard the story of Kath, her and her plan and John Robb and all, he was shocked near to death, and so was his wife. And Jock Menzies gaped and gave a mean laugh. *Ay, coarse to the bone, ill-getted I'd say if it wasn't that we came of the same bit stock. Ah well, she'll fair have to tramp to Canada, eh mother? – if she's looking for money from you.*

And Meg answered quiet *No, I wouldn't say that. I've the money all ready for them when they come.*

You could hear the sea plashing down soft on the rocks, there was such a dead silence in Tocherty house. And then Jock habbered like a cock with fits *What, give silver to one who does as she likes, and won't marry as you made the rest of us marry? Give silver to one who's no more than a—.*

And he called his sister an ill name enough, and Meg sat and smoked looking over the parks. *Ay, just that. You see, she takes after myself.*

And Jeannie squeaked *How?* and Meg answered her quiet: *She's fit to be free and to make her own choice the same as myself*

222

and the same kind of choice. *There was none of the rest of you fit to do that, you'd to marry or burn, so I married you quick. But Kath and me could afford to find out. It all depends if you've smeddum or not.*

She stood up then and put her cigarette out, and looked at the gaping gowks she had mothered. *I never married your father, you see. I could never make up my mind about Will. But maybe our Kath will find something surer . . . Here's her and her man coming up the road.*

ERIC LINKLATER

SEALSKIN TROUSERS

I AM NOT MAD. It is necessary to realise that, to accept it as a fact about which there can be no dispute. I have been seriously ill for some weeks, but that was the result of shock. A double or conjoint shock: for as well as the obvious concussion of a brutal event, there was the more dreadful necessity of recognising the material evidence of a happening so monstrously implausible that even my friends here, who in general are quite extraordinarily kind and understanding, will not believe in the occurrence, though they cannot deny it or otherwise explain – I mean explain away – the clear and simple testimony of what was left.

I, of course, realised very quickly what had happened, and since then I have more than once remembered that poor Coleridge teased his unquiet mind, quite unnecessarily in his case, with just such a possibility; or impossibility, as the world would call it. 'If a man could pass through Paradise in a dream,' he wrote, 'and have a flower presented to him as a pledge that his soul had really been there, and if he found that flower in his hand when he woke – Ay, and what then?'

But what if he had dreamt of Hell and wakened with his hand burnt by the fire? Or of Chaos, and seen another face stare at him from the looking-glass? Coleridge does not push the question far. He was too timid. But I accepted the evidence, and while I was ill I thought seriously about the whole proceeding, in detail and in sequence of detail.

I thought, indeed, about little else. To begin with, I admit, I was badly shaken, but gradually my mind cleared and my vision improved, and because I was patient and persevering – that needed discipline – I can now say that I know what happened. I have indeed, by a conscious intellectual effort, *seen and heard* what happened. This is how it began. . . .

How very unpleasant! she thought.

She had come down the great natural steps on the sea-cliff to the ledge that narrowly gave access, round the angle of it, to the western face which to-day was sheltered from the breeze and warmed by the afternoon sun. At the beginning of the week she and her fiancé, Charles Sellin, had found their way to an almost hidden shelf, a deep veranda sixty feet above the white-veined water. It was rather bigger than a billiard-table and nearly as private as an abandoned lighthouse. Twice they had spent some blissful hours there. She had a good head for heights, and Sellin was indifferent to scenery. There had been nothing vulgar, no physical contact, in their bliss together on this oceanic gazebo, for on each occasion she had been reading Héaloin's *Studies in Biology* and he Lenin's *What is to be Done?*

Their relations were already marital, not because their mutual passion could brook no pause, but rather out of fear lest their friends might despise them for chastity and so conjecture some oddity or impotence in their nature. Their behaviour, however, was very decently circumspect, and they already conducted themselves, in public and out of doors, as if they had been married for several years. They did not regard the seclusion of the cliffs as an opportunity for secret embracing, but were content that the sun should warm and colour their skin; and let their anxious minds be soothed by the surge and cavernous colloquies of the sea.

Now, while Charles was writing letters in the little fishing-hotel a mile away, she had come back to their sandstone ledge, and Charles would join her in an hour or two. She was still reading *Studies in Biology*.

But their gazebo, she perceived, was already occupied, and occupied by a person of the most embarrassing appearance. He was quite unlike Charles. He was not only naked, but obviously robust, brown-hued, and extremely hairy. He sat on the very edge of the rock, dangling his legs over the sea, and down his spine ran a ridge of hair like the dark stripe on a donkey's back, and on his shoulder-blades grew patches of hair like the wings of a bird. Unable in her disappointment to be sensible and leave at once, she lingered for a moment and saw to her relief that he was not quite naked. He wore trousers of a dark brown colour, very low at the waist, but sufficient to cover his haunches. Even so, even with that protection for her modesty, she could not stay and read biology in his company.

To show her annoyance, and let him become aware of it, she made a little impatient sound; and turning to go, looked back to see if he had heard.

He swung himself round and glared at her, more angry on the instant than she had been. He had thick eyebrows, large dark eyes, a broad snub nose, a big mouth. 'You're Roger Fairfield!' she exclaimed in surprise.

He stood up and looked at her intently. 'How do you know?' he asked.

'Because I remember you,' she answered, but then felt a little confused, for what she principally remembered was the brief notoriety he had acquired, in his final year at Edinburgh University, by swimming on a rough autumn day from North Berwick to the Bass Rock to win a bet of five pounds.

The story had gone briskly round the town for a week, and everybody knew that he and some friends had been lunching, too well for caution, before the bet was made. His friends, however, grew quickly sober when he took to the water, and in a great fright informed the police, who called out the lifeboat. But they searched in vain, for the sea was running high, until in calm water under the shelter of the Bass they saw his head, dark on the water, and pulled him aboard. He seemed none the worse for his adventure, but the police charged him with disorderly behaviour and he was fined two pounds for swimming without a regulation costume.

'We met twice,' she said, 'once at a dance and once in Mackie's when we had coffee together. About a year ago. There were several of us there, and we knew the man you came in with. I remember you perfectly.'

He stared the harder, his eyes narrowing, a vertical wrinkle dividing his forehead. ' I'm a little short-sighted too,' she said with a nervous laugh.

'My sight's very good,' he answered, 'but I find it difficult to recognise people. Human beings are so much alike.'

'That's one of the rudest remarks I've ever heard!'

'Surely not?'

'Well, one does like to be remembered. It isn't pleasant to be told that one's a nonentity.'

He made an impatient gesture. 'That isn't what I meant, and I do recognise you now. I remember your voice. You have a distinctive voice and a pleasant one. F sharp in the octave below middle C is your note.'

'Is that the only way in which you can distinguish people?'

'It's as good as any other.'

'But you don't remember my name?'

'No,' he said.

'I'm Elizabeth Barford.'

He bowed and said, 'Well, it was a dull party, wasn't it? The occasion, I mean, when we drank coffee together.'

'I don't agree with you. I thought it was very amusing, and we all enjoyed ourselves. Do you remember Charles Sellin?'

'No.'

'Oh, you're hopeless,' she exclaimed. 'What is the good of meeting people if you're going to forget all about them?'

'I don't know,' he said. 'Let us sit down, and you can tell me.'

He sat again on the edge of the rock, his legs dangling, and looking over his shoulder at her, said, 'Tell me: what is the good of meeting people?'

She hesitated, and answered, 'I like to make friends. That's quite natural, isn't it? – But I came here to read.'

'Do you read standing?'

'Of course not,' she said, and smoothing her skirt tidily over her knees, sat down beside him. 'What a wonderful place this is for a holiday. Have you been here before?'

'Yes, I know it well.'

'Charles and I came a week ago. Charles Sellin, I mean, whom you don't remember. We're going to be married, you know. In about a year, we hope.'

'Why did you come here?'

'We wanted to be quiet, and in these islands one is fairly secure against interruption. We're both working quite hard.'

'Working!' he mocked. 'Don't waste time, waste your life instead.'

'Most of us have to work, whether we like it or not.'

He took the book from her lap, and opening it read idly a few lines, turned a dozen pages and read with a yawn another paragraph.

'Your friends in Edinburgh,' she said, 'were better-off

than ours. Charles and I, and all the people we know, have got to make our living.'

'Why?' he asked.

'Because if we don't we shall starve,' she snapped.

'And if you avoid starvation – what then?'

'It's possible to hope,' she said stiffly, 'that we shall be of some use in the world.'

'Do you agree with this?' he asked, smothering a second yawn, and read from the book: *'The physical factor in a germ-cell is beyond our analysis or assessment, but can we deny subjectivity to the primordial initiatives? It is easier, perhaps, to assume that mind comes late in development, but the assumption must not be established on the grounds that we can certainly deny self-expression to the cell. It is common knowledge that the mind may influence the body both greatly and in little unseen ways; but how it is done, we do not know. Psychobiology is still in its infancy.'*

'It's fascinating, isn't it?' she said.

'How do you propose,' he asked, 'to be of use to the world?'

'Well, the world needs people who have been educated – educated to think – and one does hope to have a little influence in some way.'

'Is a little influence going to make any difference? Don't you think that what the world needs is to develop a new sort of mind? It needs a new primordial directive, or quite a lot of them, perhaps. But psychobiology is still in its infancy, and you don't know how such changes come about, do you? And you can't foresee when you *will* know, can you?'

'No, of course not. But science is advancing so quickly—'

'In fifty thousand years?' he interrupted. 'Do you think you will know by then?'

'It's difficult to say,' she answered seriously, and was

gathering her thoughts for a careful reply when again he interrupted, rudely, she thought, and quite irrelevantly. His attention had strayed from her and her book to the sea beneath, and he was looking down as though searching for something. 'Do you swim?' he asked.

'Rather well,' she said.

'I went in just before high water, when the weed down there was all brushed in the opposite direction. You never get bored by the sea, do you?'

'I've never seen enough of it,' she said. 'I want to live on an island, a little island, and hear it all round me.'

'That's very sensible of you,' he answered with more warmth in his voice. 'That's uncommonly sensible for a girl like you.'

'What sort of a girl do you think I am?' she demanded, vexation in her accent, but he ignored her and pointed his brown arm to the horizon: 'The colour has thickened within the last few minutes. The sea was quite pale on the skyline, and now it's a belt of indigo. And the writing has changed. The lines of foam on the water, I mean. Look at that! There's a submerged rock out there, and always, about half an hour after the ebb has started to run, but more clearly when there's an off-shore wind, you can see those two little whirlpools and the circle of white round them. You see the figure they make? It's like this, isn't it?'

With a splinter of stone he drew a diagram on the rock.

'Do you know what it is?' he asked. 'It's the figure the Chinese call the T'ai Chi. They say it represents the origin of all created things. And it's the sign manual of the sea.'

'But those lines of foam must run into every conceivable shape,' she protested.

'Oh, they do. They do indeed. But it isn't often you can read them. – There he is!' he exclaimed, leaning forward and staring into the water sixty feet below. 'That's him, the old villain!'

From his sitting position, pressing hard down with his hands and thrusting against the face of the rock with his heels, he hurled himself into space, and straightening in mid-air broke the smooth green surface of the water with no more splash than a harpoon would have made. A solitary razorbill, sunning himself on a shelf below, fled hurriedly out to sea, and half a dozen white birds, startled by the sudden movement, rose in the air crying 'Kittiwake! Kittiwake!'

Elizabeth screamed loudly, scrambled to her feet with clumsy speed, then knelt again on the edge of the rock and peered down. In the slowly heaving clear water she could see a pale shape moving, now striped by the dark weed that grew in tangles under the flat foot of the rock, now lost in the shadowy deepness where the tangles were rooted. In a minute or two his head rose from the sea, he shook bright drops from his hair, and looked up at her, laughing. Firmly grasped in his right hand, while he trod water, he held up an enormous blue-black lobster for her admiration. Then he threw it on to the flat rock beside him, and swiftly climbing out of the sea, caught it again and held it, cautious of its bite, till he found a piece of string in his trouser-pocket. He shouted to her, 'I'll tie its claws, and you can take it home for your supper!'

She had not thought it possible to climb the sheer face of the cliff, but from its forefoot he mounted by steps and handholds invisible from above, and pitching the tied lobster on to the floor of the gazebo, came nimbly over the edge.

'That's a bigger one than you've ever seen in your life before,' he boasted. 'He weighs fourteen pounds, I'm certain of it. Fourteen pounds at least. Look at the size of his right claw! He could crack a coconut with that. He tried to crack my ankle when I was swimming an hour ago, and got into his hole before I could catch him. But I've caught him now, the brute. He's had more than twenty years of crime, that black boy. He's twenty-four or twenty-five by the look of him. He's older than you, do you realise that? Unless you're a lot older than you look. How old are you?'

But Elizabeth took no interest in the lobster. She had retreated until she stood with her back to the rock, pressed hard against it, the palms of her hands fumbling on the stone as if feeling for a secret lock or bolt that might give her entrance into it. Her face was white, her lips pale and tremulous.

He looked round at her, when she made no answer, and asked what the matter was.

Her voice was faint and frightened. 'Who are you?' she whispered, and the whisper broke into a stammer. 'What are you?'

His expression changed and his face, with the water-drops on it, grew hard as a rock shining undersea. 'It's only a few minutes,' he said, 'since you appeared to know me quite well. You addressed me as Roger Fairfield, didn't you?'

'But a name's not everything. It doesn't tell you enough.'

'What more do you want to know?'

Her voice was so strained and thin that her words were like the shadow of words, or words shivering in the cold: 'To jump like that, into the sea – it wasn't human!'

The coldness of his face wrinkled to a frown. 'That's a curious remark to make.'

'You would have killed yourself if – if—'

He took a seaward step again, looked down at the calm green depths below, and said, 'You're exaggerating, aren't you? It's not much more than fifty feet, sixty perhaps, and the water's deep. – Here, come back! Why are you running away?'

'Let me go!' she cried, 'I don't want to stay here. I – I'm frightened.'

'That's unfortunate. I hadn't expected this to happen.'

'Please let me go!'

'I don't think I shall. Not until you've told me what you're frightened of.'

'Why,' she stammered, 'why do you wear fur trousers?'

He laughed, and still laughing caught her round the waist and pulled her towards the edge of the rock. 'Don't be alarmed,' he said. 'I'm not going to throw you over. But if you insist on a conversation about trousers, I think we should sit down again. Look at the smoothness of the water, and its colour, and the light in the depths of it: have you ever seen anything lovelier? Look at the sky: that's calm enough, isn't it? Look at that fulmar sailing past: he's not worrying, so why should you?'

She leaned away from him, all her weight against the hand that held her waist, but his arm was strong and he seemed unaware of any strain on it. Nor did he pay attention to the distress she was in – she was sobbing dryly, like a child who has cried too long – but continued talking in a light and pleasant conversational tone until the muscles of her body tired and relaxed, and she sat within his enclosing arm, making no more effort to escape, but timorously conscious of his hand upon her side so close beneath her breast.

'I needn't tell you,' he said, 'the conventional reasons for wearing trousers. There are people, I know, who sneer at all conventions, and some conventions deserve their sneering. But not the trouser-convention. No, indeed! So we can admit the necessity of the garment, and pass to consideration of the material. Well, I like sitting on rocks, for one thing, and for such a hobby this is the best stuff in the world. It's very durable, yet soft and comfortable. I can slip into the sea for half an hour without doing it any harm, and when I come out to sun myself on the rock again, it doesn't feel cold and clammy. Nor does it fade in the sun or shrink with the wet. Oh, there are plenty of reasons for having one's trousers made of stuff like this.'

'And there's a reason,' she said, 'that you haven't told me.'

'Are you quite sure of that?'

She was calmer now, and her breathing was controlled. But her face was still white, and her lips were softly nervous when she asked him, 'Are you going to kill me?'

'Kill you? Good heavens, no! Why should I do that?'

'For fear of my telling other people.'

'And what precisely would you tell them?'

'You know.'

'You jump to conclusions far too quickly: that's your trouble. Well, it's a pity for your sake, and a nuisance for me. I don't think I can let you take that lobster home for your supper after all. I don't, in fact, think you will go home for your supper.'

Her eyes grew dark again with fear, her mouth opened, but before she could speak he pulled her to him and closed it, not asking leave, with a roughly occludent kiss.

'That was to prevent you from screaming. I hate to hear people scream,' he told her, smiling as he spoke. 'But this' – he kissed her again, now gently and in a more protracted embrace – 'that was because I wanted to.'

'You mustn't!' she cried.

'But I have,' he said.

'I don't understand myself! I can't understand what has happened—'

'Very little yet,' he murmured.

'Something terrible has happened!'

'A kiss? Am I so repulsive?'

'I don't mean that. I mean something inside me. I'm not – at least I think I'm not – I'm not frightened now!'

'You have no reason to be.'

'I have every reason in the world. But I'm not! I'm not frightened – but I want to cry.'

'Then cry,' he said soothingly, and made her pillow her cheek against his breast. 'But you can't cry comfortably with that ridiculous contraption on your nose.'

He took from her the horn-rimmed spectacles she wore, and threw them into the sea.

'Oh!' she exclaimed. 'My glasses! – Oh, why did you do that? Now I can't see. I can't see at all without my glasses!'

'It's all right,' he assured her. 'You really won't need them. The refraction,' he added vaguely, 'will be quite different.'

As if this small but unexpected act of violence had brought to the boiling-point her desire for tears, they bubbled over, and because she threw her arms about him in a sort of fond despair, and snuggled close, sobbing vigorously still, he felt the warm drops trickle down his skin, and from his skin she drew into her eyes the saltness of the sea, which made her weep the more. He stroked her hair with a strong but soothing hand, and when she grew calm and lay still in his arms, her emotion spent, he sang quietly to a little enchanting tune a song that began:

> *'I am a Man upon the land,*
> *I am a Selkie in the sea,*
> *And when I'm far from every strand*
> *My home it is on Sule Skerry.'*

After the first verse or two she freed herself from his

embrace, and sitting up listened gravely to the song. Then she asked him, 'Shall I ever understand?'

'It's not a unique occurrence,' he told her. 'It has happened quite often before, as I suppose you know. In Cornwall and Brittany and among the Western Isles of Scotland; that's where people have always been interested in seals, and understood them a little, and where seals from time to time have taken human shape. The one thing that's unique in our case, in my metamorphosis, is that I am the only seal-man who has ever become a Master of Arts of Edinburgh University. Or, I believe, of any university. I am the unique and solitary example of a sophisticated seal-man.'

'I must look a perfect fright,' she said. 'It was silly of me to cry. Are my eyes very red?'

'The lids are a little pink – not unattractively so – but your eyes are as dark and lovely as a mountain pool in October, on a sunny day in October. They're much improved since I threw your spectacles away.'

'I needed them, you know. I feel quite stupid without them. But tell me why you came to the University – and how? How could you do it?'

'My dear girl – what is your name, by the way? I've quite forgotten.'

'Elizabeth!' she said angrily.

'I'm so glad, it's my favourite human name. – But you don't really want to listen to a lecture on psychobiology?'

'I want to know *how*. You must tell me!'

'Well, you remember, don't you, what your book says about the primordial initiatives? But it needs a footnote there to explain that they're not exhausted till quite late in life. The germ-cells, as you know, are always renewing themselves, and they keep their initiatives though they nearly always follow the chosen pattern except in the case

239

of certain illnesses, or under special direction. The direction of the mind, that is. And the glands have got a lot to do in a full metamorphosis, the renal first and then the pituitary, as you would expect. It isn't approved of – making the change, I mean – but every now and then one of us does it, just for a frolic in the general way, but in my case there was a special reason.'

'Tell me,' she said again.

'It's too long a story.'

'I want to know.'

'There's been a good deal of unrest, you see, among my people in the last few years: doubt, and dissatisfaction with our leaders, and scepticism about traditional beliefs – all that sort of thing. We've had a lot of discussion under the surface of the sea about the nature of man, for instance. We had always been taught to believe certain things about him, and recent events didn't seem to bear out what our teachers told us. Some of our younger people got dissatisfied, so I volunteered to go ashore and investigate. I'm still considering the report I shall have to make, and that's why I'm living, at present, a double life. I come ashore to think, and go back to the sea to rest.'

'And what do you think of us?' she asked.

'You're interesting. Very interesting indeed. There are going to be some curious mutations among you before long. Within three or four thousand years, perhaps.'

He stooped and rubbed a little smear of blood from his shin. 'I scratched it on a limpet,' he said. 'The limpets, you know, are the same to-day as they were four hundred thousand years ago. But human beings aren't nearly so stable.'

'Is that your main impression, that humanity's unstable?'

'That's part of it. But from our point of view there's something much more upsetting. Our people, you see, are quite simple creatures, and because we have relatively few beliefs, we're very much attached to them. Our life is a life of sensation – not entirely, but largely – and we ought to be extremely happy. We were, so long as we were satisfied with sensation and a short undisputed creed. We have some advantages over human beings, you know. Human beings have to carry their own weight about, and they don't know how blissful it is to be unconscious of weight: to be wave-borne, to float on the idle sea, to leap without effort in a curving wave, and look up at the dazzle of the sky through a smother of white water, or dive so easily to the calmness far below and take a haddock from the weed-beds in a sudden rush of appetite. – Talking of haddocks,' he said, 'it's getting late. It's nearly time for fish. And I must give you some instruction before we go. The preliminary phase takes a little while, about five minutes for you, I should think, and then you'll be another creature.'

She gasped, as though already she felt the water's chill, and whispered, 'Not yet! Not yet, please.'

He took her in his arms, and expertly, with a strong caressing hand, stroked her hair, stroked the roundness of her head and the back of her neck and her shoulders, feeling her muscles moving to his touch, and down the hollow of her back to her waist and hips. The head again, neck, shoulders, and spine. Again and again. Strongly and firmly his hand gave her calmness, and presently she whispered, 'You're sending me to sleep.'

'My God!' he exclaimed, 'you mustn't do that! Stand up, stand up, Elizabeth!'

'Yes,' she said, obeying him. 'Yes, Roger. Why did you call yourself Roger? Roger Fairfield?'

'I found the name in a drowned sailor's pay-book. What does that matter now? Look at me, Elizabeth!'

She looked at him, and smiled.

His voice changed, and he said happily, 'You'll be the prettiest seal between Shetland and the Scillies. Now listen. Listen carefully.'

He held her lightly and whispered in her ear. Then kissed her on the lips and cheek, and bending her head back, on the throat. He looked, and saw the colour come deeply into her face.

'Good,' he said. 'That's the first stage. The adrenalin's flowing nicely now. You know about the pituitary, don't you? That makes it easy then. There are two parts in the pituitary gland, the anterior and posterior lobes, and both must act together. It's not difficult, and I'll tell you how.'

Then he whispered again, most urgently, and watched her closely. In a little while he said, 'And now you can take it easy. Let's sit down and wait till you're ready. The actual change won't come till we go down.'

'But it's working,' she said, quietly and happily. 'I can feel it working.'

'Of course it is.'

She laughed triumphantly, and took his hand.

'We've got nearly five minutes to wait,' he said.

'What will it be like? What shall I feel, Roger?'

'The water moving against your side, the sea caressing you and holding you.'

'Shall I be sorry for what I've left behind?'

'No, I don't think so.'

'You didn't like us, then? Tell me what you discovered in the world.'

'Quite simply,' he said, 'that we had been deceived.'

'But I don't know what your belief had been.'

'Haven't I told you? – Well, we in our innocence respected you because you could work, and were willing to work. That seemed to us truly heroic. We don't work at all, you see, and you'll be much happier when you come to us. We who live in the sea don't struggle to keep our heads above water.'

'All my friends worked hard,' she said. 'I never knew anyone who was idle. We had to work, and most of us worked for a good purpose; or so we thought. But you didn't think so?'

'Our teachers had told us,' he said, 'that men endured the burden of human toil to create a surplus of wealth that would give them leisure from the daily task of bread-winning. And in their hard-won leisure, our teachers said, men cultivated wisdom and charity and the fine arts; and became aware of God. – But that's not a true description of the world, is it?'

'No,' she said, 'that's not the truth.'

'No,' he repeated, 'our teachers were wrong, and we've been deceived.'

'Men are always being deceived, but they get accustomed to learning the facts too late. They grow accustomed to deceit itself.'

'You are braver than we, perhaps. My people will not like to be told the truth.'

'I shall be with you,' she said, and took his hand. But still he stared gloomily at the moving sea.

The minutes passed, and presently she stood up and with quick fingers put off her clothes. 'It's time,' she said.

He looked at her, and his gloom vanished like the shadow of a cloud that the wind has hurried on, and exultation followed like sunlight spilling from the burning edge of a cloud. 'I wanted to punish them,' he cried, 'for robbing me of my faith, and now, by God, I'm punishing them hard. I'm robbing their treasury now, the inner vault of all their treasury! – I hadn't guessed you were so beautiful! The waves when you swim will catch a burnish from you, the sand will shine like silver when you lie down to sleep, and if you can teach the red sea-ware to blush so well, I shan't miss the roses of your world.'

'Hurry,' she said.

He, laughing softly, loosened the leather thong that tied his trousers, stepped out of them, and lifted her in his arms. 'Are you ready?' he asked.

She put her arms round his neck and softly kissed his cheek. Then with a great shout he leapt from the rock, from the little veranda, into the green silk calm of the water far below. . . .

I heard the splash of their descent – I am quite sure I heard the splash – as I came round the corner of the cliff, by the ledge that leads to the little rock veranda, our gazebo, as we called it, but the first thing I noticed, that really attracted my attention, was an enormous blue-black lobster, its huge claws tied with string, that was moving in a rather ludicrous fashion towards the edge. I think it fell over just before I left, but I wouldn't swear to that. Then I saw her book, the *Studies in Biology*, and her clothes.

Her white linen frock with the brown collar and the brown belt, some other garments, and her shoes were all there. And beside them, lying across her shoes, was a pair of sealskin trousers.

I realised immediately, or almost immediately, what had happened. Or so it seems to me now. And if, as I firmly believe, my apprehension was instantaneous, the faculty of intuition is clearly more important than I had previously supposed. I have, of course, as I said before, given the matter a great deal of thought during my recent illness, but the impression remains that I understood what had happened in a flash, to use a common but illuminating phrase. And no one, need I say? has been able to refute my intuition.

No one, that is, has found an alternative explanation for the presence, beside Elizabeth's linen frock, of a pair of sealskin trousers.

I remember also my physical distress at the discovery. My breath, for several minutes I think, came into and went out of my lungs like the hot wind of a dust-storm in the desert. It parched my mouth and grated in my throat. It was, I recall, quite a torment to breathe. But I had to, of course.

Nor did I lose control of myself in spite of the agony, both mental and physical, that I was suffering. I didn't lose control till they began to mock me. Yes, they did, I assure you of that. I heard his voice quite clearly, and honesty compels me to admit that it was singularly sweet and the tune was the most haunting I have ever heard. They were about forty yards away, two seals swimming together, and the evening light was so clear and taut that his voice might have been the vibration of an invisible bow across its coloured bands. He was singing the song that Elizabeth and I had discovered in an album of Scottish music in the little fishing-hotel where we had been living:

> *'I am a Man upon the land,*
> *I am a Selkie in the sea,*
> *And when I'm far from any strand*
> *I am at home on Sule Skerry!'*

But his purpose, you see, was mockery. They were happy, together in the vast simplicity of the ocean, and I, abandoned to the terror of life alone, life among human beings, was lost and full of panic. It was then I began to scream. I could hear myself screaming, it was quite horrible. But I couldn't stop. I had to go on screaming. . . .

MURIEL SPARK

THE SERAPH AND THE ZAMBESI

YOU MAY HAVE heard of Samuel Cramer, half poet, half journalist, who had to do with a dancer called the Fanfarlo. But, as you will see, it doesn't matter if you have not. He was said to be going strong in Paris early in the nineteenth century, and when I met him in 1946 he was still going strong, but this time in a different way. He was the same man, but modified. For instance, in those days, more than a hundred years ago, Cramer had persisted for several decades, and without affectation, in being about twenty-five years old. But when I knew him he was clearly undergoing his forty-two-year-old phase.

At this time he was keeping a petrol pump some four miles south of the Zambesi River where it crashes over a precipice at the Victoria Falls. Cramer had some spare rooms where he put up visitors to the Falls when the hotel was full. I was sent to him because it was Christmas week and there was no room in the hotel.

I found him trying the starter of a large, lumpy Mercedes outside his corrugated-iron garage, and at first sight I judged him to be a Belgian from the Congo. He had the look of north and south, light hair with canvas-coloured skin. Later, however, he told me that his father was German and his mother Chilean. It was this information rather than the 'S. Cramer' above the garage door which made me think I had heard of him.

The rains had been very poor and that December was

fiercely hot. On the third night before Christmas I sat on the stoep outside my room, looking through the broken mosquito-wire network at the lightning in the distance. When an atmosphere maintains an excessive temperature for a long spell something seems to happen to the natural noises of life. Sound fails to carry in its usual quantity, but comes as if bound and gagged. That night the Christmas beetles, which fall on their backs on every stoep with a high tic-tac, seemed to be shock-absorbed. I saw one fall and the little bump reached my ears a fraction behind time. The noises of minor wild beasts from the bush were all hushed-up, too. In fact it wasn't until the bush noises all stopped simultaneously, as they frequently do when a leopard is about, that I knew there had been any sound at all.

Overlying this general muted hum, Cramer's sundowner party progressed farther up the stoep. The heat distorted every word. The glasses made a tinkle that was not of the substance of glass, but of bottles wrapped in tissue paper. Sometimes, for a moment, a shriek or a cackle would hang torpidly in space, but these were unreal sounds, as if project-ed from a distant country, as if they were pocket-torches seen through a London fog.

Cramer came over to my end of the stoep and asked me to join his party. I said I would be glad to, and meant it, even though I had been glad to sit alone. Heat so persistent and so intense sucks up the will.

Five people sat in wicker arm-chairs drinking highballs and chewing salted peanuts. I recognized a red-haired trooper from Livingstone, just out from England, and two of Cramer's lodgers, a tobacco planter and his wife from Bulawayo. In the custom of those parts, the other two were introduced by their first names. Mannie, a short dark man of square face and build, I thought might be a Portuguese from the east coast. The woman, Fanny, was picking bits out of the frayed wicker chair and as she lifted her glass her hand shook a little, making her bracelets chime. She would be about fifty, a well-tended woman, very neat. Her grey hair, tinted with blue, was done in a fringe above a face puckered with malaria.

In the general way of passing the time with strangers in that countryside, I exchanged with the tobacco people the names of acquaintances who lived within a six-hundred-mile radius of where we sat, reducing this list to names mutually known to us. The trooper contributed his news from the region between Lusaka and Livingstone. Meanwhile an argument was in process between Cramer, Fanny and Mannie, of which Fanny seemed to be getting the better. It appeared there was to be a play or concert on Christmas Eve in which the three were taking part. I several times heard the words 'troupe of angels', 'shepherds', 'ridiculous price' and 'my girls' which seemed to be key words in the argument. Suddenly, on hearing the trooper mention a name, Fanny broke off her talk and turned to us.

'She was one of my girls,' she said, 'I gave her lessons for three years.'

Mannie rose to leave, and before Fanny followed him she picked a card from her handbag and held it out to me between her fingernails.

'If any of your friends are interested . . .' said Fanny hazily.

I looked at this as she drove off with the man, and above an address about four miles up the river I read:

> *Mme La Fanfarlo (Paris, London)*
> *Dancing Instructress. Ballet. Ballroom.*
> *Transport provided By Arrangement*

Next day I came across Cramer still trying to locate the trouble with the Mercedes.

'Are you the man Baudelaire wrote about?' I asked him.

He stared past me at the open waste veldt with a look of tried patience.

'Yes,' he replied. 'What made you think of it?'

'The name Fanfarlo on Fanny's card,' I said. 'Didn't you know her in Paris?'

'Oh, yes,' said Cramer, 'but those days are finished. She married Manuela de Monteverde – that's Mannie. They settled here about twenty years ago. He keeps a Kaffir store.'

I remembered then that in the Romantic age it had pleased Cramer to fluctuate between the practice of verse and that of belles-lettres, together with the living up to such practices.

I asked him, 'Have you given up your literary career?'

'*As* a career, yes,' he answered. 'It was an obsession I was glad to get rid of.'

He stroked the blunt bonnet of the Mercedes and added, 'The greatest literature is the occasional kind, a mere afterthought.'

Again he looked across the veldt where, unseen, a grey-crested lourie was piping 'go'way, go'way'.

'Life,' Cramer continued, 'is the important thing.'

'And do you write occasional verses?' I inquired.

'When occasion demands it,' he said. 'In fact I've just written a Nativity Masque. We're giving a performance on Christmas Eve in there.' He pointed to his garage, where a few natives were already beginning to shift petrol cans and tyres. Being members neither of the cast nor the audience, they were taking their time. A pile of folded seats had been dumped alongside.

Late on the morning of Christmas Eve I returned from the Falls to find a crowd of natives quarrelling outside the garage, with Cramer swearing loud and heavy in the middle. He held a sulky man by the shirt-sleeve, while with the other hand he described his vituperation on the hot air. Some mission natives had been sent over to give a hand with laying the stage, and these, with their standard-three school English, washed faces and white drill shorts, had innocently provoked Cramer's raw rag-dressed boys. Cramer's method, which ended with the word 'police', succeeded in sending them back to work, still uttering drum-like gutturals at each other.

The stage, made of packing-cases with planks nailed across, was being put at the back of the building, where a door led to the yard, the privy and the native huts. The space between this door and the stage was closed off by a row of black Government blankets hung on a line; this was to be the dressing-room. I agreed to come round there that evening to help with the lighting, the make-up, and the pinning on of angels' wings. The Fanfarlo's dancing pupils were to make an angel chorus with carols and dancing, while she herself, as the Virgin, was to give a representative ballet performance. Owing to her husband's very broken English, he had been given a silent role as a shepherd, supported by three other shepherds chosen for like reasons. Cramer's part was the most prominent, for he had the longest speeches, being the First Seraph. It had been agreed that, since he had written the masque, he could best deliver most of it; but I gathered there had been some trouble at rehearsals over the cost of the production, with Fanny wanting elaborate scenery as being due to her girls.

The performance was set to begin at eight. I arrived behind the stage at seven-fifteen to find the angels assembled in ballet dresses with wings of crinkled paper in various shades. The Fanfarlo wore a long white transparent skirt with a sequin top. I was helping to fix on the Wise Men's beards when I saw Cramer. He had on a toga-like garment made up of several thicknesses of mosquito-net, but not thick enough to hide his white shorts underneath. He had put on his make-up early, and this was melting on his face in the rising heat.

'I always get nerves at this point,' he said. 'I'm going to practise my opening speech.'

I heard him mount the stage and begin reciting. Above the voices of excited children I could only hear the rhythm of his voice; and I was intent on helping the Fanfarlo to paint her girls' faces. It seemed impossible. As fast as we lifted the sticks of paint they turned liquid. It was really getting abnormally hot.

'Open that door,' yelled the Fanfarlo. The back door was opened and a crowd of curious natives pressed round the entrance. I left the Fanfarlo ordering them off, for I was determined to get to the front of the building for some air. I mounted the stage and began to cross it when I was aware of a powerful radiation of heat coming from my right. Looking round, I saw Cramer apparently shouting at someone, in the attitude of his dealings with the natives that morning. But he could not advance because of this current of heat. And because of the heat I could not at first make out who Cramer was rowing with; this was the sort of heat that goes for the eyes. But as I got farther towards the front of the stage I saw what was standing there.

This was a living body. The most noticeable thing was its constancy; it seemed not to conform to the law of perspective, but remained the same size when I approached as when I withdrew. And altogether unlike other forms of life, it had a completed look. No part was undergoing a process; the outline lacked the signs of confusion and ferment which are commonly the signs of living things, and this was also the principle of its beauty. The eyes took up nearly the whole of the head, extending far over the cheekbones. From the back of the head came two muscular wings which from time to time folded themselves over the eyes, making a draught of scorching air. There was hardly any neck. Another pair of wings, tough and supple, spread from below the shoulders, and a third pair extended from the calves of the legs, appearing to sustain the body. The feet looked too fragile to bear up such a concentrated degree of being.

European residents of Africa are often irresistibly prompted to speak kitchen kaffir to anything strange.

'*Hamba!*' shouted Cramer, meaning 'Go away'.

'Now get off the stage and stop your noise,' said the living body peaceably.

'Who in hell are you?' said Cramer, gasping through the heat.

'The same as in Heaven,' came the reply, 'a Seraph, that's to say.'

'Tell that to someone else,' Cramer panted. 'Do I look like a fool?'

'I will. No, nor a Seraph either,' said the Seraph.

The place was filling with heat from the Seraph. Cramer's paint was running into his eyes and he wiped them on his net robe. Walking backward to a less hot place he cried, 'Once and for all—'

'That's correct,' said the Seraph.

'— this is my show,' continued Cramer.

'Since when?' the Seraph said.

'Right from the start,' Cramer breathed at him.

'Well, it's been mine from the Beginning,' said the Seraph, 'and the Beginning began first.'

Climbing down from the hot stage, Cramer caught his

seraphic robe on a nail and tore it. 'Listen here,' he said, 'I can't conceive of an abnormality like you being a true Seraph.'

'True,' said the Seraph.

By this time I had been driven by the heat to the front entrance. Cramer joined me there. A number of natives had assembled. The audience had begun to arrive in cars and the rest of the cast had come round the building from the back. It was impossible to see far inside the building owing to the Seraph's heat, and impossible to re-enter.

Cramer was still haranguing the Seraph from the door, and there was much speculation among the new arrivals as to which of the three familiar categories the present trouble came under, namely, the natives, Whitehall, or leopards.

'This is my property,' cried Cramer, 'and these people have paid for their seats. They've come to see a masque.'

'In that case,' said the Seraph, 'I'll cool down and they can come and see a masque.'

'*My* masque,' said Cramer.

'Ah, no, *mine*,' said the Seraph. 'Yours won't do.'

'Will you go, or shall I call the police?' said Cramer with finality.

'I have no alternative,' said the Seraph more finally still.

Word had gone round that a mad leopard was in the garage. People got back into their cars and parked at a safe distance; the tobacco planter went to fetch a gun. A number of young troopers had the idea of blinding the mad leopard with petrol and ganged up some natives to fill petrol cans from the pump and pass them chainwise to the garage.

'This'll fix him,' said a trooper.

'That's right, let him have it,' said Cramer from his place by the door.

'I shouldn't do that,' said the Seraph. 'You'll cause a fire.'

The first lot of petrol to be flung into the heat flared up. The seats caught alight first, then the air itself began to burn within the metal walls till the whole interior was flame feeding on flame. Another car-load of troopers arrived just then and promptly got a gang of natives to fill petrol cans with water. Slowly they drenched the fire. The Fanfarlo mustered her angels a little way up the road. She was trying to reassure their parents and see what was happening at the same time, furious at losing her opportunity to dance. She aimed a hard poke at the back of one of the angels whose parents were in England.

It was some hours before the fire was put out. While the corrugated metal walls still glowed, twisted and furled, it was impossible to see what had happened to the Seraph, and after they had ceased to glow it was too dark and hot to see far into the wreck.

'Are you insured?' one of Cramer's friends asked him.

'Oh yes,' Cramer replied, 'my policy covers everything except Acts of God – that means lightning or flood.'

'He's fully covered,' said Cramer's friend to another friend.

Many people had gone home and the rest were going. The troopers drove off singing 'Good King Wenceslas', and the mission boys ran down the road singing 'Good Christian Men, Rejoice'.

It was about midnight, and still very hot. The tobacco planters suggested a drive to the Falls, where it was cool. Cramer and the Fanfarlo joined us, and we bumped along the rough path from Cramer's to the main highway. There the road is tarred only in two strips to take car-wheels. The thunder of the Falls reached us about two miles before we reached them.

'After all my work on the masque and everything!' Cramer was saying.

'Oh, shut up,' said the Fanfarlo.

Just then, by the glare of our headlights I saw the Seraph again, going at about seventy miles an hour and skimming the tarmac strips with two of his six wings in swift motion, two folded over his face, and two covering his feet.

'That's him!' said Cramer. 'We'll get him yet.'

We left the car near the hotel and followed a track through the dense vegetation of the Rain Forest, where the spray from the Falls descends perpetually. It was like a convalescence after fever, that frail rain after the heat. The Seraph was far ahead of us and through the trees I could see where his heat was making steam of the spray.

We came to the cliff's edge, where opposite us and from the same level the full weight of the river came blasting into the gorge between. There was no sign of the Seraph. Was he far below in the heaving pit, or where?

Then I noticed that along the whole mile of the waterfall's crest the spray was rising higher than usual. This I took to be steam from the Seraph's heat. I was right, for presently, by the mute flashes of summer lightning, we watched him ride the Zambesi away from us, among the rocks that look like crocodiles and the crocodiles that look like rocks.

DOROTHY K. HAYNES

THOU SHALT NOT SUFFER A WITCH ...

THE CHILD SAT alone in her bedroom, weaving the fringe of the counterpane in and out of her fingers. It was a horrible room, the most neglected one of the house. The grate was narrow and rusty, cluttered up with dust and hair combings, and the floorboards creaked at every step. When the wind blew, the door rattled and banged, but the window was sealed tight, webbed, fly-spotted, a haven for everything black and creeping.

In and out went her fingers, the fringe pulled tight between nail and knuckle. Outside, the larches tossed and flurried, brilliant green under a blue sky. Sometimes the sun would go in, and rain would hit the window like a handful of nails thrown at the glass; then the world would lighten suddenly, the clouds would drift past in silver and white, and the larches would once more toss in sunshine.

'Jinnot! Jinnot!' called a voice from the yard. 'Where've you got to, Jinnot?'

She did not answer. The voice went farther away, still calling. Jinnot sat on the bed, hearing nothing but the voice which had tormented her all week.

'You'll do it, Jinnot, eh? Eh, Jinnot? An' I'll give you a sixpence to spend. We've always got on well, Jinnot. You like me better than her. She never gave you ribbons for your hair, did she? She never bought you sweeties in the village? It's not much to ask of you, Jinnot, just to say she looked at you, an' it happened. It's not as if it was telling lies. It has happened before; it has, eh, Jinnot?'

She dragged herself over to the mirror, the cracked sheet of glass with the fawn fly-spots. The door on her left hand, the window on her right, neither a way of escape. Her face looked back at her, yellow in the reflected sunlight. Her hair was the colour of hay, her heavy eyes had no shine in them. Large teeth, wide mouth, the whole face was square and dull. She went back to the bed, and her fingers picked again at the fringe.

Had it happened before? Why could she not remember properly? Perhaps it was because they were all so kind to her after it happened, trying to wipe it out of her memory. 'You just came over faint, lassie. Just a wee sickness, like. Och, you don't need to cry, you'll be fine in a minute. Here's Minty to see to you. . . .'

But Minty would not see to her this time.

The voice went on and on in her head, wheedling, in one ear and out of the other.

'Me and Jack will get married, see, Jinnot? And when we're married, you can come to our house whenever you like. You can come in, and I'll bake scones for you, Jinnot, and sometimes we'll let you sleep in our wee upstairs room. You'll do it, Jinnot, will you not? For Jack as well as for me. You like Jack. Mind he mended your Dolly for you? And you'd like to see us married thegither, would you not?

'He'd never be happy married to her, Jinnot. You're a big girl now, you'll soon see that for yourself. She's good enough in her way, see, but she's not the right kind for him. She sits and sews and works all day, but she's never a bit of fun with him, never a word to say. But he's never been used to anyone better, see, Jinnot, and he'll not look at anybody else while she's there. It's for his own good, Jinnot, and for her sake as well. They'd never be happy married.

'And Jinnot, you're not going to do her any harm. Someday you'll get married yourself, Jinnot, and you'll know. So it's just kindness . . . and she *is* like that, like what I said. Mebbe she's been the cause of the trouble you had before, you never know. So you'll do it, Jinnot, eh? You'll do it?'

She did not want to. The door rattled in the wind, and the sun shone through the dirt and the raindrops on the window. Why did she want to stay here, with the narrow bed, the choked grate, the mirror reflecting the flaked plaster of the opposite wall? The dust blew along the floor, and the chimney and the keyhole howled together. 'Jinnot! Jinnot!' went the voice again. She paid no attention. Pulling back the blankets, she climbed fully dressed into the bed, her square, suety face like a mask laid on the pillows. 'Jinnot! Jinnot!' went the voice, calling, coaxing through the height of the wind. She whimpered, and curled herself under the bedclothes, hiding from the daylight and the question that dinned at her even in the dark. 'You'll do it, Jinnot, eh? Will you? Eh, Jinnot?'

Next day, the weather had settled. A quiet, spent sun shone on the farm, the tumbledown dykes and the shabby thatch. Everything was still as a painting, the smoke suspended blue in the air, the ducks so quiet on the pond that the larches doubled themselves in the water. Jinnot stood at the door of the byre, watching Jack Hyslop at work. His brush went swish swish, swirling the muck along to the door. He was a handsome lad. No matter how dirty his work, he always looked clean. His boots were bright every morning, and his black hair glistened as he turned his head. He whistled as his broom spattered dung and dirty water, and Jinnot turned her face away. The strong, hot smell from the byre made something grip her stomach with a strong, relentless fist.

Now Minty came out of the kitchen, across the yard with a basin of pig-swill. With her arm raised, pouring out the slops, she looked at the byre door for a long minute. To the child, the world seemed to stop in space. The byreman's broom was poised in motion, his arms flexed for a forward push; his whistle went on on the same note, high and shrill; and Minty was a statue of mute condemnation, with the dish spilling its contents in a halted stream.

A moment later, Jinnot found that Jack Hyslop was holding her head on his knee. Minty had run up, her apron clutched in both hands. Beatrice, the dairymaid, was watching too, bending over her. There was a smell of the dairy on her clothes, a slight smell of sourness, of milk just on the turn, and her hair waved dark under her cap. 'There now,' she said. 'All right, dearie, all right! What made you go off like that, now?'

The child's face sweated all over, her lips shivered as the air blew cold on her skin. All she wanted now was to run away, but she could not get up to her feet. 'What was it, Jinnot?' said the voice, going on and on, cruel, kind, which was it? 'Tell me, Jinnot. Tell me.'

She could not answer. Her tongue seemed to swell and press back on her throat, so that she vomited. Afterwards, lying in bed, she remembered it all, the sense of relief when she had thrown up all she had eaten, and the empty languor of the sleep which followed. Beatrice had put her to bed, and petted her and told her she was a good girl. 'It was easy done, eh, Jinnot? You'd have thought it was real.' She gave a high, uneasy laugh. 'Aye, you're a good wee thing, Jinnot. All the same, you fair frichted me at the beginning!'

She was glad to be left alone. After her sleep, strangely

cold, she huddled her knees to her shoulders, and tried to understand. Sometime, in a few months or a few years, it did not seem to matter, Minty and Jack Hyslop were to be married. Minty was kind. Since Jinnot's mother had died, she had been nurse and foster mother, attending to clothes and food and evening prayers. She had no time to do more. Her scoldings were frequent, but never unjust. Jinnot had loved her till Beatrice came to the dairy, handsome, gay, and always ready with bribes.

'You're a nice wee girl, Jinnot. Look – will you do something for Jack and me – just a wee thing? You've done it before; I know you have. Some time, when Minty's there . . .'

And so she had done it, for the sake of sixpence, and the desire to be rid of the persistent pleading; but where she had meant to pretend to fall in a fit at Minty's glance, just to pretend, she had really lost her senses, merely thinking about it. She was afraid now of what she had done . . . was it true then, about Minty, that the way she looked at you was enough to bring down a curse?

It could not be true. Minty was kind, and would make a good wife. Beatrice was the bad one, with her frightening whispers – and yet, it wasn't really badness; it was wisdom. She knew all the terrible things that children would not understand.

Jinnot got up and put on her clothes. Down in the kitchen, there was firelight, and the steam of the evening meal. Her father was eating heartily, his broad shoulders stooped over his plate. 'All right again, lassie?' he asked, snuggling her to him with one arm. She nodded, her face still a little peaked with weakness. At the other side of the room, Minty was busy at the fireside, but she did not turn her head. Jinnot clung closer to her father.

* * *

All the air seemed to be filled with whispers.

From nowhere at all, the news spread that Jinnot was bewitched. She knew it herself. She was fascinated by the romance of her own affliction, but she was frightened as well. Sometimes she would have days with large blanks which memory could not fill. Where had she been? What had she done? And the times when the world seemed to shrivel to the size of a pinhead, with people moving like grains of sand, tiny, but much, much clearer, the farther away they seemed – who was behind it all? When had it all started?

In time, however, the trouble seemed to right itself. But now, Jack Hyslop courted Beatrice instead of Minty. Once, following them, Jinnot saw them kiss behind a hayrick. They embraced passionately, arms clutching, bodies pressed together. It had never been like that with Minty, no laughter, no sighs. Their kisses had been mere respectful tokens, the concession to their betrothal.

Minty said nothing, but her sleek hair straggled, her once serene eyes glared under their straight brows. She began to be abrupt with the child. 'Out the road!' she would snap. 'How is it a bairn's aye at your elbow?' Jinnot longed for the friendliness of the young dairymaid. But Beatrice wanted no third party to share her leisure, and Jinnot was more lonely than ever before.

Why had she no friends? She had never had young company, never played games with someone of her own age. Her pastimes were lonely imaginings, the dark pretence of a brain burdened with a dull body. She made a desperate bid to recover her audience. Eyes shut, her breathing hoarse and ragged, she let herself fall to the ground, and lay there until footsteps came running, and kind hands worked to revive her.

So now she was reinstated, her father once more mindful of her, and the household aware of her importance, a sick person in the house. The voices went on whispering around her, 'Sshh! It's wee Jinnot again. Fell away in a dead faint. Poor lassie, she'll need to be seen to . . . Jinnot – Jinnot . . . wee Jinnot . . .'

But this time, there was a difference. They waited till she waked, and then questioned her. Her father was there, blocking out the light from the window, and the doctor sat by the bedside, obviously displeased with his task. Who was to blame? Who was there when it happened? She knew what they wanted her to say; she knew herself what to tell them. 'Who was it?' pressed her father. 'This has been going on too long.' 'Who was it?' said the doctor. 'There's queer tales going around, you know, Jinnot!' 'You know who it was,' said the voice in her mind. 'You'll do it, Jinnot, eh?'

'I – I don't know,' she sighed, her eyes drooping, her mouth hot and dry. 'I . . . only . . .' she put her hand to her head, and sighed. She could almost believe she was really ill, she felt so tired and strange.

After that, the rumours started again. The voice came back to Jinnot, the urgent and convincing warning – 'She *is* like that, like what I said. . . .' For her own peace of mind, she wanted to *know*, but there was no-one she could ask. She could not trust her own judgement.

It was months before she found out, and the days had lengthened to a queer tarnished summer, full of stale yellow heat. The larches had burned out long ago, and their branches drooped in dull fringes over the pond. The fields were tangled with buttercups and tall moon daisies, but the flowers dried and shrivelled as soon as they blossomed. All the brooks were silent; and the nettles by the hedges had a curled, thirsty look. Jinnot kept away from the duckpond these days. With the water so low, the floating weeds and mud gave off a bad, stagnant smell.

Over the flowers, the bees hovered, coming and going endlessly, to and from the hives. One day, a large bumble, blundering home, tangled itself in the girl's collar, and stung her neck. She screamed out, running into the house, squealing that she had swallowed the insect, and that something with a sting was flying round in her stomach, torturing her most cruelly. They sent for the doctor, and grouped round her with advice. Later, they found the bee, dead, in the lace which had trapped it; but before that, she had vomited up half her inside, with what was unmistakably yellow bees' bodies, and a quantity of waxy stuff all mixed up with wings and frail, crooked legs.

She looked at the watchers, and knew that the time had come. 'It was Minty Fraser!' she wailed. 'It was her! She *looked* at me!' She screamed, and hid her face as the sickness once more attacked her in heaving waves.

They went to the house, and found Minty on her knees, washing over the hearthstone. One of the farm-men hauled her to her feet, and held her wrists together. 'Witch! Witch! Witch!' shouted the crowd at the door.

'What – What—'

'Come on, witch! Out to the crowd!'

'No! No, I never—'

'Leave her a minute,' roared Jack Hyslop. 'Mebbe she – give her a chance to speak!' His mouth twitched a little. At one time, he was thinking, he had been betrothed to Minty, before Beatrice told him . . . he faltered at the thought of Beatrice. 'Well, don't be rough till you're sure,' he finished lamely, turning away and leaving the business to the others. Those who sympathised with witches, he remembered, were apt to share their fate.

The women were not so blate. 'Witch! Witch!' they shrilled. 'Burn the witch! Our bairns are no' safe when folks like her is let to live!'

She was on the doorstep now, her cap torn off, her eye bleeding, her dress ripped away at the shoulder. Jinnot's father, pushing through the mob, raised his hand for the sake of order. 'Look, men! Listen, there! This is my house; there'll be no violence done on the threshold.'

'Hang her! Burn her! A rope, there!'

'No hanging till you make sure. Swim her first. If the devil floats—'

'Jinnot! Here's Jinnot!'

The girl came through a lane in the throng, Beatrice holding her hand, clasping her round the waist. She did not want to see Minty, but her legs forced her on. Then she looked up. A witch . . . she saw the blood on the face, the torn clothes, the look of horror and terrible hurt. That was Minty, who cooked her meals and looked after her and did the work of a mother. She opened her mouth and screamed, till the foam dripped over her chin.

Her father's face was as white as her own spittle. 'Take the beast away,' he said, 'and if she floats, for God's sake get rid of her as quick as you can!'

It was horrible. They all louped at her, clutching and tearing and howling as they plucked at her and trussed her for ducking. She was down on the ground, her clothes flung indecently over her head, her legs kicking as she tried to escape. 'It wasna me!' she skirled. 'It wasna me! I'm no' a witch! Aa-ah!' The long scream cut the air like a blade. Someone had wrenched her leg and snapped the bone at the ankle, but her body still went flailing about in the dust, like a kitten held under a blanket.

They had her trussed now, wrists crossed, legs crossed,

her body arched between them. She was dragged to the pond, blood from her cuts and grazes smearing the clothes of those who handled her. Her hair hung over her face and her broken foot scraped the ground. 'No! No!' she screamed. 'Ah, God . . .!' and once, 'Jinnot! Tell them it wasna me—'

A blow over the mouth silenced her, and she spat a tooth out with a mouthful of blood. She shrieked as they swung and hurtled her through the air. There was a heavy splash, and drops of green, slimy water spattered the watching faces. If Minty was a witch, she would float; and then they would haul her out and hang her, or burn her away, limb by limb.

She sank; the pond was shallow, but below the surface, green weed and clinging mud drew her down in a deadly clutch. The crowd on the bank watched her, fascinated. It was only when her yammering mouth was filled and silenced that they realised what had happened, and took slow steps to help her. By that time, it was too late.

What must it be like to be a witch? The idea seeped into her mind like ink, and all her thoughts were tinged with the black poison. She knew the dreadful aftermath; long after, her mind would be haunted by the sight she had seen. In her own nostrils, she felt the choke and snuffle of pond slime; but what must it feel like, the knowledge of strange power, the difference from other people, the danger? Her imagination played with the thrilling pain of it, right down to the last agony.

She asked Beatrice about it. Beatrice was married now, with a baby coming, and Jinnot sat with her in the waning afternoons, talking with her, woman to woman.

'I didn't like to see them set on her like yon. She never done me any harm. If it hadn't been for me—'

'Are you sure, Jinnot? Are you sure? Mind the bees, Jinnot, an' yon time at the barn door? What about them?'

'I – I don't know.'

'Well, I'm telling you. She was a witch, that one, if anybody was.'

'Well, mebbe she couldn't help it.'

'No, they can't help the power. It just comes on them. Sometimes they don't want it, but it comes, just the same. It's hard, but you know what the Bible says: "Thou shalt not suffer a witch . . ." '

She had a vision of Minty, quiet, busy, struggling with a force she did not want to house in her body. Beside this, her own fits and vomitings seemed small things. She could forgive knowing that. 'How . . . how do they first know they're witches?' she asked.

'Mercy, I don't know! What questions you ask, Jinnot! How would I know, eh? I daresay they find out soon enough.'

So that was it; they knew themselves. Her mind dabbled and meddled uncomfortably with signs and hints. She wanted to curse Beatrice for putting the idea into her head; she would not believe it; but once there, the thought would not be removed. What if she was a witch? 'I'm not,' she said to herself. 'I'm too young,' she said; but there was no conviction in it. Long before she had been bewitched, she had known there was something different about her. Now it all fell into place. No wonder the village children would not call and play with her. No wonder her father was just rather than affectionate, shielding her only because she was his daughter. And no wonder Beatrice was so eager to keep in with her, with the incessant 'Eh, Jinnot?' always on her lips.

Well, then, she was a witch. As well to know it sooner as later, to accept the bothers with the benefits, the troubles and trances with the new-found sense of power. She had never wanted to kill or curse, never in her most unhappy moments, but now, given the means, would it not be as well to try? Did her power strengthen by being kept, or did it spring up fresh from some infernal reservoir? She did not know. She was a very new witch, uncertain of what was demanded of her. Week after week passed, and she was still no farther forward.

She continued her visits to Beatrice, though the thought of it all made her grue. It angered her to see the girl sitting stout and placid at the fireside, unhaunted, unafraid. 'You'll come and see the baby when it's born, eh, Jinnot?' she would say. 'Do you like babies? Do you?' Nothing mattered to her now, it seemed, but the baby. In the dark winter nights, Jinnot made a resolve to kill her. But for Beatrice, she might never have discovered this terrible fact about herself. Beatrice was to blame for everything, but a witch has means of revenge, and one witch may avenge another.

She had no idea how to cast a spell, and there was no-one to help her. What had Minty done? She remembered the moment at the byre door, the upraised arm, and the long, long look. It would be easy. Bide her time, and Beatrice would die when the spring came.

She sat up in the attic, twining her fingers in the fringe of the bedcover, in and out, under and over. Beatrice was in labour. It had been whispered in the kitchen, spreading from mouth to mouth. Now, Jinnot sat on the bed, watching the larches grow black in the dusk. She was not aware of cold, or dirt, or darkness. All her senses were fastened on the window of Beatrice's cottage, where a light burned, and women gathered round the bed. She fixed her will, sometimes almost praying in her effort to influence fate. 'Kill her! Kill her! Let her die!' Was she talking to God, or to the devil? The thoughts stared and screamed in her mind. She wanted Beatrice to suffer every agony, every pain, and wrench, to bear Minty's pain, and her own into the bargain. All night she sat, willing pain and death, and suffering it all in her own body. Her face was grey as the ceiling, her flesh sweated with a sour smell. Outside, an owl shrieked, and she wondered for a moment if it was Beatrice.

Suddenly, she knew that it was all over. The strain passed out of her body, the lids relaxed over her eyes, her body seemed to melt and sprawl over the bed. When she woke, it was morning, and the maids were beaming with good news. 'Did you hear?' they said. 'Beatrice has a lovely wee boy! She's fair away wi' herself!'

Jinnot said nothing. She stopped her mouth and her disappointment with porridge. It did not cross her mind that perhaps, after all, she was no witch. All she thought was that the spell had not worked, and Beatrice was still alive. She left the table, and hurried over to the cottage. The door was ajar, the fire bright in the hearth, and Beatrice was awake in bed, smiling, the colour already flushing back into her cheeks.

'He's a bonny baby, Jinnot. He's lovely, eh? Eh, Jinnot?'

She crept reluctantly to the cradle. Why, he was no size at all, so crumpled, so new, a wee sliver of flesh in a bundle of white wool. She stared for a long time, half sorry for what she had to do. The baby was snuffling a little, its hands and feet twitching under the wrappings. He was so young, he would not have his mother's power to resist a witch.

She glared at him for a long minute, her eyes fixed, her lips firm over her big teeth. His face, no bigger than a lemon, turned black, and a drool of foam slavered from the mouth. When the twitching stopped, and the eyes finally uncrossed themselves, she walked out, and left the door again on the latch. She had not spoken one word.

It seemed a long time before they came for her, a long time of fuss and running about while she sat on the bed, shivering in the draught from the door. When she crossed to the window, her fingers probing the webs and pressing the guts from the plumpest insects, she saw them arguing and gesticulating in a black knot. Jack Hyslop was there, his polished hair ruffled, his face red. The women were shaking their heads, and Hyslop's voice rose clear in the pale air.

'Well, that's what she said. The wee thing had been dead for an hour. An' it was that bitch Jinnot came in an' glowered at it.'

'Och, man, it's a sick woman's fancy! A wee mite that age can easy take convulsions.'

'It wasna convulsions. My wife said Jinnot was in and out with a face like thunder. She was aye askin' about witches too, you can ask Beatrice if you like.'

'Well, she was in yon business o' Minty Fraser. Ye cannie blame her, a young lassie like that . . . mind, we sympathise about the bairn, Jacky, but—'

They went on placating him, mindful of the fact that Jinnot was the farmer's daughter. It would not do to accuse *her*, but one of the women went into the cottage, and came out wiping her eyes. 'My, it would make anybody greet. The wee lamb's lying there like a flower, that quiet! It's been a fair shock to the mother, poor soul. She's gey faur through. . . .'

They muttered, then, and drifted towards the house. Jinnot left the window, and sat again on the bed. She was not afraid, only resigned, and horribly tired of it all.

When they burst into her room, clumping over the bare boards, her father was with them. They allowed him to ask the questions. Was he angry with them, or with her? She could not guess.

'Jinnot,' he said sternly, 'what's this? What's all this?'

She stared at him.

'What's all this? Do you know what they're saying about you? They say you killed Beatrice Hyslop's bairn. Is that true, Jinnot?'

She did not answer. Her father held up his hand as the men began to growl.

'Come now, Jinnot, enough of this sulking! It's for your own good to answer, and clear yourself. Mind of what happened to Minty Fraser! Did you do anything to the baby?'

'I never touched it. I just looked at it.'

'Just looked?'

'Yes.'

A rough cry burst from Jack Hyslop. 'Is that not what Minty Fraser said? Was that not enough from her?'

'Hyslop, hold your tongue, or you lose your job.'

'Well, by God, I lose it then! There's been more trouble on this bloody farm—'

'Aye! Leave this to us!'

'We'll question the wench. If she's no witch, she's nothing to fear.'

The women had come in now, crowding up in angry curiosity. The farmer was pushed back against the wall. 'One word, and you'll swim along with her,' he was warned, and he knew them well enough to believe them. They gathered round Jinnot, barking questions at her, and snatching at the answers. Every time she paused to fidget with the fringe, they lammed her across the knuckles till her hands were swollen and blue.

'Tell the truth now; are you a witch?'

'No. No, I'm not!'

'Why did you kill the baby this morning?'

'I – I never. I can't kill folk. I—'

'You hear that? She can't kill folk! Have you ever tried?'

She cowered back from them, the faces leering at her like ugly pictures. She would tell the truth, as her father said, and be done with all this dream-like horror. 'Leave me alone!' she said. 'Leave me, and I'll tell!'

'Hurry then. Out with it! Have you ever tried to kill anybody?'

'Yes. I tried, and – and I couldn't. It was her, she started telling me I was bewitched—'

'Who?'

'Beatrice – Mistress Hyslop.'

'My God!' said Jack and her father, starting forward together.

'Hold on, there! Let her speak.'

'She said I was bewitched, an' I thought I was. I don't know if it was right . . . it was all queer, and I didn't know . . . and then, when she said about witches, she put it in my head, and it came over me I might be one. I *had* to find out—'

'There you are. She's admitting it!'

'No!' She began to shout as they laid hold of her, screaming in fright and temper till her throat bled. 'No! *Leave* me alone! I never; I tried, and I couldn't do it! I couldn't, I tell you! She *wouldn't* die. She'd have died if I'd been a witch, wouldn't she? She's a witch herself; I don't care, Jack Hyslop, she is! It was her fault Minty Fraser – oh God, no! NO!'

She could not resist the rope round her, the crossing of her limbs, the tight pull of cord on wrists and ankles. When she knew it was hopeless, she dared not resist remembering Minty's broken leg, her cuts and blood and bruises, the tooth spinning out in red spittle. She was not afraid of death, but she was mortally afraid of pain. Now, if she went quietly, there would only be the drag to the pond, the muckle splash, and the slow silt and suffocation in slime. . . .

She had no voice left to cry out when they threw her. Her throat filled with water, her nose filled, and her ears. She was tied too tightly to struggle. Down, down she went, till her head sang, and her brain nearly burst; but the pond was full with the spring rains, and her body was full-fleshed and buoyant. Suddenly, the cries of the crowd burst upon her again, and she realised that she was floating. Someone jabbed at her, and pushed her under again with a long pole, but she bobbed up again a foot away, her mouth gulping, her eyes bulging under her dripping hair. The mob on the bank howled louder.

'See, see! She's floating!'

'Witch! Burn her! Fish her out and hang her!'

'There's proof now. What are you waiting for? Out with her. See, the besom'll *no'* sink!'

So now they fished her out, untied her, and bound her again in a different fashion, hands by her side, feet together. She was too done to protest, or to wonder what they would do. She kept her eyes shut as they tied her to a stake, and she ignored the tickle of dead brushwood being piled round feet and body. She could hardly realise that she was still alive, and she was neither glad nor sorry.

They were gentle with her now, sparing her senses for the last pain. At first, she hardly bothered when the smoke nipped her eyes and her nostrils; she hardly heard the first snap of the thin twigs. It was only when the flames lapped her feet and legs that she raised her head and tried to break free. As the wood became red hot, and the flames mounted to bite her body, she screamed and writhed and bit her tongue to mincemeat. When they could not see her body through the fire, the screams still went on.

The crowd drifted away when she lost consciousness. There was no more fun to be had; or perhaps, it wasn't such fun after all. The men went back to the fields, but they could not settle to work. Jinnot's father was gnawing his knuckles in the attic, and they did not know what would happen when he came down. Beatrice tossed in a muttering, feverish sleep; and beside the pond, a few veins and bones still sizzled and popped in the embers.

GEORGE MACKAY BROWN

THE DROWNED ROSE

THERE WAS A sudden fragrance, freshness, coldness in the room. I looked up from my book. A young woman in a red dress had come in, breathless, eager, ready for laughter. The summer twilight of the far north was just beginning; it was late in the evening, after ten o'clock. The girl peered at me where I sat in the shadowy window-seat. 'You're not Johnny,' she said, more than a bit disappointed.

'No', I said, 'that isn't my name.'

She was certainly a very beautiful girl, with her abundant black hair and hazel eyes and small sweet sensuous mouth. Who was she – the merchant's daughter from across the road, perhaps? A girl from one of the farms? She was a bit too old to be one of my future pupils.

'Has he been here?' she cried. 'Has he been and gone again? The villain. He promised to wait for me. We're going up the hill to watch the sunset.' Again the flash of laughter in her eyes.

'I'm sorry,' I said, 'I'm a stranger. I only arrived this afternoon. But I assure you nobody has called here this evening.'

'Well now, and just who are you?' she said. 'And what are you doing here?'

'My name is William Reynolds,' I said. 'I'm the new schoolmaster.'

She gave me a look of the most utter sweet astonishment. 'The new—!' She shook her head. 'I'm most terribly confused,' she said. 'I really am. The queerest things are happening.'

'Sit down and tell me about it,' I said. For I liked the girl immensely. Blast that Johnny whoever-he-is, I thought; some fellows have all the luck. Here, I knew at once, was one of the few young women it was a joy to be with. I wished she would stay for supper. My mouth began to frame the invitation.

'He'll have gone to the hill without me,' she said. 'I'll wring his neck. The sun'll be down in ten minutes. I'd better hurry.'

She was gone as suddenly as she had come. The fragrance went with her. I discovered, a bit to my surprise, that I was shivering, even though it was a mild night and there was a decent fire burning in the grate.

'Goodnight,' I called after her.

No answer came back.

Blast that Johnny. I wouldn't mind stumbling to the top of a hill, breathless, with a rare creature like her, on such a beautiful night, I thought. I returned regretfully to my book. It was still light enough to read when I got to the end of the chapter. I looked out of the window at the russet-and-primrose sky. Two figures were silhouetted against the sunset on a rising crest of the hill. They stood there hand in hand. I was filled with happiness and envy.

I went to bed before midnight, in order to be fresh for my first morning in the new school.

I had grown utterly sick and tired of teaching mathematics in the junior secondary school in the city; trying to insert logarithms and trigonometry into the heads of louts whose only wish, like mine, was to be rid of the institution for ever. I read an advertisement in the educational journal for a male teacher – 'required urgently' – for a one-teacher island school in the north. There was only a month of the summer term to go. I sent in my application at once, and was appointed without even having to endure an interview. Two days later I was in an aeroplane flying over the snow-scarred highlands of Scotland. The mountains gave way to moors and firths. Then I looked down at the sea stretching away to a huge horizon; a dark swirling tide-race; an island neatly ruled into tilth and pasture. Other islands tilted towards us. The plane settled lightly on a runway set in a dark moor. An hour later I boarded another smaller plane, and after ten merry minutes flying level with kittiwakes and cormorants I was shaking hands with the island representative of the education committee. This was the local minister. I liked the Reverend Donald Barr at once. He was, like myself, a young bachelor, but he gave me a passable tea of ham-and-eggs at the manse before driving me to the school. We talked easily and well together all the time. 'They're like every other community in the world,' he said, 'the islanders of Quoylay. They're good and bad and middling – mostly middling. There's not one really evil person in the whole island. If there's a saint I haven't met him yet. One and all, they're enormously hospitable in their farms – they'll share with you everything they have. The kids – they're a delight, shy and gentle and biddable. You've made a good move, mister, coming here, if the loneliness doesn't kill you. Sometimes it gets me down, especially on a Sunday morning when I find myself preaching to half-a-dozen unmoved faces. They were very religious once, now they're reverting to paganism as fast as they can. The minister is more or less a nonentity, a useless appendage. Changed days, my boy. We used to wield great power, we ministers. We were second only to the laird, and the schoolmaster got ten pounds a year. Your remote predecessor ate the scraps from my predecessor's table. Changed days, right enough. Enjoy yourself, Bill. I know you will, for a year or two anyway.'

By this time the manse car had brought me home with my luggage, and we were seated at either side of a newly-lighted fire in the school-house parlour. Donald Barr went away to prepare his sermon. I picked a novel at random from the bookcase, and had read maybe a half-dozen pages when I had my first visitor, the girl with the abundant black hair and laughter-lighted face; the loved one; the slightly bewildered one; the looker into sunsets.

The pupils descended on the playground, and swirled round like a swarm of birds, just before nine o'clock next morning. There were twenty children in the island school, ranging in age from five to twelve. So, they had to be arranged in different sections in the single large class-room. The four youngest were learning to read from the new phonetic script. Half-a-dozen or so of the eldest pupils would be going after the summer holidays to the senior secondary school in Kirkwall; they were making a start on French and geometry. In between, and simultaneously, the others worked away at history, geography, reading, drawing, sums. I found the variety a bit bewildering, that first day.

Still, I enjoyed it. Everything that the minister had said about the island children was true. The impudence and indifference that the city children offered you in exchange for your labours, the common currency of my previous class-rooms, these were absent here. Instead, they looked at me and everything I did with a round-eyed wonderment. I expected that this would not last beyond the first weekend. Only once, in the middle of the afternoon, was there any kind of ruffling of the bright surface. With the six oldest ones I was going through a geometry theorem on the black-board. A tall boy stood up. 'Please, sir,' he said, 'that's not the way Miss McKillop taught us to do it.'

The class-room had been murmurous as a beehive. Now there was silence, as if a spell had been laid on the school.

'Please, sir, on Thursday afternoons Miss McKillop gave us nature study.' This from a ten-year-old girl with hair like a bronze bell. She stood up and blurted it out, bravely and a little resentfully.

'And what exactly did this nature study consist of?' I said.

'Please, sir,' said a boy whose head was like a hayrick and whose face was a galaxy of freckles, 'we would go to the beach for shells, and sometimes, please, sir, to the marsh for wild flowers.'

'Miss McKillop took us all,' said another boy. 'Please sir.'

Miss McKillop. . . . Miss McKillop. . . . Miss McKillop. . . . The name scattered softly through the school as if a rose had shed its petals. Indeed last night's fragrance seemed to be everywhere in the class-room. A dozen mouths uttered the name. They looked at me, but they looked at me as if some-body else was sitting at the high desk beside the blackboard.

'I see,' I said. 'Nature study on Thursday afternoons. I don't see anything against it, except that I'm a great duffer when it comes to flowers and birds and such-like. Still, I'm sure none of us will be any the worse of a stroll through the fields on a Thursday afternoon. But this Thursday, you see, I'm new here, I'm feeling my way, and I'm pretty ignorant of what should be, so I think for today we'd just better carry on the way we're doing.'

The spell was broken. The fragrance was withdrawn.

They returned to their phonetics and history and geome-try. Their heads bent obediently once more over books and jotters. I lifted the pointer, and noticed that my fist was blue

with cold. And the mouth of the boy who had first mentioned the name of Miss McKillop trembled, in the heart
of that warm summer afternoon, as he gave me the proof of
the theorem.

'Thank God for that,' said Donald Barr. He brought a chess-
board and a box of chessmen from the cupboard. He blew a
spurt of dust from them. 'We'd have grown to hate each other
after a fortnight, trying to warm each other up with politics
and island gossip.' He arranged the pieces on the board. 'I'm
very glad also that you're only a middling player, same as me.
We can spend our evenings in an amiable silence.'

We were very indifferent players indeed. None of our
games took longer than an hour to play. No victory came
about through strategy, skill, or foresight. All without exception that first evening were lost by some incredible blunder
(followed by muted cursings and the despairing fall of a fist
on the table).

'You're right,' I said after the fourth game, 'silence is the
true test of friendship.'

We had won two games each. We decided to drink a jar of
ale and smoke our pipes before playing the decider. Donald
Barr made his own beer, a nutty potent brew that crept
through your veins and overcame you after ten minutes or so
with a drowsy contentment. We smoked and sipped mostly
in silence; yet fine companionable thoughts moved through
our minds and were occasionally uttered.

'I am very pleased so far,' I said after a time, 'with this
island and the people in it. The children are truly a delight.
Mrs Sinclair who makes the school dinner has a nice touch
with stew. There is also the young woman who visited me
briefly last night. She was looking for somebody else, unfortunately. I hope *she* comes often.'

'What young woman?' said the minister drowsily.

'She didn't say her name,' I said. 'She's uncommonly good-looking, what the teenagers in my last school would call a rare chick.'

'Describe this paragon,' said Donald Barr.

I am no great shakes at describing things, especially beautiful young women. But I did my best, between puffs at my pipe. The mass of black hair. The wide hazel eyes. The red restless laughing mouth. 'It was,' I said, 'as if she had come straight into the house out of a rose garden. She asked for Johnny.'

Something had happened to the Rev. Donald Barr. My words seemed to wash the drowsiness from his face; he was like a sleeper on summer hills overcome with rain. He sat up in his chair and looked at me. He was really agitated. He knocked the ember of tobacco out of his pipe. He took a deep gulp of ale from his mug. Then he walked to the window and looked out at the thickening light. The clock on the mantelshelf ticked on beyond eleven o'clock.

'And so,' I said, 'may she come back often to the schoolhouse, if it's only to look for this Johnny.'

From Donald Barr, no answer. Silence is a test of friendship but I wanted very much to learn the name of my visitor; or rather I was seeking for a confirmation.

Donald Barr said, 'A ghost is the soul of a dead person who is earth-bound. That is, it is so much attached to the things of this world that it is unwilling to let go of them. It cannot believe it is dead. It cannot accept for one moment that its body has been gathered back into the four elements. It refuses to set out on the only road it can take now, into the kingdom of the dead. No, it is in love too much with what it has been and known. It will not leave its money and possessions. It will not forgive the wrongs that were done to it while it was alive. It clings on desperately to love.'

'I was not speaking about any ghost,' I said. 'I was trying to tell you about this very delightful lovely girl.'

'If I was a priest,' said Donald Barr, 'instead of a minister, I might tell you that a ghost is a spirit lost between this world and purgatory. It refuses to shed its earthly appetites. It will not enter the dark gate of suffering.'

The northern twilight thickened in the room while we spoke. Our conversation was another kind of chess. Yet each knew what the other was about.

'I hope she's there tonight,' I said. 'I might even prevail on her to make me some toast and hot chocolate. For it seems I'm going to get no supper in the manse.'

'You're not scared?' said Donald Barr from the window.

'No,' I said. 'I'm not frightened of that kind of ghost. It seemed to me, when we were speaking together in the school-house last night, this girl and I, that I was the wan lost one, the squeaker and gibberer, and she was a part of the ever-springing fountain.'

'Go home then to your ghost,' said Donald Barr. 'We won't play any more chess tonight. She won't harm you, you're quite right there.'

We stood together at the end of his garden path.

'Miss McKillop,' I murmured to the dark shape that was fumbling for the latch of the gate.

'Sandra McKillop,' said Donald, 'died the twenty-third of May this year. I buried her on the third of June, herself and John Germiston, in separate graves.'

'Tell me,' I said.

'No,' said Donald, 'for I do not know the facts. Never ask me for a partial account. It seemed to me they were happy. I refuse to wrong the dead. Go in peace.'

There was no apparition in the school-house that night. I went to bed and slept soundly, drugged with fresh air, ale, fellowship; and a growing wonderment.

The days passed, and I did not see the ghost again. Occasionally I caught the fragrance, a drift of sudden sweetness in the long corridor between kitchen and parlour, or in the garden or on the pebbled path between the house and the school. Occasionally a stir of cold went through the parlour late at night as I sat reading, and no heaping of peats would warm the air again for a half-hour or so. I would look up, eagerly I must confess, but nothing trembled into form and breathing out of the expectant air. It was as if the ghost had grown shy and uncertain, indicated her presence only by hints and suggestions. And in the class-room too things quietened down, and the island pupils and I worked out our regime together as the summer days passed. Only occasionally a five-year-old would whisper something about Miss McKillop, and smile, and then look sad; and it was like a small scattering of rose-petals. Apart from that everything proceeded smoothly to the final closing of books at the end of the school year.

One man in the island I did not like, and that was Henrikson who kept the island store and garage, my neighbour. A low wall separated the school garden from Henrikson's land, which was usually untidy with empty lemonade cases, oil drums, sodden cardboard boxes. Apart from the man's simple presence, which he insisted on inflicting on me, I was put out by things in his character. For example, he showed an admiration for learning and university degrees that amounted to sycophancy; and this I could not abide, having sprung myself from a race of labourers and miners and railwaymen, good people all, more solid and sound and kindly than most university people, in my experience. But the drift of Henrikson's talk was that farmers and such like, including himself, were poor creatures indeed compared to their peers who had educated themselves and got into the professions and so risen in the world. This was bad enough; but soon he began to direct arrows of slander at this person and that in the island. 'Arrows' is too open and forthright a word for it; it was more the work of 'the smiler with the knife'. Such-and-such a farmer, he told me, was in financial difficulties, we wouldn't be seeing him in Quoylay much longer. This other young fellow had run his motor-cycle for two years now without a licence; maybe somebody should do something about it; he himself had no objection to sending anonymous letters to the authorities in such a case. Did I see that half-ruined croft down at the shore? Two so-called respectable people in this island – he would mention no names – had spent a whole weekend together there at show time last summer, a married man and a farmer's daughter. The straw they had lain on hadn't even been cleaned out. . . . This was the kind of talk that went on over the low wall between school and store on the late summer evenings. It was difficult to avoid the man; as soon as he saw me weeding the potato patch, or watering the pinks, out he came with his smirkings and cap-touchings, and leaned confidentially over the wall. It is easy to say I could simply have turned my back on him; but in many ways I am a coward; and even the basest of the living can coerce me to some extent. One evening his theme was the kirk and the minister. 'I'm not wanting to criticise any friend of yours,' he said. 'I've seen him more than once in the school-house and I've heard that you visit him in the manse, and it's no business of mine, but that man is not a *real* minister, if you ask me. We're used with a different kind of preaching in this island, and a different kind of pastoral behaviour too, I assure you of that. I know for a fact that he brews – he bought two tins of malt, and hops, from the store last month. The old ministers were one and all very much against drink. What's a minister for if he doesn't keep people's feet on the true path, yes, if he doesn't warn them and counsel them in season and out of season, you know, in regard to their conduct? The old ministers that were here formerly had a proper understanding of their office. But this Mr Barr, he closes his eyes to things that are a crying scandal to the whole island. For example—'

'Mr Barr is a very good friend of mine,' I said.

'O, to be sure,' he cried. 'I know. He's an educated man and so are you too, Mr Reynolds. I spoke out of place, I'm sorry. I'm just a simple countryman, brought up on the shorter catechism and the good book. Times are changing fast. I'm sure people who have been to the university have a different way of looking at things from an old country chap. No offence, Mr Reynolds, I hope.'

A few moths were out, clinging to the stones, fluttering and birring softly on the kitchen window. I turned and went in without saying goodnight to Mr Henrikson.

And as I went along the corridor, with a bad taste in my mouth from that holy old creep across the road, I heard it, a low reluctant weeping from above, from the bedroom. I ran upstairs and threw open the door. The room was empty, but it was as cold as the heart of an iceberg, and the unmistakable fragrance clung about the window curtains and the counterpane. There was the impression of a head on the pillow, as if someone had knelt beside the bed for a half-hour to sort out her troubles in silence.

My ghost was being pierced by a slow wondering sadness.

* * *

Henrikson my neighbour was not a man to be put off by slights and reprovings. The very next evening I was fixing lures to my sillock rod in the garden, and there he was humped over the wall, obsequious and smiling.

It had been a fine day, hadn't it? And now that the school was closed for the summer, would I not be thinking of going off to Edinburgh or Brighton or Majorca for a bit of a holiday? Well, that was fine, that I liked the island so much. To tell the truth, most of the folk in Quoylay were very glad to have a quiet respectable man like me in the school, after the wild goings-on that had been just before I arrived. . . .

I was sick and tired of this man, and yet I knew that now I was to hear, in a very poisoned and biased version, the story of Sandra McKillop the school-mistress and Johnny. Donald Barr, out of compassion for the dead, would never have told me. So I threw my arms companionably over the wall and I offered Henrikson my tobacco pouch and I said, 'What kind of goings-on would that be now, Mr Henrikson?'

Miss Sandra McKillop had come to the island school straight from the teachers' training college in Scotland two years before. (I am paraphrasing Henrikson's account, removing most of the barbs, trying to imagine a rose here and there.) She was a great change from the previous teacher, a finicky perjink old maid, and that for a start warmed the hearts of the islanders to her. But it was in the school itself that she scored her great success; the children of all ages took to her at once. She was a born teacher. Every day she held them in thrall from the first bell to the last. And even after school there was a dancing cluster of them round her all the way to her front door. The stupid ones and the ugly ones adored her especially, because she made them feel accepted. She enriched their days.

She was a good-looking girl. ('I won't deny that,' said Henrikson, 'as bonny a young woman as ever I saw.') More than one of the island bachelors hung about the school gate from time to time, hoping for a word with her. Nothing doing; she was pleasant and open with them and with everybody, but love did not enter her scheme of things; at least, not yet. She was a sociable girl, and was invited here and there among the farms for supper. She gave one or two talks to the Rural Institute, about her holidays abroad and life in her training college. She went to church every Sunday morning and sang in the choir, and afterwards taught in the Sunday School. But mostly she stayed at home. New bright curtains appeared in all the windows. She was especially fond of flowers; the little glass porch at the front of the house was full all the year round with flowering plants; the school garden, that first summer after she came, was a delight. All the bees in the island seemed to forage in those flowers.

How she first met John Germiston, nobody knows. It was almost certainly during one of those long walks she took in the summer evenings of her second year. John Germiston kept a croft on the side of the Ward Hill, a poor enough place with a couple of cows and a scatter of hens. Three years before he had courted a girl from the neighbouring island of Hellya. He had sailed across and got married in the kirk there and brought his bride home, a shy creature whose looks changed as swiftly as the summer loch. And there in his croft he installed her. And she would be seen from time to time feeding the hens at the end of the house, or hanging out washing, or standing at the road-end with her basket waiting for the grocery van. But she never became part of the community. With the coming of winter she was seen less and less – a wide-eyed face in the window, a figure against the skyline looking over the sound towards Hellya. The doctor began to call regularly once a week at the croft. John Germiston let it be known in the smithy that his wife was not keeping well.

There is a trouble in the islands that is called *morbus orcadensis*. It is a darkening of the mind, a progressive flawing and thickening of the clear lens of the spirit. It is said to be induced in sensitive people by the long black overhang of winter; the howl and sob of the wind over the moors that goes on sometimes for days on end; the perpetual rain that makes of tilth and pasture one indiscriminate bog; the unending gnaw of the sea at the crags.

Soon after the new year they took the stricken girl to a hospital in the south.

Of course everyone in Quoylay was sorry for John Germiston. It is a hard thing for a young handsome man to work a croft by himself. And yet these things happen from time to time. There are a few cheerful old men in the folds of the hills, or down by the shore, who have been widowers since their twenties.

Somewhere on the hill, one evening in spring, John Germiston met Sandra McKillop. They spoke together. He brought her to his house. She stood in the door and saw the desolation inside; the rusted pot, the torn curtains, the filthy hearth. The worm had bored deep into that rose.

From that first meeting everything proceeded swiftly and inevitably. No sooner was school over for the day than Miss McKillop shook the adoring children off and was away to the croft of Stanebreck on the hill with a basket of bannocks or a bundle of clean washing. She stayed late into the evening. Sometimes they would be seen wandering together along the edge of the crags, while far below the Atlantic fell unquietly among shelving rocks and hollow caves; on and on they walked into the sunset, while near and far the crofts watched and speculated.

Night after night, late, as April brightened into May, she would come home alone. A light would go on in the school-house kitchen. She would stand in the garden for a while among her hosts of blossoms. Then she would go in and lock the door. Her bedroom window was briefly illuminated. Then the whole house was dark.

'I suppose,' said Henrikson, 'nobody could have said a thing if it had stopped there. There was suspicion – well, what do you expect, a young woman visiting a married man night after night, and her a school-teacher with a position to keep up – but I don't suppose anybody could have done a thing about it.

'But in the end the two of them got bold. They got care-less. It wasn't enough for this hussy to visit her fancy-man in his croft – O no, the bold boy takes to sallying down two or three times a week to the school-house for his supper, if you please.

'Still nobody could make a move. A person is entitled to invite another person to the house for supper, even though on one occasion at least they don't draw the curtain and I can see from my kitchen their hands folded together in the middle of the table and all that laughter going on between them.

'Mr Reynolds, I considered it my duty to watch, yes, and to report to the proper quarters if necessary.

'One Friday evening Germiston arrives at the school-house at nine o'clock. A fine evening at the beginning of May it was. The light went on in the parlour. The curtain was drawn. After an hour or so the light goes on in her bedroom. "Ah ha," says I to myself, "I've missed their farewells tonight, I've missed all the kissing in the door." . . . But I was wrong,

Mr Reynolds. Something far worse was happening. At half past five in the morning I got up to stock the van, and I saw him going home over the hill, black against the rising sun. At *half past five* in the morning.

'That same day, being an elder, I went to the manse. Mr Barr refused to do a thing about it. "Miss McKillop is a member of my church. If she's in trouble of any sort she'll come to me," he said. "I will not act on slanderous rumours. There's more than one crofter on the hill at half past five in the morning." . . . There's your modern ministers for you. And I don't care if he is your friend, Mr Reynolds, I must speak my mind about this business.

'By now the whole island was a hive of rumour.

'Neither John Germiston nor Miss McKillop could stir without some eye being on them and some tongue speculating. And yet they went on meeting one another, quite open and shameless, as if they were the only living people in an island of ghosts. They would wander along the loch shore together, hand in hand, sometimes stopping to watch the swans or the eiders, not caring at all that a dozen croft windows were watching their lingerings and kissings. Then, arms about one another, they would turn across the fields in the direction of the school-house.

'Ay, but the dog of Stanebreck was a lonely dog till the sun got up, all that month of May.

'One Tuesday morning she arrived late for school, at a quarter past nine. She arrived with the mud of the hill plastered over her stockings, and half-dead with sleep. "Hurrah," cried the bairns congregated round the locked door of the school. They knew no better, the poor innocent things. They shouted half with delight and half with disappointment when she gave them the morning off, told them to come back in the afternoon. They were not to know what manner of thing had made their teacher so exhausted.

'Of course it was no longer possible to have a woman like her for the island teacher.

'I had written to this person and that. Enquiries were under way, discreetly, you know, so as not to cause any undue sensation. I think in the end pressure would have been put on her to resign. But as things turned out it wasn't necessary.

'One night they both disappeared. They vanished as if they had been swept clean off the face of the island. The school door remained locked all the next week. John Germiston's unmilked cow bellowed in its steep field. "Ah ha," said the men in the smithy, "so it's come to this, they've run away together. . . ."

'Ten days later a fishing boat drew up the two bodies a mile west of Hellya. Their arms were round each other. The fishermen had trouble separating the yellow hair from the black hair.'

Henrikson was having difficulty with his breathing; his voice dropped and quavered and choked so that I could hardly hear his last three words. 'They were naked,' he mouthed venomously.

Moths flickered between us. The sea boomed and hushed from the far side of the hill. In a nearby croft a light came on.

'And so,' said Henrikson, 'we decided that we didn't want a woman teacher after that. That's why you're here, Mr Reynolds.'

We drifted apart, Henrikson and I, to our separate doors. Eagerly that night I wished for the vanished passion to fill my rooms: the ghost, the chill, the scent of roses. But in the school-house was only a most terrible desolation.

On fine evenings that summer, when tide and light were suitable, Donald Barr and I would fish for sillocks and cuithes from the long sloping skerry under the crag. Or we would ask the loan of a crofter's boat, if the fish were scanty there, and row out with our lines into the bay.

The evening before the agricultural show was bright and calm. We waited in the bay with dripping oars for the sun to set behind the hill. We put our rods deep into the dazzle but not one cuithe responded. Presently the sun furled itself in a cloud, and it was as if a rose had burst open over the sea's unflawed mirror. Cuithe fishing is a sport that requires little skill. Time after time we hauled our rods in burgeoning with strenuous sea fruit, until the bottom of the dinghy was a floor of unquiet gulping silver. Then the dense undersea hordes moved away, and for twenty minutes, while the rose of sunset faded and the long bay gloomed, we caught nothing.

'It must have been about here,' I said to Donald Barr, 'that they were drowned.'

He said nothing. He had never discussed the affair with me, beyond that one mention of the girl's name at the manse gate.

A chill moved in from the west; breaths of night air flawed the dark sea mirror.

'The earth-bound soul refuses to acknowledge its death,' said Donald. 'It is desperately in love with the things of this world – possessions, fame, lust. How, once it has tasted them, can it ever exist without them? Death is a negation of all that wonder and delight. It will not enter the dark door of the grave. It lurks, a ghost, round the places where it fed on earthly joys. It spreads a coldness about the abodes of the living. The five senses pulse through it, but fadingly, because there is nothing for the appetite to feed on, only memories and shadows. Sooner or later the soul must enter the dark door. But no – it will not – for a year or for a decade or for a century it lingers about the place of its passion, a rose garden or a turret or a cross-roads. It will not acknowledge that all this loveliness of sea and sky and islands, and all the rare things that happen among them, are merely shadows of a greater reality. At last the starved soul is forced to accept it, for it finds itself utterly alone, surrounded as time goes by with strange new unloved objects and withered faces and skulls. Reluctantly it stoops under the dark lintel. All loves are forgotten then. It sets out on the quest for Love itself. For this it was created in the beginning.'

We hauled the dinghy high up the beach and secured her to a rock. A few mild summer stars glimmered. The sea was dark in the bay, under the shadow of the cliff, but the Atlantic horizon was still flushed a little with reluctant sunset, and all between was a vast slow heave of gray.

'I have a bottle of very good malt whisky in the school-house,' I said. 'I think a man could taste worse things after a long evening on the sea.'

It was then that I heard the harp-like shivering cries far out in the bay. The sea thins out the human voice, purges it of its earthiness, lends it a purity and poignancy.

'Wait for me,' cried the girl's voice. 'Where are you? You're swimming too fast.'

Donald Barr had heard the voices also. Night folded us increasingly in gloom and cold as we stood motionless under the sea-bank. He passed me his tobacco pouch. I struck a match. The flame trembled between us.

'This way,' shouted a firm strong happy voice (but attenuated on the harpstrings of the sea). 'I'm over here.'

The still bay shivered from end to end with a single glad cry. Then there was silence.

The minister and I turned. We climbed over loose stones and sandy hillocks to the road. We lashed our heavy basket of cuithes into the boot of Donald Barr's old Ford. Then we got in, one on each side, and he pressed the starter.

'Earth-bound souls enact their little dramas over and over again, but each time a little more weakly,' he said. 'The reality of death covers them increasingly with its good oblivion. You will be haunted for a month or two yet. But at last the roses will lose their scent.'

The car stopped in front of the dark school-house.

IAIN CRICHTON SMITH

AT THE PARTY

A GROUP OF US was gathered in a corner of the room singing Gaelic songs. It was midnight and we were in somebody's house though we weren't sure exactly whose, except that now and again a young couple who seemed to own the place – or at least to rent it – appeared in the doorway of what seemed to be an annexe off the main room and looked around with what might have been satisfaction or apathy or even tiredness. The man was tall, bearded and wore a Red Indian hair band, the girl fair and wearing a chain of white beads at the waist.

The room was crowded with people who had arrived in cars or taxis when the rumour of a party had gone round after the poetry reading was over. Many of them were young and most were students. Two or three messengers had been sent off to buy drink but none had returned, either because they had absconded with the money or because they couldn't find any drink, a reasonable enough assumption at that time of night. Coffee, dispensed in tumblers or mugs, was circulating.

None of the real lions of the poetry reading had stayed. One was so drunk that he had to be carefully disengaged from a lamp-post around which he had entwined himself like a monkey, emitting fragmentary lines of his own verse. Another had gone off with a serious-faced girl in glasses who had spent most of her time taking down notes in a small red notebook during the proceedings. Yet another had disappeared with a dull man who worked in advertising and who had come along to find out how poetry could be used in the selling of fruit. 'My boss,' he said, 'says that before you can sell tomatoes you must think of them as women.' He repeated this statement a lot and did not realise that the laughter it evoked was not a tribute to its perception.

I sat among the Gaelic singers in a corner, a Finnish girl beside me. She had very fair fine hair, very fair fine eyelashes and blue clever eyes. I asked her about Finland and though she was unwilling to sing Finnish songs she told me about the sparse literature of the country in attractive broken English. She said there were quite a lot of Finnish girls and housewives in the city and that they met now and again in clubs. I stroked her hair and she regarded me with a cool amused gaze. Her husband apparently was a lecturer in the Scandinavian languages and she had met him at a skiing resort. He had gazed down at her solicitously while she lay spreadeagled in the snow. 'Very Victorian,' she said, 'just like God.' 'What do you think of our Gaelic songs?' I asked. She smiled but didn't answer. It occurred to me that at midnight all women are loveable.

The group around me were singing every Gaelic song they had ever heard. They sang songs about exile, about love, about war, about shepherds on distant islands. They sang with the obsessive fidelity and love of the exile. They sang with eyes closed, swaying with longing, as if they were snakes entranced by the scent and blossom of Eden. They were all young except for one man who wore a waistcoat and watch and chain and was bald. No one knew where he had come from – he didn't look like a poetry lover – and his stiff hat was clamped straight over his forehead. His hands rested gently on his stomach and he sang each song carefully and comfortably as if he were sitting at dinner. No one knew what to make of him since he didn't say anything. Now and again he would close his small eyes and then open them and look shyly and quickly around him. Most of the time he looked bovine and had an air of enigmatic satisfaction. Sometimes a song was started by someone who didn't know the words and it had to be completed by the others in their obsessed ring.

I leaned back in my corner, my head on the shoulder of the Finnish girl who was looking across towards a young bearded fellow who was strumming a guitar by himself in the opposite corner. Her face was cool and untroubled. I imagined that I was in love with her; I felt the air of sunny mornings and lemons. I said to her: 'You are so relaxed. Are you always as relaxed as this?' She told me that her child wrote poetry with large coloured crayons and that it was very good poetry too. 'In English, of course,' she said, smiling. I believed her. I believed that her child was a cool Finnish genius with fair hair and classic features. I didn't know why she was there. She reminded me of someone from the Sunday supplements. 'Do they have Sunday supplements in Finland?' I asked. She smiled. I thought of Grimm, Hans Andersen, girls in red coats meeting bowing wolves in birch woods. 'Do you write yourself?' I asked. 'No,' she said, 'I play the piano – badly.'

At that moment there was a ragged cheer such as a dispirited army seeing a glint of reinforcements might give. The drink had arrived though there wasn't much of it. We were doled out a little whisky each, holding out our mugs like refugees in some eastern country. The singing stopped for a moment and then began again. They were singing a song called *The White Swan* which is about the First World War. I drank some of the whisky and joined in. A young girl waved her empty glass like a conductor's baton and smiled at me.

And over her head I saw Miriam whom I had forgotten was there. She was standing talking to a tall bearded flat-faced poet who wore a slightly stained violet tie and a lumber jacket. He was a very bad poet though large and handsome and talkative. Miriam was wearing black which contrasted very strongly with her white miniature face and blonde hair. I tried to make out what she was saying by lip-reading but I couldn't, so I got to my feet and stumbled over to listen. They were talking about the Concept of Alienation. I listened owlishly and amusedly. Brecht and the Concept of Alienation: It's a Braw Brecht Munelicht Nicht the Nicht. He spoke freely and as if he knew a great deal about the Concept of Alienation which presumably he had made some study of. He was a very serious person and much less preferable to X, another poet who lived by quick-wittedness rather than by scholarship. Sometimes Miriam laughed delightedly, sometimes she looked grave and question-ing like a child. I wondered how long she would stay at the party.

I had met her first in a library quite by accident when she was looking for a book on the American poet Edwin Arlington Robinson and I had been able to help her as he is one of my own favourite poets. I was very lonely at that time and we began to go about together, having dinner in hotels, going to pubs though she didn't drink much. In fact she always sipped a tomato juice laced (if that is the right word) with Worcester sauce, or it may have been the other way round. Once we were invited late at night to the house of an actor who had tried to make love to her while his wife was making coffee. She had been very angry with him and had hit him over the head with a large book by George Steiner. Another time we went to visit an alcoholic woman painter who had managed to sell me a painting called Exhalations which I had barely succeeded in dragging down four flights of stairs to a taxi.

We talked a lot about literature in which I was rapidly losing interest, much preferring solidly constructed detective stories of the classical type, such as those by S. S. Van Dine. She still retained the pristine hunger for books which I had long lost. She would sit, composed and small, in the corner of a lounge bar while I made a vicious random attack on the supposedly good writing of Faulkner. She was very sensitive and sent a lot of money to Irish people. Once she had a refugee from Ireland in her flat, a ginger-haired slatternly woman who brought in her wake a husband who played the Irish bagpipes from the hip and who was eventually put out of the house by the landlady for practising on them at three in the morning after what he called a 'wet'. When that pair had left she had got hold of an Indian and his wife. Together they wore lots of beads and talked in the most beautiful Oxford accents. She was always helping 'lame ducks' and reminded me of Joan of Arc except that she was much more literate. There was some trace of Americanism in her descent which I thought accounted for her combination of innocence and experience.

I admired her a lot. I admired her sensitivity, her feeling for other people. I admired the simple, almost elegant way in which she lived. She had a very fine delicate wristwatch which recalled her best qualities – unhurried competence and fine outer appearance. I knew that she had had an unhappy upbringing. Her father had died of TB when she was very young – he had been a lecturer somewhere – and her mother of some other incurable disease. She had lots of nieces and nephews for whom she was always buying toys and though she didn't like mess of any kind she was always dressing and undressing them and taking them to the bathroom and feeding them. They would sit on her lap and pull at her necklace of brown beads. Once I was invited to her brother-in-law's house. He was a professor who was deeply involved in linguistics and whose silences were prolonged as if his researches had convinced him that language is very dangerous and should be tampered with as little as possible. She and her sister (one of three she had) kept up a bitter private running battle all the time we were there, needling each other about incidents that went back to their childhood days. I wondered whether the professor was making notes. A lot of the time, however, he retired to a large sunny room which overlooked a garden full of red and blue flowers. Perhaps he was studying their language or the language of the birds.

However my admiration for her had evaporated when one night after we had been drinking and I had taken her home in a taxi she had savagely turned on me and said as I was making some attempt to kiss her: 'You are the most selfish bugger I have ever met. You really are. Why are you taking me out? You think I'll go to bed with you. You don't care about anyone in the world except yourself. You laughed at that painter though she is on the verge of suicide. What's wrong with her painting anyway? I think it's quite good. You think I'll go to bed with you. You laughed at my brother-in-law because you think he's a pedagogue. It never occurs to you that there are people who genuinely know so much that they find it difficult to say anything at all. You think you can buy me with your money. I don't give a bugger about you. I think you're a bad artist anyway. You laughed at the photographs I showed you. You're always laughing at things, aren't you? You can't even use a tape recorder properly.' That gibe came from an incident when I was recording a Gaelic song for her, I myself doing the singing. 'Your bloody Highlands,' she said. 'All your bloody mist and your bloody principles. No wonder you've never painted anything worth a damn.' The taxi stopped. I tried to help her out but she pushed my hand away. Just as she stood on the road she added, 'And that coat you're wearing, it's bloody mediaeval.' I watched her trying to fit the key in the lock as the taxi sizzled along the blue rainy street. There were lamp-posts every few yards all down the long street brooding over the stone below them. Haloes . . . separate haloes. We entered the circles and bracelets of light. An Indian restaurant flashed by, then a huge warehouse. There was a newspaper headquarters, a shop with naked tailors' dummies and a Chinese restaurant. A drunk pawed at the air with his hands.

She knew I was there all right but she wouldn't speak to me. I went back to my corner from which the Finnish girl had disappeared perhaps to the lavatory. I hadn't known how to speak to her: instead of talking to her I had in fact been cross-examining her. On the fringe of the crowd who were by now licking the bottoms of their mugs, since the whisky had all gone, a young girl was watching me. I went across to her. I said Hello and we sat down on the floor. She told me that she had been studying literature but was now studying physics. She wasn't pretty but she was young and she had managed somehow or other to get hold of some coffee. I told her a joke about a Pakistani who had been taught to play darts. I was ready to like her since my Finnish girl had disappeared. I asked her about university and she said that she preferred physics to literature though she wasn't very practical. She said that she wrote some poetry but didn't have any with her and I silently thanked God. The last poetry book I had read I couldn't make head nor tail of: it seemed to be designed to be read either from the bottom upwards or diagonally or both simultaneously. I thought that if the poet who had climbed the lamp-post had fallen down we might have had our first concrete poet. I was astonished at the extraordinary number of charlatans in art whom I now seemed to see as if in a clear light infesting the room and other rooms all over the world.

The Gaelic singers surrounded us singing in a last fervent burst as if they sensed that the party was nearly over. The young girl looked at them tolerantly and remotely. But after all, I thought angrily, they were my people, weren't they? They had come from my world, a broken world, but a world which still provided the cohesion of song, a tradition. The other people watched, almost with envy. We were the only cohesive group there. She asked me to translate a verse and I did so:

> It is a pity that you and I were not where I would
> wish to be, in locked room with iron gates, for
> the six days of the week for seven, eight years,
> the keys lost and a blind man looking for them.

It was, according to the flowery clock on the mantelpiece, one o'clock in the morning, and I saw the poet and Miriam leaving. He put on her black cloak for her and for a brief moment she looked back at me, Napoleonic, self-possessed, frightened. The two of them had probably talked their alienation out, and now perhaps going out into the night she might feel sufficiently like Mother Courage (or the German equivalent). 'You bloody bad poet,' I thought, 'why do people never see through you?' I watched them go. I nearly went after her but I couldn't get out of the singing group. I imagined her and him in their taxi returning perhaps to her flat. I imagined the taxi going past the desolate lamp-posts. The Concept of Alienation. Well, books and plays might help, I supposed. I thought of the taxi as a hearse ticking over. Why were taxis always black, or was that just in Scotland? I imagined her leafing through her pictures of the dead and the doomed, the tubercular and the moustached, all brown with age.

The singing was growing louder. I was with my own people. The song they were singing was about an exile in the city who wished to be home. He remembered the hills, the lochs, the neighbours, the songs. I thought of the last time I had been home. It had rained all the time and I had spent a whole week reading *Reader's Digest* and books by Agatha Christie. Sometimes I had played cards with a spotty cousin. I had seen between showers the mangled body of a rabbit at the side of a road: it had been run over by a car and its guts hung out. One day I had tried to find some fool's gold on the beach but I didn't find any. I remembered the blue and white waves, the astounding Atlantic.

I left the circle. Who was I looking for? I tried to find the Finnish girl but she seemed to have gone, for the ladies' lavatory (quaintly captioned Girls in a primary tangle of colours) was open and vacant. The guitar player had also gone. I went into the darkness. As I was standing there trying to find my bearings a voice came from inside the room. 'When shall we see you again?' Blinded, I turned into the light, not recognising the voice. I went back into the room. It was the student who had changed from literature to physics and I was disappointed: I was hoping it would have been the Finnish girl. I looked at her for a long time and then said that I wasn't in the city very often. I went back into the darkness again. From the next garden a dog, probably a large one, began to bark excitedly. It sounded as if he was tearing at the wall to try and get at me. I went out into the street feeling my way as I had once done across a midnight field on the island. The singing seemed to have stopped and everyone,

I supposed, was preparing to leave. I started to walk down the street towards the centre of the city where my hotel was. I supposed the stony-faced porter would come to the door again this time. I would have preferred someone more happy-looking, especially at three in the morning.

ALASDAIR GRAY

THE CRANK
THAT MADE THE
REVOLUTION

NOWADAYS CESSNOCK IS a heavily built-upon part of industrial Glasgow, but two hundred and seventy-three years ago you would have seen something very different. You would have seen a swamp with a duck-pond in the middle and a few wretched hovels round the edge. The inmates of these hovels earned a living by knitting caps and mufflers for the inhabitants of Glasgow who, even then, wore almost nothing else. The money got from this back-breaking industry was pitifully inadequate. Old Cessnock was neither beautiful nor healthy. The only folk living there were too old or twisted by rheumatism to move out. Yet this dismal and uninteresting hamlet saw the beginning of that movement which historians call The Industrial Revolution; for here, in seventeen hundred and seven, was born Vague McMenamy, inventor of the crankshaft which made the Revolution possible.

There are no records to suggest that Vague McMenamy had parents. From his earliest days he seems to have lived with his Granny upon a diet of duck-eggs and the proceeds of the old lady's knitting. A German biographer has suggested that McMenamy's first name (Vague) was a nickname. The idea, of course, is laughable. No harder-headed, clearer-sighted individual than McMenamy ever existed, as his crankshaft proves. The learned Herr Professor is plainly ignorant of the fact that Vague is the Gaelic for Alexander. Yet it must be confessed that Vague was an introvert. While other boys were chasing the lassies or stoning each other he would stand for long hours on the edge of the duck-pond wondering how to improve his Granny's ducks.

Now, considered mechanically, a duck is not an efficient machine, for it has been designed to perform three wholly different and contradictory tasks, and consequently it does none of them outstandingly well. It flies, but not as expertly as the swallow, vulture or aeroplane. It swims, but not like a porpoise. It walks about, but not like you or me, for its legs are too short. Imagine a household appliance devised to shampoo carpets, mash potatoes and darn holes in socks whenever it feels like it. A duck is in a similar situation, and this made ducks offensive to McMenamy's dourly practical mind. He thought that since ducks spend most of their days in water they should be made to do it efficiently. With the aid of a friendly carpenter he made a boat-shaped container into which a duck was inserted. There was a hole at one end through which the head stuck out, allowing the animal to breathe, see and even eat; nonetheless it protested against the confinement by struggling to get out and in doing so its wings and legs drove the cranks which conveyed motion to a paddle-wheel on each side. On its maiden voyage the duck zig-zagged around the pond at a speed of thirty knots, which was three times faster than the maximum speed which the boats and ducks of the day had yet attained. McMenamy had converted a havering all-rounder into an efficient specialist. He was not yet thirteen years of age.

He did not stop there. If this crankshaft allowed one duck to drive a vessel three times faster than normal, how much faster would two, three or ten ducks drive it? McMenamy decided to carry the experiment as far as he could take it. He constructed a craft to be driven by every one of his Granny's seventeen ducks. It differed from the first vessel in other ways.

The first had been a conventional boat shape propelled by paddles and constructed from wood. The second was cigar-shaped with a screw propeller at the rear, and McMenamy did not order it from the carpenter, but from the blacksmith. It was made of sheet iron. Without the seventeen heads and necks sticking up through holes in the hull one would have mistaken it for a modern submarine. This is a fact worth pondering. A hundred years elapsed before The Charlotte Dundas, the world's first paddle steamer, clanked along the Forth and Clyde canal from Bowling. Fifty years after that the first ironclad screw-driven warship fired its first shot in the American Civil War. In two years the imagination of a humble cottage lad had covered ground which the world's foremost engineers took two generations to traverse in the following century. Vague was fifteen years old when he launched his second vessel. Quacking hysterically, it crossed the pond with such velocity that it struck the opposite bank at the moment of departure from the near one. Had it struck soil it would have embedded itself. Unluckily, it hit the root of a tree, rebounded to the centre of the pond, overturned and sank. Every single duck was drowned.

In terms of human achievement, McMenamy's duckboat ranks with Leonardo Da Vinci's helicopter which was designed four hundred years before the engine which could have made it fly. Economically it was disastrous. Deprived of her ducks, McMenamy's Granny was compelled to knit faster than ever. She sat in her rocking-chair, knitting and rocking and rocking and knitting and McMenamy sat opposite, brooding upon what he could do to help. He noticed that the muscular energy his Granny used to handle the needles was no greater than the energy she used to rock the chair. His Granny, in fact, was two sources of energy, one above the waist and one below, and only the upper source brought

317

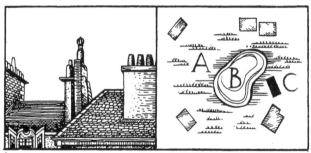

Left: Modern Cessnock shortly after implementation of the smoke abatement act.
Right: Old Cessnock from General Roy's ordnance survey of 1739. Fig. A
represents the swamp, B the duckpond, C the McMenamy hovel.

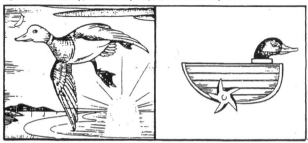

Left: Unimproved duck, after the watercolour by Peter Scott.
Right: McMenamy's Improved Duck.

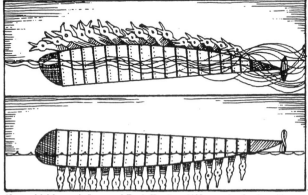

Above: McMenamy's Improved Duck Tandem .0005 seconds after launching.
Below: McMenamy's Improved Duck Tandem .05 seconds after launching. (The
ducks, though not yet drowned, have been killed by the shock.)

318

in money. If the power of her *legs and feet* could be channelled into the knitting she would work twice as fast, and his crankshaft made this possible. And so McMenamy built the world's first knitting frame, later nicknamed 'McMenamy's Knitting Granny'. Two needles, each a yard long, were slung from the kitchen ceiling so that the tips crossed at the correct angle. The motion was conveyed through crankshafts hinged to the rockers of a cast-iron rocking-chair mounted on rails below. McMenamy's Granny, furiously rocking it, had nothing to do with her hands but steer the woollen coils through the intricacies of purl and plain. When the McMenamys came to display their stock of caps and mufflers on a barrow in Glasgow's Barrowland that year, the strongest knitters in the West of Scotland, brawny big-muscled men of thirty and thirty-five, were astonished to see that old Mrs McMenamy had manufactured twice as much as they had.

Vague, however, was modest enough to know that his appliance was improvable. The power generated by a rocking-chair is limited, for it swings through a very flattened arc. His second knitting frame was powered by a see-saw. His Granny was installed on one end with the needles mounted in front of her. Hitherto, Vague had avoided operating his inventions himself, but now he courageously vaulted onto the other end and set the mighty beam swinging up and down, up and down, with a velocity enabling his Granny to turn out no less than eight hundred and ninety caps and mufflers a week. At the next Glasgow Fair she brought to market as much produce as the other knitters put together, and was able to sell at half the normal price and still make a handsome profit. The other inhabitants of Cessnock were unable to sell their goods at all. With the desperation of starving men, they set fire to the McMenamy cottage and the machinery inside it. Vague and his Granny were forced to flee across the swamp, leaving their hard earned gold to melt among the flames. They fled to the Burgh of Paisley, and placed themselves under the protection of the Provost, and from that moment their troubles were at an end.

Engraving by Shanks in Glasgow People's Palace Local History Museum showing decadence of that art before Bewick's advent. Nobody knows if it portrays Provost Coats or McMenamy's Granny.

In 1727 Paisley was fortunate in having, as Provost, an unusually enlightened philanthropist, Sir Hector Coats. (No relation to the famous thread manufacturers of the following century.) He was moved by McMenamy's story and impressed by his dedication. He arranged for Vague to superintend the construction of a large knitting mill containing no less than twenty beam-balance knitting frames. Not only that, he employed Vague and his Granny to work one of them. For the next ten years Vague spent fourteen hours a day, six days a week, swinging up and down on the opposite end of the beam from the woman who had nourished and inspired him. It is unfortunate that he had no time to devote to scientific invention, but his only holidays were on a Sunday and Sir Hector was a good Christian who took stern measures against workmen who broke the Sabbath. At the age of thirty Vague McMenamy, overcome by vertigo, fell off the see-saw never to rise again. Strangely enough his Granny survived him by twenty-two years, toiling to the last at the machine which had been named after her. Her early days in the rocking-chair had no doubt prepared her for just such an end, but she must have been a remarkable old lady.

Thirty is not an advanced age and Vague's achievement was crowded into seven years between the ages of twelve and nineteen. In that time he invented the paddle boat and the ironclad, dealt a deathblow to the cottage knitting industry, and laid the foundations of the Scottish Textile Trade. When Arkwright, Cartwright, Wainright and Watt completed their own machines, McMenamy's crankshaft was in every one of them. Truly, he was the crank that made the Revolution possible.

McMenamy's tombstone, Paisley High Kirk, engraved for the 1861 edition of Samuel Smiles's "Self Help". (This corner of the graveyard was flattened to make way for a new road in 1911.)

WILLIAM McILVANNEY

AT THE BAR

THE PUB WAS QUIET. When the big man with the ill-fitting suit came in, the barman noticed him more than he normally would have done. The suit was slightly out of fashion yet looked quite new and it was too big for him. He could have come back to it after a long illness. Yet it wasn't that either. Whatever had happened to him had tightened him but not diminished him. The charcoal grey cloth sat on him loosely but that looked like the suit's problem. You wouldn't have fancied whoever the suit might fit to come against the man who wore it.

He came up to the bar and seemed uncertain about what to order. He looked along the gantry with a bemused innocence, like a small boy in a sweet-shop.

'Sir?' the barman said.

The big man sighed and shook his head and took his time. His face looked as if it had just come off a whetstone. The cheekbones were sharp, the mouth was taut. The eyes were preoccupied with their own thoughts. His pallor suggested a plant kept out of the light. Prison, the barman thought.

'Uh-huh,' the big man said. 'Fine day. I'll have.' It seemed a momentous choice. 'A pint of heavy.'

He watched the barman pull it. Paying, he took a small wad of singles from his pocket and fingered them deliberately. He studied his change carefully. Then he retreated inside himself.

Making sure the patch of bar in front of him was clean, he spread his *Daily Record* on it and started to read, the sports pages first. His beer seemed to be for moistening his lips.

Before turning back to the television, the barman checked the pub in his quick but careful way. The afternoon was boringly in place. Old Dave and Sal were over to his left, beside the Space Invader. As usual, they were staring past each other. Dave was nursing half an inch of beer and Sal had only the lemon left from her gin and tonic, her thin lips working against each other endlessly, crocheting silence. That should be them till they went home for their tea. At the other end of the bar, Barney, the retired schoolteacher, was doing *The Times* crossword. Did he ever finish it? In the light from the window his half-pint looked as stale as cold tea.

The only other person in the pub was someone the barman didn't like. He had started to come in lately. Denim-dressed, he looked nasty-hard, a broad pitted face framed in long black hair. He was a fidgety drinker, one of those who keep looking over both shoulders as if they know somebody must be trying to take a liberty and they're determined to catch him at it. Just now, standing at the bar, he kept glancing along at the big man and seemed annoyed to get no reaction. His eyes were a demonstration looking for a place to happen. He took his pint like a penance.

The television was showing some kind of afternoon chat-show, two men talking who made the pub seem interesting. Each question sounded boring until you heard the answer and that made you want another question very quick. The barman was relieved to see Old Dave come towards the bar as if he was walking across America. It would be good if he made it before he died.

'Yes, Dave,' the barman said to encourage his progress. 'Another drink? What is this? Your anniversary?'

The barman noticed the big man had the paper open at page three. He knew what the man was seeing, having studied her this morning, a dark-haired girl called Minette with breasts like two separate states. But the big man wasn't looking at her so much as he was reading her, like a long novel. Then he flicked over to the front page, glanced, sipped his beer till it was an inch down the glass and went to the lavatory.

'Same again,' Dave said, having arrived. 'Tae hell wi' it. Ye're only young once.'

The barman laughed and turned his back on him. He had to cut more lemon. He had to find one of the lemons the pub had started getting in specially for Sal. After brief puzzlement, he did. He cut it carefully. He filled out gin, found ice, added the lemon. He turned back, put the drink on the counter, pulled a pint. As he laid the pint beside the gin and opened the tonic, pouring it, he noticed something in among the activity that bothered him. He suddenly realised what it was. The big man's pint-dish held nothing but traces of froth.

The barman was about to speak to the hard-faced man in denim when the big man walked back from the lavatory to the bar. His arrival froze the barman. The big man made to touch his paper, paused. He looked at his empty pint.

'Excuse me,' he said to the barman. 'Ah had a pint there.'

The moment crackled like an electrical storm. Even Old Dave got the message. His purse hung in his hand. He stared at the counter. The barman was wincing.

'That's right,' the man in denim said. 'Ye had a pint. But Ah drank it.'

The silence prolonged itself like an empty street with a man at either end of it. The barman knew that nobody else could interfere.

'Sorry?' the big man said.

'Ye had a pint, right enough. But Ah felt like it. So Ah drank it. That's the dinky-dory.'

So that was the story. The big man stared and lowered his eyes, looked up and smiled. It wasn't convincing. Nonchalant surrender never is. But he was doing his best to make it look as if it was.

'Oh, look,' he said. 'What does it matter? Ah can afford another one. Forget it.'

The barman was grateful but contemptuous. He didn't want trouble but he wouldn't have liked to go to sleep in the big man's head. And when the big man spoke again, he could hardly believe it.

'Look. If you need a drink, let me buy you another one. Come on. Give the man a pint of heavy.'

The barman felt as if he was pouring out the big man's blood but he did it. It was his job to keep the peace. The man in denim lifted the pint, winked at the barman.

'Cheers,' he said to the big man, smiling at him. 'Your good health. You obviously value it.'

He hadn't managed his first mouthful before the side of the big man's clenched right hand had hit the base of the glass like a demolition-ball. There was a splintered scream among the shards of exploding glass and the volleying beer.

Not unused to fast violence, the barman was stunned. The big man picked up his paper. He laid the price of a pint on the counter and nodded to the barman.

'If he's lookin' for me,' he said, 'the name's Rafferty. Cheerio. Nice shop you run.'

He went out. Lifting a dish-towel, the barman hurried round the counter and gave it to the man in denim. While he held his face together with it and the cloth saturated instantly with blood and he kept moaning, the barman found his first coherent reaction to the situation.

'You're barred,' he said.

BERNARD MacLAVERTY

THE CLINIC

IT WAS STILL DARK. He was *never* up at this time, except occasionally to catch a dawn flight. He picked up his sample, his papers and the yellow card. The bottle was warm in his hand. He was about to go out the door when he remembered. Something to read, something to pass the time. In the room with the book shelf he clicked on the light. The clock on the mantelpiece told him he was running late. He grabbed a small hardback collection of Chekhov's short stories and ran.

It was mid-November. People's Moscow-white faces told how cold it was. Breath was visible on the air. The traffic was ten times worse than he was used to. He turned off into the hospital and got lost a couple of times before he saw the Diabetic Clinic sign. He parked ages away and half hurried, half ran back. He was breathless going through the door only to find that the place was upstairs. He was about eight minutes late and apologised. The receptionist shrugged and smiled, as if to say – think nothing of it. That made him mad too. He had been so uptight trying to get there on time and now, it seemed, it didn't matter very much. If there was one thing worse than worrying, it was wasted worrying. He was asked to take a seat.

The waiting room was half full even though it was only twenty to nine. There was a row of empty seats backing onto the window. He sat down, glad not to be close enough to anyone to have to start a conversation. A Muslim woman in a black hejab talked to her mother who was similarly dressed. The language was incomprehensible to him but he was curious to know what they were talking about.

All the men's magazines were about golf or cars. He picked up *Vogue* and flicked through it. Beautiful half-naked sophisticated women clattering with jewellery. But he couldn't concentrate to read any of the text.

His letter lay face up on the chair beside him.

Your family doctor has referred you to the Diabetic Clinic to see if you are diabetic. To find this out we will need to perform a glucose tolerance test.

He remembered a crazy guy at school who had diabetes – who went into comas. But school was fifty years ago. Since being given his appointment he'd read up even more frightening stuff about your eyesight and how you could lose it. And your extremities – how in some cases they could go gangrenous and have to be lopped off.

His yellow outpatient card said *Please bring this card with you when you next attend.*

A door at the far end of the waiting room opened and screeched closed. It took about thirty or forty seconds to close, with its irritating, long, dry squeak. There was a damping device on the mechanism to make it close more slowly. But no sooner had it closed fully and the noise stopped than somebody else came through it and began the whole process over again. 'Collective responsibility is not being taken,' he wanted to yell. If he had diabetes and had to come back to this God-forsaken place then next time he'd bring an oil can. Recently in the newspaper he'd read that grumpy old men were more liable to heart attacks than old men who were not grumpy. He tried to calm down. To degrump.

*   *   *

He took out his Chekhov and looked at the list of contents. Something short. He did a quick sum, subtracting the page number from the following page number after each story. It was an old copy and the cheap paper had turned the colour of toast at the edges. The Vanguard Library edition – translated by the wonderful Constance Garnett. A nurse walked in and called people by their first names. She came to him.

'Hi, my name is Phil,' she said, 'and that's Myna at reception.' She explained what was going to happen. He had to drink a whole bottle of Lucozade and then, over the next couple of hours, every half hour in fact, he had to give both blood and urine samples. He nodded. He understood. He had grey hair, he was overweight, but he understood.

She took him into the corridor and sat him down in what looked like a wheelchair.

'Did you have any breakfast?' she said. 'A cuppa tea maybe? Some toast?'

'No. The leaflet said to come fasting.'

'Not everybody pays attention to that.'

'What a waste of everybody's time. Do people actually do that?'

'You'd be surprised,' she said.

It turned out not to be a wheelchair but a weighing machine. She calculated something against a chart on the wall.

'Did you bring a sample?'

'Yes.' He rummaged in his pocket and produced the bottle. It had returned to room temperature. *Spring water with a hint of Apple*. He handed it over and the nurse put a label on it.

'It might be a little flavoured,' he said.

'I'm not going to drink it.' She whisked it away into another room.

When he was back in his seat by the window she brought him Lucozade, a plastic glass and four lozenge-shaped paper tubs. She stuck a white label with a bar-code on each and wrote a time on the rim with her biro. He wanted to make terrible jokes about giving urine samples and her name. Phil. Phil these please. P for Phil. But he realised everybody must do this. He said, 'I hope these are not for blood.'

She laughed. She had a nice face – in her early forties.

'All at once now,' she said. He poured the Lucozade into the plastic glass and drank it. Refilled it, drank it. Halfway down he had to stop, his swallow refused to work against the sweet bubbles. Eventually he finished everything and childishly expected praise.

When she left him he tried to concentrate on his book. A story called 'The Beauties' looked feasible. Subtract one hundred and seventy-three from one hundred and eighty-three. It'd be hard with all this toing and froing – all the stabbing and pissing. All the people around him talking. He didn't think he'd read it before. That had happened several times with Turgenev – after fifty pages he'd said, 'I've read this before.' It went down so easily. Nobody gagged on Turgenev.

But Chekhov is Chekhov. He draws you in. He writes as if the thing is happening in front of your eyes. An unnamed boy of sixteen, maybe Chekhov himself, and his grandfather in a chaise are travelling through the summer heat and dust of the countryside to Rostov-on-the-Don. They stop to feed their horses at a rich Armenian's and the grandfather talks endlessly to the owner about farms and feedstuffs and manure. The place is described in minute detail down to the floors painted with yellow ochre and the flies . . . and more flies. Then tea is brought in by a barefoot girl of sixteen wearing a white kerchief and when she turns from the sideboard to hand the boy his cup she has the most wonderful face he has ever seen. He feels a wind blow across his soul.

'The Beauties' had captured him. He knew exactly what Chekhov was talking about. He was there in that room experiencing the same things.

At precisely a minute before a quarter to the hour he lifted one of his cardboard pee pots and went to the technician's laboratory. The technician was a woman with long brown hair who smiled at him. She wore a white coat. Her breast pocket had several biro ink lines descending into it. She explained what she was about to do.

'You can choose to have it done on four fingers. Or you can have it done on one finger four times. That's the choice. Four sore fingers or one very sore finger?'

He chose his middle finger and presented it – almost like an obscene gesture. He looked away, anticipating a scalpel or dagger. There was a winter tree outside. Without leaves a crow's nest was visible. There was a click and the stab was amazingly tiny – like the smallest rose thorn in the world. He hardly felt anything. The technician squeezed his finger and harvested his drop of blood into a capillary tube the size of a toothpick. When she'd finished she nodded at his cardboard container. He lifted it and sought out the lavatory.

The sign on the door indicated both men and women. Inside there were adjacent cubicles and the mother of the woman in the black hejab was coming out of the ladies' bearing her cardboard pot before her like an offering. He smiled and opened the outer door for her.

Inside the men's lavatory was a poster about 'impotence'. A man sitting on a park bench with his head in his hands. How did he discover his condition in a public park? *Talk to your doctor*, said the words.

Conjuring up a sample so soon after the one in the house took a long time. But eventually he succeeded and left it in the laboratory. The technician was working near the window. Her long hair was down her back almost to her waist.

'There you are,' he said.

'Thank you.'

The nurse brought him a plastic jug of tap water and ice.

'You might be able to give blood every time,' she said, 'but for the other you need to keep drinking this.'

He swirled the jug and poured himself some. It sounded hollow compared to ice against glass. Sipping he tried to return to the Chekhov. A distant radio was far enough away to be indistinct but it was still distracting. At the moment the only other sound was of magazine pages being turned – the kind of magazines which were looked at rather than read – *Hello!* and *OK*. Flick, flick, flick. The nurse, Phil, came in and announced a name.

'Andrew? Andrew Elliot?'

A man stood and swaggered forward responding as if he had just been chosen for a Hollywood audition. In a music-hall kind of American drawl he said, 'You caalled for *me*, lady?'

Everybody in the waiting room laughed.

He tried to return to the mood of that hot, dusty afternoon in Rostov-on-the-Don but the smile was still on his face. He couldn't concentrate.

He was at that age when things were starting to go wrong. Knee joints were beginning to scringe. Putting on socks had become a burden. Pains where there shouldn't be pains. Breathlessness. Occasional dizziness.

An immensely fat woman came in. All her weight seemed to be below her waist. Her thighs and lower belly bulged as if she'd left her bedding in her tights. Sheets, pillows, duvets.

The lot. After her, an old couple came through the doors, panting after the stairs. They sank onto chairs, incapable of speech, and sat there mouth breathing. They both had skin the colour of putty.

When he began to read again he found it awkward to turn the page because, like many people in the waiting room he had a piece of lint clenched between his chosen finger and his thumb.

The boy in 'The Beauties' when confronted with the girl in the white kerchief feels himself utterly inferior. Sunburned, dusty and only a child. But that does not stop him adoring her and having adored her his reaction is one of – sadness. Where does such perfection fit into the world? He hears the thud of her bare feet on the board floor, she disappears into a grimy outhouse which is full of the smell of mutton and angry argument. The more he watches her going about her tasks the more painful becomes his inexplicable sadness.

The first part of the story ends and Chekhov switches to another, similar incident when he has become a student. Maybe a medical student. This time he is travelling by train.

In the waiting room of the Diabetic Clinic the talk was of medical stuff.

'I have an irregular heartbeat . . .'

'Oh God help ye . . .'

'I'm just trying to keep the weight down . . .'

'Does the stick help?'

'It helps the balance . . .'

This is all in front of me, he thought.

But despite his age he felt good, felt ridiculously proud he had outlived his father who had died at the early age of forty-five. He didn't have a problem that would drive him to sit on a park bench with his head in his hands. So he felt good about that. He looked up at the clock above the posters. He picked up his pee pot and headed for the laboratory again.

This time when he looked away from the little machine which drew his blood he saw a crow settling in the branches of the tree outside. The thinnest of pinpricks and again she milked the blood from his finger into her glass capillary. This stranger was holding his hand. Her perfume radiated into his space – not perfume, but soap – maybe the smell of her shampoo. Camomile, maybe. She clipped her capillary to a little sloped rack. There were two of them now, like the double red line he'd had to rule beneath the title of his essays at school. He provided another urine sample.

When he sat down again in the waiting room he finished his jug of water and asked for another. He returned to his book. And as he read, the room gradually disappeared. Somewhere in southern Russia a train stopped at a small station on a May evening. The sun was setting and the station buildings threw long shadows. The student gets off to stretch his legs. He sees the stationmaster's daughter. She, too, is utterly captivating. As she stands talking to an old lady the youth remembers the Armenian's daughter, the girl with the white kerchief, and the sadness it brought him. Again he experiences the whoosh of feeling and tries to analyse it but cannot. Not only was the student, Chekhov, watching this exquisite woman, she was being watched by almost all the men on the platform, including a ginger telegraphist with a flat opaque face sitting by his apparatus in the station window. What chance for someone like him? The stationmaster's daughter wouldn't look at him twice.

He was struck yet again by the power of the word. Here he was – about to be told he had difficult changes to make to his life and yet by reading words on a page, pictures of Russia a hundred years ago come into his head. Not only that, but he can share sensations and emotions with this student character, created by a real man he never met and translated by a real woman he never met. It was so immediate, the choice of words so delicately accurate, that they blotted out the reality of the present. He ached now for the stationmaster's daughter the way the student aches. It's in his blood.

He paused and looked at the clock. It was time again. He gave another blood sample and when providing the urine sample he splashed the label. He patted it dry with toilet roll and hoped that the technician with the long hair wouldn't notice.

In the waiting room he returned to his book. Was the story accurate? About such feelings? Was this not about women as decoration? Neither woman in the story said anything – showed anything of her inner self – in order to be attractive. Was this not the worst of Hollywood before Hollywood was ever thought of? Audrey Hepburn – Julia Roberts – the stationmaster's daughter.

'There's the water you asked for.'
    'Oh thanks.'
    He poured himself another glass. The water was icy. With his concentration broken he looked at the posters on the wall. He could barely bring himself to read them. They made him quake for his future. But he couldn't be that bad – his doctor had referred him because he was 'borderline'. The poster warnings were for the worst cases. *Diabetic retinopathy* – can lead to permanent loss of vision. Blindness. Never to be able to read again. *Atherosclerosis* leading to *dry gangrene*. Wear well-fitting shoes, visit your chiropodist frequently. Care

for your feet. Or else you'll lose them, was the implication. Jesus. He drained the glass and poured himself another.

The door, which had been silent for a while, screeched open and a wheelchair was pushed through. A woman in her seventies, wearing a dressing gown, was being pushed by a younger woman. The screeching door must lead to the wards. When they came into the waiting area it was obvious the old woman had no legs. She wore a blue cellular blanket over her lap. She was empty to the floor. The woman pushing her sat down on a chair in front of her. From their body language they were mother and daughter.

Their talk became entangled with the Chekhov and he read the same line again and again. He needed silence.

During his final visit to give blood he tried to joke with the technician about there being no more left in that finger. This time there were two crows perched on either side of the black nest. In the lavatory he noticed that his last sample was crystal clear. The water was just going through him.

He sat and finished the Chekhov. It was a wonderful story which ended with the train moving on under a darkening sky, leaving behind the stationmaster's beautiful daughter. In the departing carriage there is an air of sadness. The last image is of the figure of the guard coming through the train beginning to light the candles.

The next thing he was aware of was hearing his name called out by a male voice. He was sitting with his eyes closed, savouring the ending of the story. He stood. The doctor smiled – he was not wearing a white coat. He had a checked shirt and was distinctly overweight – straining the buttons. He led him into an office and looked up after consulting a piece of paper.

'Well I'm pleased to say you don't have diabetes. You have

something we call impaired glucose tolerance – which could well develop into diabetes. You must begin to take some avoiding action – more exercise, better diet. Talk it over with your GP. I'll write to him with these results.'

'Thank you.'

As he walked to the head of the stairs he heard the distant door screech for one last time. He will not have to come back. No need for the oil can. He went out into the November midday and across the car park. The sun was shining. He looked up at the blue sky criss-crossed with jet trails. People travelling. Going places, meeting folk. He thought of those people he had just left who daren't misplace their outpatient cards. Above him the crows made a raucous cawing. His middle finger felt tender and bruised.

He took out his mobile and phoned his wife, dabbing the keys with his thumb. He had seen her across a dance floor forty years ago and felt the wind blow across his soul.

She sounded anxious and concerned.

'Well?'

'I'm OK,' he said.

JANICE GALLOWAY

BLOOD

HE PUT HIS knee up on her chest getting ready to pull, tilting the pliers. Sorry, he said. Sorry. She couldn't see his face. The pores on the backs of his fingers sprouted hairs, single black wires curling onto the bleached skin of the wrist, the veins showing through. She saw an artery move under the surface as he slackened the grip momentarily, catching his breath; his cheeks a kind of mauve colour, twisting at something inside her mouth. The bones in his hand were bruising her lip. And that sound of the gum tugging back from what he was doing, the jaw creaking. Her jaw. If you closed your eyes it made you feel dizzy, imagining it, and this through the four jags of anaesthetic, that needle as big as a power drill. Better to keep her eyes open, trying to focus past the blur of knuckles to the cracked ceiling. She was trying to see a pattern, make the lines into something she could recognise, when her mouth started to do something she hadn't given it permission for. A kind of suction. There was a moment of nothing while he steadied his hand, as if she had only imagined the give. She heard herself swallow and stop breathing. Then her spine lifting, arching from the seat, the gum parting with a sound like uprooting potatoes, a coolness in her mouth and he was holding something up in the metal clamp; great bloody lump of it, white trying to surface through the red. He was pleased.

There you go eh? Never seen one like that before. The root of the problem ha ha.

All his fillings showed when he laughed, holding the thing out, wanting her to look. Blood made a pool under her tongue, lapping at the back of her throat and she had to keep the head back instead. Her lips were too numb to trust: it would have run down the front of her blazer.

Rinse, he said. Cough and spit.

When she sat up he was holding the tooth out on a tissue, roots like a yellow clawhammer at the end, one point wrapping the other.

See the twist? Unusual to see something like that. Little twist in the roots.

Like a deformed parsnip. And there was a bit of flesh, a piece of gum or something nipped off between the crossed tips of bone.

Little rascal, he said.

Her mouth was filling up, she turned to the metal basin before he started singing again. *She's leaving now cos I just heard the slamming of the door* then humming. He didn't really know the words. She spat dark red and thick into the basin. When she resurfaced, he was looking at her and wiping his hands on something like a dishtowel.

Expect it'll bleed for a while, bound to be messy after that bother. Just take your time getting up. Take your time there. No rush.

She had slid to the edge of the chair, dunting the hooks and probes with having to hold on. The metal noise made her teeth sore. Her stomach felt terrible and she had to sit still, waiting to see straight.

Fine in a minute, he said. Wee walk in the fresh air. Wee walk back to school.

He finished wiping his hands and grinned, holding something out. A hard thing inside tissue. The tooth.

You made it, you have it haha. There you go. How's the jaw?

She nodded, and pointed to her mouth. This almost audible sound of a tank filling, a rising tide over the edges of the tongue.

Bleed for a while like I say. Don't worry though. Redheads always bleed worse than other folk. Haha. Sandra'll get you something: stop you making a mess of yourself.

Sandra was already away. He turned to rearrange the instruments she had knocked out of their neat arrangement on the green cloth.

Redheads, see. *Don't take your love to town.*

Maybe it was a joke. She tried to smile back till the blood started silting again. He walked over to the window as Sandra came back with a white pad in her hand. The pad had gauze over the top, very thick with a blue stripe down one side. Loops. A sanitary towel. The dentist was still turned away, looking out of the window and wiping his specs and talking. It took a minute to realise he was talking to her. It should stop in about an hour or so he was saying. Maybe three at the outside. Sandra pushed the pad out for her to take. If not by six o'clock let him know and they could give her a shot of something ok? Looking out the whole time. She tried to listen, tucking the loops at the ends of the towel in where they wouldn't be obvious, blushing when she put it up to her mouth. It was impossible to tell if they were being serious or not. The dentist turned back, grinning at the spectacles he was holding between his hands.

Sandra given you a wee special there. Least said haha. Redheads eh? *Oh Rooobeee*, not looking, wiping the same lens over and over with a cloth.

The fresh air was good. Two deep lungfuls before she wrapped her scarf round the white pad at her mouth and walked. The best way from the surgery was past the flats with bay windows and gardens. Some had trees, crocuses and bits of cane. Better than up by the building site, full of those shouting men. One of them always shouted things, whistled loud enough to make the whole street turn and look. Bad enough at the best of times. Today would have been awful. This way was longer but prettier and there was nothing to stop her taking her time. She had permission. No need to worry about getting there for some particular ring of some particular bell. Permission made all the difference. The smell of bacon rolls at the café fetched her nose: coffee and chocolate. They spoiled when they reached her mouth, heaped up with sanitary towel and the blood still coming. Her tongue wormed towards the soft place, the dip where the tooth had been, then back between tongue root and the backs of her teeth. Thick fluid. A man was crossing the road, a greyhound on a thin lead, a woman with a pram coming past the phone box. Besides, girls didn't spit in the street. School wasn't that far though, not if she walked fast. She clutched the tooth tight in her pocket and walked, head down. The pram was there before she expected it; sudden metal spokes too near her shoes before she looked up, eyes and nose over the white rim of gauze. The woman not even noticing but keeping on, ploughing up the road while she waited at the kerb with her eyes on the gutter, trying hard not to swallow. Six streets and a park to go. Six streets.

The school had no gate, just a gap in the wall with pillars on either side that led into the playground. The blacked-out window was the staff room; the others showed occasional heads, some white faces watching. The Music block was nearest. Quarter to twelve. It would be possible to wait in the practice rooms till the dinner bell in fifteen minutes and not shift till the afternoon. She was in no mood, though, not even for that. Not even for the music. It wouldn't be possible to play well. But there was no point in going home either because everything would have to be explained in triplicate when the mother got in and she never believed you anyway. It was all impossible. The pad round her mouth was slimy already, the wet going cold further at the far sides. She could go over and ask Mrs McNiven for another towel and just go anyway, have a lie-down or something but that meant going over to the other block, all the way across the playground again and the faces looking out knowing where you were going because it was the only time senior girls went there. And this thing round her mouth. Her stomach felt terrible too. She suddenly wanted to be in the music rooms, soothing herself with music. Something peaceful. Going there made her feel better just because of where it was. Not like at home. You could just go and play to your heart's content. That would be nice now, right now this minute, going up there and playing something: the Mozart she'd been working on, something fresh and clean. Turning, letting the glass door close, she felt her throat thicken, closing over with film. And that fullness that said the blood was still coming. A sigh into the towel stung her eyes. The girls' toilets were on the next landing.

Yellow. The light, the sheen off the mirrors. It was always horrible coming here. She could usually manage to get through the days without having to, waiting till she got home and drinking nothing. Most of the girls did the same, even just to avoid the felt-tip drawings on the girls' door – mostly things like split melons only they weren't. All that pretending you couldn't see them on the way in and what went with them, GIRLS ARE A BUNCH OF CUNTS still visible under the diagonal scores of the cleaners' Vim. Impossible to argue against so you made out it wasn't there, swanning past the word CUNTS though it radiated like a black sun all the way from the other end of the corridor. Terrible. And inside, the yellow lights always on, nearly all the mirrors with cracks or warps. Her own face reflected yellow over the nearside row of sinks. She clamped her mouth tight and reached for the towel loops. Its peeling away made her mouth suddenly cold. In her hand, the pad had creased up the centre, ridged where it had settled between her lips and smeared with crimson on the one side. Not as bad as she had thought, but the idea of putting it back wasn't good. She wrapped it in three paper towels instead and stuffed it to the bottom of the wire bin under the rest, bits of paper and God knows what, then leaned over the sinks, rubbing at the numbness in her jaw, rinsing out. Big, red drips when she tried to open her mouth. And something else. She watched the slow trail of red on the white enamel, concentrating. Something slithered in her stomach, a slow dullness that made it difficult to straighten up again. Then a twinge in her back, a recognisable contraction. That's what the sweating was, then, the churning in her gut. It wasn't just not feeling well with the swallowing and imagining things. Christ. It wasn't supposed to be due for a week yet. She'd have to use that horrible toilet paper and it would get sore and slip about all day. Better that than asking Mrs McNiven for two towels, though, anything was better than asking Mrs McNiven. The cold tap spat water along the length of one blazer arm. She was turning it the wrong way. For a frightening moment, she couldn't think how to turn it off then managed, breathing out, tilting forward. It would be good to get out of here, get to something fresh and clean, Mozart and the white room upstairs. She would patch something together and just pretend she wasn't bleeding so much, wash her hands and be fit for things. The white keys.

She pressed her forehead against the cool concrete of the facing wall, swallowing. The taste of blood like copper in her mouth, lips pressed tight.

The smallest practice room was free. The best one: the rosewood piano and the soundproofing made it feel warm. There was no one in either of the other two except the student who taught cello. She didn't know his name, just what he did. He never spoke. Just sat in there all the time waiting for pupils, playing or looking out of the window. Anything to avoid catching sight of people. Mr Gregg said he was afraid of the girls and who could blame him haha. She'd never understood the joke too well but it seemed to be right enough. He sometimes didn't even answer the door if you knocked or made out he couldn't see you when he went by you on the stairs. It was possible to count yourself alone, then, if he was the only one here. It was possible to relax. She sat on the piano stool, hunched over her stomach, rocking. C major triad. This piano had a nice tone, brittle and light. The other two made a fatter, fuzzier noise altogether. This one was leaner, right for the Mozart anyway. Descending chromatic scale with the right hand. The left moved in the blazer pocket, ready to surface, tipping something soft. Crushed tissue, something hard in the middle. The tooth. She had almost forgotten about the tooth. Her back straightened to bring it out, unfold the bits of tissue to hold it up to the light. It had a ridge about a third of the way down, where the glaze of enamel stopped. Below it, the roots were huge, matte like suede. The twist was huge, still bloody where they crossed. Whatever it was they had pulled out with them, the piece of skin, had disappeared. Hard to accept her body had grown this thing. Ivory. She smiled and laid it aside on the wood slat at the top of the keyboard, like a misplaced piece of inlay. It didn't match. The keys were whiter.

Just past the hour already. In four minutes the bell would go and the noise would start: people coming in to stake claims on the rooms, staring in through the glass panels on the door. Arpeggios bounced from next door. The student would be warming up for somebody's lesson, waiting. She turned back to the keys, sighing. Her mouth was filling up again, her head thumping. Fingers looking yellow when she stretched them out, reaching for chords. Her stomach contracted. But if she could just concentrate, forget her body and let the notes come, it wouldn't matter. You could get past things that way, pretend they weren't there. She leaned towards the keyboard, trying to be something else: a piece of music. Mozart, the recent practice. Feeling for the clear, clean lines. Listening. She ignored the pain in her stomach, the scratch of paper towels at her thighs, and watched the keys, the pressure of her fingers that buried or released them. And watching, listening to Mozart, she let the music get louder, and the door opened, the abrupt tearing sound of the doorseals seizing her stomach like a fist. The student was suddenly there and smiling to cover the knot on his forehead where the fear showed, smiling fit to bust, saying, Don't stop, it's lovely; Haydn isn't it? and she opened her mouth not able to stop, opened her mouth to say Mozart. It's Mozart – before she remembered.

Welling up behind the lower teeth, across her lips as she tilted forwards to keep it off her clothes. Spilling over the white keys and dripping onto the clean tile floor. She saw his face change, the glance flick to the claw roots in the tissue before he shut the door hard, not knowing what else to do. And the bell rang, the steady howl of it as the outer doors gave, footfalls in the corridor gathering like an avalanche. They would be here before she could do anything, sitting dumb on the piano stool, not able to move, not able to breathe, and this blood streaking over the keys, silting the action. The howl of the bell. This unstoppable redness seeping through the fingers at her open mouth.

IRVINE WELSH

THE GRANTON
STAR CAUSE

IT HIT BOAB COYLE hard, right in the centre of his chest. He stood at the bar, open-mouthed, as his mate Kev Hyslop explained the position to him.

– Sorry, Boab, but we aw agree. We cannae guarantee ye a game. Wuv goat Tambo n wee Grant now. This team's gaun places.

– Gaun places!? Gaun places!? Churches League Division Three! It's a kick aboot, ya pretentious cunt. A fuckin kick aboot!

Kev did not like Boab's stroppy response. Surely the Granton Star cause was bigger than any one individual's ego. After all, in an open vote, he had been the one entrusted with the captain's armband for the season. The Star were challenging for promotion to Division Two of the Edinburgh Churches League. Additionally, they were only three games away from a cup-final appearance at City Park – with nets – in the Tom Logan Memorial Trophy. The stakes were high, and Kev wanted to be the man who skippered the Star to cup glory in their own backyard. He knew, though, that part of his responsibilities involved making unpopular decisions. Friendships had to be put on the back burner.

– Yir bound tae be disappointed mate . . .

– Disappointed!? Too fuckin right ah'm disappointed. Which cunt washes the strips nearly every week? Eh? Boab pleaded, pointing to himself.

– C'moan Boab, huv another pint . . .

– Stick yir fuckin pint up yir erse! Some mates yous, eh? Well fuck yis! Boab stormed out of the pub as Kev turned to the rest of the boys and shrugged.

Before returning home, Boab went for a few unenjoyable pints of lager on his own in two other pubs. He brimmed with resentment when he thought of Tambo, who had had his eye on Boab's number 10 jersey ever since the posing cunt had got involved with the Star at the start of the season. Orange-juice drinking bastard. It had been a mistake to fill the side with wankers like that. It was, after all, just a kick about; a laugh with the mates. *Fresh orange n lemonade. Fresh orange n lemonade.* Tambo's nasal tones grated mercilessly in his head.

In the pubs Boab visited, he failed to recognise anybody. This was unusual. Additionally, auld drunkards who normally plagued him, looking for company, or to cadge a pint, avoided him like he was a leper.

Boab's mother was hoovering when her son returned home. As soon as she heard him at the door, however, she switched the machine off. Doreen Coyle looked conspiratorially at her husband, Boab senior, who shifted his considerable bulk in his chair and cast the *Evening News* onto the coffee table.

– Ah want a wee word, son, Boab senior said.

– Eh? Boab was somewhat alarmed by the challenging and confrontational tone of his father's voice.

But before Boab senior could speak, Doreen started to rant nervously

– S'no likesay wir tryin tae git rid ay ye, son. S'no likesay that at aw.

Boab stood there, a sense of foreboding cutting through his bemusement.

– That's enough, Doreen, Boab's father said, with a hint of irritation. – Thing is, son, it's time ye wir ootay this hoose.

Yir twinty-three now, which is far too auld fir a laddie tae be steyin wi his ma n faither. A mean, ah wis away tae sea wi the Merchant Navy at seventeen. It's jist no natural, son, d'ye understand?

Boab said nothing. He couldn't think straight. His father continued.

– Dinnae want yir mates tae think thit yir some kinday queer felly, now dae ye? Anyway, yir ma n me's no gittin any younger. Wir ent'rin a funny phase in oor lives, son. Some might say ... Boab Coyle looked at his wife, – ... a dangerous phase. Yir ma n me son, we need time tae sort oot oor lives. Tae git it the gither, if ye ken whit ah mean. You've goat a lassie, wee Evelyn. You ken the score! Boab senior winked at his son, examining his face for a sign of understanding. Although none was apparent, he carried on. – Yir problem is, son, yir huvin yir cake n eatin it. N whae suffers? Ah'll tell ye whae. Muggins here, Boab senior pointed to himself. – Yir ma n me. Now ah ken it's no that easy tae find somewhair tae stey these days, especially whin yuv hud everybody else, like muggins here, runnin aroond eftir ye. Bit we'll no say nowt aboot that. Thing is, me n yir ma, wir prepared tae gie ye two weeks' grace. Jist as long as ye make sure that yir ootay here within a fortnight.

Somewhat stunned, Boab could only say, – Aye ... right ...

– Dinnae think thit wir tryin tae git rid ay ye, son. It's jist thit yir faither n me think thit it wid be mutually advantageous, tae baith parties, likesay, if ye found yir ain place.

– That's it, Doe, Boab's faither sang triumphantly. – Mutually advantageous tae baith parties. Ah like that. Any brains you n oor Cathy've got, son, they definitely come fae yir ma thair, nivir mind muggins here.

Boab looked at his parents. They seemed somehow different. He had always regarded his auld man as a fat, wheezing, chronic asthmatic, and his auld girl as a blobby woman in a tracksuit. Physically they looked the same, but he could, for the first time, detect an unsettling edge of sexuality about them which he'd previously been oblivious to. He saw them for what they were: sleazy, lecherous bastards. He now realised that the look they gave him when he took Evelyn upstairs for sex, was not of embarrassment or resentment, but one of anticipation. Far from concerning themselves with what he was doing, it gave them the chance to do their own thing.

Evelyn. Once he talked to her things would be better. Ev always understood. Ideas of formal engagement and marriage, so long pooh-poohed by Boab, now fluttered through his mind. He'd been daft not to see the possibilities in it before. Their own place. He could watch videos all evening. A ride every night. He'd get another club; fuck the Star! Evelyn could wash the strips. Suddenly buoyant again, he went out, down to the call-box at the shops. He already felt like an intruder in his parents' home.

Evelyn picked up the phone. Boab's spirits rose further at the prospect of company. The prospect of understanding. The prospect of sex.

– Ev? Boab. Awright?

– Aye.

– Fancy comin ower?

– . . .

– Eh? Ev? Fancy comin ower, likesay?

– Naw.

– How no? Something wasn't right. A shuddering anxiety shot through Boab.

– Jist dinnae.

– But how no? Ah've hud a bad day, Ev. Ah need tae talk tae ye.

– Aye. Well, talk tae yir mates well.

– Dinnae be like that, Ev! Ah sais ah've hud a hard day! Whit is it? Whit's wrong?

– You n me. That's whit's wrong.

– Eh?

– Wir finished. Finito. Kaput. Endy story. Goodnight Vienna.

– Whit've ah done, Ev? Whit've ah done? Boab could not believe his ears.

– You ken.

– Ev . . .

– It's no whit yuv done, it's whit yuv no done!

– But Ev . . .

– Me n you Boab. Ah want a guy what kin dae things fir ays. Somebody whae kin really make love tae a woman. No some fat bastard whae sits oan ehs erse talkin aboot fitba n drinkin pints ay lager wi his mates. A real man, Boab. A sexy man. Ah'm twinty Boab. Twinty years auld. Ah'm no gaun tae tie masel doon tae a slob!

– Whit's goat intae you? Eh? Evelyn? Yuv nivir complained before. You n me. Ye wir jist a daft wee lassie before ye met me. Nivir knew whit a ride wis, fir fuck sake . . .

– Aye! Well that's aw changed! Cos ah've met somebody, Boab Coyle! Mair ay a fuckin man thin you'll ivir be!

– . . . Eh? . . . Eh? . . . WHAE? . . . WHAE IS THE CUUUHHNNT!

– That's fir me tae ken n you tae find oot!

– Ev . . . how could ye dae this tae ays . . . you n me, Ev . . . it wis eywis you n me . . . engagement n that . . .

– Sorry, Boab. Bit ah've been wi you since ah wis sixteen.

Ah might huv kent nowt aboot love then, bit ah sure as fuck ken a bit mair now!

– YA FAAHKIN SLAG! . . . YA HORRIBLE FUCKIN HING-OOT! . . .

Evelyn slammed the receiver down.

– Ev . . . Ev . . . Ah love ye . . . Boab spoke those words for the first time, down a dead telephone line.

– SLAAHT! FAAHKIN SLAAAHHT! He smashed the receiver around in the box. His segged brogues booted out two glass panels and he tried to wrench the phone from its mounting.

Boab was unaware that a police squad-car had pulled up outside the phone-box.

Down at the local police station, the arresting officer, PC Brian Cochrane, was typing up Boab's statement when Duty Sergeant Morrison appeared. Boab sat in depressed silence at the foot of the desk while Cochrane typed with two fingers.

– Evening, sarge, PC Cochrane said.

The sergeant mumbled something which may or may not have been 'Brian', not pausing to look around. He put a sausage roll into the microwave. When he opened the cupboard above the oven, Morrison was angered to note that there was no tomato sauce. He despised snacks without ketchup. Upset, he turned to PC Cochrane.

– Thir's nae fuckin ketchup, Brian. Whae's turn wis it tae git the provisions?

– Eh . . . sorry sarge . . . slipped up, the constable said, embarrassed. – Eh . . . busy night, sarge, likes.

Morrison shook his head sadly and let out a long exhalation of breath.

– So what've we goat the night, Brian?

– Well, there's the rapist, the guy who stabbed the boy at

the shopping centre and this comedian here, he pointed at Boab.

– Right . . . ah've already been doon n hud a word wi the rapist. Seems a nice enough young felly. Telt ays the daft wee hoor wis askin fir it. S'the wey ay the world, Brian. The guy who knifed the boy . . . well, silly bugger, but boys will be boys. What aboot this tube-stake?

– Caught him smashin up a phone-box.

Sergeant Morrison clenched his teeth shut. Trying to contain a surge of anger which threatened to overwhelm him, he spoke slowly and deliberately: – Get this cowboy doon tae the cells. Ah want a wee word wi this cunt.

Somebody else wanting a wee word. Boab was beginning to feel that these 'wee words' were never to his advantage.

Sergeant Morrison was a British Telecom shareholder. If one thing made him more angry than snacks without tomato ketchup, it was seeing the capital assets of BT, which made up part of his investment, depreciated by wanton vandalism.

Down in the cells, Morrison pummelled Boab's stomach, ribs and testicles. As Boab lay lying groaning on the cold, tiled floor, the sergeant smiled down at him.

– Ye ken, it jist goes tae show ye the effectiveness ay they privatisation policies. Ah would nivir huv reacted like that if ye hud smashed up a phone-box when they were nationalised. Ah know it's jist the same really; vandalism meant increased taxes for me then, while now it means lower dividends. Thing is, ah feel like ah've goat mair ay a stake now, son. So ah don't want any lumpen-proletarian malcontents threatening ma investment.

Boab lay moaning miserably, ravaged by sickening aches and oppressed by mental torment and anguish.

Sergeant Morrison prided himself on being a fair man. Like the rest of the punters detained in the cells, Boab was given his cup of stewed tea and jam roll for breakfast. He couldn't touch it. They had put butter and jam on together. He couldn't touch the piece but was charged with breach of the peace, as well as criminal damage.

Although it was 6.15 a.m. when he was released, he felt too fragile to go home. Instead, he decided to go straight to his work after stopping off at a cafe for a scrambled-egg roll and a cup of coffee. He found a likely place and ordered up.

After his nourishment, Boab went to settle the bill.

– One pound, sixty-five pence. The cafe owner was a large, fat, greasy man, badly pock-marked.

– Eh? Bit steep, Boab counted out his money. He hadn't really thought about how much money he had, even though the police had taken it all from him, with his keys and shoe-laces, and he'd had to sign for them in the morning.

He had one pound, thirty-eight pence. He counted out the money. The cafe proprietor looked at Boab's unshaven, bleary appearance. He was trying to run a respectable estab-lishment, not a haven for dossers. He came from behind the counter and jostled Boab out of the door.

– Fuckin wise cunt . . . wide-o . . . ye kin see the prices . . . ah'll fuckin steep ye, ya cunt . . .

Out in the cold, blue morning street, the fat man punched Boab on the jaw. More through fatigue and disorientation than the power of the blow, Boab fell backwards, cracking his head off the pavement.

He lay there for a while, and began weeping, cursing God, Kev, Tambo, Evelyn, his parents, the police and the cafe owner.

Despite being physically and mentally shattered, Boab put in a lot of graft that morning, to try and forget his worries and make the day pass quickly. Normally, he did very little lifting, reasoning that as he was the driver, it wasn't really his job. Today, however, he had his sleeves rolled up. The first flit his crew worked on saw them take the possessions of some rich bastards from a big posh house in Cramond to a big posh house in the Grange. The other boys in the team, Benny, Drew and Zippo, were far less talkative than usual. Normally Boab would have been suspicious of the silence. Now, feeling dreadful, he welcomed the respite it offered.

They got back to the Canonmills depot at 12.30 for dinner. Boab was surprised to be summoned into the office of Mike Rafferty, the gaffer.

– Sit doon, Boab. I'll come straight to the point, mate, Rafferty said, doing anything but. – Standards, he said enigmatically, and pointed to the Hauliers and Removals Association plaque on the wall, bearing a logo which deco-rated each one of his fleet of lorries. – Counts for nothing now. It's all about price these days, Boab. And all these cowboys, who have fewer overheads and lower costs, they're trimming us, Boab.

– Whit ur ye tryin tae say?

– We've goat tae cut costs, Boab. Where can ah cut costs? This place? He looked out of the glass and wooden box of an office and across the floor of the warehouse. – We're tied doon tae a five-year lease here. No. It has to be capital and labour costs. It's aw doon tae market positioning, Boab. We have to find our niche in the market. That niche is as a quality firm specialising in local moves for the As, Bs and Cs.

– So ah'm sacked? Boab asked, with an air of resignation.

Rafferty looked Boab in the eye. He had recently been on a training course entitled: 'Positively Managing The Redundancy Scenario.'

– Your post is being made redundant, Boab. It's important to remember that it's not the person we make redundant, it's the post. We've overstretched ourselves, Boab. Got geared up for continental removals. Tried, and I have to say failed, to compete with the big boys. Got a wee bit too carried away by 1992, the single market and all that. I'm going to have to let the big lorry go. We also need to lose a driver's job. This isnae easy, Boab, but it has tae be last one in, first one out. Now ah'll put it around in the trade that I know of a reliable driver who's looking for something, and obviously, ah'll give you an excellent reference.

– Obviously, said Boab, with sarcastic bitterness.

Boab left at lunchtime and went for a pint and a toastie down the local pub. He didn't bother to go back. As he sat and drank alone, a stranger approached him, sitting down next to him, even though plenty free seats were available. The man looked in his fifties, not particularly tall, yet with a definite presence. His white hair and white beard reminded Boab of a folk singer, the guy from the Corries, or maybe the boy in the Dubliners.

– Yuv fucked this one up, ya daft cunt, the man said to him, raising a pint of eighty shilling to his lips.

– Eh? What? Boab was surprised again.

– You. Boab Coyle. Nae hoose, nae joab, nae burd, nae mates, polis record, sair face, aw in the space ay a few ooirs. Nice one, he winked and toasted Boab with his pint. This angered, but intrigued Boab.

– How the fuck dae you ken? Whae the fuckin hell ur you?

The man shook his head, – It's ma fuckin business tae ken. Ah'm God.

– Way tae fuck ya auld radge! Boab laughed loudly, throwing his head back.

– Fuckin hell. Another wise cunt, said the man tiredly. He then trudged out a spiel with the bored, urbane air of someone who had been through all this more times than they cared to remember.

– Robert Anthony Coyle, born on Friday the 23rd of July, 1968, to Robert McNamara Coyle and Doreen Sharp. Younger brother of Cathleen Siobhain Shaw, who is married to James Allan Shaw. They live at 21 Parkglen Crescent in Gilmerton and they have a child, also called James. You have a sickle-shaped birthmark on your inner thigh. You attended Granton Primary School and Ainslie Park Secondary, where you obtained two SCE O Grades, in Woodwork and Technical Drawing. Until recently, you worked in furniture removals, lived at hame, hud a bird called Evelyn, whom you couldn't sexually satisfy, and played football for Granton Star, like you made love, employing little effort and even less skill.

Boab sat totally deflated. There seemed to be an almost translucent aura around this man. He spoke with certainty and conviction. Boab almost believed him. He didn't know what to believe anymore.

– If you're God, what ur ye daein wastin yir time oan me?

– Good question, Boab. Good question.

– Ah mean, thir's bairns starvin, likesay, oan telly n that. If ye wir that good, ye could sort aw that oot, instead ay sitting here bevvyin wi the likes ay me.

God looked Boab in the eye. He seemed upset.

– Jist hud oan a minute, pal. Lit's git one thing straight. Every fuckin time ah come doon here, some wide-o pills ays up aboot what ah should n shouldnae be fuckin daein. Either that or ah huv tae enter intae some philosophical fuckin discourse wi some wee undergraduate twat aboot the nature ay masel, the extent ay ma omnipotence n aw that shite. Ah'm gittin a wee bit fed up wi aw this self-justification; it's no for yous cunts tae criticise me. Ah made yous cunts in

369

ma ain image. Yous git oan wi it; yous fuckin well sort it oot. That cunt Nietzsche wis wide ay the mark whin he sais ah wis deid. Ah'm no deid; ah jist dinnae gie a fuck. It's no fir me tae sort every cunt's problems oot. Nae other cunt gies a fuck so how should ah? Eh?

Boab found God's whingeing pathetic. – You fuckin toss. If ah hud your powers . . .

– If you hud ma powers ye'd dae what ye dae right now: sweet fuck all. You've goat the power tae cut doon oan the pints ay lager, aye?

– Aye, bit . . .

– Nae buts aboot it. You've goat the power tae git fit and make a mair positive contribution tae the Granton Star cause. You hud the power tae pey mair attention tae that wee burd ay yours. She wis tidy. Ye could've done a loat better there, Boab.

– Mibbe ah could, mibbe ah couldnae. Whit's it tae you?

– Ye hud the power tae git oot fae under yir ma n dad's feet, so's they could huv a decent cowp in peace. Bit naw. No selfish cunt Coyle. Jist sits thair watchin *Coronation Street* n *Brookside* while they perr cunts ur gaun up the waws wi frustration.

– S 'nane ay your business.

– Everything's ma business. Ye hud the power tae fight back against the fat cunt fi the cafe. Ye jist lit the cunt panel ye, fir a few fuckin pence. That wis ootay order, bit ye lit the cunt git away wi it.

– Ah wis in a state ay shock . . .

– And that cunt Rafferty. Ye didnae even tell the cunt tae stick his fuckin joab up his erse.

– So what! So fuckin what!

– So ye hud they powers, ye jist couldnae be bothered usin thum. That's why ah'm interested in ye Boab. You're jist like me. A lazy, apathetic, slovenly cunt. Now ah hate bein like this, n bein immortal, ah cannae punish masel. Ah kin punish you though, mate. That's whit ah intend tae dae.

– But ah could . . .

– Shut it cunt! Ah've fuckin hud it up tae ma eyebaws wi aw this repentence shite. Vengeance is mine, n ah intend tae take it, oan ma ain lazy n selfish nature, through the species ah created, through thir representative. That's you.

God stood up. Although he was almost shaking with anger, Boab saw that this was not easy for him. He could still be talked out of doing whatever he was going to do. – Ye look jist like ah always imagined . . . Boab said sycophantically.

– That's cause ye've nae imagination, ya daft cunt. Ye see ays n hear ays as ye imagine ays. Now you're fuckin claimed, radge.

– Bit ah'm no the worst . . . Boab pleaded. – . . . Whit aboot the murderers, the serial killers, dictators, torturers, politicians . . . the cunt's thit shut factories doon tae preserve thir profit levels . . . aw they greedy rich bastards . . . what aboot thaim? Eh?

– Might git round tae they cunts, might no. That's ma fuckin business. You've hud it cunt! Yir a piece ay slime, Coyle. An insect. That's it! An insect . . . God said, inspired. – . . . ah'm gaunny make ye look like the dirty, lazy pest thit ye are!

God looked Boab in the eye again. A force of invisible energy seemed to leave his body and travel a few feet across the table, penetrating Boab through to his bones. The force pinned him back in his chair, but it was over in a second, and all Boab was left with was a racing heartbeat and a sweating brow, genitals and armpits. The whole performance seemed to take it out of God. He stood up shakily in his chair and looked at Boab. – Ah'm away tae ma fuckin kip, he wheezed, turning and leaving the pub.

Boab sat there, mind racing, feverishly trying to rationalise what had happened to him. Kevin came into the pub for a quick pint a few minutes after this. He noted Boab, but was reluctant to approach him, after Boab's outburst in the pub the day before.

When Kevin eventually did come over, Boab told him that he had just met God, who was going to turn him into an insect.

– You dinnae half talk some shite, Boab, he told his distraught friend, before leaving him.

That evening, Kevin was at home alone, eating a fish supper. His girlfriend was on a night out with some friends. A large bluebottle landed on the edge of his plate. It just sat there, looking at him. Something told him not to swat it.

The bluebottle then flew into a blob of tomato sauce on the edge of the plate, and soared up to the wall before Kev could react. To his astonishment, it began to trace out KEV against the white woodchip paper. It had to make a second journey to the sauce to finish what it had started. Kev shuddered. This was crazy, but there it was; his name, spelt by an insect . . .

– Boab? Is that really you? Fuckin hell! Eh, buzz twice fir aye, once fir naw.

Two buzzes.

– Did eh, what's his name, did God dae this?

Two buzzes.

– Whit the fuck ur ye gaunny dae?

Frantic buzzing.

– Sorry Boab . . . kin ah git ye anything? Scran, likesay?

They shared the fish supper. Kev had the lion's share, Boab

sat near the edge of the plate licking at a little bit of fish, grease and sauce.

Boab stayed with Kev Hyslop for a few days. He was encouraged to lie low, in case Julie, Kev's girlfriend, discovered him. Kev threw the fly-spray away. He bought a pot of ink and some notepaper. He'd pour some ink into a saucer, and let Boab trace out some laborious messages on the paper. One, particuarly, was written in anxiety: CUNT OF A SPIDER IN BATHROOM. Kev flushed the spider down the toilet. Whenever he came in from work, Kev was concerned that something might have happened to Boab. He could not relax until he heard that familiar buzz.

From his location behind the bedroom curtains, Boab plotted revenge. He'd all but absolved Kev for dropping him from the Star, on account of his kindness. However, he was determined to get back at his parents, Evelyn, Rafferty, and the others.

It wasn't all bad being a bluebottle. The power of flight was something he'd have hated to have missed; there had been few greater pleasures than soaring around outside. He also gained a taste for excrement, its rich, sour moistness tantalising his long insect tongue. The other bluebottles who crowded onto the hot shite were not so bad. Boab was attracted to some of them. He learned to appreciate the beauty of the insect body; the sexy, huge, brown eyes, the glistening external skeleton, the appealing mosaic of blue and green, the rough, coarse hairs and the shimmering wings which refracted the sun's golden light.

One day, he flew over by Evelyn's, and caught sight of her leaving the house. He followed her, to her new boy-friend's place. The guy was Tambo, who'd displaced Boab in the Granton Star line-up. He found himself buzzing involuntarily. After watching them fuck like rabbits in every conceivable position, he flew down into the cat's litter tray, checking first that the creature was asleep in its basket.

He munched at a skittery turd not properly buried in the gravel. He then flew into the kitchen, and puked the shire into a curry that Tambo had made. He made several journeys.

The next day Tambo and Evelyn were violently ill with food-poisoning. Observing them feverish and sick gave Boab a sense of power. This encouraged him to fly over to his old workplace. When he got there, he lifted some smaller granules of blue rat-poison from a matchbox on the floor, and inserted them into Rafferty's cheese salad sandwich.

Rafferty was very sick the next day, having to go to casualty and get his stomach pumped. The doctor reckoned he'd been given rat-poison. In addition to feeling terrible physically, Rafferty was also devastated with paranoia. Like most bosses, who are regarded with at best contempt and at worst hated by all their subordinates, except the most cringing sycophants, he imagined himself to be popular and respected. He wondered: Who could have done this to me?

Boab's next journey was to his parents' home. This was one journey he wished he hadn't made. He took up a position high on the wall, and tears condensed in his massive brown eyes as he surveyed the scene below him.

His father was clad in a black nylon body-stocking with a hole at the crotch. His arms were outstretched with his hands on the mantelpiece and his legs spread. Boab senior's flab rippled in his clinging costume. Boab's mother was naked, apart from a belt which was fastened so tightly around her body it cut sharply into her wobbling flesh, making her look like a pillow tied in the middle with a piece of string. Attached to the belt was a massive latex dildo, most of which was in Boab senior's anus. Most, but still not enough for Boab senior.

– Keep pushin Doe . . . keep pushin . . . ah kin take mair . . . ah *need* mair . . .

– Wir nearly at the hilt already . . . yir an awfay man, Boab Coyle . . . Doreen grunted and sweated, pushing further, smearing more KY jelly around Boab senior's flabby arse and onto the still-visible part of the shaft.

– The questionin, Doe . . . gies the questionin . . .

– Tell ays whae it is! Tell ays ya fuckin philandering bastard! Doreen screeched, as Boab the bluebottle shuddered on the wall.

– Ah'll nivir talk . . . Boab senior's wheezing tones concerned Doreen.

– Ye awright, Boab? Mind yir asthma n that . . .

– Aye . . . aye . . . keep up the questionin, Doreen . . . the crocodile clips, GIT THE CROC CLIPS DOE! Boab senior filled his cheeks with air.

Doreen took the first clip from the mantelpiece and attached it to one of Boab senior's nipples. She did the same with the other one. The third clip was a larger one, and she snapped it harshly onto his wizened scrotum. Turned on by his screams, she pushed the dildo in further.

– Tell ays, Boab! WHAE HUV YE BEEN SEEIN?

– AAAGGHHH . . . Boab senior screamed, then whispered, – . . . Dolly Parton.

– Whae? Ah cannae hear ye, Doreen said, menacingly.

– DOLLY PARTON!

– That fuckin slut . . . ah knew it . . . whae else?

– Anna Ford . . . n that Madonna . . . bit jist the once . . .

– SCUMBAG! BASTARD! YA DIRTY FUCKIN PRICK! . . . Ye ken whit this means!

– No the shite, Doe . . . ah cannae eat yir shite . . .

– Ah'm gaunny shite in your mooth, Boab Coyle! It's whit wi baith want! Dinnae deny it!

– Naw! Don't shite in ma mooth . . . don't . . . shite in ma mooth . . . shite in ma mooth . . . SHITE IN MA MOOTH!

Boab saw it all now. While he was mechanically relieving himself upstairs by skill-lessly poking Evelyn in the missionary position, his parents were trying to cram the three-piece suite up each other's arses. The very thought of them have a sexuality had repulsed him; now it shamed him in a different way. There was one aspect, however, where it was like father, like son. He knew he could not trust himself to see his mother's shite. It would be too arousing, that succulent, hot sour faeces, all going into his father's mouth. Boab felt his first conscious twinges of an Oedipus complex, at twenty-three years old, and in a metamorphosised state.

Boab sprang from the wall and swarmed around them, flying in and out of their ears.

– Shite . . . that fuckin fly . . . Doreen said. Just then, the phone went. – Ah'll huv tae git it! Boab. Stey thair. It'll be oor Cathy. She'll jist pester us aw night if ah dinnae answer now. Don't go away. She undid the belt, leaving the dildo in Boab's senior's arse. He was at peace, his muscles stretched, but holding the latex rod comfortably and securely. He felt filled, complete, and alive.

Boab junior was exhausted after his efforts and retreated back to the wall. Doreen grabbed the telephone receiver.

– Hiya Cathy. How are you doin, love? . . . Good . . . Dad's fine. How's the wee felly? . . . Aw, the wee lamb! N Jimmy . . . Good. Listen love, wir jist sitting doon tae oor tea. Ah'll phone ye back in aboot half an hour, n will huv a proper blether . . . Right love . . . Bye the now.

Doreen's reactions were quicker than the weary Boab's.

She picked up the *Evening News* as she put down the phone and sprang over to the wall. Boab didn't see the threat until the rolled newspaper was hurtling towards him. He took off, but the paper caught him and knocked him back against the wall at great speed. He felt excruciating pain as parts of his external skeletal structure cracked open.

– Got ye, ya swine, Doreen hissed.

Boab tried to regain the power of flight, but it was useless. He dropped onto the carpet, falling down the gap between the wall and the sideboard. His mother crouched down onto her knees, but she couldn't see Boab in the shadows.

– Tae hell wi it, the hoover'll git it later. That fly wis a bigger pest thin young Boab, she smiled, clipping on the belt and pushing the dildo further into Boab senior's arse.

That night, the Coyles were awakened by the sound of groaning. They went tentatively down the stairs and found their son lying battered and bloodied, under the sideboard in the front room, suffering from terrible injuries.

An ambulance was called for, but Boab junior had slipped away. The cause of death was due to massive internal injuries, similar to the type someone would sustain in a bad car crash. All his ribs were broken, as were both his legs and his right arm. His skull had fractured. There was no trail of blood and it was inconceivable that Boab could have crawled home from an accident or a severe kicking in that condition. Everyone was perplexed.

Everyone except Kev, who began drinking heavily. Due to this problem, Kev became estranged from Julie, his girlfriend. He has fallen behind on the mortgage payments on his flat. There are to be further redundancies at the north Edinburgh electronics factory where he works. Worst of all for Kev, he is going through a lean spell in front of goal. He tries to console himself by remembering that all strikers have such barren periods, but he knows that he has lost a yard in pace. His position as captain, and even his place in the Star line-up, can no longer be considered unassailable. Star are not going to be promoted this year due to a bad slump in form and Muirhouse Albion almost contemptuously dismissed them at the quarter-final stage of the Tom Logan Memorial Trophy.

JACKIE KAY

MY DAUGHTER
THE FOX

WE HAD A NIGHT of it, my daughter and I, with the foxes screaming outside. I had to stroke her fur and hold her close all night. She snuggled up, her wet nose against my neck. Every time they howled, she'd startle and raise her ears. I could feel the pulse of her heart beat on my chest, strong and fast. Strange how eerie the foxes sounded to me; I didn't compare my daughter's noises to theirs. Moonlight came in through our bedroom window; the night outside seemed still and slow, except for the cries of the foxes. It must have been at least three in the morning before we both fell into a deep sleep, her paw resting gently on my shoulder. In my dream I dreamt of being a fox myself, of the two of us running through the forest, our red bushy tails flickering through the dark trees, our noses sniffing rain in the autumn air.

In the morning I sat her in her wooden high chair and she watched me busy myself around the kitchen. I gave her a fresh bowl of water and a raw egg. She cracked the shell herself and slurped the yellow yolk in one gulp. I could tell she was still a little drowsy. She was breathing peacefully and slowly, her little red chest rising and falling. Her eyes literally followed me from counter to counter to cupboard, out into the hall to pick up the post from the raffia mat and back again. I poured her a bowl of muesli and put some fresh blueberries in it. She enjoys that. Nobody tells you how flattering it is, how loved you feel, your child following your every move like that. Her beady eyes watched me open my post as if it was the most interesting thing anybody could do. The post was dull as usual, a gas bill and junk. I sighed, went to the kitchen bin and threw everything in but the bill. When I turned back around, there she still was, smiling at me, her fur curling around her mouth. Her eyes lit up, fierce with love. When she looked at me from those deep dark eyes of hers, straight at me and through me, I felt more understood than I have ever felt from any look by anybody.

Nobody says much and nothing prepares you. I've often wondered why women don't warn each other properly about the horrors of childbirth. There is something medieval about the pain, the howling, the push-push-pushing. In the birthing room next door, the November night my daughter was born, I heard a woman scream, 'Kill me! Just kill me!' That was just after my waters had broken. An hour later I heard her growl in a deep animal voice, 'Fucking shoot me!' I tried to imagine the midwife's black face. We were sharing her and she was running back and forth between birthing stations. She held my head and said, 'You're in control of this!' But I felt as if my body was exploding. I felt as if I should descend down into the bowels of the earth and scrape and claw. Nothing prepares you for the power of the contractions, how they rip through your body like a tornado or an earthquake. Then the beautiful, spacey peace between contractions where you float and dream away out at sea.

Many of my friends were mothers. I'd asked some, 'Will it hurt?' and they'd all smiled and said, 'A bit.' A bit! Holy Mary, Mother of God. I was as surprised as the Jamaican midwife when my daughter the fox came out. I should have known, really. Her father was a foxy man, sly and devious, and, I found out later, was already seeing two other women when he got me pregnant, that night under the full moon. On our way up north for that weekend, I saw a dead fox on the hard shoulder. It was lying, curled, and the red of the blood was much darker than the red of the fur. When we made love in the small double bed in Room 2 at the bed-and-breakfast place by Coniston Water, I could still see it, the dead fox at the side of the road. It haunted me all the way through my pregnancy. I knew the minute I was pregnant, almost the second the seed had found its way up. I could smell everything differently. I smelt an orange so strongly I almost vomited.

When the little blue mark came, of course it couldn't tell me I was carrying a fox, just that I was pregnant. And even the scans didn't seem to pick anything up, except they couldn't agree whether or not I was carrying a girl or a boy. One hospital person seemed sure I was carrying a son. It all falls into place now of course, because that would have been her tail. Once they told me the heart was beating fine and the baby seemed to be progressing, but that there was something they couldn't pick up. She was born on the stroke of midnight, a midnight baby. When she came out, the stern Jamaican midwife, who had been calm and in control all during the contractions, saying, 'Push now, that's it, and again,' let out a blood-curdling scream. I thought my baby was dead. But no, midwives don't scream when babies are stillborn. They are serious, they whisper. They scream when foxes come out a woman's cunt though, that's for sure. My poor daughter was terrified. I could tell straight away. She gave a sharp bark and I pulled her to my breast and let her suckle.

It's something I've learnt about mothers: when we are loved we are not choosy. I knew she was devoted to me from the start. It was strange; so much of her love was loyalty. I knew that the only thing she shared with her father was red hair. Apart from that, she was mine. I swear I could see

383

my own likeness, in her pointed chin, in her high cheeks, in her black eyes. I'd hold her up in front of me; her front paws framing her red face, and say, 'Who is mummy's girl, then?'

I was crying when she was first born. I'd heard that many mothers do that – cry straight from the beginning. Not because she wasn't what I was expecting, I was crying because I felt at peace at last, because I felt loved and even because I felt understood. I didn't get any understanding from the staff at the hospital. They told me I had to leave straight away; the fox was a hazard. It was awful to hear about my daughter being spoken of in this way, as if she hadn't just been born, as if she didn't deserve the same consideration as the others. They were all quaking and shaking like it was the most disgusting thing they had ever seen. She wasn't even given one of those little ankle-bracelet name tags I'd been so looking forward to keeping all her life. I whispered her name into her alert ear. 'Anya,' I said. 'I'll call you Anya.' It was the name I'd chosen if I had a girl and seemed to suit her perfectly. She was blind when she was born. I knew she couldn't yet see me, but she recognized my voice; she was comforted by my smell. It was a week before her sight came.

They called an ambulance to take me home at three in the morning. It was a clear, crisp winter's night. The driver put on the sirens and raced through the dark streets screaming. I had to cover my daughter's ears. She has trembled whenever she's heard a siren ever since. When we arrived at my house in the dark, one of the men carried my overnight bag along the path and left it at my wooden front door. 'You'll be all right from here?' he said, peering at my daughter, who was wrapped in her very first baby blanket. 'Fine,' I said, breathing in the fresh night air. I saw him give the driver an odd look, and then they left, driving the ambulance slowly up my street and off. The moon shone still, and the stars sparkled and fizzed in the sky. It wasn't what I'd imagined, arriving home from hospital in the dark, yet still I couldn't contain my excitement, carrying her soft warm shape over my door step and into my home.

When I first placed her gently in the little crib that had been sitting empty for months, I got so much pleasure. Day after endless day, as my big tight round belly got bigger and tighter, I'd stared into that crib hardly able to believe I'd ever have a baby to put in it. And now at last I did, I lay her down and covered her with the baby blanket, then I got into bed myself. I rocked the crib with my foot. I was exhausted, so bone tired, I hardly knew if I really existed or not. Not more than half an hour passed before she started to whine and cry. I brought her into bed with me and she's never been in the crib since. She needs me. Why fight about these things? Life is too short. I know her life will be shorter than mine will. That's the hardest thing about being the mother of a fox. The second hardest thing is not having anyone around who has had the same experience. I would so love to swap notes on the colour of her shit. Sometimes it seems a worrying greenish colour.

I'll never forget the look on my mother's face when she first arrived, with flowers and Baby-Gros and teddy bears. I'd told her on the phone that the birth had been fine, and that my daughter weighed three pounds, which was true. 'Won't she be needing the incubator, being that small?' she'd asked, worried. 'No,' I'd said. 'They think she's fine.' I hadn't said any more, my mother wasn't good on the phone. I opened the front door and she said, 'Where is she, where is she?' her eyes wild with excitement. My daughter is my mother's first grandchild. I said, 'Ssssh, she's sleeping. Just have a wee peek.' I felt convinced that as soon as she saw her it wouldn't matter and she would love her like I did.

How could anybody not see Anya's beauty? She had lovely dark red fur, thick and vivid, alive. She was white under her throat. At the end of her long bushy tail she had a perfect white tail-tip. Her tail was practically a third of the length of her body. On her legs were white stockings. She was shy, slightly nervous of strangers, secretive, and highly intelligent. She moved with such haughty grace and elegance that at times she appeared feline. From the minute I gave birth to my daughter the fox, I could see that no other baby could be more beautiful. I hoped my mother would see her the same way.

We tiptoed into my bedroom where Anya was sleeping in her crib for her daytime nap. My mother was already saying, 'Awwww,' as she approached the crib. She looked in, went white as a sheet, and then gripped my arm. 'What's going on?' she whispered, her voice just about giving out. 'Is this some kind of a joke?'

It was the same look on people's faces when I took Anya out in her pram. I'd bought a great big Silver Cross pram with a navy hood. I always kept the hood up to keep the sun or the rain out. People could never resist sneaking a look at a baby in a pram. I doubt that many had ever seen daughters like mine before. One old friend, shocked and fumbling for something to say, said, 'She looks so like you.' I glowed with pride. 'Do you think so?' I said, squeaking with pleasure. She did look beautiful, my daughter in her Silver Cross pram, the white of her blanket against the red of her cheeks. I always made her wear a nappy when I took her out in the pram though she loathed nappies.

It hurt me that her father never came to see her, never took the slightest bit of interest in her. When I told him that on the stroke of midnight I'd given birth to a baby fox, he actually denied being her father. He thought I was lying, that I'd done something with our real daughter and got Anya in her place. 'I always thought you were off your fucking rocker. This proves it! You're barking! Barking!' he screamed down the phone. He wouldn't pay a penny towards her keep. I should have had him DNA tested, but I didn't want to put myself through it. Nobody was as sympathetic to me as I thought they might be. It never occurred to me to dump Anya or disown her or pretend she hadn't come from me.

But when the baby stage passed, everything changed. My daughter didn't like being carried around in the pouch, pushed in the pram or sat in her high chair. She didn't like staying in my one-bedroom ground-floor flat in Tottenham either. She was constantly sitting by the front door waiting for me to open it to take her out to Clissold Park, or Finsbury Park or Downhills Park. But I had to be careful during the day. Once a little child came running up to us with an ice-cream in her hand, and I stroked the little girl's hair. Anya was so jealous she growled at her and actually bared her teeth.

Soon she didn't want me to be close to anyone else. I had to call friends up before they came around to tell them for God's sake not to hug me in front of Anya or she would go for them. She'd gone for my old friend Adam the night he raised his arms to embrace me as he came in our front door. Anya rushed straight along the hall and knocked him right over. She had him on his back with her mouth snarling over his face. Adam was so shaken up I had to pour him a malt. He drank it neat and left, I haven't seen or heard of him since.

Friends would use these incidents to argue with me. 'You can't keep her here forever,' they'd say. 'You shouldn't be in a city for a start.'

'You'll have to release her.'

They couldn't imagine how absurd they sounded to me.

London was full of foxes roaming the streets at night. I was always losing sleep listening to the howls and the screams of my daughter's kind. What mother gives her daughter to the wilds? Aileen offered to drive us both to the north of Scotland and release her into Glen Strathfarrar, where she was convinced Anya would be safe and happy – the red deer and the red fox and the red hills.

But I couldn't bring myself to even think of parting with my daughter. At night, it seemed we slept even closer, her fur keeping me warm. She slept now with her head on the pillow, her paw on my shoulder. She liked to get right under the covers with me. It was strange. Part of her wanted to do everything the same way I did: sleep under covers, eat what I ate, go where I went, run when I ran, walk when I walked; and part of her wanted to do everything her way. Eat from whatever she could snatch in the street or in the woods. She was lazy; she never really put herself out to hunt for food. She scavenged what came her way out of a love of scavenging, I think. It certainly wasn't genuine hunger, she was well fed. I had to stop her going through my neighbour's bin for the remains of their Sunday dinner. Things like that would embarrass me more than anything. I didn't mind her eating a worm from our garden, or a beetle. Once she spotted the tiny movement of a wild rabbit's ear twitching in our garden. That was enough for Anya. She chased the rabbit, killed it, brought it back and buried it, saving it for a hungry day. It thrilled me when she was a fox like other foxes, when I could see her origins so clearly. Anya had more in common with a coyote or a grey wolf or a wild dog than she had with me. The day she buried the rabbit was one of the proudest moments in my life.

But I had never had company like her my whole life long.

With Anya, I felt like there were two lives now: the one before I had her and the one after, and they seemed barely to connect. I didn't feel like the same person even. I was forty when I had Anya, so I'd already lived a lot of my life. All sorts of things that had mattered before I had her didn't matter any more. I wasn't so interested in my hair, my weight, clothes. Going out to parties, plays, restaurants, pubs didn't bother me. I didn't feel like I was missing anything. Nor did I feel ambitious any more. It all seemed stupid wanting to be better than the others in the same ring, shallow, pointless. I called in at work and extended my maternity leave for an extra three months. The thought of the office bored me rigid. It was Anya who held all of my interest.

At home, alone, I'd play my favourite pieces of music to her and dance round the room. I'd play her Mozart's piano concertos, I'd play her Chopin, I'd play Ella Fitzgerald and Louis Armstrong. Joni Mitchell was Anya's favourite. I'd hold her close and dance, 'Do you want to dance with me, baby, well come on.' Anya's eyes would light up and she'd lick my face. 'All I really, really want our love to do is to bring out the best in me and in you too.' I sang along. I had a high voice and Anya loved it when I sang, especially folk songs. Sometimes I'd sing her to sleep. Other times I'd read her stories. I'd been collecting stories about foxes. My best friend, Aileen, had bought Anya *Brer Rabbit*. No fox ever came off too well in the tales or stories. 'Oh, your kind are a deceptive and devious lot,' I'd say, stroking her puffed out chest and reading her another Brer Rabbit tale. She loved her chest being stroked. She'd roll on her back and put both sets of paws in the air.

But then I finally did have to go back to work. I left Anya alone in the house while I sat at my computer answering emails, sipping coffee. When I came home the first time, the wooden legs of the kitchen chairs were chewed right through; the paint on the kitchen door was striped with claw marks. I had to empty the room of everything that could be damaged, carrying the chairs through to the living room, moving the wooden table, putting my chewed cookery books in the hall. I put newspapers on the floor. I left Anya an old shoe to chew. I knew that no nursery would take her, no childminder. I couldn't bring myself to find a dog-walker: Anya was not a dog! It seemed so unfair. I was left to cope with all the problems completely on my own. I had to use my own resources, my own imagination. I left her an old jumper of mine for the comfort of my smell while I was out working, knowing that it would be chewed and shredded by the time I came home. When I tried to tell my colleagues about Anya's antics, they would clam up and look uncomfortable, exchanging awkward looks with each other when they thought I wasn't looking. It made me angry, lonely.

Sometimes it felt as if there was only Anya and me in the world, nobody else mattered really. On Sundays, I'd take her out to Epping Forest and she'd make me run wild with her, running through the lime trees and hornbeams, through beech trees and old oaks, chasing rabbits. The wind flew through my hair and I felt ecstatically happy. I had to curb the impulse to rip off my clothes and run with Anya naked through the woods. My sense of smell grew stronger over those Sundays. I'd stand and sniff where Anya was sniffing, pointing my head in the same direction. I grew to know when a rabbit was near. I never felt closer to her than out in the forest running. But of course, fit as I was, fast as I was, I could never be as fast as Anya. She'd stop and look round for me and come running back.

I don't think anybody has ever taught me more about myself than Anya. Once, when she growled at the postman,

I smacked her wet nose. I felt awful. But five minutes later she jumped right onto my lap and licked my face all over, desperate to be friends again. There's nothing like forgiveness, it makes you want to weep. I stroked her long, lustrous fur and nuzzled my head against hers and we looked straight into each other's eyes, knowingly, for the longest time. I knew I wasn't able to forgive like Anya could. I just couldn't. I couldn't move on to the next moment like that. I had to go raking over the past. I couldn't forgive Anya's father for denying her, for making promises and breaking them like bones.

One morning I woke up and looked out of the window. It was snowing; soft dreamy flakes of snow whirled and spiralled down to the ground. Already the earth was covered white, and the winter rose bushes had snow clinging to the stems. Everything was covered. I got up and went to get the milk. Paw footprints led up to our door. The foxes had been here again in the night. They were driving me mad. I sensed they wanted to claim Anya.

I fetched my daughter her breakfast, some fruit and some chicken. I could tell she wasn't herself. Her eyes looked dull and her ears weren't alert. She gave me a sad look that seemed to last an age. I wasn't sure what she was trying to tell me. She walked with her elegant beauty to the door and hit it twice with her paw. Then she looked at me again, the saddest look you ever saw. Perhaps she'd had enough. Perhaps she wanted to run off with the dog fox that so often hung and howled around our house.

I couldn't actually imagine my life without her now, that was the problem. They never tell you about that either. How the hardest thing a mother has to do is give her child up, let them go, watch them run.

Much later that night when we were both in bed, we heard

them again; one of the most common sounds in London now, the conversations of the urban fox. Anya got up and stood at my bedroom window. She howled back. Soon four of them were out in the back garden, their bright red fur even more dramatic against the snow. I held my breath in when I looked at them. They looked strange and mysterious, different from Anya. They were stock-still, lit up by the moonlight. I stared at them for a long time and they stared back. I walked slowly through to the kitchen in my bare feet. I stood looking at the back door for some minutes. I pulled the top bolt and then the bottom one. I opened the door and I let her out into the night.

JAMES ROBERTSON

OLD MORTALITY

'ARE YOU COLD?' Alec asked. 'You mustn't get a chill.'

'I'm all right,' Liz said. 'It was just a shiver. You know, one of those shivers? Just standing here in front of this . . . this bloody great stone. Your family.'

'They're not as bad as all that,' he said.

'It scares me, though,' she said, 'and that's the truth. I mean, when I think about everything. What we're going to do. And then here's this thing that represents generations of your family and there's nothing on it. Absolutely nothing.'

'Well, I hope you weren't expecting some big message,' he said. 'You're right, there is nothing. It's a lovely place, that's all. No mystery, no revelation. I just wanted to show it to you.'

'But there are people here,' she said. 'Can't you feel them?'

'No,' he said. 'It's just a graveyard, sweetheart.'

'There's more to it than that,' she said. She reached for his hand. 'There has to be.'

'No,' he said, 'this is it. A field full of bones. This is where everybody ends up.'

She shivered again, although there was still warmth in the air. 'I think we're being watched,' she said.

'What?' He glanced round. 'Who by?'

'I don't know. I just feel it.'

He tried not to laugh. When Liz came out with things like this, which she'd been doing a lot lately, it made him uneasy. It was amusing, but he felt it could get out of hand

and then it wouldn't be funny at all. But also it made him feel manly, sensible, down-to-earth. It sent a wave of love rushing through him. He would have been embarrassed, though, if anyone else had heard her.

They had been visiting his parents for the weekend. They didn't go very often: work and other commitments left them with little time or energy to make the journey north, and there was also the fact that Liz felt intimidated by Alec's mother. But there'd been a particular reason for making this trip: to tell them about the baby they were expecting. They weren't married, and Liz had anticipated a fuss, an argument about 'doing the right thing'. In fact, all had gone well. Alec's mother had seemed genuinely pleased about becoming a grandmother. Liz felt that perhaps a turning point in the relationship had been reached.

Then on the way back south Alec had turned off the main road in order to introduce Liz to his ancestors. He'd never taken her there before. The place was a ruined church with an ancient burial ground, right on the edge of the firth. To get to it you left the dual carriageway and followed a single-track road down to the water. There were fine old trees, beech and ash, and a big house, with three cars in the drive, that had presumably once been the manse. Through an iron kissing-gate was the roofless church, surrounded by old gravestones and tablets set at odd angles like wreckage bobbing in a green sea. The kirk's west gable-end rose to a small belfry which would once have housed a single monotonous summoning bell. A sign at the boarded up door warned of the danger of falling masonry.

The gravestones were thick with moss, their inscriptions faded and often indecipherable. There was the usual assortment of symbols found in old Scottish kirkyards: urns, skulls, bones, shrouds. Towards the water was a section filled with more recent stones, polished ones from the fifties and sixties that seemed out of place, as if they had been transferred from another cemetery. Between the boundary dyke and the sea a few sheep were grazing a strip of rough pasture. It was early evening in October. The grass was thick and springy, and there was birdsong among the stones and in the great trees shading the parking area. It was, Alec thought, all very peaceful.

'I wish we hadn't come,' Liz said. 'I'm frightened.'

'What's the matter?' he said. He tried not to sound impatient. 'What are you frightened of?'

'Nothing.'

He thought she was avoiding the question, but then she said it again. 'Nothing. That's exactly what.'

His ancestors had once been big shots in the area. Landed gentry. They had been rich at a time when almost nobody else was. Each generation had followed the pattern of the previous one. The eldest son inherited the big house and the younger ones went off to die in far-flung bits of the Empire, while the daughters were married to the sons of other rich families. The wives – all the wives – produced eight, or ten, or twelve children, or died in the attempt. Even the good breeders expired long before their husbands. Their annual pregnancies and early deaths were what perpetuated the system. Nothing lasts, though. One laird died unexpectedly young. There were debts and death duties. Limbs started to break off the family tree: the stout trunk began to crack and crumble. The big house was now long gone, and Alec's parents lived miles away in a new housing development. Alec felt, when he was being cynical, that he was a twig at the end of a fallen branch rotting on the ground.

The ancestral plot was a patch enclosed by a foot-high

cast-iron fretted fender. Various centuries-old tablets lay half-submerged in the soft turf. The main feature was an upright sandstone slab, eight feet high and ten feet wide, at the base of which, presumably, the family lay packed one on top of another. The sandstone had weathered so much that only a few words were still legible: BELOVED . . . DIED . . . TAKETH . . . TRUST. Alec ran his fingers over the face of the stone, but the names that had once been there could no longer be felt any more than they could be read. He knew it was the right spot because his grandfather had brought him to it twenty-five years before. 'Pay attention,' his grandfather had said. 'This will be standing long after you and I are both gone. This is where we come from.'

He could read a few of the names back then. There had been an ALEXANDER, which had made him feel sure that his grandfather must be right. *This is where we come from*: he'd imagined troll-like people who looked a bit like him crawling from a hole under the slab. Twenty-five years and nothing much had changed. And yet everything had changed: his grandfather was dead – cremated – Alec was grown up, and the names on the stone were all gone. And he didn't feel the connection anymore.

Something else was different. Beyond the kirkyard, beyond the sheep, beyond the splash of the shoreline, a group of oil rigs rested in the water like great metallic birds. They brought them in from the North Sea fields for refitting or when demand for oil fell and some distant accounting procedure drove them into the firth like birds sheltering from a storm. Alec thought them majestic. The vast structures, all intestinal pipes and rust-coloured legs and craning steel beaks and claws, seemed to be in sympathy with the gravestones, as if they themselves were already becoming monuments to aching toil and hard-earned rest.

'I love it here,' Alec said. He moved behind her, put his arms around her waist and gently turned her to face the water. He felt the bump beneath her shirt and rubbed it with the palm of one hand. 'Beautiful, isn't it?'

Liz said, 'Yes, in a way. But ugly too. Those things out there, they're like monsters.' She turned again to the family monument. 'You know what really scares me?'

'No.'

'The finality of it. This great blank . . . nothing.'

'The End,' he said, and gave a little laugh.

'You don't believe in anything, do you?' she said. 'Not God, not something else after this, nothing at all.'

'Nope,' he said.

'I just can't imagine it,' she said. 'Not feeling, not existing. It doesn't make sense.'

'I believe in you and I believe in me,' he said. 'I can feel us both. That makes sense.'

'What about love?' she said. 'Don't you believe in love?'

'Well, I suppose so, but . . . it's not really something you *believe* in, is it? It's just there.'

'But it has a power. It can make things happen. We know that.'

'Are you going to burst into song, Liz?'

'No I fucking am not.' She kicked him lightly on the shin with her heel. 'I'm just . . . everything just feels . . .'

'What?'

'Empty,' she said.

He let her go and she walked down towards the sea. He wondered if she was trying to tell him something about the baby. If there was something wrong. If she didn't want to go through with it.

Down below, where his forebears had been, it *was* empty. He felt that all right. Their minds and bones long since crumbled away. Ideas and work and knowledge and endurance, all mince for the worms. But there was a comfort in that. One day, there'd be nothing more to face, to deal with. He thought of the morning, Monday, and how tired, almost immediately, he would be.

He was about to call to Liz, ask her if she was feeling sick, if she was warm enough, if everything was going to be all right, when she gave a little yelp of surprise. She was twenty yards away, at the entrance to a stone enclosure – some other family's plot. 'Alec?' she said – quite quietly, but a light breeze had got up off the firth and her voice carried to him as if she were speaking in his ear – 'Alec, come here.'

The body of an old man was stretched on top of one of the tablets inside the enclosure. He was wearing a heavy black coat with mud splatters around the hem, and trousers with mud encrusted round the ankles. He had old working boots on his feet. On the ground beside him was a Tesco carrier bag with the wooden shaft of some implement protruding from it. His mouth was open and his right arm was flung to the side so that the hand trailed over the edge of the tablet. His skin looked blue beneath the white bristles of his beard.

'Oh, Jesus,' Alec said.

Liz had her hand to her mouth. 'I knew it,' she said. 'I knew someone was watching us.'

'I don't think so, sweetheart,' Alec said. 'I think he's dead.'

He stepped forward and listened. His own heart was pounding so hard he couldn't hear if the old man was breathing. He reached out and gingerly touched the coat at the shoulder. It felt damp and cold. He smelt something unpleasant, mouldy. He shook the shoulder.

The man jerked upright, and Alec jumped away. 'What? What?' the old man said, and went into a fit of coughing. Alec came back and started slapping his back. 'I'm sorry,' he said. 'Don't worry, it's all right. God, I'm sorry. We thought you were dead.'

'Dead?' the old man said. 'I'm not dead. Stop hitting me. What makes you think I'm dead?'

'You don't look very well,' Liz said.

'I was working. I just needed a kip. Who are you?'

'We're visitors,' Alec said. 'We're looking at the graves. Do you look after them then?'

'Look after what?'

'The graves.'

'Oh.' He paused. 'Aye, I do. After a fashion.' Another pause, as if he was weighing the information he had just given them. 'Not just these ones. I look after lots of grave-yards, all over the country. I do repairs.'

Alec and Liz exchanged glances. The old man appeared confused, disorientated. He swung his feet to the ground, cleared his throat and spat.

'Sorry, lass,' he said, less roughly. 'Always have to do that when I've had a kip.'

'I'm sorry we disturbed you,' Liz said.

'Well, it's done now. Need to get on anyway. Finish up for the day.'

The three of them came out of the enclosure together. The old man looked at the sky as if assessing the chances of rain. He spat again.

'What is it you repair?' Alec asked. 'The gravestones?'

'Aye, of course,' the old man said. 'Do you think I'm going to manage the kirk single-handed?' He was more impatient with Alec than he was with Liz. 'The stones, man, the stones. Plenty of them. Somebody's got to do it, get them back to how they were. See?' He opened the Tesco bag and took out a mallet and a stone chisel. 'Tools of the trade, man. That's all I need. Anybody could do it, really.'

'Oh, right,' Alec said. He glanced at Liz again.

'Once the names are gone, you see,' the old man said, 'that's it. Oblivion.' He looked directly at Liz, as if he suddenly recognised her. 'What are *you* doing here? You're too bonnie to hang about a place like this.'

Liz shrugged. She was about to speak when Alec butted in. The old man was beginning to irritate him.

'My ancestors are here.' Alec pointed to the sandstone slab. 'I wanted to show her our stone.'

The old man peered over at the slab. 'Oh aye,' he said, 'I mind that one. How do you ken it's yours?'

'What do you mean?'

'How do you ken it's your stone. There's no names on it.'

'My grandfather told me,' Alec said. 'He brought me here years ago. I remember.'

'You remember, do you?' Something like a sneer slid into the old man's voice. 'Your grandfather? Ach well. If you remember.'

'Yes, he does,' Liz said. She moved closer to Alec. 'He does.'

'Ach well,' the old man said again. 'That's all right then.'

'There were names on it then,' Alec said. 'But they're all gone now.'

'That's right,' the old man said. 'All gone. Nothing more I can do about *them*.'

Liz shivered against Alec. He could tell she was still frightened. There was something about the old man that even he found unsettling.

'Well, I'd better get on.' The man put his tools back in the plastic bag and set off towards the shore, where the newer graves were. They saw him spit on the grass again. After a minute his head bobbed down behind a shiny black stone and they heard the *chink*, *chink* of his chisel.

Alec screwed up his face at Liz. 'What was that all about?'

'I don't know,' Liz said. 'He seems . . .'

'He's nuts,' Alec said. 'Probably harmless, but nuts. Nobody goes around repairing gravestones. Not like that. With their tools in a carrier bag? And where's his car? He can't have walked here.'

'Maybe he lives nearby,' Liz said. She pointed at the former manse in the trees. 'Like there.'

'I don't think so. Did you get a whiff of him? He's a tramp. A tramp who's lost the place, thinks he's a stonemason.'

'That's sad,' she said. 'Maybe we ought to tell someone.'

'What would we say? That we met an old tramp in a graveyard and we think he's a bit sad? Forget it. Who'd give a fuck about that?'

They stood together, holding hands, looking out at the rigs. Alec tried to count them, but some were hidden behind others, and he kept having to start again. A dozen at least. Liz was doing the same, or maybe just staring, he couldn't tell. Why was that, if he loved her? And if she was going to have his baby? How could he be so close to her and yet not tell?

The breeze blowing off the water was cool now. The day was starting to fade, and out on the rigs amber and yellow lights were coming on.

'Time to go,' Alec said.

'Do you think we should offer him a lift?' Liz asked, as they started back to the car.

'Who? The old fellow? No chance,' Alec said.

Liz said, 'Wait a minute. Listen.'

They heard a sheep bleating, and gulls crying, but the *chink, chink* noise had stopped.

'Go and see if he's all right,' she said. 'He might have keeled over again.'

'He'll be fine,' Alec said.

'No, go and check,' she insisted. 'I couldn't bear it if we left him here and he'd collapsed. We'll both go.'

But there was no sign of him. They separated, searching through the newer gravestones, calling out, 'Hello, hello,' but he had gone. They came together again by the stone he had been working on.

'He must have had a bike,' Alec said. 'He said he was finishing up for the day. He'll stay up the road somewhere.'

'He didn't have a bike,' Liz said. Then she said, 'Oh, look!'

All the lettering on the shiny black stone had been chiselled away. They could tell where it had been because there were six deep gouges across the face of the stone. On the ground was a heap of chips. The breeze was already dispersing dust across the grass.

'Bloody hell!' Alec said.

Liz stood shaking her head. 'Do you think he did that? He can't have, can he?'

'He must have. There's been nobody else here.'

'But that's terrible. That's sacrilege.'

'Vandalism. The old bastard.'

'Maybe it's some family thing,' Liz said. 'That must be what it is. An old feud. Maybe somebody did something awful to him, something he could never forgive, and this is his way of repaying them.'

'Doesn't matter,' Alec said. 'It still doesn't give him the right. And anyway, this isn't the only one. Look, here. And here.'

They separated and moved among the stones again, finding more and more of them defaced, the names and dates of people obliterated. Every time they found one they shouted out in amazement. They only stopped, and came back together, when it grew so gloomy that it was easier to hear than to see each other.

'He said he did repairs,' Alec said.

'Yes,' Liz said. 'But that's not what he meant. He said . . .'

'What?' Alec said when she didn't finish.

'Something else,' Liz said. 'What was it?'

'We should report him,' Alec said. 'Nobody has the right to do that.' He heard the anger in his voice and wondered at it. He felt Liz clutch at his arm. 'That's what the weather does,' he said. 'The wind and the rain. That's what *they* do. Not some old tramp with a hammer and chisel.'

'I'd like to go now,' Liz said. 'Can we go?'

'Yes, yes, of course.' She looked so pale and weary that he needed to say something, to reassure her.

'I'll look after you,' he said. 'You don't need to be afraid.'

'I know,' she said. But they hurried to the car, and Alec started the engine at once, as if something were pursuing them. He switched on the headlights. The night had swallowed up the day and he felt as if it might swallow them. He wondered where the old man had gone. He thought, maybe he's hiding in the back of the car with his chisel, just waiting till we drive off before he attacks. He ridiculed the thought as soon as it arrived, but he kept it to himself.

He took a last look at the firth before swinging the car round. The lights on the oil rigs stretched towards them across the water in wavy amber lines. The rigs could have been giant floating houses, each one with giant children running up and down stairs, and a man and a woman of ordinary size, coming home from work, exhausted, dividing the labours, one tidying rooms and drawing curtains while the other prepared dinner for their giant children. But it was an illusion, a childish fancy. They were just oil rigs, waiting for the signal from someone hundreds or maybe thousands of miles away that would send them back out to sea.

A. L. KENNEDY

NIGHT GEOMETRY AND THE AND THE GARSCADDEN TRAINS

ONE QUESTION.

Why do so many trains stop at Garscadden? I don't mean stop. I mean finish. I mean terminate. Why do so many trains terminate at Garscadden?

Every morning I stand at my station, which isn't Garscadden, and I see them: one, two, three, even four in a row, all of them terminating at Garscadden. They stop and no one gets off, no one gets on; their carriages are empty, and then they pull away again. They leave. To go to Garscadden. To terminate there.

I have never understood this. In the years I have waited on the westbound side of my station, the number of trains to Garscadden has gradually increased; this increase being commensurate with my lack of understanding. The trees across the track put out leaves and drop leaves; the seasons and the trains to Garscadden pass and I do not understand.

It's stupid.

So many things are stupid, though. Like the fact that the death of my mother's dog seemed to upset me more than the death of my mother. And I loved my mother more than I loved her dog. The stupidity of someone being killed by the train that might normally take them home, things like that. There seems to be so much lack of foresight, so much carelessness in the world. And people can die of carelessness. They lack perspective.

I do, too. I know it. I am the most important thing in my

life. I am central to whatever I do and those whom I love and care for are more vital to my existence than statesmen, or snooker players, or Oscar nominees, but the television news and the headlines were the same as they always are when my mother died and theirs were the names and faces that I saw. Nations didn't hold their breath and the only lines in the paper for her were the ones I had inserted.

Inserted. Horrible word. Like putting her in a paper grave.

To return to the Garscadden trains, they are not important in themselves; they are only important in the ways they have affected me. Lack of perspective again, you see? Naturally, they make me late for work, but there's altogether more to them than that. It was a Garscadden train that almost killed my husband.

Of course you don't know my husband, Duncan, and I always find him difficult to describe. I carry his picture with me sometimes; more to jog my memory than through any kind of sentiment. I do love him. I do love him, even now. I love him in such a way that it seems, before I met him, I was waiting to love him. But I remember what I remember and that isn't his face.

Esau was an hairy man. I remember my mother saying that. It always sounded more important than just saying he was born with lots of hair. I only mention Esau now, because Duncan wasn't hairy at all.

He had almost no eyebrows, downy underarm hair and a disturbingly naked chest. We used to go walking together as newly weds, mainly on moorland and low hills where he'd been as a scout. The summers were usually brief, unsettled, the way you'd expect, but the heat across the moors could be remarkable. It seems to be a quality of moors. The earth is warm and sweaty under the wiry grass, the heather bones are brilliant white and the sun swings, blinding, over-head. You walk in a cloud of wavering air and tiny, black insects.

On such days – hot days – Duncan would never wear a T-shirt. Not anything approaching it. He would put on a shirt, normally pale blue or white, roll the sleeves up high on his arms and wear the whole thing loose and open like a jacket, revealing a thin, vulnerable chest. Sensible boots, socks, faded khaki shorts and the shirt flapping: he would look like those embarrassing forties photographs of working class men at the beach or in desert armies. He had a poverty stricken chest, pale with little boy's skin.

There was hair on his head, undoubtedly, honey brown and cut short enough to subdue the natural curl, but his face was naked. I remember him washing and brushing his teeth, but I don't believe he ever shaved. There was no need.

Duncan, you might also notice, is in the past tense – not because he's dead, because he's over. I call him my husband because I've never had another one and everything I tell you will only show you how he was. Today I am a different person and he will be, too. Whatever I describe will be part of our past. I used to want to own his past. I used to want to look after him retrospectively. This was during the time when our affair had turned into marriage but still had something to do with love. In fact, there was a lot of love about. I mean that.

My clearest memory of him comes from about that time. I don't see it, because I never looked at it. I only remember a feeling, safe and complete, of lying with him, eyes closed, and whispering that I wanted to own his past; that I wanted to own him, too.

It was strange. However we flopped together, however haphazardly we decided to come to rest, the fit would always be the same.

His right arm, cradling my neck.

My head on his shoulder.

My right arm across his chest.

My left arm, tucked away between us with my hand resting quietly on his thigh. Not intending to cause disturbance, merely resting, proprietary.

In these pauses, we would doze together before sleeping and dreaming apart and we would whisper. We always whispered, very low and very soft, as if we were afraid of disturbing each other.

'I love you.'
   'Uh hu.'
   'I do love you.'
   'I know that. I feel that. I love you, too.'
   'I want to look after you.'
   'You can't.'
   'Why not.'
   'Because I'm looking after you.'
   'That's alright, then.'
   'I love you.'
   'Uh hu.'
   'I do love you.'

And, finally, we would be quiet and sleepy and begin to breathe in unison. I've noticed since, if you're very close to anything for long enough, you'll start to breathe in unison. Even my mother's dog, when he slept with his head on my lap, would eventually breathe in time with me. There was more to it than that with Duncan, of course.

I sometimes imagined our hearts beat together, too. It's silly, I know, but we felt close then. Closer than touch.

This positioning, our little bit of night geometry, this came to be important in a way I didn't like because it changed. I didn't like it then, as much as I now don't like to remember the two of us together and almost asleep, because, by fair means or foul, you can't replace that. Intensity is easy, it's the simple nearness that you'll miss.

The change happened one evening on a Sunday. We had cocoa in bed. I made it in our little milk pan and I whisked it with our little whisk, to make it creamy, and we drank it sitting up against the pillows and ate all butter biscuits, making sure we didn't drop any crumbs. There is nothing worse than a bed full of crumbs. And we put away the cocoa mugs and we turned out the lights and that was fine. Very nice.

But when we slowed to a stop, when we terminated, the geometry had changed. I didn't really think about it because it was so nicely changed.

My right arm around his neck.

His head against my shoulder.

His one arm tucked between us very neat, and the other, just resting, doing nothing much, just being there.

It all felt very pleasant. The good weight of him, snuggled down there, the smell of his hair when I kissed the top of his head. I did that. I told him I could never do enough, or be enough, or give enough back and I kissed the top of his head. I told him I belonged to him. I think he was asleep.

I told him anyway and he was my wee man, then, and I couldn't sleep for wanting to look after him.

The following morning, I waited on the westbound platform and the smell of him was still on me, even having washed. All that day when I moved in my clothes, combed

413

my hair, his smell would come round me as if he'd just walked through the room.

It was good, that. Not unheard of in itself, hardly uncommon, in fact. It wasn't unknown for me to leave my bed and dress without washing in order to keep what I could of the night before, but you'll understand that, this time, I was remembering something special, I thought, unique.

Now I realise that you can never be sure that anything is unique. You can never be sure you know enough to judge. I mean, when Pizarro conquered the Incas, they thought he was a god – his men, too – when really Spain was full of Spaniards just like him. Eventually you see you were mistaken, but look what you've had to lose in order to learn.

I thought that the way I met Duncan was unique.

Wrong.

Not in the place: a bar. Not in the time: round about eight. Not in the circumstances: two friends of friends, talking at a wee, metal table when the rest of the conversation dipped. It was a bit of a boring evening to tell the truth.

We all left on the bell for last orders and there was the usual confusion about coats – who was sitting on whose jacket, who'd lost gloves. Duncan and I were a little delayed, quite possibly not by chance.

'I'm going to call you tomorrow. Ten o'clock. What's your number?'

'What?'

'What number could I get you on, tomorrow at ten o'clock?'

'In the morning?'

'Yes, in the morning.'

'Well, I would be at work, then.'

'I know that, what's the number?'

I gave him the office number and he went away. I don't even think he said goodbye.

At a quarter to eleven, the following day, he called McSwiggin and Jones and was put through to me. I had some idea that he might be in need of advice. McSwiggin and Jones accepted payment from various concerns with money to call in the debts of various individuals without it. Debt, as Mr McSwiggin often said, could be very democratic – Mrs Gallacher with two small boys, no husband and her loan from the Social Fund turned down was in debt. And so was Peru. Perhaps, I thought, Duncan was in debt.

'What do you mean, in debt?'

'I mean, who do you owe money? I can't help you if it's on our books. I mean I can, but not really, you know.'

'No, I don't know. I owe my brother a fiver, since you ask.'

'Mm hm.'

'And that's it. I don't have any debts, just a bit of an overdraft which doesn't count. I want to see you tonight. I could bring my bank statement with me if you'd like.'

'Look, I'm sorry, but you're wasting my time, aren't you?'

'I'm sorry if you feel that way. I thought we got on well together.'

'Ring me at home tomorrow evening. This is ridiculous and I'm at work.'

He called at the end of the week and we went out for a coffee on the Sunday afternoon. Before I had time to ask he told me that he and Claire, his partner from the pub, were only friends. They'd been at school together which is why they'd seemed so close the other evening.

When Duncan and I were married, quite a while later, Claire was at the little party afterwards. She smiled quietly when she saw me, danced with Duncan once and then left. I had to ask who she was because she looked so familiar, but I couldn't remember her name.

So, Duncan and I were married and we were unique. Although men and women often marry as an expression of various feelings and beliefs and although they often go to bed together before, during and after marriage, the thing with Duncan and me was unrepeatable, remarkable and entirely unique. So I thought.

No one had ever married us before and we had never married each other. It was tactfully assumed that the going to bed had happened with other partners in other times, but they had never managed to reach the same conclusion. We were one flesh, one collection of jokes and habits and one smell. Even now, I know, the smell of my sweat and the taste of my mouth are not the same as they were before I met him. He will always be that much a part of me, whether I like it or not.

Even when two different friends in two different ladies toilets in two different bars told me that Claire and Duncan had been sleeping and staying awake together for months before I met him, I didn't mind. I didn't mind if they had continued to see each other after we met. I was flattered he had taken the trouble to lie. It didn't matter because he had left her for me and we had made each other unique.

Finally, of course, I realised the most original things about us were our fingerprints. Nothing of what we did was ever new. I repeated the roles that Duncan chose to give me in his head – wicked wife, wounded wife, the one he would always come back to, the one he had to leave and I never even noticed. I always felt like me. For years, I never knew that when he rested with his head on my shoulder, all wee and snuggled up, it was helping him to ease his guilt. Once or twice a year, it was his body's way of saying he'd been naughty, but he was going to be a good boy from now on.

And I was a good wife. I even answered the telephone with a suitably unexpected voice, to give his latest girlfriend her little shiver before she hung up. Like a good wife should.

All the time I thought I was just being married when, really, Duncan was turning me into Claire and the ones before and after Claire.

I lived with the only person I've met who can snore when he's wide awake, who soaked his feet until they looked like a dead man's, then rubbed them to make them peel. I've washed hundreds of towels, scaley with peelings from his feet. I've cooked him nice puddings, nursed him through the 'flu, stopped him trimming his fringe with the kitchen scissors and have generally been a good wife. Never knowing how Duncan saw me inside his head. It seems I was either a victim, an obstacle or a safety net. I wasn't me. He took away me.

But it wasn't his fault, not really. It was the E numbers in his yoghurt, or his role models when he was young. It was a compulsion. Duncan, the wee pet lamb, would chase after anything silly enough to show him a half inch of leg. From joggers to lady bicyclists to the sad looking Scottish Nationalist who sold papers round the pubs in his kilt. Duncan couldn't help it. It wasn't his fault.

I sound like an idiot, not seeing how things were for so long. I felt like an idiot, too. Nothing makes you feel more stupid than finding out you were wrong when you thought you were loved. The first morning after I discovered, it wasn't good to wake up. Over by the wall in the bedroom there was a wardrobe with a mirror in the door. I swung my legs out of bed and just sat. There I was; reflected; unrecognisable. I looked for a long while until I could tell it was me: pale and slack, round shouldered and dank-haired, varicose veins, gently mapping their way. You would have to really love me to like that and Duncan, of course, no longer loved me at all. I could have felt sorry for him, if I hadn't felt so sorry for myself.

I considered the night before and letting his head rest on my shoulder, knowing what I finally knew. It was as if I wasn't touching him, only pressing against his skin through a coating of other women. I'd felt his breath on my collar bone and found it difficult not to retch.

It had taken about a month to fit all the pieces together in my head. Nothing silly like lipstick on collars, or peroxide blonde hairs along his lapels: it was all quite subtle stuff. He would suddenly become more crumpled, as if he had started sleeping in his shirts, while his trousers developed concertina creases and needed washing much more regularly. The angle of the passenger seat in the car would often change and, opening the door in the morning, there would be that musty smell. And yet, for all the must and wrinkles, the fluff all over his jackets, as if they'd been thrown on the floor, Duncan would be taking pains with his appearance. When he walked out of the flat he'd never looked better and when he returned he'd never looked worse. Life seemed to be treating him very roughly, which perhaps explained his sudden interest in personal hygiene, the increasingly frequent washing and the purchase of bright, new Saint Michael's underwear. It's all very obvious now, but it wasn't then. Even though it had been repeating itself for years.

Duncan's infidelity didn't have all the implications it might have today. I didn't take a blood test, although I've watched for signs of anything since. Still, you can imagine the situation in the first few weeks of both of us constantly washing away the feel of his current mistress. We went through a lot of soap.

I suppose that I should have left him, or at least made it clear that I'd found him out. I should have made sure that we both knew that I knew what he knew. Or whatever it was you were meant to make sure of. I didn't know. To tell the truth, it didn't really seem important. It was to do with him and things to do with him didn't seem important any more. I couldn't see why he should know what was going on inside my head when, through all the episodes of crumpled shirts and then uncrumpled shirts and even the time when he tried for a moustache, I had never had any idea of what Duncan was thinking.

I stayed and, for a long time, things were very calm. We finished with all of our washing, started to sleep at night and I managed to get the dryer to chew up six pairs of rainbow coloured knickers. Duncan went back to being just a little scruffy and always coming home for tea.

It wasn't going to last, I knew. It would maybe be a matter of months before the whole performance started up again and I wasn't sure how I would react to that. In the meantime I sorted out my past. I still worked at McSwiggin and Jones, but only for three days out of seven and instead of spending the rest of my week on housework or other, silly, things I started to sit on the bed a lot and stare at that mirror door. I bought some books on meditation and, at night, when I felt Duncan sleeping, I used to breathe the way they told me to – independently. It wasn't easy, crumpling up a marriage and throwing it away, looking for achievements I'd made that weren't to do with being a wife, but I don't think I did too badly. For a while I was a bit depressed, but only a bit.

My future, and this surprised me, was much harder to redefine. All the hopes you collect: another good holiday abroad, a proper fitted kitchen, children, a child. Your future creates an atmosphere around you and mine was surprisingly beautiful. Duncan and I, retired, would grow closer and closer, more and more serene, there would be grandchildren, picnics, gardening and fine, white hair. There would be trust and understanding, dignity in sickness and not dying alone. We would leave good things behind us when we were gone. I can't imagine where it all came from, I only know that it was hard to give away.

Then, one Monday morning, there was an incident involving my husband and a Garscadden train.

I went down, as usual, to stand on the westbound platform, this time in a hard, grey wind, the black twigs and branches over the line, oily and dismal with the damp. I waited in the little, orange shelter, read the walls and watched the Garscadden trains. There were three, and a Not In Service and, for the first time in my life, I gave up the wait. I turned around, walked away from the shelter and went home. I wished it would rain. I wanted to feel rain on my face.

The hall still smelt of the toast for breakfast. I took off my coat and went into the bedroom, needing to look in the mirror again, and there they were, in bed with the fire on, nice and cosy: Duncan and a very young lady I had never met before. They seemed to be taking the morning off. Duncan ducked his head beneath the bedclothes, as if I wouldn't know it was him, and she stared at the shape he made in the covers and then she stared at me.

I don't believe I said a single word. There wasn't a word I could say. I don't remember going to the kitchen, but I do remember being there, because I reached into one of the drawers beside the sink and I took out a knife. To be precise, my mother's old carving knife. I was going to run back to the bedroom and do what you would do with a carving knife, maybe to one of them, maybe to both, or perhaps just cut off his prick. That thought occurred.

That thought and several others and you shouldn't pause for thought on these occasions. I did and that was it. In the end I tried to stab the knife into the worksurface, so that he would see it there, sticking up, and know that he'd had a near miss. The point slid across the formica and my hand went down on the blade, so that all of the fingers began to bleed. When Duncan came in, there was blood everywhere and my hand was under the tap and I'm sure he believed I'd tried to kill myself. The idea seemed to disturb him, so I left it at that.

He drove me to and from the hospital and stayed that night in the flat, but, when he was sure I felt stable again, he went away and we began the slow division of our memories and ornaments. It was all done amicably, with restraint, but we haven't kept in touch.

And that, I suppose, is the story of how my husband was almost killed by one Garscadden train too many. It is also the story of how I learned that half of some things is less than nothing at all and that, contrary to popular belief, people, many people, almost all the people, live their lives in the best way they can with generally good intentions and still leave absolutely nothing behind.

There is only one thing I want more than proof that I existed and that's some proof, while I'm here, that I exist. Not being an Olympic skier, or a chat show host, I won't get my wish. There are too many people alive today for us to notice every single one.

But the silent majority and I do have one memorial, at least. The Disaster. We have small lives, easily lost in foreign droughts, or famines; the occasional incendiary incident, or a wall of pale faces, crushed against grillework, one Saturday afternoon in Spring. This is not enough.

LEILA ABOULELA

THE MUSEUM

AT FIRST SHADIA was afraid to ask him for his notes. The earring made her afraid. And the straight long hair that he tied up with a rubber band. She had never seen a man with an earring and such long hair. But then she had never known such cold, so much rain. His silver earring was the strangeness of the West, another culture-shock. She stared at it during classes, her eyes straying from the white scribbles on the board. Most times she could hardly understand anything. Only the notation was familiar. But how did it all fit together? How did *this* formula lead to this? Her ignorance and the impending exams were horrors she wanted to escape. His long hair, a dull colour between yellow and brown, different shades. It reminded her of a doll she had when she was young. She had spent hours combing that doll's hair, stroking it. She had longed for such straight hair. When she went to Paradise she would have hair like that. When she ran it would fly behind her; if she bent her head down it would fall over like silk and sweep the flowers on the grass. She watched his pony-tail move as he wrote and then looked up at the board. She pictured her doll, vivid suddenly after years, and felt sick that she was day-dreaming in class, not learning a thing.

The first days of term, when the classes started for the MSc in Statistics, she was like someone tossed around by monstrous waves. Battered, as she lost her way to the different lecture rooms, fumbled with the photocopying machine, could not find anything in the library. She could scarcely hear or eat or see. Her eyes bulged with fright, watered from the cold. The course required a certain background, a background she didn't have. So she floundered, she and the other African students, the two Turkish girls, and the men from Brunei. Asafa, the short, round-faced Ethiopian, said, in his grave voice, as this collection from the Third World whispered their anxieties in grim Scottish corridors, the girls in nervous giggles, 'Last year, last year a Nigerian on this very same course committed suicide. *Cut his wrists.*'

Us and them, she thought. The ones who would do well, the ones who would crawl and sweat and barely pass. Two predetermined groups. Asafa, generous and wise (he was the oldest), leaned and whispered to Shadia, 'The Spanish girl is good. Very good.' His eyes bulged redder than Shadia's. He cushioned his fears every night in the university pub; she only cried. Their countries were next-door neighbours but he had never been to Sudan, and Shadia had never been to Ethiopia. 'But we meet in Aberdeen!', she had shrieked when this information was exchanged, giggling furiously. Collective fear had its euphoria.

'That boy Bryan,' said Asafa, 'is excellent.'

'The one with the earring?'

Asafa laughed and touched his own unadorned ear. 'The earring doesn't mean anything. He'll get the Distinction. He did his undergraduate here, got First Class Honours. That gives him an advantage. He knows all the lecturers, he knows the system.'

So the idea occurred to her of asking Bryan for the notes of his graduate year. If she strengthened her background in stochastic processes and time series, she would be better able to cope with the new material they were bombarded with every day. She watched him to judge if he was approachable.

Next to the courteous Malaysian students, he was devoid of manners. He mumbled and slouched and did not speak with respect to the lecturers. He spoke to them as if they were his equals. And he did silly things. When he wanted to throw a piece of paper in the bin, he squashed it into a ball and from where he was sitting he aimed it at the bin. If he missed, he muttered under his breath. She thought that he was immature. But he was the only one who was sailing through the course.

The glossy handbook for overseas students had explained about the 'famous British reserve' and hinted that they should be grateful, things were worse further south, less 'hospitable'. In the cafeteria, drinking coffee with Asafa and the others, the picture of 'hospitable Scotland' was something different. Badr, the Malaysian, blinked and whispered, 'Yesterday our windows got smashed; my wife today is afraid to go out.'

'Thieves?' asked Shadia, her eyes wider than anyone else's.

'Racists,' said the Turkish girl, her lipstick chic, the word tripping out like silver, like ice.

Wisdom from Asafa, muted, before the collective silence, 'These people think they own the world . . .' and around them the aura of the dead Nigerian student. They were ashamed of that brother they had never seen. He had weakened, caved in. In the cafeteria, Bryan never sat with them. They never sat with him. He sat alone, sometimes reading the local paper. When Shadia walked in front of him he didn't smile. 'These people are strange . . . One day they greet you, the next day they don't . . .'

On Friday afternoon, as everyone was ready to leave the room after Linear Models, she gathered her courage and spoke to Bryan. He had spots on his chin and forehead, was taller than her, restless, as if he was in a hurry to go somewhere else. He put his calculator back in its case, his pen in his pocket. She asked him for his notes and his blue eyes behind his glasses took on the blankest look she had ever seen in her life. What was all the surprise for? Did he think she was an insect, was he surprised that she could speak?

A mumble for a reply, words strung together. So taken-aback, he was. He pushed his chair back under the table with his foot.

'Pardon?'

He slowed down, separated each word, 'Ah'll have them for ye on Monday.'

'Thank you.' She spoke English better than him! How pathetic. The whole of him was pathetic. He wore the same shirt every blessed day. Grey stripes and white.

On the weekends, Shadia never went out of the halls and unless someone telephoned long distance from home, she spoke to no one. There was time to remember Thursday nights in Khartoum, a wedding to go to with Fareed, driving in his red Mercedes. Or the club with her sisters. Sitting by the pool drinking lemonade with ice, the waiters all dressed in white. Sometimes people swam at night, dived in the water dark like the sky above. Here, in this country's week-end of Saturday and Sunday, Shadia washed her clothes and her hair. Her hair depressed her. The damp weather made it frizz up after she straightened it with hot tongs. So she had given up and now wore it in a bun all the time, tightly pulled back away from her face, the curls held down by pins and Vaseline Tonic. She didn't like this style, her corrugated hair, and in the mirror her eyes looked too large. The mirror in the public bathroom, at the end of the corridor to her room, had printed on it 'This is the face of someone with HIV.' She had written about this mirror to her sister, something foreign and sensational like hail and cars driving on the left. But she hadn't written that the mirror made her feel as if she had left her looks behind in Khartoum.

On the weekends, she made a list of the money she had spent, the sterling enough to keep a family alive back home. Yet she might fail her exams after all that expense, go back home empty-handed without a degree. Guilt was cold like the fog of this city. It came from everywhere. One day she forgot to pray in the morning. She reached the bus-stop and then realised that she hadn't prayed. That morning folded out like the nightmare she sometimes had, of discovering that she had gone out into the street without any clothes.

In the evening, when she was staring at multidimensional scaling, the telephone in the hall rang. She ran to answer it. Fareed's cheerful greeting. 'Here, Shadia, Mama and the girls want to speak to you.' His mother's endearments, 'They say it's so cold where you are . . .'

Shadia was engaged to Fareed. Fareed was a package that came with the 7Up franchise, the paper factory, the big house he was building, his sisters and widowed mother. Shadia was going to marry them all. She was going to be happy and make her mother happy. Her mother deserved happiness after the misfortunes of her life. A husband who left her for another woman. Six girls to bring up. People felt sorry for her mother. Six girls to educate and marry off. But your Lord is generous, each of the girls, it was often said, was lovelier than the other. They were clever too: dentist, pharmacist, architect, and all with the best of manners.

'We are just back from looking at the house,' Fareed's turn again to talk. 'It's coming along fine, they're putting the tiles down . . .'

'That's good, that's good,' her voice strange from not talking to anyone all day.

'The bathroom suites. If I get them all the same colour for us and the girls and Mama, I could get them on a discount. Blue, the girls are in favour of blue,' his voice echoed from one continent to another. Miles and miles.

'Blue is nice. Yes, better get them all the same colour.' He was building a block of flats, not a house. The ground-floor flat for his mother and the girls until they married, the first floor for him and Shadia. The girls' flats on the two top floors would be rented out. When Shadia had first got engaged to Fareed, he was the son of a rich man. A man with the franchise for 7Up and the paper factory which had a monopoly in ladies' sanitary towels. Fareed's sisters never had to buy sanitary towels; their house was abundant with boxes of *Pinky*, fresh from the production line. But Fareed's father died of an unexpected heart attack soon after the engagement party (500 guests at the Hilton). Now Shadia was going to marry the rich man himself. You are a lucky, lucky girl, her mother said, and Shadia rubbed soap in her eyes so that Fareed would think she had been weeping his father's death.

There was no time to talk about her course on the telephone, no space for her anxieties. Fareed was not interested in her studies. He had said, 'I am very broad-minded to allow you to study abroad. Other men would not have put up with this . . .' It was her mother who was keen for her to study, to get a post-graduate degree from Britain and then have a career after she got married. 'This way,' her mother had said, 'you will have your in-laws' respect. They have money but you will have a degree. Don't end up like me. I left my education to marry your father and now . . .' Many conversations ended with her mother bitter, with her mother saying, 'No one suffers like I suffer,' and making Shadia droop. At night her mother sobbed in her sleep, noises that woke Shadia and her sisters.

No, on the long-distance line, there was no space for her worries. Talk about the Scottish weather. Picture Fareed, generously perspiring, his stomach straining the buttons of his shirt. Often she had nagged him to lose weight with no success. His mother's food was too good; his sisters were both overweight. On the long-distance line, listen to the Khartoum gossip as if listening to a radio play.

On Monday, without saying anything, Bryan slid two folders across the table towards her as if he did not want to come near her, did not want to talk to her. She wanted to say, 'I won't take them till you hand them to me politely.' But smarting, she said, 'Thank you very much.' *She* had manners. *She* was well brought up.

Back in her room, at her desk, the clearest handwriting she had ever seen. Sparse on the pages, clean. Clear and rounded like a child's, the tidiest notes. She cried over them, wept for no reason. She cried until she wetted one of the pages, stained the ink, blurred one of the formulas. She dabbed at it with a tissue but the paper flaked and became transparent. Should she apologise about the stain, say that she was drinking water, say that it was rain? Or should she just keep quiet, hope he wouldn't notice? She chided herself for all that concern. *He* wasn't concerned about wearing the same shirt every day. She was giving him too much attention thinking about him. He was just an immature and closed-in sort of character. He probably came from a small town; his parents were probably poor, low class. In Khartoum, she never mixed with people like that. Her mother liked her to be friends with people who were higher up. How else was she and her sisters going to marry well? She must study the notes and stop crying over this boy's handwriting. His handwriting had nothing to do with her, nothing to do with her at all.

Understanding after not understanding is fog lifting, is pictures swinging into focus, missing pieces slotting into place. It is fragments gelling, a sound vivid whole, a basis to build on. His notes were the knowledge she needed, the gaps. She struggled through them, not skimming them with the carelessness of incomprehension, but taking them in, making them a part of her, until in the depth of concentration, in the late hours of the nights, she lost awareness of time and place and at last when she slept she became epsilon and gamma and she became a variable making her way through discrete space from state i to state j.

It felt natural to talk to him. As if now that she had spent hours and days with his handwriting, she knew him in some way. She forgot the offence she had taken when he had slid his folders across the table to her, all the times he didn't say hello.

In the computer room, at the end of the statistical packages class, she went to him and said, 'Thanks for the notes. They are really good. I think I might not fail, after all. I might have a chance to pass.' Her eyes were dry from all the nights she had stayed up. She was tired and grateful.

He nodded and they spoke a little about the Poisson distribution, queuing theory. Everything was clear in his mind, his brain was a clear pane of glass where all the concepts were written out boldly and neatly. Today, he seemed more at ease talking to her, though he still shifted about from foot to foot, avoided her eyes.

He said, 'Do ye want to go for a coffee?'

She looked up at him. He was tall and she was not used to speaking to people with blue eyes. Then she made a mistake. Perhaps because she had been up late last night, she made that mistake. Perhaps there were other reasons for that mistake. The mistake of shifting from one level to another.

She said, 'I don't like your earring.'

The expression in his eyes, a focusing, no longer shifting away. He lifted his hand to his ear and tugged the earring off. His earlobe without the silver looked red and scarred.

She giggled because she was afraid, because he wasn't smiling, wasn't saying anything. She covered her mouth with her hand then wiped her forehead and eyes. A mistake was made and it was too late to go back. She plunged ahead, careless now, reckless, 'I don't like your long hair.'

He turned and walked away.

The next morning, Multivariate Analysis, and she came in late, dishevelled from running and the rain. The professor whose name she wasn't sure of (there were three who were Mc something) smiled unperturbed. All the lecturers were relaxed and urbane, in tweed jackets and polished shoes. Sometimes she wondered how the incoherent Bryan, if he did pursue an academic career, was going to transform himself into a professor like that. But it was none of her business.

Like most of the other students, she sat in the same seat in every class. Bryan sat a row ahead which was why she could always look at his hair. But he had cut it, there was no pony-tail today! Just his neck and the collar of the grey- and white-striped shirt.

Notes to take down. *In discriminant analysis, a linear combination of variables serves as the basis for assigning cases to groups . . .*

She was made up of layers. Somewhere inside, deep inside, under the crust of vanity, in the untampered-with essence, she would glow and be in awe, and be humble and think, this is just for me, he cut his hair for me. But there were other layers, bolder, more to the surface. Giggling. Wanting to catch hold of a friend. Guess what? You wouldn't *believe* what this idiot did!

Find a weighted average of variables . . . The weights are estimated so that they result in the best separation between the groups.

After the class he came over and said very seriously, without a smile, 'Ah've cut my hair.'

A part of her hollered with laughter, sang, you stupid boy, you stupid boy, I can see that, can't I?

She said, 'It looks nice.' She said the wrong thing and her face felt hot and she made herself look away so that she would not know his reaction. It was true though, he did look nice, he looked decent now.

She should have said to Bryan, when they first held their coffee mugs in their hands and were searching for an empty table, 'Let's sit with Asafa and the others.' Mistakes follow mistakes. Across the cafeteria, the Turkish girl saw them together and raised her perfect eyebrows; Badr met Shadia's eyes and quickly looked away. Shadia looked at Bryan and he was different, different without the earring and the ponytail, transformed in some way. If he would put lemon juice on his spots . . . but it was none of her business. Maybe the boys who smashed Badr's windows looked like Bryan, but with fiercer eyes, no glasses. She must push him away from her. She must make him dislike her.

He asked her where she came from and when she replied, he said, 'Where's that?'

'Africa,' with sarcasm. 'Do you know where *that* is?'

His nose and cheeks under the rim of his glasses went red. Good, she thought, good. He will leave me now in peace.

He said, 'Ah know Sudan is in Africa; I meant where exactly in Africa.'

'North-east, south of Egypt. Where are *you* from?'

'Peterhead. It's north of here. By the sea.'

It was hard to believe that there was anything north of Aberdeen. It seemed to her that they were on the northernmost corner of the world. She knew better now than to imagine sun-tanning and sandy beaches for his 'by the sea'. More likely dismal skies, pale bad-tempered people shivering on the rocky shore.

'Your father works in Peterhead?'

'Aye, he does.'

She had grown up listening to the proper English of the BBC World Service only to come to Britain and find people saying 'yes' like it was said back home in Arabic, *aye*.

'What does he do, your father?'

He looked surprised, his blue eyes surprised, 'Ma' dad's a joiner.'

Fareed hired people like that to work on the house. Ordered them about.

'And your mother?' she asked.

He paused a little, stirred sugar in his coffee with a plastic spoon. 'She's a lollipop lady.'

Shadia smirked into her coffee, took a sip.

'My father,' she said proudly, 'is a doctor, a specialist.' Her father was a gynaecologist. The woman who was his wife now had been one of his patients. Before that, Shadia's friends had teased her about her father's job, crude jokes that made her laugh. It was all so sordid now.

'And my mother,' she blew the truth up out of proportion, 'comes from a very big family. A ruling family. If you British hadn't colonised us, my mother would have been a princess now.'

'Ye walk like a princess,' he said.

What a gullible, silly boy! She wiped her forehead with her hand, said, 'You mean I am conceited and proud?'

'No, Ah didnae mean that, no . . .' The packet of sugar he was tearing open tipped from his hand, its contents scattered over the table. 'Ah shit . . . sorry . . .' He tried to scoop up the sugar and knocked against his coffee mug, spilling a little on the table.

She took out a tissue from her bag, reached over and mopped up the stain. It was easy to pick up all the bits of sugar with the damp tissue.

'Thanks,' he mumbled and they were silent. The cafeteria was busy, full of the humming, buzzing sound of people talking to each other, trays and dishes. In Khartoum, she avoided being alone with Fareed. She preferred it when they were with others: their families, their many mutual friends. If they were ever alone, she imagined that her mother or her sister was with them, could hear them, and spoke to Fareed with that audience in mind.

Bryan was speaking to her, saying something about rowing on the river Dee. He went rowing on the weekends, he belonged to a rowing club.

To make herself pleasing to people was a skill Shadia was trained in. It was not difficult to please people. Agree with them, never dominate the conversation, be economical with the truth. Now here was someone whom all these rules needn't apply to.

She said to him, 'The Nile is superior to the Dee. I saw your Dee, it is nothing, it is like a stream. There are two Niles, the Blue and the White, named after their colours. They come from the south, from two different places. They travel for miles over countries with different names, never knowing they will meet. I think they get tired of running alone, it is such a long way to the sea. They want to reach the sea so that they can rest, stop running. There is a bridge in Khartoum and under this bridge the two Niles meet and if you stand on the bridge and look down you can see the two waters mixing together.'

'Do ye get homesick?' he asked and she felt tired now, all this talk of the river running to rest in the sea. She had never talked like that before. Luxury words, and the question he asked.

'Things I should miss I don't miss. Instead I miss things I didn't think I would miss. The *azan*, the Muslim call to prayer from the mosque, I don't know if you know about it. I miss that. At dawn it used to wake me up. I would hear *prayer is better than sleep* and just go back to sleep, I never got up to pray.' She looked down at her hands on the table. There was no relief in confessions, only his smile, young, and something like wonder in his eyes.

'We did Islam in school,' he said. 'Ah went on a trip to Mecca.' He opened out his palms on the table.

'What!'

'In a book.'

'Oh.'

The coffee was finished. They should go now. She should go to the library before the next lecture and photocopy previous exam papers. Asafa, full of helpful advice, had shown her where to find them.

'What is your religion?' she asked.

'Dunno, nothing I suppose.'

'That's terrible! That's really terrible!' Her voice was too loud, concerned.

His face went red again and he tapped his spoon against the empty mug.

Waive all politeness, make him dislike her. Badr had said,

437

even before his windows got smashed, that here in the West they hate Islam. Standing up to go, she said flippantly, 'Why don't you become a Muslim then?'

He shrugged, 'Ah wouldnae mind travelling to Mecca; I was keen on that book.'

Her eyes filled with tears. They blurred his face when he stood up. In the West they hate Islam and he . . . She said, 'Thanks for the coffee' and walked away but he followed her.

'Shadiya, Shadiya,' he pronounced her name wrong, three syllables instead of two, 'there's this museum about Africa. I've never been before. If you'd care to go, tomorrow . . .'

No sleep for the guilty, no rest, she should have said no, I can't go, no I have too much catching up to do. No sleep for the guilty, the memories come from another continent. Her father's new wife, happier than her mother, fewer worries. When Shadia visits she offers fruit in a glass bowl, icy oranges and guava, soothing in the heat. Shadia's father hadn't wanted a divorce, hadn't wanted to leave them, he wanted two wives not a divorce. But her mother had too much pride, she came from fading money, a family with a 'name'. Of the new wife her mother says, bitch, whore, the dregs of the earth, a nobody.

Tomorrow, she need not show up at the museum, even though she said that she would. She should have told Bryan she was engaged to be married, mentioned it casually. What did he expect from her? Europeans had different rules, reduced, abrupt customs. If Fareed knew about this . . . her secret thoughts like snakes . . . Perhaps she was like her father, a traitor. Her mother said that her father was devious. Sometimes Shadia was devious. With Fareed in the car, she would deliberately say, 'I need to stop at the grocer; we need things at home.' At the grocer he would pay for

438

all her shopping and she would say, 'No, you shouldn't do that, no, you are too generous, you are embarrassing me.' With the money she saved, she would buy a blouse for her mother, nail varnish for her mother, a magazine, imported apples.

It was strange to leave her desk, lock her room and go out on a Saturday. In the hall the telephone rang. It was Fareed. If he knew where she was going now . . . Guilt was like a hard-boiled egg stuck in her chest. A large cold egg.

'Shadia, I want you to buy some of the fixtures for the bathrooms. Taps and towel hangers. I'm going to send you a list of what I want exactly and the money . . .'

'I can't, I can't.'

'What do you mean you can't? If you go into any large department store . . .'

'I can't. I wouldn't know where to put these things, how to send them.'

There was a rustle on the line and she could hear someone whispering, Fareed distracted a little. He would be at work this time in the day, glass bottles filling up with clear effervescent, the words 7Up written in English and Arabic, white against the dark green.

'You can get good things, things that aren't available here. Gold would be good. It would match . . .'

Gold. Gold toilet seats!

'People are going to burn in Hell for eating out of gold dishes; you want to sit on gold!'

He laughed. He was used to getting his own way, not easily threatened, 'Are you joking with me?'

'No.'

In a quieter voice, 'This call is costing . . .'

She knew, she knew. He shouldn't have let her go away.

She was not coping with the whole thing, she was not handling the stress. Like the Nigerian student.

'Shadia, gold-coloured, not gold. It's smart.'

'Allah is going to punish us for this; it's not right . . .'

'Since when have you become so religious!'

Bryan was waiting for her on the steps of the museum, familiar-looking against the strange grey of the city, streets where cars had their headlamps on in the middle of the afternoon. He wore a different shirt, a navy-blue jacket. He said, not looking at her, 'Ah was beginning to think you wouldnae turn up.'

There was no entry fee to the museum, no attendant handing out tickets. Bryan and Shadia walked on soft carpets, thick blue carpets that made Shadia want to take off her shoes. The first thing they saw was a Scottish man from Victorian times. He sat on a chair surrounded with possessions from Africa, over-flowing trunks, an ancient map strewn on the floor of the glass cabinet. All the light in the room came from this and other glass cabinets, gleamed on the wax. Shadia turned away, there was an ugliness in the life-like wispiness of his hair, his determined expression, the way he sat. A hero who had gone away and come back, laden, ready to report.

Bryan began to conscientiously study every display cabinet, read the posters on the wall. She followed him around and thought that he was studious, careful and studious, that was why he did so well in his degree. She watched the intent expression on his face as he looked at everything. For her the posters were an effort to read, the information difficult to take in. It had been so long since she had read anything outside the requirements of the course. But she persevered, saying the words to herself, moving her lips . . . *During the*

18th and 19th centuries, north-east Scotland made a dispropor-
tionate impact on the world at large by contributing so many
skilled and committed individuals … In serving an empire
they gave and received, changed others and were themselves
changed and often returned home with tangible reminders of
their experiences.

The tangible reminders were there to see, preserved in spite of the years. Her eyes skimmed over the disconnected objects out of place and time. Iron and copper, little statues. Nothing was of her, nothing belonged to her life at home, what she missed. Here was Europe's vision, the clichés about Africa: cold and old.

She had not expected the dim light and the hushed silence. Apart from Shadia and Bryan, there was only a man with a briefcase, a lady who took down notes, unless there were others out of sight on the second floor. Something electrical, the heating or the lights, gave out a humming sound like that of an air-conditioner. It made Shadia feel as if they were in an aeroplane without windows, detached from the world outside.

'He looks like you, don't you think?' she said to Bryan. They stood in front of a portrait of a soldier who died in the first year of this century. It was the colour of his eyes and his hair. But Bryan did not answer her, did not agree with her. He was preoccupied with reading the caption. When she looked at the portrait again, she saw that she was mistaken. That strength in the eyes, the purpose, was some-thing Bryan didn't have. They had strong faith in those days long ago.

Biographies of explorers who were educated in Edin-burgh; doctors, courage, they knew what to take to Africa: Christianity, commerce, civilisation. They knew what they wanted to bring back; cotton watered by the Blue Nile, the

Zambezi river. She walked after Bryan, felt his concentration, his interest in what was before him and thought, 'In a photograph we would not look nice together.'

She touched the glass of a cabinet showing papyrus rolls, copper pots. She pressed her forehead and nose against the cool glass. If she could enter the cabinet, she would not make a good exhibit. She wasn't right, she was too modern, too full of mathematics.

Only the carpet, its petroleum blue, pleased her. She had come to this museum expecting sunlight and photographs of the Nile, something to appease her homesickness, a comfort, a message. But the messages were not for her, not for anyone like her. A letter from West Africa, 1762, an employee to his employer in Scotland. An employee trading European goods for African curiosities. *It was great difficulty to make the natives understand my meaning, even by an interpreter, it being a thing so seldom asked of them, but they have all undertaken to bring something and laughed heartily at me and said, I was a good man to love their country so much* . . .

Love my country so much. She should not be here; there was nothing for her here. She wanted to see minarets, boats fragile on the Nile, people. People like her father. Times she had sat in the waiting room of his clinic, among pregnant women, the pain in her heart because she was going to see him in a few minutes. His room, the air-conditioner and the smell of his pipe, his white coat. When she hugged him, he smelled of Listerine Mouthwash. He could never remember how old she was, what she was studying. Six daughters, how could he keep track? In his confusion, there was freedom for her, games to play, a lot of teasing. She visited his clinic in secret, telling lies to her mother. She loved him more than she loved her mother. Her mother who did everything for her, tidied her room, sewed her clothes from *Burda* magazine.

Shadia was twenty-five and her mother washed everything for her by hand, even her pants and bras.

'I know why they went away,' said Bryan. 'I understand why they travelled.' At last he was talking. She had not seen him intense before. He spoke in a low voice, 'They had to get away, to leave here . . .'

'To escape from the horrible weather . . .' she was making fun of him. She wanted to put him down. The imperialists who had humiliated her history were heroes in his eyes.

He looked at her. 'To escape . . .' he repeated.

'They went to benefit themselves,' she said. 'People go away because they benefit in some way . . .'

'I want to get away,' he said.

She remembered when he had opened his palms on the table and said, 'I went on a trip to Mecca.' There had been pride in his voice.

'I should have gone somewhere else for the course,' he went on. 'A new place, somewhere down south.'

He was on a plateau, not like her. She was punching and struggling for a piece of paper that would say she was awarded an MSc from a British university. For him the course was a continuation.

'Come and see,' he said, and he held her arm. No one had touched her before, not since she had hugged her mother goodbye. Months now in this country and no one had touched her.

She pulled her arm away. She walked away, quickly up the stairs. Metal steps rattled under her feet. She ran up the stairs to the next floor. Guns, a row of guns aiming at her. They had been waiting to blow her away. Scottish arms of centuries ago, gun-fire in service of the empire.

Silver muzzles, a dirty grey now. They must have shone pretty once, under a sun far away. If they blew her away now, where would she fly and fall? A window that looked out at the hostile sky. She shivered in spite of the wool she was wearing, layers of clothes. Hell is not only blazing fire, a part of it is freezing cold, torturous ice and snow. In Scotland's winter you live a glimpse of this unseen world, feel the breath of it in your bones.

There was a bench and she sat down. There was no one here on this floor. She was alone with sketches of jungle animals, words on the wall. A diplomat away from home, in Ethiopia in 1903, Asafa's country long before Asafa was born. *It is difficult to imagine anything more satisfactory or better worth taking part in than a lion drive. We rode back to camp feeling very well indeed. Archie was quite right when he said that this was the first time since we have started that we have really been in Africa – the real Africa of jungle inhabited only by game, and plains where herds of antelope meet your eye in every direction.*

'Shadiya, don't cry.' He still pronounced her name wrong because she had not shown him how to say it properly.

He sat next to her on the bench, the blur of his navy jacket blocking the guns, the wall-length pattern of antelope herds. She should explain that she cried easily; there was no need for the alarm on his face. His awkward voice, 'Why are ye crying?' He didn't know, he didn't understand. He was all wrong, not a substitute . . .

'They are telling you lies in this museum,' she said. 'Don't believe them. It's all wrong. It's not jungles and antelopes, it's people. We have things like computers and cars. We have 7Up in Africa and some people, a few people, have bathrooms with golden taps . . . I shouldn't be here with you. You shouldn't talk to me . . .'

He said, 'Museums change; I can change . . .'

He didn't know it was a steep path she had no strength for.

He didn't understand. Many things, years and landscapes, gulfs. If she was strong she would have explained and not tired of explaining. She would have patiently taught him another language, letters curved like the epsilon and gamma he knew from mathematics. She would have showed him that words could be read from right to left. If she was not small in the museum, if she was really strong, she would have made his trip to Mecca real, not only in a book.

ALI SMITH

FIDELIO AND BESS

A YOUNG WOMAN is ironing in a kitchen in a prison. But she's not a prisoner, no. Her father's the chief gaoler; she just lives here. A young man comes into the kitchen and tells her he's decided that he and she are going to marry. I've chosen you, he says. She is desultory with him. She suggests to the audience that he's a bit of a fool. Then she sings a song to herself. It's Fidelio I've chosen, it's Fidelio I'm in love with, she sings. It's Fidelio who's in love with me. It's Fidelio I want to wake up next to every morning.

Her father comes home. Then, a moment later, so does Fidelio himself, who looks suspiciously like a girl dressed as a boy, and who happens to be wreathed in chains. Not that Fidelio's a prisoner, no. Apparently the chains have been being repaired by a blacksmith (whom we never see), and Fidelio, the girl's father's assistant, has brought the mended chains back to the gaol.

But it seems that Fidelio isn't much interested in marrying the boss's daughter. Fidelio, instead, is unnaturally keen to meet a mysterious prisoner who's being kept in the deepest, darkest underground cell in the prison. This particular prisoner has been down there for two years and is receiving almost no food or water any more. This is on the prison governor's orders; the prison governor wants him starved to death. He's clearly a man who's done great wrong, Fidelio says, fishing for information – or made great enemies, which is pretty much the same thing, the gaoler says, leaning magnanimously back in his kitchen chair. Money, he says. It's the answer to everything. The girl looks at Fidelio. Don't let *him* see that dying prisoner, the girl says. He couldn't stand it, he's just a boy, he's such a gentle boy. Don't subject him to such a cruel sight. On the contrary, Fidelio says. Let me see him. I'm brave enough and I'm strong enough.

But then the prison governor announces to the gaoler, in private, that he has just decided to have this prisoner killed. *I'm* not murdering him, the gaoler says when the governor tells him to. Okay, I'll do it myself, the prison governor says. I'll take pleasure in it. And I'll give you a bag of gold if you go and dig a grave for him in the old well down there in his cell.

It's agreed. In the next Act the gaoler will take the boy Fidelio down to the deep dungeon and they'll dig the grave for the man who, we've begun to gather, is Fidelio's imprisoned husband. Meanwhile, as the First Act draws to a close, Fidelio has somehow managed to get all the other prisoners in the place released our of the dark of their cells into the weak spring sun in the prison yard for a little while.

They stagger out into the light. They stand about, ragged, dazed, heartbreakingly hopeful. They're like a false resurrection. They look up at the sunlight. Summertime, they sing, and the living is easy. Fish are jumping and the cotton is high.

Then they all look at each other in amazement.

Fidelio looks bewildered.

The gaoler shakes his head.

The conductor's baton droops.

The orchestra in the pit stops playing. Instruments pause in mid-air.

The girl who was doing the ironing at the beginning is singing too. She's really good. She shrugs at her father as if she can't help it, can't do anything about it. Your daddy's rich, she sings, and your mammy's good-looking.

Then a man arrives in a cart pulled by a goat. He stops the cart in the middle of the stage. Everybody crowds round him. He's black. He's the only black person on the stage. He looks very poor and at the same time very impressive. When the song finishes he gets out of the cart. He walks across the stage. He's got a limp. It's quite a bad limp. He tells them all that he's looking for Bess. Where is she? He's heard she's here. He's not going to stop looking for her until he finds her. He glances at the gaoler; he regards Fidelio gravely for a moment. He nods to the girl. He approaches a group of prisoners. Is this New York? he says. Is she here?

Yeah, but, you say. Come on. I mean.

But what? I say.

You can't, you say.

Can't what? I say.

Culture's fixed, you say. That's why it's culture. That's how it gets to be art. That's how it works. That's why it works. You can't just change it. You can't just alter it when you want or because you want. You can't just revise things for your own pleasure or whatever.

Actually I can do anything I like, I say.

Yeah, but you can't revise Fidelio, you say. No one can.

Fidelio's all about revision, I say. Beethoven revised Fidelio several times. Three different versions. Four different overtures.

You know what I mean. No one can just, as it were, interject Porgy into Fidelio, you say.

Oh, *as it were*, I say.

You don't say anything. You stare straight out, ahead, through the windscreen.

Okay. I know what you mean, I say.

You start humming faintly, under your own breath.

But I don't think interject is quite the right word to use there, I say.

I say this because I know there's nothing that annoys you more than thinking you've used a word wrongly. You snort down your nose.

Yes it is, you say.

I don't think it's quite the right usage, I say.

It is, you say. Anyway, I didn't say interject. I said inject.

I lean forward and switch the radio on. I keep pressing the channel button until I hear something I recognise.

It's fine for you to do that, you say, but if you're going to, can you at least, before we get out of the car, return it to the channel to which it was originally tuned?

I settle on some channel or other, I've no idea what.

Which channel was it on? you say.

Radio 4, I say.

Are you sure? you say.

Or 3, I say.

Which? you say.

I don't know, I say.

You sigh.

Gilbert O'Sullivan is singing the song about the people who are hurrying to the register office to get married. *Very shortly now there's going to be an answer from you. Then one from me.* I sing along. You sigh out loud again. The sigh lifts the hair of your fringe slightly from your forehead.

You're so pretty when you sigh like that.

When we arrive at the car park you reach over to my side of the radio and keep the little button pressed in until the radio hits the voices of a comedy programme where celebrities have one minute exactly to talk about a subject, with no repetitions. If they repeat themselves, they're penalised. An audience is killing itself laughing.

When you're sure it's Radio 4, you switch the radio off.

We are doomed as a couple. We are as categorically doomed as when Clara in Porgy and Bess says: *Jake, you ain't plannin' to take de Sea Gull to de Blackfish Banks, is you? It's time for de September storms.* No, the Sea Gull, a fictional boat, moored safe and ruined both at once in its own eternal bay, is less doomed than we are. We're as doomed as the Cutty Sark itself, tall, elegant, real, mundanely gathering the London sky round its masts and making it wondrous, extraordinary, for the people coming up out of the underground train station in the evening, the ship-of-history gracious against the sky for all the people who see it and all the people who don't even notice it any more because they're so used to seeing it, and just two months to go before there'll be nothing left of it but a burnt-out hull, a scoop of scorched plankwork.

We are doomed on land and doomed on sea, you and me; as doomed holding on to each other's arms on the underground as we are arguing about culture in your partner's car; as doomed in a bar sitting across from each other or side by side at the cinema or the opera or the theatre; as doomed as we are when we're pressed into each other in the various beds in the various near-identical rooms we go to, to have the sex that your partner doesn't know about us having. Of all the dooms I ever thought I might come to I never reckoned on middle-classness. You and me, holding hands below the seats at Fidelio, an opera you've already seen, already taken your partner to; and it all started so anarchically, so happily, all heady public kissing in King's Cross station. *Mir ist so wunderbar.* That's me in the £120-a-night bed, and you through in the bathroom, thoroughly cleaning your teeth.

I've read in the sleeve notes for the version of Fidelio I have on CD that at an early point in the opera, when all four people, the girl, the thwarted young man, the woman dressed as a boy and the gaoler, are singing about happiness and everybody is misunderstanding everybody else and believing a different version of things to be true, that this is where 'backstairs chat turns into the music of the angels'. *How wonderful it is to me. Something's got my heart in its grip. He loves me, it's clear. I'm going to be happy.* Except, wunderbar here doesn't mean the usual simple wonderful. It means full of wonder, strange. *How strange it is to me.* I wish I could remember her name, the ironing girl who loves Fidelio, the light-comedy act-opener, the girl for whom there's no real end to it, the girl who has to accept – with nothing more than an alas, which pretty soon modulates into the same song everyone else is singing – what happens when the boy Fidelio is suddenly revealed as the wife Leonore, and everybody stands round her in awe at her wifely faithfulness, her profound self-sacrifice. *O namenlose.*

Which is worse to her, the ironing girl? That Fidelio is really Leonore, a woman, not the boy she thought he was? Or that her beloved Fidelio is someone else's wife, after all, and so, in this opera about the sacredness of married love, will never, ever be hers?

Oh my Leonore, Florestan, the husband, the freed prisoner, says to Fidelio after she's unearthed him, after she's flung herself between him and certain death, between him and the drawn blade of the prison governor. Point of catharsis. Point of truth. After she does this, everything in the whole world changes for the better.

Oh my Leonore, what have you done for me?

Nothing, nothing, my Florestan, she answers.

Lucky for her she had a gun on her, that's what I say, otherwise they'd both be dead.

Oh, I got plenty o' nuttin. And nuttin's plenty fo' me.

It's famously unresolved, you know, I say. Even though its ending seems so celebratory, so C-major, so huge and comforting and sure, there's still a sense, at the back of it all, that lots of things haven't been resolved. Look at the ironing girl, for instance. She's not resolved, is she? Beethoven called it his 'child of sorrow'. He never wrote another opera after it.

Half a year ago you'd never heard of Fidelio, you say.

Klemperer conducted it at two really extraordinarily different times in history, I say.

I am flicking through the little book that comes with the version of Fidelio you've just given me. The new CD is one of my Christmas presents. Christmas is in ten days' time. We have just opened our Christmas presents, in a bedroom in a Novotel. I bought you a really nice French-looking jumper, with buttons at one side of the neck. I know that you'll probably drop it in a litter bin on your way home.

Imagine, I say. Imagine conducting it in 1915 in the middle of the First World War. Then imagine the strangeness of conducting it in the 1960s, when every single scene must have reminded people of the different thing it meant, for a German conductor, the story of all the people starved and tyranted, buried alive, for being themselves, for saying the truth, for standing up to the status quo.

Tyranted's not a word, you say in my ear.

You say it lovingly. You are holding me in your arms. We are both naked. You are warm behind me. You make my back feel blessed, the way you are holding me. I can feel the curve of your breasts at each of my shoulder blades.

Imagine all the things that Florestan must have meant,

then, I say, to those people, in that audience in 1915, then 1961.

It's an opera, you say. It's nothing to do with history.

Yes, but it is, I say. It's post-Napoleonic. That's obvious. Imagine what it meant to its audience in 1814. Imagine watching the same moment in this opera at different times in history. Take the moment when Fidelio asks whether she can give the prisoner a piece of old bread. It's the question of whether one starving man can have a piece of mercy. All the millions of war dead are in it there, crowding behind that one man. And the buried, unearthed truth. And the new day dawning, and all the old ghosts coming out of the ground.

Uh huh, you say.

What if Fidelio had been written by Mozart? I say.

It wasn't, you say.

The knockabout there'd have been with Fidelio in her boy's clothes, I say. The swagger Mozart would have given Rocco. The good joke the girl who's ironing at the start would have become, and the boy too, who thinks he can just marry her because he's made up his mind he wants to.

You yawn.

Though there's something really interesting in the way Beethoven doesn't force those characters to be funny, I say. The ironing girl, what's her name? There's something humane in the way they're not just, you know, played for laughs.

You kiss the back of my neck. You use your teeth on my shoulder. It's allowed, you biting me. I quite like to be gently bitten. I'm not allowed to bite you, though, in case it marks you.

I still have no idea whether you like being gently bitten or not.

Not long after we'd met, when I said I'd never heard much,

456

didn't know much about Beethoven, you played me some on your iPod. When I said I thought it sounded like Jane Austen crossed with Daniel Libeskind, you looked bemused, like I was a clever child. When I said that what I meant was that it was like different kinds of architecture, as if a classically eighteenth-century room had suddenly morphed into a postmodern annexe, you shook your head and kissed me to make me stop talking. I closed my eyes into the kiss. I love your kiss. Everything's sorted, and obvious, and understood, and civilised, your kiss says. It's a shut-eye lie, I know it is, because the music I didn't know before I knew you makes me open my eyes in a place of no sentimentality, where light itself is a kind of shadow, where everything is fragment-slanted. A couple of months later, when I said I thought you could hear the whole of history in it, all history's grand-nesses and sadnesses, you'd looked a bit annoyed. You'd taken the iPod off my knee and disconnected its head-phones from their socket. When I'd removed the dead headphones from my ears you'd rolled them up carefully and tucked them into the special little carrying-case you keep them in. You'd said you were getting a migraine. Impatience had crossed your face so firmly that I had known, in that instant, that now we were actually a kind of married, and that our marriedness was probably making your real rela-tionship more palatable.

Sometimes a marriage needs three hearts beating as one.

I've met your partner. She's nice. I can tell she's quite a nice person. She knows who I am but she doesn't know who I am. Her clothes smell overwhelmingly of the same washing powder as yours.

Ten days before Christmas, smelling of sex in a rented bed, with half an hour to go before you have to get the half past ten train home, I hold the new Fidelio in my hands.

I think of the ironing girl, holding up the useless power of her own huge love to Fidelio in the First Act like a chunk of dead stone she thinks is full of magic. I think of Fidelio herself, insufferably righteous. I think about how she makes her first entrance laden with chains that aren't actually binding her to anything.

I open the plastic box and I take out one of the shiny discs. I hold it up in front of us and we look at our reflection, our two heads together, in the spectrum-split plastic of the first half of the opera.

So is marriage a matter of chains? I say.

Eh? you say.

Or a matter of the kind of faithfulness that brings dead things back to life? I say.

I have absolutely no idea what you're talking about, you say.

I lean my head back on your collarbone and turn it so that my mouth touches the top of your arm. I feel with my teeth the front of your shoulder.

Don't bite me, you say.

Marzelline. That's her name.

Gershwin wrote six prayers to be sung simultaneously, for the storm scene in Porgy and Bess. As an opera, Porgy and Bess did comparatively badly at the box office. So did the early versions of Fidelio; it wasn't till 1814 that audiences were ready to acclaim it. At the end of one, all the prisoners are free and all the self-delusion about love is irrelevant. At the end of the other, there's nothing to do but go off round the world, on one good leg and one ruined leg, in search of the lost beloved. I guess you got me fo' keeps, Porgy, Bess says, before she's gone, gone, gone, gone, gone, gone, gone.

Will I dress as a boy and stand outside your house, all its windows lit for your Christmas party, its music filtering out into the dark? Will I stand in the dark and take a pick or a spade to the hard surface of the turf of your midwinter back lawn? Will I dig till I'm covered in dust and earth, till I uncover the whole truth, the house of dust under the ground? Will I shake the soil off the long iron chain fixed to the slab of rock deep in the earth beneath the pretty lavenders, the annuals and perennials of your suburban garden?

It is Saturday night. It is summertime on a quiet hot street in a port town. A man plays a sleepy lament on a piano. Some men play dice. A woman married to a fisherman is rocking a baby to sleep. Her husband takes the baby out of her arms and sings it his own version of a lullaby. A woman is a some time thing, he sings. The baby cries. Everybody laughs.

Porgy arrives home. He's a cripple; he rides in a cart pulled by a goat. He goes to join in the dice game. A man arrives with a woman in tow; the man is Crown and the woman is Bess. His job is the unloading and loading of cargo from ships. Her job is to be his, and to keep herself happy on happy dust, drugs. These dice, Porgy says shaking them, are my morning and my evening stars. An' just you watch 'em rise and shine for this poor beggar.

But Crown is high on drink and dust. When he loses at dice he starts a fight. He kills someone with a cotton hook. Get out of here, Bess tells him, the police will be here any minute. At the mention of the police, everybody on the street disappears except the dead man, the dead man's mourning wife, and Bess, who finds all the doors of all the houses shut against her.

Then, unexpectedly, one door opens. It's the door of Porgy, the cripple. She's about to go in, but at the last moment she doesn't. She turns and looks at the side of the stage instead. Everything on stage stops, holds its breath.

The orchestra stops.

A white girl has entered from the wings. She is standing, lost-looking, over by the edge of the set.

Bess stares at her. Porgy, still at his door, stares at her. Serena, the dead man's wife, stares at her. The dead man, Robbins, opens his eyes and puts his head up and stares at her.

The doors of the other houses on the set open; the windows open. All the other residents of Catfish Row look out. They come out of the houses. They're sweating, from the heat under the stage-lights, under the hot summer night. They stand at a distance, their sweat glistening, their eyes on the white girl with the iron in her hand.

The girl starts to sing.

A brother has come to seek her brothers, she sings. To help them if she can with all her heart.

Everybody on stage looks to Porgy, the cripple. He looks to Bess, who shrugs, then nods.

Porgy nods too. He opens his door wider.

ANDREW O'HAGAN

KEEPSAKES

LOFTY BROGAN WORKED as a fishmonger in the Salt-market. People said he was the fastest skinner in Glasgow, but he couldn't do jokes like the other guys. This manic lady came to the stall every morning and told them she wanted kippers. 'I'm Geetha from Parnie Street,' she said on that particular day. 'And my name means "song".'

'You're in the right place,' Elaine the boss said. 'Lofty here's a lovely singer, aren't you, darling?' He wrapped the kippers in some greaseproof paper. The boss had lipstick on her teeth. 'Come on, Geetha,' she went on to say, 'why don't you change it up a bit today? We've got all the stuff here for a fish stew.'

'Cacciucco,' Lofty said.

'Red mullet. A bit of sole. Clams.'

'I can't cope with fancy fish,' Geetha said.

Elaine told her she was making a mistake. 'You're a great cook, and you're going to turn into a kipper if you eat any more.'

Geetha opened her purse and picked out the usual amount.

'She used to run the best Indian restaurant in Argyle Street,' Elaine said when the lady walked off with her bag. 'I feel sorry for her.'

There was too much history, Lofty thought.

He was OK working at the Fish Plaice, but it wasn't his trade. He'd served his time as a joiner. He liked Elaine, that was all, and building sites were a nightmare. The main thing he cared about was European cities. He saved up all his spare cash so that he could fly off to these places, the emptier the better. At work, he hardly spoke. He knew about mussels and whelks, how long to cook a John Dory, and he got nice looks over the iceboxes. Elaine called him Angel Eyes. The market did poultry as well as fish, and he could sell squabs as fast as he could sell an octopus, so she had no complaints. Some things he said, his work mates didn't get. The day before the lockdown, he combed his blond hair into a quiff and wrote an ad for a boyfriend. Elaine was excited about the ad, but he told her it was no big deal, just a dating profile. 'You're nice-looking, Lofty,' she said to him during the break, 'and tall. You should've stuck in at school. That way you wouldn't be renting rooms and paying these extortionate rents.'

'You took all the houses. All the prospects.' Elaine was standing under a sign that said, 'Want Fresher Fish? Buy a Boat.'

'What you on about?'

'You seniors,' Lofty said. 'And now we're stuck.'

'I'll seniors you,' she said, before adding something about his mother. 'An educated woman like that. How'd you get to be so spoiled?'

'Oh, yeah,' he said. 'Totally spoiled. We've had two "once in a generation" crises in a dozen years. Spoiled rotten.'

The pet shop closed the next morning. The guy never sold anything anyway: the animals were just his pals. But he said he'd watched 'Newsnight' and everybody was going into quarantine, so, against the rules, he released his canaries on Glasgow Green. 'Oh, my God,' Lofty said, 'are you tipping your goldfish into the Clyde?' Next door to Pet Emporium, the Empire Bar hung on until lunchtime, then closed. By the end of the week, the street was deserted and nothing was happening on Grindr. The flat Lofty rented looked down on the Green, and it was strange for him to see that nobody was outside the courthouse. The smoke from the Polmadie furnace had stopped dead.

He didn't like calling his mother. Half the time she'd just talk about the past or go on about money. 'You're addicted to being awkward,' she said to him that afternoon. 'Nothing's ever your fault.'

'What?'

'It must be such a comfort.'

'My life is a result of your decisions.'

'Oh, get a grip. You're 27 years old.'

'I didn't want to be a joiner. I didn't think I'd stay at the market.'

'You're always late to the party,' she said. 'Why not throw your own party? Why not fill it with people you care about and show some commitment?'

'Because you drank all the Champagne,' he said.

He didn't call her for another 10 days, and when he did a nurse answered. She said that his mother couldn't come to the phone, that things were pretty bad, and later that day they took her in an ambulance to the Royal Infirmary. It ended very quickly after that. There was nothing he could do, and then it was too late to do anything. A doctor had called his older brother in London, who then rang Lofty, but he wouldn't pick up. Daniel had been nothing to him for years – Dan was away. Dan was out of it.

They had a spat when their father died in 2015. Lofty accused his brother of stealing a briefcase from their parents' flat. 'That's the maddest accusation I've ever heard,' Dan texted him at the time, but Lofty just ignored it. Then Dan ranted and raved to their mother, before blocking him, which made Lofty feel victorious. It was obvious Dan was guilty and out of control, not only about the theft but about everything. Dan had always acted as if his family was a total drain on his concentration. The one time Lofty went to see him, they nearly had a fight in the middle of Notting Hill Gate. After drinking at a private club, Dan started shouting in the street about Lofty being 'toxic and self-righteous, unreachably angry'. Whatever. Lofty spat on the ground right next to him.

'Your life is a joke, Dan. All this cash. You make me sick.' Their mother later told Lofty she'd heard about the argument. He knew that she and his brother agreed: it was Lofty who had the problem. They were 'on the same page', or into the same books. They used words like 'dysfunctional'. People had 'issues'. After the thing with the briefcase, his mother sent him a book in the post called 'How to Be Free of Yourself'. Lofty never worked out if she took him seriously about the theft. She never brought it up, not once. He felt detached in a whole new way and was tearful as he left his flat, banging the door. He carried the toolbox down the stairs and thought of it as doing weights.

It would take an hour to get to her place. In the Salt-market, all the shutters were down. The virus was like a revolution in the brain, like a brand-new argument. A man was slumped outside the Old Ship Bank pub with his head between his knees. Lofty passed the solicitors' office and looked up at No. 175. His father had been obsessed with tales of their Irish ancestors – including a few young footballers who were among the first to play for Glasgow Celtic, Molly Brogan who sold flowers at St Enoch's, the prizefighters, the shebeeners and the first Alexander Brogan, a part-time chemist who poisoned his wife. They'd all lived there, 'the five Alexanders.' The first came from Derry in 1848 and went straight from the ship to the Parish Relief. Lofty stood back in the middle of the road. It said '1887' at the top of the crow-stepped gable, and he realized the building must've replaced an older one. The Brogans: up there with their Papist utensils and their strong views about how to survive.

He crossed the river and went up Victoria Road. He noticed the post office was still open. He looked at his watch. The removal guy said they would do it quickly and maintain social distancing and be out of the flat by 2 o'clock. How did people keep their distance while carrying a three-piece suite? He changed hands; the toolbox was heavy. He reached the park and suddenly felt he should sit down on a bench. After taking out his phone, he swiped for a bit. 'No, no, nope,' he said. 'Not with that face.' He went onto Instagram and posted a selfie with the trees behind him. Within minutes, Elaine had 'liked' it and posted a comment, two thumbs and a love heart.

He blocked her, then lit a cigarette, then deleted his account. A policeman got out of a van and walked over to a group of schoolgirls sitting on the grass. 'What's your plans?' he heard the officer saying.

'Just sitting,' one of them said.

'It's time to move on, I'm afraid.'

'That's right! It's not your grass!' Lofty shouted. He stood up and the officer looked at him and the girls giggled.

'Are you OK, sir?' the policeman asked.

He walked away with the heavy toolbox. It was the only thing his father had left him, the toolbox and the stuff inside.

There were ferns in her front garden. The key was under a brick. He unlocked the storm doors and saw the hall was pretty empty, except for an unplugged telephone in the corner and personal things here and there, framed certificates in boxes. It was a small flat, perfectly proportioned, with tiled fireplaces in the living room and both bedrooms.

There was a shadow on the carpets where the beds had been, the sofa was gone, plus the dining table, the TV, all her side tables, rugs and lamps. He wasn't keeping any of it. He'd told the guys to take it all away and do what they liked with it. In the corner of the kitchen, he found a wooden stool he remembered from childhood that his mother painted with blue gloss. He opened the toolbox and took out a hacksaw, pausing to replace the blade. He cut up the stool and then he found some newspaper. He lit a fire in the living room. At one point he had three fires going – one in each room. He started emptying the bags. He would let one fire die down while building another, using a shovel to scoop the hot ashes into a bucket he'd found in the backcourt. Late in the evening, he found bottles from her departed drinks trolley and drank Pernod by the neck. He put the other bottles out. In one of the bags in the hall he found a long dripping string of rosary beads. God knows how many buckets he took outside, but there was a heap of ashes cooling in the backcourt. It must have been midnight when he put a coil of TV cables into the living-room fire, an old telephone directory, and then he opened the last of the black bin bags and found it – the briefcase.

He sat cross-legged and opened it, the fire leaping beside him and bouncing shadows around the room. 'Who, Me?' it said on a leaflet, the first of many inside the briefcase from Alcoholics Anonymous. He read each one and slugged the Pernod. He found a series of postcards from Oban – the old man's solo holiday destination – and in each one he went on about the weather before he signed off, 'with love'. Lofty worried he might be like him but enjoyed the way the postcards turned the flame green. In a zipped compartment he found letters and birth certificates going back years, and a school photograph with different writing on the back:

468

'Alexander and Daniel, St Ninians, 1989'. He looked at his brother's face and knew for a certainty that he'd never see him again.

He took a Stanley knife and cut the soft leather into strips. The smell of it burning gave a whole new feel to his mother's front room. Eventually there was nothing much left, the wooden frames had all crackled away, and he'd twisted the screws out of the walls with pliers and tossed them into the bucket. Eventually, in the middle of the night, he took a scraper and removed layers of wallpaper. The last layer before the plaster was pink with white flowers, and he threw bunches of it into the fire. He decided he would wait for all the ashes in the backcourt to become cold, and then he'd put a load of them into the empty toolbox, go to the post office in the morning and post it to Daniel's London address. It was the least he could do. About 4 a.m. he could hear birds chirping loudly in the street.

He took out his father's favourite chisel. It had a faded stamp on the metal part – 'J. Tyzack and Son, Sheffield, 1879'. He put it in the fire and then walked to the living-room window. It didn't matter that the steel would be left over. He felt he had done his best. There was music outside. The lights in people's flats seemed bright at that hour, and he wondered if everyone was up. Here and there, remains had gone from houses or care homes without funerals or anything. 'I wonder if she knew,' he said. Then he placed his hands on the cold glass and thought of Malmo in the spring.

ACKNOWLEDGMENTS

LEILA ABOULELA: 'The Museum' from *Coloured Lights* © Leila Aboulela 2001, 2005. Reproduced with permission from Birlinn Limited.

IAIN CRICHTON SMITH: 'At the Party' from *The Red Door: The Complete English Stories 1949–76* © Iain Crichton Smith, 2001. Reproduced with permission from Birlinn Limited.

JANICE GALLOWAY: 'Blood' by Janice Galloway, © Janice Galloway, 1992. Reproduced with permission from Penguin Random House UK. Penguin Random House US.

ALASDAIR GRAY: 'The Crank That Made the Revolution', first published in *The Scottish Field*, 1971, and published in slightly amended form in *Unlikely Stories, Mostly* © Alasdair Gray 1951, 1997. Reproduced with permission from Canongate Books, Ltd.

DOROTHY K. HAYNES: 'Thou Shalt Not Suffer a Witch' © Dorothy K. Haynes, 2001. First published in the UK by Black & White Publishing, an imprint of Bonnier Books UK Ltd. Reproduced with permission.

JACKIE KAY: 'My Daughter the Fox' from *Wish I Was Here* © Jackie Kay, 2010. Reproduced with permission from Macmillan Publishers International Limited.

A. L. KENNEDY: 'Night Geometry and the Garscadden Trains' © A. L. Kennedy, 1990. Reproduced with permission from Antony Harwood Ltd.

ERIC LINKLATER: 'Sealskin Trousers' by Eric Linklater

Titles in Everyman's Library Pocket Classics